aye, and gomorrah

aye, and gomorrah

STORIES

samuel r. delany

Vintage Books
A Division of Random House, Inc.
New York

FIRST VINTAGE BOOKS EDITION, April 2003

The stories in this collection have been previously published, as follows:

"Of Doubts and Dreams," in *Distant Stars*, Bantam Books, New York, 1981.

"The Star Pit," in *Worlds of Tomorrow*, New York, 1967, © Galaxy Publishing Corporation 1967.*

"Corona," *The Magazine of Fantasy and Science Fiction*, New York, 1967, © Mercury Press Inc. 1967.*

"Aye, and Gomorrah . . . ," in *Dangerous Visions*, Doubleday, New York, 1967, © Harlan Ellison 1967 for *Dangerous Visions*.*

"Driftglass," in *If*, New York, 1967, © Galaxy Publishing Corporation 1967.*

"We, in Some Strange Power's Employ, Move on a Rigorous Line," in *The Magazine of Fantasy and Science Fiction*, New York, 1968, © Mercury Press Inc. 1968.*

"Cage of Brass," in *If*, New York, 1968, © Galaxy Publishing Corporation 1968.*

"High Weir," In *If*, New York, 1968, © Galaxy Publishing Corporation 1968.*

"Time Considered as a Helix of Semi-precious Stones," in *New Worlds*, No. 185, London, 1968.*

"Omegahelm," first published in a slightly different form, as "Stars in My Pocket Like Grains of Sand" in *Beyond This Horizon*, Christopher Carrell ed., London, 1973. (This story does not form a part of the novel *Stars in My Pocket Like Grains of Sand*.)

"Prismatica," first published in *The Magazine of Fantasy and Science Fiction*, New York, 1977, © Mercury Press Inc. 1977.

"Ruins," an altered version of the story "In the Ruins" in *Algol*, No. 13, New York, 1968, © Andrew Porter 1968.

"Dog in a Fisherman's Net," in *Quark No. 3*, New York, 1971, © Coronet Communications, Inc. 1971.*

"Night and the Loves of Joe Dicostanzo," in *Alchemy & Academe*, Doubleday, New York, 1970, © Anne McCaffrey for *Alchemy & Academe* 1971.*

"Among the Blobs," in *Mississippi Review* 47/8, Volume 16, Nos 2 & 3, 1988, © *Mississippi Review* 1988.

"Tapestry," (under the title "The Unicorn Tapestry"), in *New American Review* 9, April 1970, Copyright © 1970 by New American Library, New York, 1970.

*These stories subsequently published in the collection *Driftglass*, New American Library, 1971. All stories appear here by permission of the author and his agents, Henry Morrison, Inc.

To
Sara Delany
and in memory of
Margaret Carey Boyd Delany,
Sara Ophelia Fitzgerald Boyd, *and*
Samuel R. Delany, Sr.

contents

Aye, there was destruction.

My God! Oh, my God!

And burning. And death and the sounds of death and burning.

Was Sodom destroyed?

Aye, and Gomorrah to six miles around it. The river beneath it boiled in the streets. The mountain vomited rock on the orchards. And no one now can live upon the place.

Oh, my city! What city may I found? Where now must I go make me a home?

aye, and gomorrah

the star pit

Two glass panes with dirt between and little tunnels from cell to cell: when I was a kid I had an ant colony.

But once some of our four-to-six-year-olds built an ecologarium, with six-foot plastic panels and grooved aluminum bars to hold corners and top down. They put it out on the sand.

There was a mud puddle against one wall so you could see what was going on underwater. Sometimes segment worms crawling through the reddish earth hit the side so their tunnels were visible for a few inches. In hot weather the inside of the plastic got coated with mist and droplets. The small round leaves on the litmus vines changed from blue to pink, blue to pink as clouds coursed the sky and the pH of the photosensitive soil shifted slightly.

The kids would run out before dawn and belly down naked in the cool sand with their chins on the backs of their hands and stare in the half-dark till the red mill wheel of Sigma lifted over the bloody sea. The sand was maroon then, and the flowers of the crystal plants looked like rubies in the dim light of the giant sun. Up the beach the jungle would begin to whisper while somewhere an aniwort would start warbling. The kids would giggle and poke each other and crowd closer.

Then Sigma-prime, the second member of the binary, would flare like thermite on the water, and crimson clouds would bleach from coral, through peach, to foam. The kids, half on top of each other now, lay like a pile of copper ingots with sun streaks in their hair—even on little Antoni, my oldest, whose hair was black and curly like bubbling oil (like his mother's), the down on the small of his two-year-old back was a white haze across the copper if you looked that close to see.

More children came to squat and lean on their knees, or kneel with their noses an inch from the walls, to watch, like young magicians, as things were born, grew, matured, and other things were born. Enchanted at their own construction, they stared at the miracle in their live museum.

A small, red seed lay camouflaged in the silt by the lake/puddle. One evening as white Sigma-prime left the sky violet, it broke open into a brown larva as long and of the same color as the first joint of Antoni's thumb. It flipped and swirled in the mud a couple of days, then crawled to the first branch of the nearest crystal plant to hang, exhausted, head down, from the tip. The brown flesh hardened, thickened, grew shiny, black. Then one morning the children saw the onyx chrysalis crack, and by second dawn there was an emerald-eyed flying lizard buzzing at the plastic panels.

"Oh, look, Da!" they called to me. "It's trying to get out!"

The speed-hazed creature butted at the corner for a few days, then settled at last to crawling around the broad leaves of the miniature shade palms.

When the season grew cool and there was the annual debate over whether the kids should put tunics on—they never stayed in them more than twenty minutes anyway—the jewels of the crystal plant misted, their facets coarsened, and they fell like gravel.

There were little four-cupped sloths, too, big as a six-year-old's fist. Most of the time they pressed their velvety bodies against the walls and stared longingly across the sand with their retractable eye-clusters. Then two of them swelled for about three weeks. We thought at first it was some bloating infection. But one evening we saw a couple of litters of white velvet balls half hidden by the low leaves of the shade palms. The parents were occupied now and didn't pine to get out.

There was a rock half in and half out of the puddle, I remember, covered with what I'd always called mustard-moss when I saw it in the wild. Once it put out a brush of white hairs. Then, one afternoon, the children ran to collect all the adults they could drag over. "Look! Oh, Da! Da, Ma, look!" The hairs had detached themselves and were walking around the water's edge, turning end over end along the soft soil.

I had to leave for work in a few minutes and haul some spare drive parts out to Tau Ceti. But when I got back five days later, the hairs had taken root, thickened and were already putting out the small round leaves of litmus vines. Among the new shoots, lying on her back, claws curled over her wrinkled belly, eyes cataracted like the foggy jewels of the crystal plant—she'd dropped her wings like cellophane days ago—was the flying lizard. Her pearl throat still pulsed, but as I watched, it stopped. Before she died, however, she had managed to deposit, nearly camouflaged in the silt by the puddle, a scattering of red seeds.

I remember getting home from another job where I'd been doing the maintenance on the shuttle-boats for a crew putting up a ring station to circle a planet itself circling Aldebaran. I was gone a long time on that one. When I left the landing complex and wandered out toward the tall weeds at the edge of the beach, I still didn't see anybody.

Which was just as well because the night before I'd put on a real winner with the crew to celebrate the completion of the station. That morning I'd taken a couple more drinks at the landing bar to undo last night's damage. Never works.

The swish of frond on frond was like clashed rasps. Sun on the sand reached out fingers of pure glare and tried to gouge my eyes. I was glad the home-compound was deserted because the kids would have asked questions I didn't want to answer; the adults wouldn't ask anything, which was even harder.

Then, down by the ecologarium, a child screeched. And screeched again. Then Antoni came hurtling toward me, half running, half on all fours, and flung himself on my leg. "Oh, Da! Da! Why, oh why, Da?"

I'd kicked my boots off and shrugged my shirt back at the compound porch, but I still had my overalls on. Antoni had two fists full of my pants leg and wouldn't let go. "Hey, kid-boy, what's the matter?"

When I finally got him on my shoulder, he butted his blubber wet face against my collarbone. "Oh, Da! Da! It's crazy, it's all cra*aaa-zy*!" His voice rose to lose itself in sobs.

"What's crazy, kid-boy? Tell Da."

Antoni held my ear and cried while I walked down to the plastic enclosure.

They'd put a small door in one transparent wall with a two-number combination lock that was supposed to keep this sort of thing from happening. I guess Antoni learned the combination from watching the older kids; or maybe he just figured it out.

One of the young sloths had climbed over and wandered across the sand about three feet.

"See, Da! It crazy, it bit me. Bit me, Da!" Sobs became sniffles as he showed me a puffy, bluish place on his wrist centered on which was a tiny crescent of pinpricks. Then he pointed jerkily to the creature.

It was shivering, and bloody froth spluttered from its lip flaps. All the while it was digging futilely at the sand with its clumsy cups, eyes retracted. Now it fell over, kicked, tried to right itself, breath going like a flutter valve. "It can't take the heat," I explained, reaching down to pick it up.

It snapped at me, and I jerked back. "Sunstroke, kid-boy. Yeah, it is crazy."

Suddenly it opened its mouth wide, let out all its air, and didn't take in any more.

"It's all right now," I said.

Two more of the baby sloths were at the door, front cups over the sill, staring with bright, black eyes. I pushed them back with a piece of seashell and closed the door.

Antoni kept looking at the white fur ball on the sand. "Not crazy now?"

"It's dead," I told him.

"Dead because it went outside, Da?"

I nodded.

"And crazy?" He made a fist and ground something already soft and wet around his upper lip.

I decided to change the subject, which was already too close to something I didn't like to think about. "Who's been taking care of you, anyway?" I asked. "You're a mess, kid-boy. Let's go and fix up that arm. They shouldn't leave a fellow your age all by himself." We started back to the compound. Those bites infect easily, and this one was swelling.

"Why it go crazy? Why it die when it go outside, Da?"

"Can't take the light," I said as we reached the jungle. "They're animals that live in shadow most of the time. The plastic cuts out the ultraviolet rays, just like the leaves that shade them when they run loose in the jungle. Sigma-prime's high on ultraviolet. That's why you're so good-looking, kid-boy. I think your ma told me their nervous systems are on the surface, all that fuzz. Under the ultraviolet, the enzymes break down so quickly that—does this mean anything to you at all?"

"*Uh-uh*." Antoni shook his head. Then he came out with, "Wouldn't it be nice, Da—" he admired his bite while we walked "—if some of them could go outside, just a few?"

That stopped me. There were sunspots on his blue-black hair. Fronds reflected faint green on his brown cheek. He was grinning, little, and wonderful. Something that had been anger in me a lot of times momentarily melted to raging tenderness, whirling about him like the dust in the light striking down at my shoulders, raging to protect my son. "I don't know about that, kid-boy."

"Why not?"

"It might be pretty bad for the ones who had to stay inside," I told him. "I mean after a while."

"Why?"

I started walking again. "Come on, let's fix your arm and get you cleaned up."

I washed the wet stuff off his face, and scraped the dry stuff from beneath it, which had been there at least two days. Then I got some antibiotic into him.

"You smell funny, Da."

"Never mind how I smell. Let's go outside again." I put down a cup of black coffee too fast. It and my hangover had a fight in my stomach. I tried to ignore it and do a little looking around. But I still couldn't find anybody. That got me mad. I mean he's independent, sure: he's mine. But he's only two.

Back on the beach we buried the dead sloth in sand; then, through the ecologarium's fogged and dripping walls, I pointed out the new, glittering stalks of the tiny crystal plants. At the bottom of the pond, in the jellied mass of ani-wort eggs, you could see the tadpole forms quivering already. An orange-fringed shelf fungus had sprouted nearly eight inches since it had been just a few black spores on a pile of dead leaves two weeks back.

"Grow up," Antoni chirped, with nose and fists against the plastic. "Everything grow up, and up."

"That's right."

He grinned at me. "I grow!"

"You sure as hell do."

"You grow?" Then he shook his head, twice: once to say no, and the second time because he got a kick from shaking his hair around—there was a lot of it. "You don't grow. You don't get any bigger. Why don't you grow?"

"I do too," I said indignantly. "Just very slowly."

Antoni turned around, leaned on the plastic and moved one toe at a time in the sand—I can't do that—watching me.

"You have to grow all the time," I said. "Not necessarily get bigger. But inside your head you have to grow, kid-boy. For us human-type people that's what's important. And that kind of growing never stops. At least it shouldn't. You can grow, kid-boy; or you can die. That's the choice you've got, and it goes on all of your life."

He looked back over his shoulder. "Grow up, all the time, even if they can't get out."

"Yeah," I said. And was uncomfortable all over again. I started pulling off my overalls for something to do. "Even—" The zipper got stuck. "God*damn* it—if you can't get out." *Rnrnrnrnrn*—it came loose.

T he rest got back that evening. They'd been on a group trip around the foot of the mountain. I did a little shouting to make sure my point got across about leaving Antoni alone. Didn't do much good. You know those family arguments:

He didn't want to come. We weren't going to force—

So what. He's got to learn to do things he doesn't want—

Like some other people I could mention!

Now look—

It's a healthy group. Don't you want him to grow up a healthy—

I'll be happy if he just grows up period. No food, no medical—

But the server was chock full of food. He knows how to use it—

Look, when I got home the kid's arm was swollen all the way up to his elbow!

And so on and so forth, with Antoni sitting in the middle looking confused. When he got confused enough, he ended it all by announcing matter-of-factly: "Da smell funny when he came home."

Everyone got quiet. Then someone said, "Oh, Vyme, you didn't come home that way again! I mean, in front of the children . . ."

I said a couple of things I was sorry for later and stalked off down the beach—on a four-mile hike.

Times I got home from work? The ecologarium? I guess I'm just leading up to this one.

The particular job had taken me a hectic week to get. It was putting back together a battleship that was gutted somewhere off Aurigae. Only when I got there, I found I'd already been laid off. That particular war was over—they're real quick now. So I scraped and lied and browned my way into a repair gang that was servicing a traveling replacement station, generally had to humiliate myself to get the job because every other drive mechanic from the battleship fiasco was after it too. Then I got canned the first day because I came to work . . . smelling funny. It took me another week to hitch a ride back to Sigma. Didn't even have enough to pay passage, but I made a deal with the pilot I'd do half the driving for him.

We were an hour out, and I was at the controls when something I'd never heard of happening happened. We came *this* close to ramming another ship. Consider how much empty space there is; the chances are infinitesimal. On top of that, every ship should be broadcasting an identification beam at all times.

But this big, bulbous keeler-intergalactic slid by so close I could *see* her through the front viewport. Our inertia system went nuts. We jerked around in the stasis whirl from the keeler. I slammed on the video-intercom and shouted, "You great big stupid . . . *stupid* . . ." so mad and scared I couldn't say anything else.

The golden piloting the ship stared at me from the view-screen with mildly surprised annoyance. I remember his face was just slightly less Negroid than mine.

Our little Serpentina couldn't hurt him. But had we been even a hundred meters closer we might have ionized. The other pilot came bellowing from behind the sleeper curtain and started cursing me out.

"Damn it," I shouted, "it was one of those . . ." and lost all the profanity I know to my rage—"golden . . ."

"This far into galactic center? Come off it. They should be hanging out around the Star Pit!"

"It was a keeler drive," I insisted. "It came right in front of us." I stopped because the control stick was shaking in my hand. You know the Serpentina colophon? They have it in the corner of the view-screen and raised in plastic on the head of the control knobs. Well, it got pressed into the ham of my thumb so you could make it out for an hour, I was squeezing the control rod that tight.

When he set me down, I went straight to the bar to cool off. And got into a *really* stupid argument that turned into a shoving match with some guy probably just visiting. I mean, *I'd* never seen him before. When I reached the beach I was broke; I had a bloody nose (he'd shoved pretty high there once); I was sick and furious.

It was just after first sunset, and the kids were squealing around the ecologarium. Then one little girl I didn't even recognize ran up to me and jerked my arm. "Da, oh, Da! Come look! The ani-worts are just about to—"

I pushed her, and she sat down, surprised, on the sand.

I just wanted to get to the water and splash something cold on my face, because every minute or so it would start to burn.

Another bunch of kids grabbed me, shouting, "Da, Da! The ani-worts, Da!" and tried to pull me over.

First I took two steps with them. Then I just swung my arms. I didn't make a sound. But I put my head down and barreled against the plastic wall. Kids screamed. Aluminum snapped; the plastic cracked and went down. My boots were still on, and I kicked and kicked at red earth and sand. Shade palms went down and the leaves tore under my feet. Crystal plants broke like glass rods beneath a piece of plastic. A swarm of lizards flittered up around my head. Some of the red was Sigma; some was what burned behind my face.

I remember I was still shaking and watching water run out of the broken lake, then soak in so that the wet tongue of sand expanded a little, raised just a trifle around the edge. Then I looked up to see the kids coming back down the beach, crying, shouting, afraid and clustered around Antoni's ma. She walked steadily toward me— steady because she was a woman and they were children. But I saw the same fear in her face. Antoni was on her shoulder. Other grown-ups were coming behind her.

Antoni's ma was a biologist, and I think she had suggested the ecologarium to the kids in the first place. When she looked up from the ruin I'd made, I knew I'd broken something of hers too.

An odd expression got caught in the features of her—I remember it, oh-so-beautiful—face, with compassion alongside the anger, contempt alongside the fear. "Oh, for pity's sake, Vyme," she cried, not loudly at all. "Won't you ever grow up?"

I opened my mouth, but everything I wanted to say was too big and stayed wedged in my throat.

"Grow up?" Antoni repeated and reached for a lizard that buzzed his head. "Everything stop growing up, now." He looked down again at the wreck I'd made. "All broken. Everything get out."

"He didn't mean to break it," she said to the others for me, then knifed my gratitude with a look. "We'll put it back together."

She put Antoni on the sand and picked up one of the walls.

After they got started, they let me help. A lot of the plants were broken. And only the ani-worts who'd completed metamorphosis could be saved. The flying lizards were too curious to get far away, so we—they—netted them and got them back inside. I guess I didn't help *that* much. And I wouldn't say I was sorry.

They got just about everything back except the sloths.

We couldn't find them. We searched for a long time, too.

The little sun was down so they should have been all right. They can't negotiate the sand with any speed so couldn't have reached the jungle. But there were no tracks, no nothing. We even dug in the sand to see if they'd buried themselves. It wasn't till more than a dozen years later I found out where they went.

For the present I accepted Antoni's mildly adequate, "They just must of got out again."

Not too long after that I left the procreation group. Went off to work one day, didn't come back. But like I said to Antoni, you either grow or die. I didn't die.

Once I considered returning. But there was another war—and suddenly there wasn't anything to return to. Some of the group got out alive. Antoni and his ma didn't. I mean there wasn't even any *water* left on the planet.

When I finally came to the Star Pit, myself, I hadn't had a drink in years. But working there on the galaxy's edge did something to me—something to the part that grows I'd once talked about on the beach with Antoni.

If it did it to me, it's not surprising it did it to Ratlit and the rest.

(And I remember a black-eyed creature pressed against the plastic wall, staring across impassable sands.)

Perhaps it was knowing this was as far as you could go.

Perhaps it was the golden.

Golden? I hadn't even joined the group yet when I first heard the word. I was sixteen and a sophomore at Luna Vocational. I was born in a city called New York on a planet called Earth. Luna is its one satellite. You've heard of the system, I'm sure. That's where we all came from. A few other things about it are well known. Unless you're an anthropologist, though, I doubt you've ever been there. It's way the hell off the main trading routes and pretty primitive. I was a drive-mechanics major, on scholarship, living in and studying hard. All morning in Practical Theory (a ridiculous name for a ridiculous class, I thought then) we'd been putting together a model keeler-intergalactic drive. Throughout those dozens of helical inserts and superinertia organus sensitives, I had been silently cursing my teacher, thinking, about like everyone else in the class, "So what if they can fly these jalopies from one galaxy to another. Nobody will ever be able to ride in them. Not with the Psychic and Physiologic shells hanging around this cluster of the universe."

Back in the dormitory I was lying on my bed, scraping graphite lubricant from my nails with the end of my slide rule and half reading at a folded-back copy of *The Stellar Mechanic* when I saw the article and the pictures.

Through some freakish accident, two people had been discovered who didn't crack up at twenty thousand light-years off the galactic rim, who didn't die at twenty-five thousand.

They were both psychological freaks with some incredible hormone imbalance in their systems. One was a little Oriental girl; the other was an older man, blond and big-boned, from a cold planet circling Cygnus-beta: golden. They looked sullen as hell, both of them.

Then there were more articles, more pictures, in the economic journals, the sociology student-letters, the legal bulletins, as various fields began acknowledging the impact that the golden and the sudden birth of intergalactic trade were having on them. The head of some commission summed it up with the statement: "Though interstellar travel has been with us for three centuries, intergalactic trade has been an impossibility, not because of mechanical limitations, but rather because of barriers that till now we have not even been able to define. Some psychic shock causes insanity in any human— or for that matter, any intelligent species or perceptual machine or computer—that goes more than twenty thousand light-years from the galactic rim; then complete physiological death, as well as recording breakdown in computers that might replace human crews. Complex explanations have been offered, none completely satisfactory, but the base of the problem seems to be this: as the nature of space and time are relative to the concentration of matter in a given area of the continuum, the nature of reality itself operates by the same, or similar, laws. The averaged mass of all the stars in our galaxy controls the 'reality' of our microsector of the universe. But as a ship leaves the galactic rim, 'reality' breaks down and causes insanity and eventual death for any crew, even though certain mechanical laws—though not all—appear to remain, for reasons we don't understand, relatively constant. Save for a few barbaric experiments done with psychedelics at the dawn of spatial travel, we have not even developed a vocabulary that can deal with 'reality' apart from its measurable, physical expression. Yet, just when we had to face the black limit of intergalactic space, bright resources glittered within. Some few of us whose sense of reality has been shattered by infantile, childhood, or prenatal trauma, whose physiological orientation makes life in our interstellar society painful or impossible—not all, but a few of these golden . . ." at which point there was static, or the gentleman coughed, ". . . can make the crossing and return."

The name golden, sans noun, stuck.

Few was the understatement of the millennium. Slightly less than one human being in thirty-four thousand is a golden. A couple of people had pictures of emptying all mental institutions by just shaking them out over the galactic rim. Didn't work like that. The particular psychosis and endocrine setup were remarkably specialized. Still, back then there was excitement, wonder, anticipation, hope, admiration in the word: admiration for the ones who could get out.

"Golden?" Ratlit said when I asked him. He was working as a grease monkey out here in the Star Pit over at Poloscki's. "Born with the word. Grew up with it. Weren't no first time with me. Though I remember when I was about six, right after the last of my parents was killed, and I was hiding out with a bunch of other lice in a broke-open packing crate in an abandoned freight yard near the ruins of Helios on Creton VI—that's where I was born, I think. Most of the city had been starved out by then, but somebody was getting food to us. There was this old crook-back character who was hiding too. He used to sit on the top of the packing crate and bang his heels on the aluminum slats and tell us stories about the stars. Had a couple of rags held with twists of wire for clothes, missing two fingers off one hand; he kept plucking the loose skin under his chin with those grimy talons. And he talked about them. So I asked, 'Golden what, sir?' He leaned forward so that his face was like a mahogany bruise on the sky, and croaked. 'They've been *out*, I tell you, seen more than ever you or I. Human and inhuman, kid-boy, mothered by women and fathered by men, still they live by their own laws and walk their own ways!'" Ratlit and I were sitting under a streetlamp with our feet over the Edge, where the fence had broken. His hair was like breathing flame in the wind; his single earring glittered. Star-flecked infinity dropped away below our boot soles, and the wind created by the stasis field that held our atmosphere down—we call it the "world-wind" out here because it's never cold and never hot and like nothing on any world—whipped his black shirt back from his bony chest as we gazed on galactic night between our knees. "I guess that was back during the second Kyber war," he concluded.

"Kyber war?" I asked. "Which one was that?"

Ratlit shrugged. "I just know it was fought over possession of a couple of tons of di-allium; that's the polarized element the golden brought back from Lupe-galaxy. They used y-adna ships to fight it— that's why it was such a bad one. I mean worse than usual."

"Y-adna? That's a drive I don't know anything about."

"Some golden saw the plans for them in a civilization in Magellanic-9."

"Oh," I said. "And what was Kyber?"

"It was a weapon, a sort of fungus the golden brought back from some overrun planet on the rim of Andromeda. It's deadly. Only they were too stupid to bring back the antitoxin."

"That's golden for you."

"Yeah. You ever notice about golden, Vyme? I mean just the word. I found out all about it from my publisher, once. It's semantically unsettling."

"Really?" I said. "So are they. Unsettling I mean."

I'd finished a rough, rough day installing a rebuilt keeler in a quantum transport hull that just wasn't big enough. The golden having the job done stood over my shoulder the whole time, and every hour he'd come out with the sort of added instruction that would make the next sixty-one minutes miserable. But I did it. The golden paid me in cash and without a word climbed into the lift, and two minutes later, while I was still washing the grease off, the damn five-hundred-ton hulk began to whistle for takeoff.

Sandy, a young fellow who'd come looking for a temporary mechanic's job three months back (but hadn't given me cause to fire him yet), barely had time to pull the big waldoes out of the way and go scooting into the shock chamber when the three-hundred-meter doofus tore loose from the grapplers. And Sandy, who, like a lot of these youngsters drifting around from job to job, is usually sort of quiet and vague, got loud and specific. ". . . two thousand pounds of nonshockproof equipment out there . . . ruin it all if he could . . . *I'm* not expendable, I don't care what a . . . these golden out here . . ." while the ship hove off where only the golden go. I just flipped on the "not open" sign, left the rest of the grease where it was, left the hangar, and hunted up Ratlit.

So there we were, under that streetlamp, sitting on the Edge, in the world-wind.

"Golden," Ratlit said under the roar. "It would be much easier to take if it were grammatically connected to something: golden ones, golden people. Or even one gold, two golden."

"Male golden, female goldene?"

"Something like that. It's not an adjective, it's not a noun. My publisher told me that for a while it was written with a dash after it that stood for whatever it might modify."

I remembered the dash. It was an uneasy joke, a fill-in for that cough. Golden *what*? People had already started to feel uncomfortable. Then it went past joking and back to just "golden."

"Think about that, Vyme. Just golden: one, two, or three of them."

"That's something to think about, kid-boy," I said.

Ratlit had been six during the Kyber war. Square that and add it once again for my age now. Ratlit's? Double six and add one. I like kids; and they like me. But that may be because my childhood left me a lot younger at forty-two than I should be. Ratlit's had left him a lot older than any thirteen-year-old has a right to be.

"No golden took part in the war," Ratlit said.

"They never do." I watched his thin fingers get all tangled together.

After two divorces, my mother ran off with a salesman and left me and four siblings with an alcoholic aunt for a year. Yeah, they still have divorces, monogamous marriages and stuff like that where I was born. Like I say, it's pretty primitive. I left home at fifteen, made it through vocational school on my own, and learned enough about what makes things fly to end up—after that disastrous marriage I told you about earlier—with my own repair hangar on the Star Pit.

Compared with Ratlit I had a stable childhood.

That's right, he lost the last parent he remembered when he was six. At seven he was convicted of his first felony—after escaping from Creton VI. But part of his treatment at hospital *cum* reform school *cum* prison was to have the details lifted from his memory. "Did something to my head back there. That's why I never could learn to read, I think." For the next couple of years he ran away from one foster group after the other. When he was eleven, some guy took him home from Play Planet where he'd been existing under the boardwalk on discarded hot dogs, souvlakia, and falafel. "Fat, smoked perfumed cigarettes; name was Vivian?" Turned out to be the publisher. Ratlit stayed for three months, during which time he dictated a novel to Vivian. "Protecting my honor," Ratlit explained. "I had to do *something* to keep him busy."

The book sold a few hundred thousand copies as a precocious curiosity among many. But Ratlit had split. The next years he was involved as a shill in some illegality I never really understood. He didn't either. "But I bet I made a million, Vyme! I earned at least a million." It's possible. At thirteen he still couldn't read or write, but his travels had gained him fair fluency in three languages. A couple of weeks ago he'd wandered off a stellar tramp, dirty and broke, here at the Star Pit. And I'd gotten him a job as grease monkey over at Poloscki's.

Ratlit leaned his elbows on his knees, his chin in his hands. "Vyme, it's a shame."

"What's a shame, kid-boy?"

"To be washed up at my age. A has-been! To have to grapple with the fact that this—" he spat at a star—"is it."

He was talking about golden again.

"You still have a chance." I shrugged. "Most of the time it doesn't come out till puberty."

He cocked his head up at me. "I've been pubescent since I was nine, buster."

"Ex*cuse* me."

"I feel cramped in, Vyme. There's all that night out there to grow up in, to explore."

"There was a time," I mused, "when the whole species was confined to the surface, give or take a few feet up or down, of a single planet. You've got the whole galaxy to run around in. You've seen a lot of it, yeah. But not all."

"But there are billions of galaxies out there. I want to see them. In all the stars around here there hasn't been one life form discovered that's based on anything but silicon or carbon. I overheard two golden in a bar once, talking: there's something in some galaxy out there that's big as a star, neither dead nor alive, and sings. I want to *hear* it, Vyme!"

"Ratlit, you can't fight reality."

"Oh, go to sleep, grandpa!" He closed his eyes and bent his head back until the cords of his neck quivered. "What is it that makes a golden? A combination of physiological and psychological . . . what?"

"It's primarily some sort of hormonal imbalance as well as an environmentally conditioned thalamic/personality response—"

"Yeah. Yeah." His head came down. "And that X-chromosome heredity nonsense they just connected up with it a few years back. But all I know is *they* can take the stasis shift from galaxy to galaxy, whereas you and I, Vyme, if we get more than twenty thousand light-years off the rim, we're dead."

"Insane at twenty thousand," I corrected. "Dead at twenty-five."

"Same difference." He opened his eyes. They were large, green, and mostly pupil. "You know, I stole a golden belt once. Rolled it off a staggering slob about a week ago who came out of a bar and collapsed on the corner. I went across the Pit to the Calle-J where nobody knows me and wore it around for a few hours, just to see if I felt different."

"You did?" Ratlit had lengths of gut that astounded me about once a day.

"I didn't. But people walking around me did. Wearing that two-inch band of yellow metal around my waist, nobody in the worlds could tell I wasn't a golden, just walking by on the street, without talking to me awhile, or making hormone tests. And wearing that belt, I learned just how much I hated golden. Because I could suddenly see, in almost everybody who came by, how much they hated me while I had that metal belt on. I threw it over the Edge." Suddenly he grinned. "Maybe I'll steal another one."

"You really hate them, Ratlit?"

He narrowed his eyes at me and looked superior.

"Sure, I talk about them," I told him. "Sometimes they're a pain to work for. But it's not their fault we can't take the reality shift."

"I'm just a child," he said evenly, "incapable of such fine reasoning. I hate them." Ratlit looked back at the night. "How can you stand to be trapped by anything, Vyme?"

Three memories crowded into my head when he said that.

First: I was standing at the railing of the East River—runs past this New York I was telling you about—at midnight, looking at the illuminated dragon of the Manhattan Bridge that spanned the water, then at the industrial fires flickering in bright, smoky Brooklyn, and then at the template of mercury streetlamps behind me bleaching out the playground and most of Houston Street; then, at the reflections in the water, here like crinkled foil, there like glistening rubber; at last, looked up at the midnight sky itself. It wasn't black but dead pink, without a star. This glittering world made the sky a roof that pressed down on me so I almost screamed. . . . That time the next night I was twenty-seven light-years away from Sol on my first star-run.

Second: I was visiting my mother after my first few years out. I was looking in the closet for something when this contraption of plastic straps and buckles fell on my head.

"What's this, Ma?"

She smiled with a look of idiot nostalgia and crooned, "Why that's your little harness, Vymey. Your first father and I would take you on picnics up at Bear Mountain and put you in that and tie you to a tree with about ten foot of cord so you wouldn't get—" I didn't hear the rest because of the horror that suddenly flooded me, thinking of myself tied up in that thing. Okay, I was twenty and had just joined that beautiful procreation group a year back on Sigma and was the proud father of three and expecting two more. The hundred and sixty-three of us had the whole beach and nine miles of jungle and half a mountain to ourselves; maybe I was seeing Antoni caught up in that thing, trying to catch a bird or a beetle or a wave—with only ten feet of cord. I hadn't worn clothes for anything but work in a twelvemonth, and I was chomping to get away from the incredible place I had grown up in called an apartment and back to wives, husbands, kids, and civilization. Anyway, it was pretty terrible.

The third? After I had left the proke-group—fled them, I suppose, guilty and embarrassed over something I couldn't name, still having nightmares once a month that woke me screaming about what was going to happen to the kids, even though I knew one point of group marriage was to prevent the loss of one, two, or three parents being traumatic—still wondering if I wasn't making the same mistakes my parents made, hoping my brood wouldn't turn out like me, or worse like the kids you sometimes read about in the paper (like Ratlit, though I hadn't met him yet), horribly suspicious that no matter how different I tried to be from my sires, it was just the same thing all over again. . . . Anyway, I was on the ship bringing me to the Star Pit for the first time. I'd gotten to talking to a golden who, as golden go, was a pretty regular gal. We'd been discussing inter- and intragalactic drives. She was impressed I knew so much. I was impressed that she could use them and know so little. She was digging in a very girl-way the six-foot-four, two hundred-

and-ten-pound drive mechanic with mildly grimy fingernails and that was me. I was digging in a very boy-way the slim, amber-eyed young lady who had seen it *all*. From the view deck we watched the immense, artificial disk of the Star Pit approach, when she turned to me and said, in a voice that didn't sound cruel at all, "This is as far as you go, isn't it?" And I was frightened all over again, because I knew that on about nine different levels she was right.

Ratlit said: "I know what you're thinking." A couple of times when he'd felt like being quiet and I'd felt like talking I may have told him more than I should. "Well, cube that for me, dad. That's how trapped *I* feel!"

I laughed, and Ratlit looked very young again. "Come on," I said. "Let's take a walk."

"Yeah." He stood. The wind fingered at our hair. "I want to go see Alegra."

"I'll walk you as far as Calle-G," I told him. "Then I'm going to go to bed."

"I wonder what Alegra thinks about this business? I always find Alegra a very good person to talk to," he said sagely. "Not to put you down, but her experiences are a little more up-to-date than yours. You have to admit she has a modern point of view. Plus the fact that she's older." Than Ratlit anyway. She was fifteen.

"I don't think being 'trapped' ever really bothered her," I said. "Which may be a place to take a lesson from."

By Ratlit's standards Alegra had a few things over me. In my youth kids took to dope in their teens, twenties. Alegra was born with a three-hundred-milligram-a-day habit on a bizarre narcotic that combined the psychedelic qualities of the most powerful hallucinogens with the addictiveness of the strongest depressants. I can sympathize. Alegra's mother was addicted, and the tolerance was passed with the blood plasma through the placental wall. Ordinarily a couple of complete transfusions at birth would have gotten the newborn child straight. But Alegra was also a highly projective telepath. She projected the horrors of birth, the glories of her infantile hallucinated world on befuddled doctors; she was given her drug. Without too much difficulty she managed to be given her drug every day since.

Once I asked Alegra when she'd first heard of the golden, and she came back with this horror story. A lot were coming back from Tiber-44 cluster with psychic shock. The mental condition of golden is pretty delicate, and sometimes very minor conflicts nearly ruin them. Anyway, the government that was sponsoring the importation of micro-microsurgical equipment from some tiny planet in that galaxy, to protect its interests, hired Alegra, age eight, as a psychiatric therapist. "I'd concretize their fantasies and make them work them through. In just a couple of hours I'd have 'em back to their old, mean, stupid selves again. Some of them were pretty nice when they came to me." But there was a lot of work for her; projective telepaths are rare. So they started withholding her drug to force her to work harder, then rewarding her with increased dosage. "Up till then," she told me, "I might have kicked it. But when I came away, they had me on double what I used to take. They pushed me past the point where withdrawal would be fatal. But I *could* have kicked it, up till then, Vyme." That's right. Age eight.

Oh, yeah. The drug was imported by golden from Cancer-9, and most of it goes through the Star Pit. Alegra came here because illegal imports are easier to come by, and you can get it for just about nothing—if you want it. Golden don't use it.

The wind lessened as Ratlit and I started back. Ratlit began to whistle. In Calle-K the first night lamp had broken so that the level street was a tunnel of black.

"Ratlit?" I asked. "Where do you think you'll be, oh, in say five years?"

"Quiet," he said. "I'm trying to get to the end of the street without bumping into the walls, tripping on something, or some other catastrophe. If we get through the next five minutes all right, I'll worry about the next five years." He began whistling again.

"Trip? Bump the walls?"

"I'm listening for echoes." Again he commenced the little jets of music.

I put my hands in my overall pouch and went on quietly while Ratlit did the bat bit. Then there was a catastrophe, though I didn't realize it at the time:

Into the circle of light from the remaining lamp at the other end of the street walked a golden.

His hands went up to his face, and he was laughing. The sound skittered in the street. His belt was low on his belly the way the really down and broke—

I just thought of a better way to describe him. The resemblance struck me immediately. He looked like Sandy, my mechanic—who is short, twenty-four years old, muscled like an ape, and wears his worn-out work clothes even when he's off duty. ("I just want this job for a while, boss. I'm not staying out here at the Star Pit. As soon as I save up a little, I'm gonna make it back in toward galactic center. It's funny out here, like dead." He gazes up through the opening in the hangar roof where there are no clouds and no stars either. "Yeah. I'm just gonna be here for a little while."

("Fine with me, kid-boy."

(That was three months back, like I say. He's still with me. He works hard too, which puts him a cut above a lot of characters out here. Still, there was something about Sandy . . .) On the other hand Sandy's face is also hacked up with acne. His hair is always nap short over his wide head. But in these aspects, the golden was exactly Sandy's opposite, come to think of it. Still, there was something about the golden . . .

He staggered, went down on his knees still laughing, then collapsed. By the time we reached him, he was silent. With the toe of his boot Ratlit nudged the hand from the belt buckle.

It flopped, palm up, on the pavement. The little fingernail was three-quarters of an inch long, the way a lot of the golden wear it. (Like his face, the nails on Sandy's fingers are masticated wrecks. Still, something . . .)

"Now isn't that something." Ratlit shook his head. "What do you want to do with him, Vyme?"

"Nothing," I said. "Let him sleep it off."

"Leave him so somebody can come along and steal his belt?" Ratlit grinned. "I'm not that nasty."

"Weren't you just telling me how much you hated golden?"

"I'd be nasty to whoever stole the belt and wore it. Nobody but a golden should be hated that much."

"Ratlit, let's go."

But Ratlit had already kneeled down and was shaking the golden's shoulder. "Let's get him to Alegra's and find out what's the matter with him."

"He's just drunk."

"Nope," Ratlit said. " 'Cause he don't smell funny."

"Look. Get back." I hoisted the golden up and laid him across my neck, fireman's carry. "Start moving," I told Ratlit. "I think you're crazy."

Ratlit grinned. "Thanks. Maybe he'll be grateful and lay some lepta on me for taking him in off the street."

"You don't know golden," I said. "But if he does, split it with me."

"Sure."

Two blocks later we reached Alegra's place. (But like I say, Sandy, though well built, is little; so I didn't have much trouble carrying him.) Halfway up the sagging stairs Ratlit said, "She's in a good mood."

"I guess she is." The weight across my shoulders was becoming pleasant.

I can't describe Alegra's place. I can describe a lot of places like it; and I can describe it before she moved in because I knew a derelict named Drunk-roach who slept on that floor before she did. You know what never-wear plastics look like when they wear out? What non-rust metals look like when they rust through? It was a shabby crack-walled cubicle with dirt in the corners and scars on the windowpane when Drunk-roach had his pile of blankets in the corner. But since the hallucinating projective telepath took it over, who knows what it had become.

Ratlit opened the door on an explosion of classical beauty.

"Come in," she said, accompanied by symphonic arrangement

scored on twenty-four staves, with full chorus. "What's that you're carrying, Vyme? Oh, it's a golden!"

And before me, dizzying tides of yellow.

"Put him down, put him down quick, and let's see what's wrong!"

Hundreds of eyes, spotlights, glittering lenses; I lowered him to the mattress in the corner.

"Ohhh . . ." breathed Alegra.

And the golden lay on orange silk pillows in a teak barge drawn by swans, accompanied by flutes and drums.

"Where did you find him?" she hissed, circling against the ivory moon on her broom.

We watched the glowing barge, hundreds of feet below, sliding down the silvered waters between the crags.

"We just picked him up off the street," Ratlit said. "Vyme thought he was drunk. But he don't smell."

"Was he laughing?" Alegra asked.

Laughter rolled and broke on the rocks.

"Yeah," Ratlit said. "Just before he collapsed."

"Then he must be from the Un-dok expedition that just got back."

Mosquitoes darted at us through wet fronds. Insects reeled among the leaves, upsetting droplets that fell like cut glass as, barely visible beyond the palms, the barge drifted on the sweltering, bright river.

"That's right," I said, backpaddling frantically to avoid a hippopotamus that threatened to upset my kayak. "I'd forgotten they'd just come in."

"Okay." Ratlit's breath clouded his lips. "I'm out of it. Let me in. Where did they come back from?"

The snow hissed beneath the runners, as we looked after the barge, nearly at the white horizon.

"Un-dok, of course," Alegra said. The barking grew fainter. "Where did you think?"

White eclipsed to black, and the barge was a spot gleaming in galactic night, flown on by laboring comets.

"Un-dok is the furthest galaxy reached yet," I told Ratlit. "They just got back last week."

"Sick," Alegra added.

I dug my fingers against my abdomen to grab the pain.

"They all came back sick—"

Fever heated blood-bubbles in my eyes: I slipped to the ground, my mouth wide, my tongue like paper on my lips . . .

Ratlit coughed. "All *right*, Alegra. Cut it out! You don't have to be so dramatic!"

"Oh, I'm dreadfully sorry, Ratty, Vyme."

Coolth, water. Nausea swept away as solicitous nurses hastily put the pieces back together until everything was beautiful, or so austerely horrible it could be appreciated as beauty.

"Anyway," she went on, "they came back with some sort of disease they picked up out there. Apparently it's not contagious, but they're stuck with it for the rest of their lives. Every few days they suddenly have a blackout. It's preceded by a fit of hysterics. It's just one of those stupid things they can't do anything about yet. It doesn't hurt their being golden."

Ratlit began to laugh. Suddenly he asked, "How long are they passed out for?"

"Only a few hours," Alegra said. "It must be terribly annoying."

And I began to feel mildly itchy in all sorts of unscratchable places, my shoulder blades, somewhere down my ear, the roof of my mouth. Have you ever tried to scratch the roof of your mouth?

"Well," Ratlit said, "let's sit down and wait it out."

"We can talk," Alegra said. "That way it won't seem like such a long . . ." and hundreds of years later she finished ". . . time."

"Good," Ratlit said. "I wanted to talk to you. That's why I came up here in the first place."

"Oh, fine!" Alegra said. "I love to talk. I want to talk about love. Loving someone—" (an incredible yearning twisted my stomach, rose to block my throat) "—I mean really loving someone—" (the yearning brushed the edge of agony) "—means you are willing to admit the person you love is not what you first fell in love with, not the image you first had; and you must be able to like them still for being as close to that image as they are, and avoid disliking them for being so far away."

And through the tenderness that suddenly obliterated all hurt, Ratlit's voice came from the jeweled mosaics shielding him: "Alegra, I want to talk about loneliness."

"I'm on my way home, kids," I said. "Tell me what happens with Prince Charming when he wakes up." They kept on talking while I went through the difficulties of finding my way out without Alegra's help. When my head cleared, halfway down the stairs, I couldn't tell you if I'd been there five minutes or five years.

When I got to the hangar next morning, Sandy was filing the eight-foot prongs on the conveyor. "You got a job coming in about twenty minutes," he called down from the scaffold.

"I hope it's not another of those rebuilt jobs."

"Yep."

"Hell," I said. "I don't want to see another one for six weeks."

"All he wants is a general tune-up. Maybe two hours."

"Depends on where it's been," I said. "Where *has* it been?"

"Just back from—"

"Never mind." I started toward the office cubicle. "I think I'll put the books in order for the last six months. Can't let it go forever."

"Boss!" Sandy protested. "That'll take all day!"

"Then I better get started." I leaned back out the door. "Don't disturb me."

Of course as soon as the shadow of the hull fell over the office window I came out in my overalls, after giving Sandy five minutes to get it grappled and himself worried. I took the lift up to the one-fifty catwalk. When I stepped out, Sandy threw me a grateful smile from his scar-ugly face. The golden had already started his instructions. When I reached them and coughed, the golden turned to me and continued talking, not bothering to fill me in on what he had said before, figuring Sandy and I would put it together. You could tell this golden had made his pile. He wore an immaculate blue tunic, with bronze codpiece, bracelets, and earrings. His hair was the same bronze, his skin was burned red-black, and his blue-gray eyes and tight-muscled mouth were proud, proud, proud. While I finished getting instructions, Sandy quietly got started unwelding the eight-foot seal of the organum so we could get to the checkout circuits.

Finally the golden stopped talking—that's the only way you could tell he was finished—and leaned his angular six and a half feet against the railing, clicking his glossy, manicured nails against the pipe a few times. He had that same sword-length pinky nail, all white against his skin. I climbed out on the rigging to help Sandy.

We had been at work ten minutes when a kid, maybe eighteen or nineteen, barefoot and brown, black hair hacked off shoulder length, a rag that didn't fit tucked around under his belt, and dirty, came wandering down the catwalk. His thumbs were rubbing the yellow metal links: golden.

First I thought he'd come from the ship. Then I realized he'd just stalked into the hangar from outside and come up on the lift.

"Hey, brother!" The kid who was golden hooked his thumbs in his belt, as Sandy and I watched the dialogue from the rigging on the side of the hull. "I'm getting tired of hanging around this Star Pit. Just about broke as well. Where you running to?"

The man who was golden clicked his nails again. "Go away, distant cousin."

"Come on, brother, give me a berth on your lifeboat out of this dungheap to someplace worthwhile."

"Go away, or I'll kill you."

"Now, brother, I'm just a youngster adrift in this forsaken quarter of the sky. Come on, now—"

Suddenly the blond man whirled from the railing, grabbed up a four-foot length of pipe leaning beside him, and swung it so hard it hissed. The black-haired ragamuffin leapt back and from under his rag snatched something black that, with a flick of that long nail, grew seven inches of blade. The bar swung again, caught the shoulder of the boy, then clattered against the hull. He shrieked and came straight forward. The two bodies locked, turned, fell. A gurgle, and the man's hands slipped from the neck of the ragamuffin. The boy scrambled back to his feet. Blood bubbled and popped on the hot blade.

A last spasm caught the man; he flipped over, smearing the cat-walk, rolled once more, this time under the rail, and dropped—two hundred and fifty feet to the cement flooring.

Flick. Off went the power in the knife. The golden wiped pow-dered blood on his thigh, spat over the rail and said softly, "No rel-ative of mine." Flick. The blade itself disappeared. He started down the catwalk.

"Hey!" Sandy called, when he got his voice back up into his throat. "What about . . . I mean you . . . well, your ship!" There are no familial inheritance laws among golden—only rights of plunder.

The golden glanced back. "I give it to you," he sneered. His shoulder must have been killing him, but he stepped into the lift like he was walking into a phone booth. That's a golden for you.

Sandy was horrified and bewildered. Behind his pitted ugliness there was that particularly wretched amazement only the totally vulnerable get when hurt.

"That's the first time you've ever seen an incident like that?" I felt sorry for him.

"Well, I wandered into Gerg's Bar a couple of hours after they had that massacre. But the ones who started it were drunk."

"Drunk or sober," I said. "Believe me, it doesn't make *that* much difference to the way a man acts." I shook my head. "I keep forget-ting you've only been here three months."

Sandy, upset, looked down at the body on the flooring. "What about him? And the ship, boss?"

"I'll call the wagon to come scrape him up. The ship is yours."

"Huh?"

"He gave it to you. It'll stand up in court. It just takes one wit-ness. Me."

"What am I gonna do with it? I mean I would have to haul it to a junk station to get the salvage. Look, boss, I'm gonna give it to you. Sell it or something. I'd feel sort of funny with it anyway."

"I don't want it. Besides, then I'd be involved in the transaction and couldn't be a witness."

"I'll be a witness." Ratlit stepped from the lift. "I caught the whole bit when I came in the door. Great acoustics in this place. He whistled again. The echo came back. Ratlit closed his eyes for a moment. "Ceiling is . . . a hundred and twenty feet overhead, more or less. How's that, huh?"

"Hundred and twenty-seven," I said.

Ratlit shrugged. "I need more practice. Come on, Sandy, you give it to him, and I'll be a witness."

"You're a minor," Sandy said. Sandy didn't like Ratlit. I used to think it was because Ratlit was violent and flamboyant where Sandy was stolid and ugly. Even though Sandy kept protesting the temporariness of his job to me, I remember, when I first got to the Star Pit, those long-dying thoughts I'd had about leaving. It was a little too easy to see Sandy a mechanic here thirty years from now. I wasn't the only one it had happened to. Ratlit had been a grease monkey here three weeks. You tell me where he was going to be in three more. "Aren't you supposed to be working at Poloscki's?" Sandy said, turning back to the organum.

"Coffee break," Ratlit said. "If you're going to give it away, Sandy, can I have it?"

"So you can claim salvage? Hell, no!"

"I don't want it for salvage. I want it for a present."

Sandy looked up again.

"Yeah. To give to someone else. Finish the tune-up and give it to me, okay?"

"You're nuts, kid-boy," Sandy said. "Even if I gave you the ship, what you gonna pay for the work with?"

"Aw, it'll only take a couple of hours. You're half done anyway. I figured you'd throw in the tune-up along with it. If you really want the money, I'll get it to you a little at a time. Vyme, what sort of professional discount will you give me? I'm just a grease monkey, but I'm still in the business."

I whacked the back of his red head between a-little-too-playfully and not-too-hard. "Come on, kid-boy," I said. "Help me take care of puddles downstairs. Sandy, finish it up, huh?"

Sandy grunted and plunged both hands back into the organum.

As soon as the lift door closed, Ratlit demanded, "You gonna give it to me, Vyme?"

"It's Sandy's ship," I said.

"You tell him, and he will."

I laughed. "You tell me how your golden turned out when he came to. I assume that's who you want the ship for. What sort of fellow was he?"

Ratlit hooked his fingers in the mesh wall of the lift cage and leaned back. "There're only two types of golden." He began to swing from side to side. "Mean ones and stupid ones." He was repeating a standard line around the Star Pit.

"I hope yours is stupid," I said, thinking of the two who'd just ruined Sandy's day and upset mine.

"Which is worse?" Ratlit shrugged. That's the rest of the line. When a golden isn't being outright mean, he exhibits the sort of nonthinkingness that gets other people hurt—you remember the one that nearly rammed my ship, or the ones who didn't bother to bring back the Kyber antitoxin? "But this one—" Ratlit stood up—"is unbelievably stupid."

"Yesterday you hated them. Today you want to give one a ship?"

"He doesn't have one," Ratlit explained calmly, as though that warranted all change of attitude. "And because he's sick, it'll be hard for him to find work unless he has one of his own."

"I see." We bounced on the silicon cushion. I pushed open the door and started for the office. "What all went on after I left? I must have missed the best part of the evening."

"You did. Will I really need that much more sleep when I pass thirty-five?"

"Cut the cracks and tell me what happened."

"Well—" Ratlit leaned against the office doorjamb while I dialed necrotics. "Alegra and I talked a little after you left, till finally we realized the golden was awake and listening. Then he told us we were beautiful."

I raised an eyebrow. "*Mmmm?*"

"That's what we said. And he said it again, and that watching us talk and think and build was one of the most beautiful things he'd ever seen. 'What *have* you seen?' we asked him. And he began to tell us." Ratlit stopped breathing, something built up, then, at once, it came out: "Oh, Vyme, the places he's been! The things he's done! The landscapes he's starved in, the hells where he's had to lie down and go to sleep he was that tired, or the heavens he's soared through screaming! Oh, the things he told us about! And Alegra made them almost real so we could all be there again, just like she used to do when she was a psychiatrist! The stories, the places, the things . . . "

"Sounds like it was really something."

"It was nothing!" he came back vehemently. "It was all in the tears that wash your eyes, in the humming in your ears, in the taste of your own saliva. It was just a hallucination, Vyme! It wasn't real." Here his voice started cracking between the two octaves that were after it. "But that thing I told you about . . . huge . . . alive and dead at the same time, like a star . . . way in another galaxy. Well, he's *seen* it. And last night, it wasn't real of course, but . . . I almost heard it . . . sing!" His eyes were huge and green and bright. I felt envious of anyone who could pull that reaction from kids like Alegra and Ratlit.

"So, we decided—" Ratlit's voice fixed itself on the proper side of middle C—"after he went back to sleep, and we lay awake talking awhile longer, that we'd try and help him get back out there. Because it's . . . wonderful."

"That's fascinating." When I finished my call, I stood up from the desk. I'd been sitting on the corner. "After work I'll buy you dinner, and you can tell me about the things he showed you."

"He's still there, at Alegra's," Ratlit said—helplessly, I realized after a moment. "I'm going back there right after work."

"Oh," I said. I didn't seem to be invited.

"It's just a shame," Ratlit said when we came out of the office, "that he's *so* stupid." He glanced at the mess staining the concrete that had been a golden and shook his head.

I'd gone back to the books when Sandy stepped in. "All finished. What say we knock off for a beer or something, huh, boss?"

"All right," I said, surprised. Sandy was usually as social as he was handsome. "Want to talk about something?"

"Yeah." He looked relieved.

"That business this morning got to your head, huh?"

"Yeah," he repeated.

"There is a reason," I said as I made ready to go. "It's got something to do with the psychological part of being a golden. Meanness and stupidity, like everyone says. But however it makes them act here, it protects them from complete insanity at the twenty thousand light-year limit."

"Yeah. I know." Sandy had started stepping uncomfortably from one boot to the other. "But that's not what I wanted to talk about."

"It isn't?"

"*Um-um.*"

"Well?" I asked after a moment.

"It's that kid, the one you're gonna give the ship to."

"Ratlit?"

"Yeah."

"I haven't made up my mind about giving him the ship," I lied. "Besides, legally it's yours."

"You'll give it to him," Sandy said. "And I don't care. I mean not about the ship. But, boss, I gotta talk to you about that kid-boy."

Something about Sandy . . .

I'd never realized he'd thought of Ratlit as more than a general nuisance. Also, he seemed sincerely worried about me. I was curious. It took him all the way to the bar and through two beers—while I drank hot milk with honey—before he tongued and chewed what he wanted to say into shape.

"Boss, understand, I'm nearer Ratlit than you. Not only my age. My life's been more like his than yours has. You look at him like a son. To me, he's a younger brother: I taught him all the tricks. I don't understand him completely, but I see him clearer than you do. He's had a hard time, but not as hard as you think. And he's gonna take you—and I don't mean money—for everything he can."

Where the hell that came from I didn't know and didn't like. "He won't take anything I don't want to give."

"Boss?" Sandy asked suddenly. "You got kids of your own?"

"Nine," I said. "Did have. I don't see the ones who're left now, for which their parents have always been just as happy—except one. And she was sensible enough to go along with the rest, while she was alive."

"Oh." Sandy got quiet again. Suddenly he went scrambling in his overall pouch and pulled out a three-inch porta-pix. Those great, greasy hands that I was teaching to pick up an eggshell through a five-hundred-to-one-ratio waldo were clumsily fumbling at the push-pull levers. "I got kids," he said. "See. Seven of them."

And on the porta-pix screen was a milling, giggling group of little apes that couldn't have been anybody else's. All the younger ones lacked was acne. They even shuffled back and forth from one foot to the other. They began to wave, and the speaker in the back chirped: "Hi, Da! Hello, Da! Da, Mommy says to say we love you! Da, Da, come home soon!"

"I'm not with them now," he said throatily. "But I'm going back soon as I get enough money so I can take them all out of that hellhole they're in now and get the whole family with a decent-sized proke-group. They're only twenty-three adults there now, and things were beginning to rub. That's why I left in the first place. It was getting so nobody could talk to anyone else. That's pretty rough on all our kids, thirty-two when I left. But soon I'll be able to fix that."

"On the salary I'm paying you?" This was the first I'd heard of any of this; that was my first reaction. My second, which I didn't voice, was: Then why the hell don't you take that ship and sell it somehow! Over forty and self-employed, the most romantic become momentarily practical.

Sandy's fist came down hard on the bar. "That's what I'm trying to *say* to you, boss! About you, about Ratlit. You've all got it in your heads that this, out here, is it. The end. Sure, you gotta accept limitations, but the right ones. Sure, you have to admit there are certain directions in which you cannot go. But once you do that, you find there are others where you can go as far as you want. Look, I'm not gonna hang around the Star Pit all my life! And if I make my way back toward galactic center, make enough money so I can go home, raise my family the way I want, that's going forward, forward even from here. Not back."

"All right," I said. Quiet Sandy had surprised me. I still wondered why he wasn't breaking his tail to get salvage on that ship that had just fallen into his hands, if getting back home with money in his pocket was that important. "I'm glad you told me about yourself. Now how does it all tie up with Ratlit?"

"Yeah. Ratlit." He put the porta-pix back in his overall pouch. "Boss, Ratlit is the kid your own could be. You want to give him the advice, friendship, and concern he's never had, that you couldn't give yours. But Ratlit is also the kid I was about ten, fifteen years ago, started no place, with no destination, and no values to help figure out the way, mixed up in all the wrong things, mainly because he's not sure where the right ones are."

"I don't think you're that much like Ratlit," I told him. "I think you may wish you were. You've done a lot of the things Ratlit's done? Ever write a novel?"

"Wrote a trilogy," Sandy said. "It was lousy. But it pushed some things off my chest. So I got something out of it, even if nobody else did—which is what's important. Because now I'm a better mechanic for it, boss. Until I admit to myself what I can't do, it's pretty hard to work on what I can. Same goes for Ratlit. You too. That's growing up. And one thing you can't do is help Ratlit by giving him a ship he can't fly."

Growing up brought back the picture. "Sandy, did you ever build an ecologarium when you were a kid?"

"No." The word had the puzzled inflection that means, *Don't-even-know-what-one-is.*

"I didn't either," I told him. Then I grinned and punched him on the shoulder. "Maybe you're a little like me, too? Let's get back to work."

"Another thing," Sandy said, not looking very happy as he got off the stool. "Boss, that kid's gonna hurt you. I don't know how, but it's gonna seem like he hunted for how to make it hurt most, too. *That's* what I wanted to tell you, boss."

I was going to urge him to take the ship, but he handed me the keys back in the hangar before I could say anything, and walked away. When people who should be clearing up their own problems start giving you advice . . . well, there was something about Sandy I didn't like.

If I can't take long walks at night with company, I take them by myself. I was strolling by the Edge, the world-wind was low, and the Stellarplex, the huge heat-gathering mirror that's hung nine thousand miles off the Pit, was out. It looks vaguely like the moon used to look from Earth, only twice as big, perfectly silver, and during the three and a half days it faces us it's always full.

Then, up ahead where the fence was broken, I saw Ratlit kicking gravel over the Edge. He was leaning against a lamppost, his shirt ballooning and collapsing at his back.

"Hey, kid-boy! Isn't the golden still at Alegra's?"

Ratlit saw me and shrugged.

"What's the matter?" I asked when I reached him. "Ate dinner yet?"

He shrugged again. His body had the sort of ravenous metabolism that shows twenty-four hours without food. "Come on. I promised you a meal. Why so glum?"

"Make it something to drink."

"I know about your phony ID," I told him. "But we're going to eat. You can have milk, just like me."

No protests, nor dissertations on the injustice of liquor laws. He started walking with me.

"Come on, kid-boy, talk to gramps. Don't you want your ship anymore?"

Suddenly he clutched my forearm with white, bony fingers. My forearm is pretty thick, and he couldn't get his hands around it. "Vyme, you've got to make Sandy give it to me now! You've got to!"

"Kid-boy, talk to me."

"Alegra." He let go. "And the golden. Hate golden, Vyme. Always hate them. Because if you start to like one, and then start hating again, it's worse."

"What's going on? What are they doing?"

"He's talking. She's hallucinating. And neither one pays any attention to *me*."

"I see."

"You don't see. You don't understand about Alegra and me."

Then I was the only one who'd met the both of them who didn't. "I know you're very fond of each other." More could be said.

Ratlit said more. "We don't even like each other that much, Vyme. But we *need* each other. Since she's been here, I get her medicine for her. She's too sick to go out much, now. And when I have bad changes, or sometimes bright recognitions, it doesn't matter, I bring them to her, and she builds pictures of them for me, and we explore them together and . . . learn about things. When she was a psychiatrist for the government, she learned an awful lot about how people tick. And she's got an awful lot to teach me, things I've got to know." Fifteen-year-old ex-psychiatrist drug addicts? Same sort of precocity that produces thirteen-year-old novelists. Get used to it. "I need her now almost as much as she needs her . . . medicine."

"Have you told the golden you've got him a ship?"

"You didn't say I could have it yet."

"Well, I say so right now. Why don't we go back there and tell him he can be on his way? If we put it a little more politely, don't you think that'll do the trick?"

He didn't say anything. His face just got back a lot of its life.

"We'll go right after we eat. What the hell, I'll buy you a drink. I may even have one with you."

Alegra's was blinding when we arrived. "Ratlit, oh, you're back! Hello, Vyme! I'm so glad you're both here! Everything is beautiful tonight."

"The golden," Ratlit said. "Where's the golden?"

"He's not here." A momentary throb of sadness, dispelled with tortuous joy. "But he's coming back!"

"Oh," Ratlit said. His voice echoed through the long corridors of golden absence winding the room. "'Cause I got a ship for him. All his. Just had a tune-up. He can leave anytime he wants to."

"Here's the keys," I said, taking them from my pouch for dramatic effect. "Happen to have them right here."

As I handed them to Ratlit there were fireworks, applause, a fanfare of brasses. "Oh, that's wonderful. Wonderful! Because guess what, Ratlit. Guess what, Vyme?"

"I don't know," Ratlit said. "What?"

"I'm a golden too!" Alegra cried from the shoulders of the cheering crowd that pushed its way through more admiring thousands.

"Huh?"

"I, me, myself am actually an honest-to-goodness golden. I just found out today."

"You can't be," Ratlit said. "You're too old for it just to show up now."

"Something about my medicine," Alegra explained. "It's dreadfully complicated." The walls were papered with anatomical charts, music by Stockhausen. "Something in my medicine kept it from coming out until now, until a golden could come to me, drawing it up and out of the depths of me, till it burst out, beautiful and wonderful and . . . golden! Right now he's gone off to Carlson Labs with a urine sample for a final hormone check. They'll let him know in an hour, and he'll bring back my golden belt. But he's sure already. And when he comes back with it, I'm going to go with him to the far galaxies, as his apprentice. We're going to find a cure for his sickness and something that will make it so I won't need my medicine anymore. He says if you have all the universe to roam around in, you can find anything you look for. But you need it *all*— not just a cramped little cluster of a few billion stars off in a corner by itself. Oh, I'm free, Ratlit, like you always wanted to be! While you were gone, he . . . well, did something to me that was . . . *golden*! It triggered my hormonal imbalance." The image came in through all five senses. Breaking the melodious ecstasy came the clatter of keys as Ratlit hurled them at the wall.

I left feeling pretty odd. Ratlit had started to go too, but Alegra called him back. "Oh, now don't go on like that, Ratty! Act your age. Won't you stay and do me one little last favor?"

So he stayed. When I untangled myself from the place and was walking home, I kept on remembering what Alegra had said about love.

Work next day went surprisingly smoothly. Poloscki called me up about ten and asked if I knew where Ratlit was because he hadn't been at work that day. "You're sure the kid isn't sick?"

I said I'd seen him last night and that he was probably all right. Poloscki made a disgusted sound and hung up.

Sandy left a few minutes early, as he'd been doing all week, to run over to the post office before it closed. He was expecting a letter from his group, he said. I felt strange about having given the ship away out from under him. It was sort of an immature thing to do. But he hadn't said anything about wanting it, and Ratlit was still doing Alegra favors, so maybe it would all work out for the best.

I thought about visiting Alegra that evening. But there was the last six months' paperwork, still not finished. I went into the office, plugged in the computer, and got ready to work late.

I was still at it sometime after eleven when the entrance light blinked, which meant somebody had opened the hangar door. I'd locked it. Sandy had the keys so he could come in early. So it was Sandy. I was ready for a break and all set to jaw with him awhile. He was always coming back to do a little work at odd hours. I waited for him to come into the office. But he didn't.

Then the needle on the power gauge, which had been hovering near zero with only the drain of the little office computer, swung up to seven. One of the big pieces of equipment had been cut in.

There was some cleanup work to do, but nothing for a piece that size. Frowning, I switched off the computer and stepped out of the office. The first great opening in the hangar roof was mostly blocked with the bulk of Ratlit's/Sandy's/my ship. Stellarplex light curved smoothly over one side, then snarled in the fine webbing of lifts, catwalks, haul-lines, and grappler rigging. The other two openings were empty, and thirty-meter circles of silver dropped through assembly riggings to the concrete floor. Then I saw Sandy.

He stood just inside the light from the last opening, staring up at the Stellarplex, its glare lost in his ruined face. As he raised his left hand—when it started to move I thought it looked too big—light caught on the silver joints of the master-gauntlet he was wearing. I knew where the power was going.

As his hand went above his head, a shadow fell over him as a fifteen-foot slave talon swung from the darkness, its movement aping the master-glove. He dropped his hand in front of his face, fingers curved. Metal claws lowered about him, beginning to quiver. Something about . . . he was trying to kill himself!

I started running toward those hesitant, gaping claws, leaped into the grip, and reached over his shoulder to slap my forearm into the control glove, just as he squeezed. Like I said, my forearm is big, but when those claws came together, it was a tight fit. Sandy was crying.

"You stupid," I shouted, "inconsiderate, bird-brained, infantile—" at last I got the glove off "—puerile . . ." Then I said, "What the hell is the matter with you?"

Sandy was sitting on the floor now, his head hung between his shoulders. He stank.

"Look," I said, maneuvering the talon back into place with the gross-motion controls of the gauntlet's wrist, "if you want to go jump off the Edge, that's fine with me. Half the gate's down anyway. But don't come here and mess up my tools. You can squeeze your own head up a little, but you're not going to bust up my glove here. You're fired. Now tell me what's wrong."

"I knew it wasn't going to work. Wasn't even worth trying. I knew . . ." His voice was getting all mixed up with the sobs. "But I thought maybe . . ." Beside his left hand was the porta-pix, its screen cracked. And a crumpled piece of paper.

I turned off the glove, and twenty feet overhead the talons stopped humming. I picked up the paper and smoothed it out. I didn't mean to read it all the way through.

Dear Sanford,

Things have been difficult since you left but not too hard and I guess a lot of pressure is off everybody since you went away and the kids are getting used to your not being here though Bobbi-D cried a lot at first. She doesn't now. We got your letter and were glad to hear things had begun to settle down for you though Hank said you should have written before this and was very mad though Mary tried to calm him down but he just said, "When he married you all he married me too, damn it, and I've got just as much right to be angry at him as you have," which is true, Sanford, but I tell you what he said because it's a quote and I think you should know exactly what's being said, especially since it expresses something we all feel on one level or another. You said you might be able to send us a little money, if we wanted you home, which I think would be very good, the money I mean, though Laura said if I put that in the letter she would divorce us, but she won't, and like Hank I've got a right to say what I feel which is, Yes, I think you should send money, especially after that unpleasant business just before you left. But we are all agreed we do not want you to come back. And would rather not have the money if that's what it meant.

That is hard but true. As you can gather, your letter caused quite an upset here. I would like—which makes me different from the others but is why they wanted me to write this letter—to hear from you again and keep track of what you are doing because I used to love you very much and I never could hate you. But like Bobbi-D, I have stopped crying.

Sincerely—

The letter was signed "Joseph." In the lower corner were the names of the rest of the men and women of the group.

"Sandy?"

"I knew they wouldn't take me back. I didn't even really try, did I? But—"

"Sandy, get up."

"But the *children*," he whispered. "What's gonna happen to the children?"

And there was a sound from the other end of the hangar. Three stories up the side of the ship in the open hatchway, silvered by Stellarplex light, stood the golden, the one Ratlit and I had found on the street.

You remember what he looked like.

He and Alegra must have sneaked in while Sandy and I were struggling with the waldo. Probably they wanted to get away as soon as possible before Ratlit made real trouble, or before I changed my mind and got the keys back. All this ship-giving had been done without witnesses. The sound was the lift rising toward the hatchway. "The children . . ." Sandy whispered again.

The door opened, and a figure stepped out in the white light. Only it was Ratlit! It was Ratlit's red hair, his gold earring, his bouncy run as he started for the hatch. And there were . . . links of yellow metal around his wrist!

Baffled, I heard the golden call: "Everything checks out inside, brother. She'll fly us anywhere."

And Ratlit cried, "I got the grapples all released, cousin. Let's go!" Their voices echoed down through the hangar. Sandy raised his head, squinting.

As Ratlit leapt into the hatch, the golden caught his arm around the boy's shoulder. They stood a moment, gazing at one another, then Ratlit turned to look down into the hangar, back on the world he was about to leave. I couldn't tell if he knew we were there or not. Even as the hatch swung closed, the ship began to whistle.

I hauled Sandy back into the shock chamber. I hadn't even locked the door when the thunder came and my ears nearly split. I think the noise surprised Sandy out of himself. It broke something up in my head, but the pieces were falling wrong.

"Sandy," I said, "we've got to get going!"

"*Huh?*" He was fighting the drunkenness and probably his stomach too.

"I don't wanna go nowhere—"

"You're going anyway. I'm sure as hell not going to leave you all alone."

———

Wh" hen we were halfway up the stairs I figured she wasn't there. I felt just the same. Was she with them in the ship—?

"My medicine. Please can't you get my medicine? I've got to have my medicine, please, please . . . please."

I could just hear the small, high voice when I reached the door. I pushed it open.

Alegra lay on the mattress, pink eyes wide, white hair frizzled around her balding skull. She was incredibly scrawny, her uncut nails black as Sandy's nubs without the excuse of hours in a graphite-lubricated gauntlet. The translucency of her pigmentless skin under how-many-days of dirt made my flesh crawl. Her face drew in around her lips like the flesh about a scar. "My medicine, Vyme—is that you? You'll get my medicine for me, Vyme? Won't you get my medicine?" Her mouth wasn't moving, but the voice came on. She was too weak to project on any but the aural level. It was the first time I'd seen Alegra without her cloak of hallucination, and it brought me up short.

"Alegra," I said when I got hold of myself. "Ratlit and the golden went off on the ship!"

"Ratlit. Oh, nasty Ratty, awful little boy! He wouldn't get my medicine. But you'll get it for me, won't you, Vyme? I'm going to die in about ten minutes, Vyme. I don't want to die. Not like this. The world is so ugly and painful now. I don't want to die here."

"Don't you have any?" I stared around the room I hadn't seen since Drunk-roach lived there. It was a lot worse. Dried garbage, piled first in one corner, now covered half the floor. The rest was littered with papers, broken glass, and a spilled can of something unrecognizable for the mold.

"No. None here. Ratlit gets it from a man who hangs out in Gerg's over on Calle-X. Oh, Ratlit used to get it for me every day, such a nice little boy, every day he would bring me my lovely medicine, and I never had to leave my room at all. You go get it for me, Vyme!"

"It's the middle of the night, Alegra! Gerg's is closed, and Calle-X is all the way across the Pit anyway. I couldn't even get there in ten minutes, much less find this character and come back!"

"If I were well, Vyme, I'd fly you there in a cloud of light pulled by peacocks and porpoises, and you'd come back to hautboys and tambourines, bringing my beautiful medicine to me, in less than an eye's blink. But I'm sick now. And I'm going to die."

There was a twitch in the crinkled lid of one pink eye.

"Alegra, what happened!"

"Ratlit's insane!" she projected with shocking viciousness. I heard Sandy behind me catch his breath. "Insane at twenty thousand light-years, dead at twenty-five."

"But his golden belt—"

"It was mine! It was my belt, and he stole it. And he wouldn't get my medicine. Ratlit's not a golden. *I'm* a golden, Vyme! I can go anywhere, anywhere at all! I'm a golden golden golden. . . . But I'm sick now. I'm so sick."

"But didn't the golden know the belt was yours?"

"Him? Oh, he's so incredibly stupid! He would believe anything. The golden went to check some papers and get provisions and was gone all day, to get my belt. But you were here that night. I asked Ratlit to go get my medicine and take another sample to Carlson's for me. But neither of them came back till I was very sick, very weak. Ratlit found the golden, you see, told him that I'd changed my mind about going, and that he, Ratlit, was a golden as well, that he'd just been to Carlson's. So the golden gave him my belt and off they went."

"But how in the world would he believe a kid with a story like that?"

"You know how stupid a golden can be, Vyme. As stupid as they can be mean. Besides, it doesn't matter to him if Ratlit dies. He doesn't care if Ratlit was telling the truth or not. The golden will live. When Ratlit starts drooling, throwing up blood, goes deaf first and blind last, and dies, the golden won't even be sad. He's too stupid to feel sad. That's the way golden are. But I'm sad, Vyme, because no one will bring me my medicine."

My frustration had to lash at something; she was there. "You mean you didn't know what you were doing to Ratlit by leaving,

Alegra? You mean you didn't know how much he wanted to get out, and how much he needed you at the same time? You couldn't see what it would do to him if you deprived him of the thing he needed and rubbed his nose in the thing he hated both at once? You couldn't guess that he'd pull something crazy? Oh, kid-girl, you talk about golden. You're the stupid one!"

"Not stupid," she projected quietly. "*Mean,* Vyme. I knew he'd try to do something. I just didn't think he'd succeed. Ratlit is really such a child."

The frustration, spent, became rolling sadness. "Couldn't you have waited just a little longer, Alegra? Couldn't you have worked out the leaving some other way, not hurt him so much?"

"I wanted to get out, Vyme, to keep going and not be trapped, to be free. Like Ratlit wanted, like you want, like Sandy wants, like the golden. Only I was cruel. I had the chance to do it, and I took it. Why is that bad, Vyme? Unless, of course, that's what being free means."

A twitch in the eyelid again. It closed. The other stayed open.

"Alegra—"

"I'm a golden, Vyme. A golden. And that's how golden are. But don't be mad at me, Vyme. Don't. Ratlit was mean too, not to give me my medi—"

The other eye closed. I closed mine too and tried to cry, but my tongue was pushing too hard on the roof of my mouth.

Sandy came to work the next day, and I didn't mention his being fired. The teletapes got hold of it, and the headlines tried to make the thing as sordid as possible:

X-CON TEENAGER
(they didn't mention his novel)
SLAYS JUNKY SWEETHEART! DIES HORRIBLY!

They didn't mention the golden either. They never do.

Reporters pried around the hangar awhile, trying to get us to say the ship was stolen. Sandy came through pretty well. "It was his ship," he grunted, putting lubricant in the gauntlets. "I gave it to him."

"What are you gonna give a kid like that a ship for? Maybe you loaned it to him. 'Dies horrible death in borrowed ship.' That sounds okay."

"Gave it to him. Ask the boss." He turned back toward the scaffolding. "He witnessed."

"Look, even if you liked the kid, you're not saving him anything by covering up."

"I didn't like him," Sandy said. "But I gave him the ship."

"Thanks," I told Sandy when they left, not sure what I was thanking him for but still feeling very grateful. "I'll do you a favor back."

A week later Sandy came in and said, "Boss, I want my favor."

I narrowed my eyes against his belligerent tone. "So you're gonna quit at last. Can you finish out the week?"

He looked embarrassed, and his hands started moving around in his overall pouch. "Well, yeah. I am gonna leave. But not right away, boss. It is getting a little hard for me to take, out here."

"You'll get used to it," I said. "You know there's something about you that's, well, a lot like me. I learned. You will too."

Sandy shook his head. "I don't think I want to." His hand came out of his pocket. "See, I got a ticket." In his soiled fingers was a metal-banded card. "In four weeks I'm going back in from the Star Pit. Only I didn't want to tell you just now, because, well, I did want this favor, boss."

I was really surprised. "You're not going back to your group," I said. "What are you going to do?"

Sandy shrugged. "Get a job, I don't know. There're other groups. Maybe I've grown up a little bit." His fists went way down into his pouch, and he started to shift his weight back and forth on his feet. "About that favor, boss."

"What is it?"

"I got to talking to this kid outside. He's really had it rough,

Vyme." That was the first and last time Sandy ever called me by name, though I'd asked him to enough times before. "And he could use a job."

A laugh got all set to come out of me. But it didn't, because the look on his ugly face, behind the belligerence, was so vulnerable and intense. Vulnerable? But Sandy had his ticket; Sandy was going on.

"Send him to Poloscki's," I said. "Probably needs an extra grease monkey. Now let me get back to work, huh?"

"Could you take him over there?" Sandy said very quickly. "That's the favor, boss."

"Sandy, I'm awfully busy." I looked at him again. "Oh, all right."

"Hey, boss?" Sandy said as I slid from behind the desk. "Remember that thing you asked me if I ever had when I was a kid?"

It took a moment to come back to me. "You mean an ecologarium?"

"Yeah. That's the word." He grinned. "The kid-boy's got one. He's right outside, waiting for you."

"He's got it with him?"

Sandy nodded.

I walked toward the hangar door, picturing some kid lugging around a six-by-six plastic cage.

Outside the boy was sitting on a fuel hydrant. I'd put a few trees there, and the "day"-light from the illumination tubes arcing the street dappled the gravel around him.

He was about fourteen, with copper skin and curly black hair. I saw why Sandy wanted me to go with him about the job. Around his waist, as he sat hunched over on the hydrant with his toes spread on the metal base-flange, was a wide-linked, yellow belt: golden.

He was looking through an odd jewel-and-brass thing that hung from a chain around his neck.

"Hey."

He looked up. There were spots of light on his blue-black hair. "You need a job?"

He blinked.

"My name's Vyme. What's yours?"

"You call me An." The voice was even, detached, with an inflection that is golden.

I frowned. "Nickname?"

He nodded.

"And really?"

"Androcles."

"Oh." My oldest kid is dead. I know it because I have all sorts of official papers saying so. But sometimes it's hard to remember. And it doesn't matter whether the hair is black, white, or red. "Well, let's see if we can put you to work somewhere. Come on." An stood up, eyes fixed on me, suspicion hiding behind high glitter. "What's the thing around your neck?"

His eyes struck it and bounced back to my face. "Cousin?" he asked.

"Huh?" Then I remembered the golden slang. "Oh, sure. First cousins. Brothers if you want."

"Brother," An said. Then a smile came tumbling out of his face, silent and volcanic. He began loping beside me as we started off toward Poloscki's. "This—" he held up the thing on his chain—"is an ecologarium. Want to see?" His diction was clipped, precise, and detached. But when an expression caught on his face, it was unsettlingly intense.

"Oh, a little one. With microorganisms?"

An nodded.

"Sure. Let's have a look."

The hair on the back of his neck pawed the chain as he bent to remove it.

I held it up to see.

Some blue liquid, a fairly large air bubble, and a glob of black-speckled jelly filled a transparent globe, the size of an eyeball. It was set in two rings, one within the other, pivoted so that it turned in all directions. Mounted on the outside ring was a curved tube with a pin-sized lens. The tube was threaded into a bushing, and I guess you used it to look at what was going on in the sphere.

"Self-contained," explained An. "The only thing needed to keep the whole thing going is light. Just about any frequency will do, except way up on the blue end. And the shell cuts that out."

I looked through the brass eyepiece.

I'd swear there were over a hundred life forms with five to fifty stages each: spores, zygotes, seeds, eggs, growing and developing through larvae, pupae, buds, reproducing through sex, syzygy, fission.

Beside me An said: "The whole ecological cycle takes about two minutes. . . ."

Spongy masses like red lotuses clung to the air bubble. Every few seconds one would expel a cloud of black things like wrinkled bits of carbon paper into the gas where they were attacked by tiny motes I could hardly see even with the lens. Black became silver. It fell back to the liquid like globules of mercury, and coursed toward the jelly that was emitting a froth of bubbles. Something in the froth made the silver beads reverse direction. They reddened, sent out threads and alveoli, until they reached the main bubble again as lotuses.

The reason the lotuses didn't crowd each other out was because every eight or nine seconds a swarm of green paramecia devoured most of them. I couldn't tell where they came from; I never saw one of them split or get eaten, but they must have had something to do with the thorn-balls—if only because there were either thorn-balls or paramecia floating in the liquid, but never both at once.

A black spore in the jelly wiggled, then burst the surface as a white worm. Exhausted, it laid a couple of eggs, rested until it developed fins and a tail, then swam to the bubble where it laid more eggs among the lotuses. Its fins grew larger, its tail shriveled, splotches of orange and blue appeared, till it took off like a weird butterfly to flit around the inside of the bubble. The motes that silvered the black offspring of the lotus must have eaten the parti-colored fan because it just grew thinner and frailer till it disappeared. The eggs by the lotus would hatch into bloated fish forms that swam back through the froth to vomit a glob of jelly on the mass at the bottom, then collapse. The first eggs didn't do much except turn into black spores when they were covered with enough jelly.

All this was going on amidst a kaleidoscope of frail, wilting flowers and blooming jeweled webs, vines and worms, warts and jellyfish, symbiotes and saprophytes, while rainbow herds of algae careened back and forth like glittering confetti. One rough-rinded galoot, so big you could see him *without* the eyepiece, squatted on the wall, feeding on jelly, batting its eye-spots while tides surged through its quivering tears of gills.

I blinked as I took it from my eye.

"That looks complicated." I handed it back to him.

"Not really." He slipped it around his neck. "Took me two weeks with a notebook to get the whole thing figured out. You saw the big fellow?"

"The one who winked?"

"Yes. Its reproductive cycle is about two hours, which trips you up at first. Everything else goes so fast. But once you see him mate with the thing that looks like a spider web with sequins—same creature, different sex—and watch the offspring aggregate into paramecia, then dissolve again, the whole thing falls into—"

"One creature!" I said. "The whole thing is a single creature!"

An nodded vigorously. "Has to be to stay self-contained." The grin on his face whipped away like a snapped window shade. A very serious look was underneath. "Even after I saw the big fellow mate, it took me a week to understand it was all one."

"But if goofus and the fishnet have paramecia—" I began. It seemed logical when I made the guess.

"You've seen one before."

I shook my head. "Not like that one, anyway. I once saw something similar, but it was much bigger—about six feet across."

An's seriousness was replaced by horror. I mean he really started to shake. "How could you . . . *ever* even *see* all the . . . stuff inside, much less *catalogue* it? You say . . . *this* is complicated?"

"Hey, relax. Relax!" I said. He did. Like that. "It was much simpler," I explained and went on to describe the one our kids had made, so many years ago, as best I remembered.

"Oh," An said at last, his face set in its original impassivity. "It wasn't microorganisms. Simple. Yes." He looked at the pavement.

"Very simple." When he looked up, another expression had scrambled his features. It took a moment to identify. "I don't see the point at all." There was surprising physical surety in the boy's movement; his nervousness was a cat's, not a human's. But it was one of the psychological qualities of golden.

"Well," I said, "it showed the kids a picture of the way the cycles of life progress."

An rattled his chain. "That is why they gave us these things. But everything in the one you had was so primitive. It wasn't a very good picture."

"Don't knock it," I told him. "When I was a kid, all I had was an ant colony. I got my infantile *Weltanschauung* watching a bunch of bugs running around between two plates of glass. I think I would have been better prepared by a couple of hungry rats on a treadmill. Or maybe a torus-shaped fish tank alternating sharks with schools of piranhas: Get them all chasing around after each other real fast—"

"Ecology wouldn't balance," An said. "You'd need snails to get rid of the waste. Then a lot of plants to reoxygenate the water, and some sort of herbivore to keep down the plants because they'd tend to choke out everything since neither the sharks nor the piranhas would eat them." Kids and their damned literal minds. "If the herbivores had some way to keep the sharks off, then you might do it."

"What's wrong with the first one I described?"

The explanation worked around the muscles of his face. "The lizards, the segment worms, the plants, ani-worts—all their cycles were completely circular. They were born, grew up, reproduced, maybe took care of the kids awhile, then died. Their only function was reproduction. That's a pretty awful picture." He made an unintelligible face.

There was something about this wise-alecky kid who was golden, younger than Alegra, older than Ratlit, I liked.

"There are stages in here—" An tapped his globe with his pinky nail—"that don't get started on their most important functions till after they've reproduced and grown up through a couple more metamorphoses as well. Those little green worms are a sterile end stage of the blue feathery things. But they put out free phosphates that the algae live on. Everything else, just about, lives on the algae—except the thorn-balls. They eat the worms when they die. There're phagocytes in there that ingest the dust-things when they get out of the bubble and start infecting the liquid." All at once he got very excited. "Each of us in the class got one of these! They made us figure them out! Then we had to prepare these report tapes on whether the reproductive process was the primary function in life or an adjunctive one." Something white frothed at the corners of his mouth. "I think grown-ups should just *leave* their kids the hell *alone,* go on and do something *else,* stop bothering us! That's what I said! That's what I *told* them!" He stopped, his tongue flicked the foam at the cusp of his lips; he seemed all right again.

"Sometimes," I said evenly, "if you leave them alone and forget about them, you end up with monsters who aren't kids anymore. If you'd been left alone, you wouldn't have had a chance to put your two cents in in the first place, and you wouldn't have that thing around your neck." And he was really trying to follow what I was saying. A moment past his rage, his face was as open and receptive as a two-year-old's. God, I want to stop thinking about Antoni!

"That's not what I mean." An wrapped his arms around his shoulders and bit on his forearm pensively.

"An—you're not stupid, kid-boy. You're cocky, but I don't think you're mean. You're golden." There was all my resentment, out now, Ratlit. There it was, Alegra. I didn't grow up with the word, so it meant something different to me.

An looked up to ingest my meaning. The toothmarks were white on his skin, then red around that.

"How long have you been one?"

He watched me, arms still folded. "They found out when I was seven."

"That long ago?"

"Yes." He turned and started walking again. "I was very precocious."

"Oh." I nodded. "Just about half your life, then. How's it been, little brother, being a golden?"

An dropped his arms. "They take you away from your group a

lot of times." He shrugged. "Special classes. Training programs. I'm psychotic."

"I never would have guessed." What would you call Ratlit? What would you call Alegra?

"I know it shows. But it gets us through the psychic pressures at the reality breakdown at twenty thousand light-years. It really does. For the past few years, though, they've been planting the psychosis artificially, pretty far down in the preconscious, so it doesn't affect our ordinary behavior as much as it does the older ones. They can use this process on anybody whose hormone system is even close to golden. They can get a lot more and a lot better quality golden that way than just waiting for us to pop up by accident."

As I laughed, something else struck me. "Just what do you need a job out here for, though? Why not hitch out with some cousin or get a job on one of the intergalactics as an apprentice?"

"I have a job in another galaxy. There'll be a ship stopping for me in two months to take me out. A whole lot of Star Pits have been established in galaxies halfway to Un-dok. I'll be going back and forth, managing roboi-equipment, doing managerial work. I thought it would be a good idea to get some practical experience out here before I left."

"Precocious," I nodded. "Look, even with roboi-equipment you have to know one hell of a lot about the inside of how many different kinds of keeler drives? You're not going to get that kind of experience in two months as a grease monkey. And roboi-equipment? I don't even have any in my place. Poloscki's got some, but I don't think you'll get your hands on it."

"I know a good deal already," An said with strained modesty.

"Yeah?" I asked him a not too difficult question and got an adequate answer. Made me feel better that he didn't come back with something really brilliant. I did know more than he did. "Where'd you learn?"

"They gave me the information the same way they implanted my psychosis."

"You're pretty good for your age." Dear old Luna Vocational! Well, maybe educational methods have improved. "Come to think of it, I was just as old as you when I started playing around with those keeler models. Dozens and dozens of helical inserts—"

"And those oily organum sensitives in all that graphite? Yes, brother! But I've never even had my hands in a waldo."

I frowned. "Hell, when I was younger than you, I could—" I stopped. "Of course, with roboi-equipment, you don't need them. But it's not a bad thing to know how they work, just in case."

"That's why I want a job." He hooked one finger on his chain. "Brother-in-law Sandy and I got to talking, so I asked him about working here. He said you might help me get in someplace."

"I'm glad he did. My place only handles big ships, and it's all waldo. Me and an assistant can do the whole thing. Poloscki's place is smaller, but handles both inter- and intragalactic jobs, so you get more variety and a bigger crew. You find Poloscki, say I sent you, tell what you can do and why you're out here. Belt or no, you'll probably get something better than a monkey."

"Thanks, brother."

We turned off Calle-D. Poloscki's hangar was ahead. Dull thunder sounded over the roof as a ship departed.

"As soon as I despair of the younger generation," I told him, "one of you kids comes by and I start to think there's hope. Granted you're a psychopath, you're a lot better than some of your older, distant relations."

An looked up at me, apprehensive.

"You've never had a run-in with some of your cousins out here. But don't be surprised if you're dead tomorrow and your job's been inherited by some character who decided to split your head open to check on what's inside. I try to get used to you, behaving like something that isn't even up to savage. But, boy-kid, can your kind really mess with a guy's picture of the universe."

"And what the hell do you expect us to act like?" An shot back. Spittle glittered on his lips again. "What would *you* do if you were trapped like *us*?"

"Huh?" I said questioningly. "*You*, trapped?"

"Look." A spasm passed over his shoulders. "The psycho-technician who made sure I was properly psychotic *wasn't* a golden, *brother*! You *pay* us to bring back the weapons, dad! *We* don't fight your damn wars, *grampa*! You're the ones who take us away from our groups, say we're *too* valuable to submit to *your* laws, then deny us our heredity because we don't *breed* true, no-relative-of-*mine*!"

"Now, wait a minute—!"

An snatched the chain from around his neck and held it taut in front of him. His voice ground to a whisper, his eyes glittered. "I strangled one of my classmates with this chain, the one I've got in my hands now." One by one, his features blanked all expression. "They took it away from me for a week, as punishment for killing that little girl." The whisper stopped decibels above silence, then went on evenly. "Out here, nobody will punish me. And my reflexes are faster than yours."

Fear lashed my anger as I followed the insanity flickering in his eyes.

"Now!" He made a quick motion with his hands; I ducked. "I give it to you!" He flung the chain toward me. Reflexively I caught it. An turned away and stalked into Poloscki's.

When I burst through the rattling hangar door at my place, the lift was coming down. Sandy yelled through the mesh walls, "Did he get the job?"

"Probably," I yelled back, going toward the office.

I heard the cage settle on the silicon cushion. Sandy was at my side a moment later, grinning. "So how do you like my brother-in-law, Androcles?"

"Brother-in-law?" I remembered An using the phrase, but I'd thought it was part of the slang golden. Something about the way Sandy said it though. "He's your *real* brother-in-law?"

"He's Joey's kid brother. I didn't want to say anything until after you'd met him." Sandy came along with me toward the office door. "Joey wrote me again and said since An was coming out here he'd tell him to stop by and see me and maybe I could help him out."

"Now how the hell am I supposed to know who Joey is?" I pushed open the door. It banged the wall.

"He's one of my husbands, the one who wrote me that letter you told me you'd read."

"Oh, yeah. Him." I started stacking papers.

"I thought it was pretty nice of him after all that to tell An to look me up when he got out here. It means that there's still somebody left who doesn't think I'm a complete waste. So what do you think of Androcles?"

"He's quite a boy." I scooped up the mail that had come in after lunch, started to go through it but put it down to hunt for my coveralls.

"An used to come visit us when he got his one weekend a month off from his training program as golden," Sandy was going on. "Joey's and An's parents lived in the reeds near the estuary. But we lived back up the canyon by Chroma Falls. An and Joey were pretty close, even though Joey's my age and An was only eight or nine back then. I guess Joey was the only one who really knew what An was going through, since they were both golden."

Surprised and shocked, I turned back to the desk. "You were married to a golden?" One of the letters on the top of the pile was addressed to Alegra from Carlson's Labs. I had a carton of the kids' junk in the locker and had gotten their mail—there wasn't much—sent to the hangar, as though I were waiting for somebody to come for it.

"Yeah," Sandy said, surprised at my surprise. "Joey."

So I wouldn't stand there gaping, I picked up Alegra's letter.

"Since the traits that are golden are polychromazoic, it dies out if they only breed with each other. There's a big campaign back in galactic center to encourage them to join heterogeneous prokegroups."

"Like bluepoint Siamese cats, huh?" I ran my blackened thumbnail through the seal.

"That's right. But they're *not* animals, boss. I remember what they put that kid-boy through for psychotic reinforcement of the factors that were golden to make sure they stuck. It tore me up to hear him talk about it when he'd visit us."

I pulled a porta-pix out of Alegra's envelope. Carlson's tries to personalize its messages.

"I'm sure glad they can erase the conscious memory from the kids' minds when they have to do that sort of stuff."

"Small blessings and all that." I flipped the porta-pix on.

Personalized but mass produced: ". . . blessed addit . . ." the little speaker echoed me. Poloscki and I had used Carlson's a couple of times. I guess every other mechanic up here had too. The porta-pix had started in the middle. Now it hummed back to the beginning.

"You know," Sandy went on, "Joey was different, yeah, sort of dense about some things . . ."

"Alegra," beamed the chic, grandmotherly type Carlson's always uses for messages of this sort, "we were so glad to receive the urine sample you sent us by Mr. Ratlit last Thursday . . ."

". . . even so, Joey was one of the sweetest men or women I've ever known. He was the easiest person in the group to live with. Maybe it was because he was away a lot . . ."

". . . and now, just a week later—remember, Carlson's gives results immediately and confirms them by personalized porta-pix in seven days—we are happy to tell you that there will be a blessed addition to your group. However . . ."

". . . All right, he was different, reacted funny to a lot of things. But nothing like this rank destructive stupidity you find out here at the Star Pit . . ."

". . . the paternity is not Mr. Ratlit's. If you are interested, for your eugenic records, in further information, please send us other possible urine samples from the men in your group, and we will be glad to confirm paternity . . ."

". . . I can't understand the way people act out here, boss. And that's why I'm pushing on."

". . . Thank you so much for letting us give you this wonderful news. Remember, when in doubt, call Carlson's."

I said to Sandy, "You were married with—you loved a golden?"

Unbidden, the porta-pix began again. "Alegra . . ." I flipped it off without looking.

"Sandy," I said, "you were hired because you were a fair mechanic and you kept off my back. Do what you're paid for. Get out of here."

"Oh. Sure, boss." Sandy backed quickly from the office.

I sat down.

Maybe I'm old-fashioned, but when someone runs off and abandons a sick girl like that, it gets me. That was the trip to Carlson's, the last little favor Ratlit never came back from. On-the-spot results, and formal confirmation in seven days. In her physical condition, pregnancy would have been as fatal as the withdrawal. And she was too ill for any abortive method I know of not to kill her. On-the-spot results. Ratlit must have known all that too when he got the results back, the results that Alegra was probably afraid of, the results she sent him to find. Ratlit knew Alegra was going to die anyway.

And so he stole a golden belt.

"Loving someone, I mean really loving someone . . ." Alegra had said.

When someone runs off and leaves a sick girl like that, there's got to be a reason.

It came together for me like two fissionables. The explosion cut some moorings in my head I thought were pretty solidly fixed.

I pulled out the books, plugged in the computer, unplugged it, put the books away, and stared into the ecologarium in my fist.

Among the swimming, flying, crawling things, mating, giving birth, growing, changing, busy at whatever their business was, I picked out those dead-end green worms. I hadn't noticed them before because they were at the very edge of things, bumping against the wall. After they released their free phosphates and got tired of butting at the shell, they turned on one another and tore themselves to pieces.

Fear and anger is a bad combination in me.

I came close to being killed by a golden once, through that meanness and stupidity.

The same meanness and stupidity that killed Alegra and Ratlit.

And now when this damn kid threatened to—I mean at first I had *thought* he was threatening to—

|reached Gerg's a few minutes after the "day"-lights went out and the streetlamps came on. But I'd stopped in nearly a dozen places on the way. I remember trying to explain to a sailor from a star-shuttle who was just stopping over at the Star Pit for the first time and was all upset because one woman golden had just attacked another with a broken glass; I remember saying to the three-headed bulge of his shoulder, ". . . an ant colony! You know what it is, two pieces of glass with dirt between them, and you can see all the little ants make tunnels and hatch eggs and stuff. When I was a kid, I had an ant colony. . . ." I started to shake my hand in his face. The chain from the ecologarium was all tangled up in my fingers.

"Look." He caught my wrist and pushed it down on the counter. "It's all right now, pal. Just relax."

"You look," I said as he turned away. "When I was a kid, all I had was an *ant* colony!"

He turned back and leaned his rusty elbow on the bar. "Okay," he said affably. Then he made the most stupid and frustrating mistake he possibly could have just then. "What about your aunt?"

"My mother—"

"I thought you were telling me about your aunt?"

"Naw," I said. "My aunt, she drank too much. This is about my mother."

"All right. Your mother then."

"My mother, see, she always worried about me, getting sick and things. I got sick a lot when I was a little kid. She made me mad! Used to go down and watch the ships take off from the place they called the Brooklyn Navy Yards. They were ships that went to the stars."

The sailor's Oriental face grinned. "Yeah, me too. Used to watch 'em when I was a kid."

"But it was raining, and she wouldn't let me go."

"Aw, that's too bad. Little rain never hurt a kid. Why didn't she call up and have it turned off so you could go out? Too busy to pay attention to you, huh? One of my old men was like that."

"Both of mine were," I said. "But not my ma. She was all over me all the time when she was there. But she made me mad!"

He nodded with real concern. "Wouldn't turn off the rain."

"Naw, couldn't. You didn't grow up where I did, narrow-minded, dark-side world. No modern conveniences."

"Off the main trading routes, huh?"

"Way off. She wouldn't let me go out, and that made me mad."

He was still nodding.

"So I broke it!" My fist came down hard on the counter, and the plastic globe in its brass cage clacked on the wood. "Broke it! Sand, glass all over the rug, on the windowsill!"

"What'd you break?"

"Smashed it, stamped on it, threw sand whenever she tried to make me stop!"

"Sand? You lived on a beach? We had a beach when I was a kid. A beach is nice for kids. What'd you break?"

"Let all the damn bugs out. Bugs in everything for days. Let 'em all out."

"Didn't have no bugs on our beach. But you said you were off the main trading routes."

"Let 'em *out*!" I banged my fist again. "Let *every*body out, whether they like it or not! It's their problem whether they make it, not mine! Don't care, I don't—" I was laughing now.

"She let you out, and you didn't care?"

My hand came down on top of the metal cage, hard. I caught my breath at the pain. "On our beach," I said, turning my palm up to look. There were red marks across it. "There weren't any bugs on our beach." Then I started shaking.

"You mean you were just putting me on, before, about the bugs. Hey, are you all right?"

". . . broke it," I whispered. Then I smashed fist and globe and chain into the side of the counter. "Let 'em *out*!" I whirled away, clutching my bruised hand against my stomach.

"*Watch* it, kid-boy!"

"I'm not a kid-boy!" I shouted. "You think I'm some stupid, half-crazy kid!"

"So you're older than me. Okay?"

"I'm not a kid anymore!"

"So you're ten years older than Sirius, all right? Quiet down, or they'll kick us out."

I bulled out of Gerg's. A couple of people came after me because I didn't watch where I was going. I don't know who won, but I remember somebody yelling, "Get out! Get out!" It may have been me.

I remember later, staggering under the mercury streetlamp, the world-wind slapping my face, stars swarming back and forth below me, gravel sliding under my boots, the toes inches over the Edge. The gravel clicked down the metal siding, the sound terribly clear as I reeled in the loud wind, shaking my arm against the night.

As I brought my hand back, the wind lashed the cold chain across my cheek and the bridge of my nose. I lurched back, trying to claw it away. But it stayed all tangled on my fingers while the globe swung, gleaming in the streetlight. The wind roared. Gravel chattered down the siding.

Later, I remember the hangar door ajar, stumbling into the darkness, so that in a moment I was held from plummeting into nothing only by my own footsteps, as black swerved around me. I stopped when my hip hit a workbench. I pawed around under the lip of the table till I found a switch. In the dim orange light, racked along the back of the bench in their plastic shock-cases, were the row of master-gauntlets. I slipped one out and slid my hand into it.

"Who's over there?"

"Go 'way, Sandy." I turned from the bench, switched up the power on the wrist controls. Somewhere in the dark above, a fifteen-foot slave-hand hummed to life.

"Sorry, buster. This isn't Sandy. Put that down and get away from there."

I squinted as the figure approached in the orange light, hand extended. I saw the vibra-gun and didn't bother to look at the face.

Then the gun went down. "Vyme, baby? That you? What the hell you doing here this hour of the night?"

"Poloscki?"

"Who'd you think it was?"

"Is this your—?" I looked around, shook my head. "But I thought it was my—" I shook my head again.

Poloscki sniffed. "Hey, have you been a naughty kid-boy, tonight!"

I swung my hand, and the slave-hand overhead careened twenty feet.

The gun jumped. "Look, you mess up my waldo and I *will* kill you, don't care who you are! Take that thing off."

"Very funny." I brought the talon down where I could see it clawing shadow.

"Come on, Vyme. I'm serious. Turn it off and put it down. You're a mess now, and you don't know what you're doing."

"That kid, the golden. Did you give him a job?"

"Sure. He said you sent him. Smart little so-and-so. He rehulled some yacht with the roboi-anakatasthasizer, just to show me what he could do. If I knew a few more people who could handle them that well, I'd go all roboi. He's not worth a damn with a waldo, but as long as he's got that little green light in front of him, he's fine."

I brought the talons down another ten feet so that the great spider claw hung between us. "Well, I happen to be very handy with a waldo, Poloscki."

"Vyme, you're gonna get *hur-rrrt* . . ."

"Poloscki," I said, "will you stop coming on like an overprotective aunt? I don't need another one."

"You're very drunk, Vyme."

"Yeah. But I'm no clumsy kid-boy who's going to mess up your equipment."

"If you do, you'll be—"

"Shut up and watch." I pulled the chain out of my pouch and tossed it onto the concrete floor. In the orange light you couldn't tell whether the cage was brass or silver.

"What's that?"

The claw came down, and the fine-point tips, millimeters above the floor, closed on the ecologarium.

"Oh, hey! I haven't seen one of those since I was ten. What are you going to do with it? Those are five-hundred-to-one strength, you know. You're gonna break it."

"That's right. Break this one too."

"Aw, come on. Let me see it first."

I lifted the globe. "Could be an eggshell," I said. "Drunk or sober I can handle this damn equipment, Poloscki."

"I haven't seen one for years. Used to have one."

"You mean it wasn't spirited back from some distant galaxy by golden, from some technology beyond our limited ken?"

"Product of the home spiral. Been around since the 'fifties."

I raised it over Poloscki's extended hand.

"They're supposed to be very educational. What do you want to break it for?"

"I never saw one."

"You came from someplace off the routes, didn't you? They weren't that common. Don't break it."

"I want to."

"Why, Vyme?"

Something got wedged in my throat. "Because I want to get out, and if it's not that globe, it's gonna be somebody's head." Inside the gauntlet my hand began to quiver. The talons jerked. Poloscki caught the globe and jumped back.

"Vyme—!"

"I'm hanging here at the Edge." My voice kept getting caught on the things in my throat. "I'm useless, with a bunch of monsters and fools!" The talons swung, contracted, clashed on each other. "And then when the children . . . when the *children* get so bad you can't even reach . . ." The claw opened, reached for Poloscki, who jumped back in the half-dark.

"Damn it, Vyme—"

". . . can't even reach the children anymore." The talon stopped shaking, came slowly back, knotting. "I want to break something and get out. Very childishly, yes. Because nobody is paying any attention to me." The claw jumped. "Even when I'm trying to help. I *don't* want to hurt anybody any*more*. I *swear* it, so help me, I swear—"

"Vyme, take off the glove and listen!"

I raised the slave-hand because it was about to scrape the cement.

"Vyme, I want to pay some attention to you." Slowly Poloscki walked back into the orange light. "You've been sending me kids for five years now, coming around and checking up on them, helping them out of the stupid scrapes they get in. They haven't all been Rat-lits. I like kids too. That's why I take them on. I think what you do is pretty great. Part of me loves kids. Another part of me loves you."

"Aw, Poloscki . . ." I shook my head. Somewhere disgust began.

"It doesn't embarrass me. I love you a little and wouldn't mind loving you a lot. More than once I've thought about asking you to start a group."

"*Please,* Poloscki. I've had too many weird things happen to me this week. Not tonight, huh?" I then turned the power off in the glove.

"Love shouldn't frighten you, no matter when or how it comes, Vyme. Don't run from it. A marriage between us? Yeah, it would be a little hard for somebody like you, at first. But you'd get used to it before long. Then when kids came around, there'd be two of—"

"I'll send Sandy over," I said. "He's the big-hearted marrying kind. Maybe he's about ready to try again." I pulled off the glove.

"Vyme, don't go out like that. Stay for just a minute!"

"Poloscki," I said, "I'm just not that goddamned drunk!" I threw the glove on the table.

"Please, Vyme."

"You're gonna use your gun to keep me here?"

"Don't be like—"

"I hope the kids I send over here appreciate you more than I do right now. I'm sorry I busted in here. Good night!"

I turned from the table.

Nine thousand miles away the Stellarplex turned too. Circles of silver dropped through the roof. Behind the metal cage of the relaxed slave-claw I saw Poloscki's large, injured eyes, circles of crushed turquoise, glistening now.

And nine feet away someone said, "Ma'am?"

Poloscki glanced over her shoulder. "An, you awake?"

An stepped into the silver light, rubbing his neck. "That office chair is pretty hard, sister."

"He's here?" I asked.

"Sure," Poloscki said. "He didn't have anyplace to stay so I let him sleep in the office while I finished up some work in the back. Vyme, I meant what I said. Leave if you want, but not like this. Untwist."

"Poloscki," I said, "you're very sweet, you're fun in bed, and a good mechanic too. But I've been there before. Asking me to join a group is like asking me to do something obscene. I know what I'm worth."

"I'm also a good businesswoman. Don't think that didn't enter my head when I thought about marrying you." An came and stood beside her. He was breathing hard, the way an animal does when you wake it all of a sudden.

"Poloscki, you said it, I didn't: I'm a mess. That's why I'm not with my own group now."

"You're not always like this. I've never seen you touch a drop before."

"For a while," I said, "it happened with disgusting frequency. Why do you think my group dropped me?"

"Must have been a while ago. I've known you a long time. So you've grown up since then. Now it only happens every half-dozen years or so. Congratulations. Come have some coffee. An, run into the office and plug in the pot. I showed you where it was." An turned like something blown by the world-wind and was gone in shadow. "Come on," Poloscki said. She took my arm, and I came with her. Before we left the light, I saw my reflection in the polished steel tool cabinet.

"Aw, no." I pulled away from her. "No, I better go home now."

"Why? An's making coffee."

"The kid. I don't want the kid to see me like this."

"He already has. Won't hurt him. Come on."

When I walked into Poloscki's office, I felt I didn't have a damn thing left. No. I had one. I decided to give it away.

When An turned to me with the cup, I put my hands on his shoulders. He jumped, but not enough to spill the coffee. "First and last bit of alcoholic advice for the evening, kid-boy. Even if you *are* crazy, don't go around telling people who are not golden how they've trapped you. That's like going to Earth and complimenting a nigger on how well he sings and dances and his great sense of rhythm. He may be able to tap seven with one hand against thirteen with the other while whistling a tone row. It still shows a remarkable naïveté about the way things are." That's *one* of the other things known throughout the galaxy about the world I come from. When I say primitive, I mean primitive.

An ducked from under my hands, put the coffee on the desk, and turned back. "I didn't say you trapped us."

"You said we treated you lousy and exploited you, which we may, and that this trapped you—"

"I said you exploited us, which you do, *and* that we were trapped. I *didn't* say by what."

Poloscki sat down on the desk, picked up my coffee and sipped it.

I raised my head. "All right. Tell me how you're trapped."

"Oh, I'm sorry," Poloscki said. "I started drinking your coffee—"

"Shut up. How are you trapped, An?"

An moved his shoulders around as though he was trying to get them comfortable. "It started in the Tyber-44 cluster. Golden were coming back with really bad psychic shock."

"Yes. I heard about it. That was a few years back."

An's face started to twitch. The muscles around his eyes twisted below the skin. "*Something* out there . . ."

I put my hand on the back of his neck, my thumb in the soft spot behind his ear, and began to stroke, the way you get a cat to calm down. "Take it easy. Just tell me."

"Thanks," An said and bent his head forward. "We found them first in Tyber-44, but then they turned up all *over,* on half the planets in every galaxy that could support any life, and a lot more that shouldn't have been able to at all." His breathing grew coarser. I kept rubbing, and it slowed again. "I guess we have such a funny psychology that working with them, studying them, even thinking about them too much . . . There was something about them that changes our sense of reality. On a fundamental and immediate biological level, they break through barriers involving the very conservation of energy and matter. The shock was bad."

"An," I said, "to be trapped, there has to be somewhere you can't go. For it to bug you, there has to be something else around that can."

An nodded under my hand, then straightened up. "I'm all right now. Just tired. You want to know where and what?"

Poloscki had put down the coffee now and was dangling the chain. An whirled to stare.

"Where?" he said. "Other universes."

"Galaxies farther out?" asked Poloscki.

"No. Completely different matrices of time and space." Staring at the swinging ball seemed to calm him even more. "No physical or temporal connection to this one at all."

"A sort of parallel—"

"Parallel? Hell!" It was almost a drawl. "There's nothing parallel about them. Out of the billions-to-the-billionth of them, most are hundreds of times the size of ours and empty. There are a few, though, whose entire spatial extent is even smaller than this galaxy. Some of them are completely dense to us, because even though there seems to be matter in them, distributed more or less as in this universe, there's no electromagnetic activity at all. No radio waves, no heat, no light." The globe swung; the voice was a whisper.

I closed my fist around the globe and took it from Poloscki. "How do you know about them? Who brings back the information? Who is it who can get out?"

Blinking, An looked back at me.

When he told me, I began to laugh. To accommodate the shifting reality tensions, the psychotic personality that is golden is totally labile. An laughed with me, not knowing why. He explained through his torrential hysteria how with the micro-microsurgical techniques from Tyber-44 they had read much of the information from a direct examination of the creature's nervous system, which covered its surface like velvet. It could take intense cold or heat, a range of pressure from vacuum to hundreds of pounds per square millimeter; but a fairly small amount of ultraviolet destroyed the neural synapses, and it died. They were small and deceptively organic because in an organic environment they appeared to breathe and eat. They had four sexes, two of which carried the young. They had clusters of retractable sense organs that first appeared to be eyes, but were sensitive to twelve distinct senses, stimulation for three of which didn't even exist in our continuum. They traveled around on four suction cups when using kinetic motion for ordinary traversal of space, were small, and looked furry. The only way to make them jump universes was to scare the life out of them. At which point they . . . vanished.

An kneaded his stomach under his belt to ease the pain from so much laughter. "Working with them at Tyber-44 just cracked up a whole bunch of golden." He leaned against the desk, panting and grinning. "They had to be sent home for therapy. We still can't think about them directly, but it's easier for us to control what we think about than for you; that's part of being golden. I even had one of them for a pet, up until yesterday. The damn creatures are either totally apathetic, or vicious. Mine was a baby, all white and soft." He held out his arms. "Yesterday it bit me and disappeared." On his wrist there was a bluish place centered on which was a crescent of pinpricks. "Lucky it was a baby. The bites infect easily."

Poloscki started drinking from my cup again as An and I started laughing all over.

As I walked back that night, black coffee slopped in my belly.

There are certain directions in which you cannot go. Choose one in which you can and move as far as you want. Sandy said that? He did. And there was something about Sandy, very much like someone golden. It doesn't matter how, he's going on.

Under a streetlamp I stopped and lifted up the ecologarium. The reproductive function, was it primary or adjunctive? If, I thought with the whiskey lucidity always suspect at dawn, you consider the whole ecological balance a single organism, it's adjunctive, a vital reparative process along with sleeping and eating, to the primary process which is living, working, growing. I put the chain around my neck.

I was still half-soused, and it felt bad. But I howled. Androcles, is drunken laughter appropriate to mourn all my dead children? Perhaps not. But tell me, Ratlit; tell me, Alegra: What better way to launch my live ones who are golden into night? I don't know. I know I laughed. Then I put my fists into my overall pouch and crunched homeward along the Edge, while on my left the world-wind roared.

—New York
October 1965

corona

Pa ran off to Mars Colony before Buddy was born. Momma drank. At sixteen Buddy used to help out in a 'copter repair shop outside St. Gable below Baton Rouge. Once he decided it would be fun to take a 'copter, some bootleg, a girl named Dolores-Jo, and sixty-three dollars and eighty-five cents to New Orleans. Nothing taken had ever, by any interpretation, been his. He was caught before they raised from the garage roof. He lied about his age at court to avoid the indignity of reform school. Momma, when they found her, wasn't too sure ("Buddy? Now, let me see, that's Laford. And James Robert Warren—I named him after my third husband who was not living with me at the time—now little James, he came along in . . . two thousand and thirty-*two*, I do believe. Or thirty-*four*—you sure now, it's Buddy?") when he was born. The constable was inclined to judge him younger than he was, but let him go to grown-up prison anyway. Some terrible things happened there. When Buddy came out three years later, he was a gentler person than before; still, when frightened, he became violent. Shortly, he knocked up a waitress six years his senior. Chagrined, he applied for emigration to one of Uranus' moons. In twenty years, though, the colonial economy had stabilized. They were a lot more stringent with applicants than in his Pa's day: colonies had become almost respectable. They'd started barring people with jail records and things like that. So he went to New York instead and eventually got a job as an assistant servicer at the Kennedy spaceport.

There was a nine-year-old girl in a hospital in New York at that time who could read minds and wanted to die. Her name was Lee.

Also there was a singer named Bryan Faust.

Slow, violent, blond Buddy had been at Kennedy over a year when Faust's music came. The songs covered the city, sounded on every radio, filled the title selections on every jukebox and Scopitone. They shouted and whispered and growled from the wall speaker in the spacehangar. Buddy ambled over the catwalk while the cross-rhythms, sudden silences, and moments of pure voice were picked up by jangling organ, whining oboe, bass, and cymbals. Buddy's thoughts were small and slow. His hands, gloved in canvas, his feet, in rubber boots, were big and quick.

Below him the spaceliner filled the hangar like a tuber an eighth of a mile long. The service crew swarmed the floor, moving over the cement like scattered ball bearings. And the music—

"Hey, kid."

Buddy turned.

Bim swaggered toward him, beating his thigh to the rhythms in the falls of sound. "I was just looking for you, kid." Buddy was twenty-four, but people would call him "kid" well after he was thirty. He blinked a lot.

"You want to get over and help them haul down that solvent from upstairs? The damn lift's busted again. I swear, they're going to have a strike if they don't keep the equipment working right. Ain't safe. Say, what did you think of the crowd outside this morning?"

"Crowd?" Buddy's drawl snagged on a slight speech defect. "Yeah, there was a lot of people, huh. I been down in the maintenance shop since six o'clock, so I guess I must've missed most of it. What was they here for?"

Bim got a lot of what-are-you-kidding-me on his face. Then it turned to a tolerant smile. "For Faust." He nodded toward the speaker: the music halted, lurched, then Bryan Faust's voice roared out for love and the violent display that would prove it real. "Faust came in this morning, kid. You didn't know? He's been making it down from moon to moon through the outer planets. I hear he broke 'em up in the asteroids. He's been to Mars, and the last thing

I heard, they love him on Luna as much as anywhere else. He arrived on Earth this morning, and he'll be up and down the Americas for twelve days." He thumbed toward the pit and shook his head: "That's his liner." Bim whistled. "And did we have a hell of a time! All them kids, thousands of 'em, I bet. And people old enough to know better, too. You should have seen the police! When we were trying to get the liner in here, a couple of hundred kids got through the police block. They wanted to pull his ship apart and take home the pieces. You like his music?"

Buddy squinted toward the speaker. The sounds jammed into his ears, pried around his mind, loosening things. Most were good things, touched on by a resolved cadence, a syncopation caught up again, feelings sounded on too quickly for him to hold, but good feelings. Still, a few of them . . .

Buddy shrugged, blinked. "I like it." And the beat of his heart, his lungs, and the music coincided. "Yeah. I like that." The music went faster; heart and breathing fell behind; Buddy felt a surge of disorder. "But it's . . . strange." Embarrassed, he smiled over his broken tooth.

"Yeah. I guess a lot of other people think so too. Well, get over there with those solvent cans."

"Okay." Buddy turned off toward the spiral staircase. He was on the landing, about to go up, when someone yelled down, "Watch it—!"

A ten-gallon drum slammed the walkway five feet from him. He whirled to see as the casing split—

(Faust's sonar drums slammed.)

—and solvent, oxidizing in air, splattered.

Buddy screamed and clutched his eye. He had been working with the metal rasp that morning, and his gloves were impregnated with steel flakes and oil. He ground his canvas palm against his face.

(Faust's electric bass ground against a suspended dissonance.)

As he staggered down the walk, hot solvent rained on his back. Then something inside went wild, and he began to swing his arms.

(The last chorus swung toward the close. And the announcer's voice, not waiting for the end, cut over. "All *right* all you little people *out* there in music land . . .")

"What in the—"

"Jesus, what's wrong with—"

"What happened? I told you the damn lift was broken!"

"Call the infirmary! Quick! Call the—"

Voices came from the level above, the level below. And footsteps. Buddy turned on the ramp and screamed and swung.

"Watch it! What's with that guy—"

"Here, help me hold . . . *Owww*!"

"He's gone berserk! Get the doc up from the infirm—"

(". . . *that* was Bryan Faust's mind-*twisting*, brain-*blowing*, brand-new release, *Corona*! And you know it will be a *hit* . . . *!*")

Somebody tried to grab him, and Buddy hit out. Blind, rolling from the hips, he tried to apprehend the agony with flailing hands. And couldn't. A flashbulb had been jammed into his eye socket and detonated. He knocked somebody else against the rail, and staggered, and shrieked.

(". . . And he's come down to Earth at *last*, all you baby-mommas and baby-poppas! The little man from Ganymede who's been putting *the* music of *the* spheres through *so* many changes this past year arrived *in* New York this morning. And all *I* want to say, Bryan . . .")

Rage, pain, and music.

(". . . is, how do you *dig* our Earth!")

Buddy didn't even feel the pressure hypo on his shoulder. He collapsed as the cymbals died.

Lee turned and turned the volume knob till it clicked.

In the trapezoid of sunlight over the desk from the high, small window, open now for August, lay her radio, a piece of graph paper with an incomplete integration for the area within the curve $X^4+Y^4=K^4$, and her brown fist. Smiling, she tried to release the tension the music had built.

Her shoulders lowered, her nostrils narrowed, and her fist fell over on its back. Still, her knuckles moved to *Corona*'s remembered rhythm.

The inside of her dark forearm was webbed with raw pink. There were a few marks on her right arm too. But those were three years old; from when she had been six.

Corona!

She closed her eyes and pictured the rim of the sun. Centered in the flame, with the green eyes of his German father and the high cheekbones of his Arawak mother, was the impudent and insouciant, sensual and curious face of Bryan Faust. The brassy, four-color magazine with its endless hyperbolic prose was open on her bed behind her.

Lee closed her eyes tighter. If she could reach out, and perhaps touch—no, not him; that would be too much—but someone standing, sitting, walking near him, see what seeing him close was like, hear what hearing his voice was like, through air and light: she reached out her mind, reached for the music. And heard—

—your daughter getting along?

They keep telling me better and better every week when I go to visit her. But, oh, I swear, I just don't know. You have no idea how we hated to send her back to that place.

Of course I know! She's your own daughter. And she's such a cute little thing. And so smart. Did they want to run some more tests?

She tried to kill herself. Again.

Oh, *no!*

She's got scars on her wrist halfway to her elbow! What am I doing wrong? The doctors can't tell me. She's not even ten. I can't keep her here with me. Her father's tried; he's about had it with the whole business. I know because of a divorce a child may have emotional problems, but that a little girl, as intelligent as Lee, can be so—confused! She had to go back, I know she had to go back. But what is it I'm doing wrong? I hate myself for it, and sometimes, just because she can't tell me, I hate her—

Lee's eyes opened. She smashed the table with her fists, tightening the muscles of her cheeks to hold in the tears. All musical beauty was gone. She breathed once more. For a while she looked up at the window, its glass door swung wide. The bottom sill was seven feet from the floor.

She pressed the button for Dr. Gross and went to the bookshelf. She ran her fingers over the spines: *Charlotte's Web, The Secret in the Ivory Charm, The Decline of the West, The Wind in the Wil—*

She turned at the sound of the door unbolting.

"You buzzed for me, Lee?"

"It happened. Again. Just about a minute ago."

"I noted the time as you rang."

"Duration, about forty-five seconds. It was my mother, and her friend who lives downstairs. Very ordinary. Nothing worth noting down."

"And how do you feel?"

She didn't say anything, but looked at the shelves.

Dr. Gross walked into the room and sat down on her desk. "Would you like to tell me what you were doing just before it happened?"

"Nothing. I'd just finished listening to the new record. On the radio."

"Which record?"

"The new Faust song, *Corona*."

"Haven't heard that one." He glanced down at the graph paper and raised an eyebrow. "This yours, or is it from one of your books?"

"You told me to ring for you every time I . . . got an attack, didn't you?"

"Yes—"

"I'm doing what you want."

"Of course, Lee. I didn't mean to imply you hadn't been keeping your word. Want to tell me something about the record? What did you think of it?"

"The rhythm is very interesting. Five against seven when it's there. But a lot of the beats are left out, so you have to listen hard to get it."

"Was there anything, perhaps in the words, that may have set off the mind reading?"

"His colonial Ganymede accent is so thick that I missed most of the lyrics, even though it's basically English."

Dr. Gross smiled. "I've noticed the colonial expressions are slipping into a lot of young people's speech since Faust has become so popular. You hear them all the time."

"I don't." She glanced up at the doctor quickly, then back to the books.

Dr. Gross coughed; then he said, "Lee, we feel it's best to keep you away from the other children at the hospital. You tune in most frequently on the minds of people you know, or those who've had similar experiences and reactions to yours. All the children in the hospital are emotionally disturbed. If you were to suddenly pick up all their minds at once, you might be seriously hurt."

"I wouldn't!" she whispered.

"You remember you told us about what happened when you were four, in kindergarten, and you tuned into your whole class for six hours? Do you remember how upset you were?"

"I went home and tried to drink the iodine." She flung him a brutal glance. "I remember. But I hear Mommy when she's all the way across the city. I hear strangers too, lots of times! I hear Mrs. Lowery, when she's teaching down in the classroom! I hear her! I've heard people on other planets!"

"About the song, Lee—"

"You want to keep me away from the other children because I'm smarter than they are! I know. I've heard you think too—"

"Lee, I want you to tell me more about how you felt about this new song—"

"You think I'll upset them because I'm so smart. You won't let me have any friends!"

"What did you feel about the song, Lee?"

She caught her breath, holding it in, her lids batting, the muscle in the back of her jaw leaping.

"What did you *feel* about the song; did you like it, or did you dislike it?"

She let the air hiss through her lips. "There are three melodic motifs," she began at last. "They appear in descending order of rhythmic intensity. There are more silences in the last melodic line. His music is composed of silence as much as sound."

"Again, what did you feel? I'm trying to get at your emotional reaction, don't you see?"

She looked at the window. She looked at Dr. Gross. Then she turned toward the shelves. "There's a book here, a part in a book, that says it, I guess, better than I can." She began working a volume from the half-shelf of Nietzsche.

"What book?"

"Come here." She began to turn the pages. "I'll show you."

Dr. Gross got up from the desk. She met him beneath the window.

Dr. Gross took it and, frowning, read the title heading: "*The Birth of Tragedy from the Spirit of Music* . . . death lies only in these dissonant tones—"

Lee's head struck the book from his hand. She had leapt on him as though he were a piece of furniture and she a small beast. When her hand was not clutching his belt, shirt front, lapel, shoulder, it was straining upward. He managed to grab her just as she grabbed the window ledge.

Outside was a nine-story drop.

He held her by the ankle as she reeled in the sunlit frame. He yanked, and she fell into his arms, shrieking, "Let me die!"

They went down on the floor together, he shouting, "No!" and the little girl crying. Dr. Gross stood up, now panting.

"I want to die!" She lay on the green vinyl, curling around the sound of her own sobs, pulling her hands over the floor to press her stomach. "I want to die. . . ."

"Lee, isn't there *any* way you can understand this? Yes, you've been exposed to more than any nine-year-old's mind should be able to bear. But you've got to come to terms with it somehow! That isn't the answer, Lee. I wish I could back it up with something. If you let me help, perhaps I can—"

She shouted, with her cheek pressed to the floor, "But you can't help! Your thoughts, they're just as clumsy and imprecise as the others! How can you—*you*—help people who're afraid and confused because their own minds have formed the wrong associations! How! I don't want to have to stumble around in all your insecurities and fears as well! I'm not a child! I've lived more years and places than any ten of you! Just go away and let me alone—"

Rage, pain, and music.

"Lee—"

"Go away! Please!"

Dr. Gross, upset, swung the window closed, locked it, left the room, locked the door.

Rage, pain . . . below the chaos she was conscious of the infectious melody of *Corona*. Somebody—not her—somebody else was being carried into the hospital, drifting in the painful dark, dreaming over the same sounds. Exhausted, still crying, she let it come.

The man's thoughts, she realized through her exhaustion, to escape pain had taken refuge in the harmonies and cadences of *Corona*. She tried to hide her own mind there. And twisted violently away. There was something terrible there. She tried to pull back, but her mind followed the music down.

The terrible thing was that someone had once told him not to put his knee on the floor.

Fighting, she tried to push it aside to see if what was underneath was less terrible. ("Buddy, stop that whining and let your momma alone. I don't feel good. Just get out of here and leave me *alone*!" The bottle shattered on the doorjamb by his ear, and he fled.)

She winced. There couldn't be anything that bad about putting your knee on the floor. And so she gave up and let it swim toward her—suds wound on the dirty water. The water was all around him. Buddy leaned forward and scrubbed the wire brush across the wet stone. His canvas shoes were already soaked.

"Put your blessed knee on the floor, and I'll get you! Come on, move your . . ." Somebody, not Buddy, got kicked. "And don't let your knee touch that floor! Don't, I say." And got kicked again.

They waddled across the prison lobby, scrubbing. There was a sign over the elevator: Louisiana State Penal Correction Institute, but it was hard to make out because Buddy didn't read very well.

"Keep up with 'em, kid. Don't you let 'em get ahead'n you!" Bigfoot yelled. "Just 'cause you little, don't think you got no special privileges." Bigfoot slopped across the stone.

"When they gonna get an automatic scrubber unit in here?" somebody complained. "They got one in the county jail."

"This Institute—" Bigfoot lumbered up the line—"was built in nineteen hundred and *forty*-seven! We ain't had no escape in ninety-four years. We run it the same today as when it was builded back in nineteen hundred and *forty*-seven. The first time it don't do its job right of keepin' you all inside—then we'll think about running it different. Get on back to work. *Watch* that knee!"

Buddy's thighs were sore, his insteps cramped. The balls of his feet burned, and his pants cuffs were sopping.

Bigfoot had taken off his slippers. As he patrolled the scrubbers, he slapped the soles together, first in front of his belly, then behind his heavy buttocks. *Slap* and *slap*. With each slap, one foot hit the soapy stone. "Don't bother looking up at me. You look at them stones! But don't let your knee touch the floor."

Once, in the yard latrine, someone had whispered, "Bigfoot? You watch him, kid! Was a preacher, with a revival meeting back in the swamp. Went down to the Emigration Office in town back when they was taking everyone they could get and demanded they make him Pope or something over the colony on Europa they was just setting up. They laughed him out of the office. Sunday, when everyone came to meeting, they found he'd sneaked into the town, busted the man at the Emigration Office over the head, dragged him out to the swamp, and nailed him up to a cross under the meeting tent. He tried to make everybody pray him down. After they prayed for about an hour, and nothing happened, they brought Bigfoot here. He's a trustee now."

Buddy rubbed harder with his wire brush.

"Let's see you rub a little of the devil out'n them stones. And don't let me see your knee touch the—"

Buddy straightened his shoulders. And slipped.

He went over on his backside, grabbed the pail; water splashed over him, sluiced beneath. Soap stung his eyes. He lay there a moment.

Bare feet slapped toward him. "Come on, kid. Up you go, and back to work."

With eyes tight, Buddy pushed himself up.

"You sure are one clums—"

Buddy rolled to his knees.

"I *told* you not to let your knee touch the floor!"

Wet canvas whammed his ear and cheek.

"Didn't I?"

A foot fell in the small of his back and struck him flat. His chin hit the floor, and he bit his tongue, hard. Holding him down with his foot, Bigfoot whopped Buddy's head back and forth, first with one shoe, then the other. Buddy, blinded, mouth filled with blood, swam on the wet stone, tried to duck away.

"Now don't let your knees touch the floor *again*. Come on, back to work, all of you." The feet slapped away.

Against the sting, Buddy opened his eyes. The brush lay just in front of his face. Beyond the wire bristles he saw a pink heel strike in suds.

His action took a long time to form. *Slap* and *slap*. On the third *slap*, he gathered himself to his feet, leapt. He landed on Bigfoot's back, pounding with the brush. He hit three times, then he tried to scrub off the side of Bigfoot's face.

The guards finally pulled him off. They took him to a room where there was an iron bed with no mattress and strapped him, ankles, wrist, neck, and stomach, to the frame. He yelled for them to let him up. They said they couldn't because he was still violent. "How'm I gonna eat!" he demanded. "You gonna let me up to eat?"

"Calm down a little. We'll send someone in to feed you."

A few minutes after the dinner bell rang that evening, Bigfoot looked into the room. Ear, cheek, neck, and left shoulder were bandaged. Blood had seeped through at the tip of his clavicle to the size of a quarter. In one hand Bigfoot held a tin plate of rice and fatback, in the other an iron spoon. He came over, sat on the edge of Buddy's bed, and kicked off one canvas shoe. "They told me I should come in and feed you, kid." He kicked off the other one. "You real hungry?"

When they unstrapped Buddy four days later, he couldn't talk. One tooth was badly broken, several others chipped. The roof of his mouth was raw; the prison doctor had to take some stitches in his tongue.

Lee gagged on the taste of iron.

Somewhere in the hospital, Buddy lay in the dark, terrified, his eye stinging, his head filled with the beating rhythms of *Corona*.

Her shoulders bunched; she worked her jaw and tongue against the pain that Buddy remembered. She wanted to die.

Stop it! she whispered and tried to wrench herself from the inarticulate terror that Buddy, cast back by pain and the rhythm of a song to a time when he was not twice her age, remembered. Oh, stop it! But no one could hear her, the way she could hear Buddy, her mother, Mrs. Lowery in the schoolroom . . .

Perhaps it was the music. Perhaps it was because she had exhausted every other way. Perhaps it was because the only place left to look for a way out was back inside Buddy's mind—

—when he wanted to sneak out of the cell at night to join a card game down in the digs where they played for cigarettes, he would take a piece of chewing gum and the bottle cap from a Dr Pepper and stick it over the bolt in the top of the door. When they closed the doors after free-time, it still fitted into place, but the bolt couldn't slide in—

Lee looked at the locked door of her room. She could get the chewing gum in the afternoon period when they let her walk around her own floor. But the soft-drink machine by the elevator only dispensed in cups. Suddenly she sat up and looked at the bottom of her shoe. On the toe and heel were the metal taps that her mother had made the shoemaker put there so they wouldn't wear so fast.

She went to the cot and began to work the tap loose on the frame.

———

Buddy lay on his back, afraid. After they had drugged him, they had brought him into the city. He didn't know where he was. He couldn't see, and he was afraid.

Something fingered his face. He rocked his head to get away from the spoon—

"*Shhh*! It's all right. . . ."

Light struck one eye. There was still something wrong with the other. He blinked.

"You're all right," she—it was a *she* voice, though he still couldn't make out a face—told him again. "You're not in jail. You're not in the . . . the joint anymore. You're in New York. In a hospital. Something's happened to your eye. That's all."

"My eye . . ."

"Don't be afraid anymore. Please. Because I can't stand it."

It was a kid's voice. He blinked again, reached up to rub his vision clear.

"Watch out," she said. "You'll get—"

His eye itched, and he wanted to scratch it. So he shoved at the voice.

"Hey!"

Something stung him, and he clutched at his thumb with his other hand.

"I'm sorry," she said. "I didn't mean to bite your finger. But you'll hurt the bandage. I've pulled the one away from your right eye. There's nothing wrong with that. Just a moment." Something cool swabbed his blurred vision.

It came away.

The cutest little colored girl was kneeling on the edge of the bed with a piece of wet cotton wool in her hand. The light was nowhere near as bright as it had seemed. A nightlight glowed over the mirror above the basin. "You've got to stop being so frightened," she whispered. "You've *got* to."

Buddy had spent a good deal of his life doing what people told him, when he wasn't doing the opposite on purpose.

The girl sat back on her heels. "That's better."

He pushed himself up in the bed. There were no straps. Sheets hissed over his knees. He looked at his chest. Blue pajamas: the buttons were in the wrong holes by one. He reached down to fix them, and his fingers closed on air.

"You've only got one eye working so there's no parallax for depth perception."

"Huh?" He looked up again.

She wore shorts and a red and white polo shirt.

He frowned. "Who you?"

"Dianne Lee Morris," she said. "And you're—" Then she frowned too. She scrambled from the bed, took the mirror from over the basin and brought it back to the bed. "Look. Now who are you?"

He reached up to touch with grease-crested nails the bandage that sloped over his left eye. Short, yellow hair lapped the gauze. His forefinger went on to the familiar scar through the tow hedge of his right eyebrow.

"Who are you?"

"Buddy Magowan."

"Where do you live?"

"St. Gab—" He stopped. "A hun' ni'tee' stree' 'tween Se'on and Thir' A'nue."

"Say it again."

"A hundred an' nineteenth street between Second an' Third Avenue." The consonants his night-school teacher at P.S. 125 had laboriously inserted into his speech this past year returned.

"Good. And you work . . . ?"

"Out at Kennedy. Service assistant."

"And there's nothing to be afraid of."

He shook his head, "Naw," and grinned. His broken tooth reflected in the mirror. "Naw. I was just having a bad . . . dream."

She put the mirror back. As she turned, suddenly she closed her eyes and sighed.

"What'sa matter?"

She opened them again. "It's stopped. I can't hear inside your head anymore. It's been going on all day."

"Huh? What do you mean?"

"Maybe you read about me in the magazine. There was a big article about me in *New Times* a couple of years ago. I'm in the hospital too. Over on the other side, in the psychiatric division. Did you read the article?"

"Didn't do much magazine reading back then. Don't do too much now, either. What'd they write about?"

"I can hear and see what other people are thinking. I'm one of the three they're studying. I do it best of all of them. But it only comes in spurts. The other one, Eddy, is an idiot. I met him when we were getting all the tests. He's older than you and even dumber. Then there's Mrs. Lowery. She doesn't hear. She just sees. And sometimes she can make other people hear her. She works in the school here at the hospital. She can come and go as she pleases. But I have to stay locked up."

Buddy squinted. "You can hear what's in my head?"

"Not now. But I could. And it was . . ." Her lip began to quiver; her brown eyes brightened. ". . . I mean when that man tried to . . . with the . . ." And overflowed. She put her fingers on her chin and twisted. ". . . when he . . . cutting in your . . ."

Buddy saw her tears, wondered at them. "Aw, honey—" he said, reached to take her shoulder—

Her face struck his chest, and she clutched his pajama jacket. "It hurt *so* much!"

Her grief at his agony shook her.

"I had to stop you from hurting! Yours was just a dream, so I could sneak out of my room, get down here, and wake you up. But the others, the girl in the fire, or the man in the flooded mine . . . those weren't dreams! I couldn't do anything about them. I couldn't stop the hurting there. I couldn't stop it at all, Buddy! I wanted to. But one was in Australia and the other in Costa Rica!" She sobbed against his chest. "And one was on Mars! And I couldn't get to Mars. I couldn't!"

"It's all right," he whispered, uncomprehending, and rubbed her rough hair. Then, as she shook in his arms, understanding swelled. "You came . . . down here to wake me up?" he asked.

She nodded against his pajama jacket.

"Why?"

She shrugged against his belly. "I . . . I don't . . . maybe the music."

After a moment he asked, "Is this the first time you ever done something about what you heard?"

"It's not the first time I ever tried. But it's the first time it ever . . . worked."

"Then why did you try again?"

"Because . . ." She was stiller now. ". . . I hoped maybe it would hurt less if I could get—through." He felt her jaw moving as she spoke. "It does." Something in her face began to quiver. "It does hurt less." He put his hand on her hand, and she took his thumb.

"You knew I was . . . was awful scared?"

She nodded. "I knew, so I was scared just the same."

Buddy remembered the dream. The back of his neck grew cold, and the flesh under his thighs began to tingle. He remembered the reality behind the dream—and held her more tightly and pressed his cheek to her hair. "Thank you." He couldn't say it any other way, but it didn't seem enough. So he said it again more slowly. "*Thank you.*"

A little later she pushed away, and he watched her sniffling face with depthless vision.

"Do you like the song?"

He blinked. And realized the insistent music still worked through his head. "You can—hear what I'm thinking again?"

"No. But you were thinking about it before. I just wanted to find out."

Buddy thought awhile. "Yeah." He cocked his head. "Yeah. I like it a lot. It makes me feel . . . good."

She hesitated, then let out: "Me *too!* I think it's beautiful. I think Faust's music is so—" and she whispered the next word as though it might offend—"*alive!* But with life the way it should be. Not without pain, but with pain contained, ordered, given form and meaning so that it's almost all right again. Don't you feel that way?"

"I . . . don't know. I *like* it . . ."

"I suppose," Lee said a little sadly, "people like things for different reasons."

"You like it a lot." Buddy looked down and tried to understand how she liked it. And failed. Tears had darkened his pajamas. Not wanting her to cry again, he grinned when he looked up. "You know, I almost saw him this morning."

"Faust? You mean you saw Bryan Faust?"

He nodded. "Almost. I'm on the service crew out at Kennedy. We were working on his liner when . . ." He pointed to his eye.

"*His* ship? *You* were?" The wonder in her voice was perfectly childish, and enchanting.

"I'll probably see him when he leaves," Buddy boasted. "I can get in where they won't let anybody else go. Except people who work at the port."

"I'd give—" she remembered to take a breath—"anything to see him. Just anything in the world!"

"There was a hell of a crowd out there this morning. They almost broke through the police. But I could've just walked up and stood at the bottom of the ramp when he come down. If I'd thought about it."

Her hands made little fists on the edge of the bed as she gazed at him.

"Yeah, I'll probably see him when he goes." This time he found his buttons and began to put them into the proper holes.

"I wish I could see him too!"

"I suppose Bim—he's foreman of the service crew—he'd let us through the gate, if I said you were my sister." He looked back up at her brown face. "Well, maybe my cousin."

"Would you take me? Would you really take me?"

"Sure." Buddy reached out to tweak her nose, missed. "You did something for me. I don't see why not, if they'd let you leave—"

"Mrs. Lowery!" Lee whispered and stepped back from the bed.

"—the hospital. Huh?"

"They know I'm gone! Mrs. Lowery is calling for me. She says she's seen me, and Dr. Gross is on his way. They want to take me back to my room." She ran to the door.

And it opened. "Lee, *there* you are! Are you all right?" In the doorway Dr. Gross grabbed her arm as she tried to twist away.

"Let me *go*!"

"Hey!" bellowed Buddy. "What are you doin' with that little girl!" He bounded up in the middle of the bed, shedding sheets.

Dr. Gross's eyes widened. "I'm taking her back to her room. She's a patient in the hospital. She should be in another wing."

"She wanna go?" Buddy demanded, swaying over the blankets.

"She's very disturbed!" Dr. Gross countered at Buddy, towering on the bed. "We're trying to help her, don't you understand? I don't know who you are, but we're trying to keep her alive. She has to go back!"

Lee shook her head against the doctor's hip. "Oh, Buddy . . ."

He leapt over the foot of the bed, swinging. Or at any rate, he swung once. He missed wildly because of the parallax. Also because he pulled the punch in, half-completed, to make it seem a floundering gesture. He was not in the Louisiana State Penal Correction Institute: the realization had come the way one only realized the tune playing in the back of the mind when it stops. "Wait!" Buddy said.

Outside the door the doctor was saying, "Mrs. Lowery, take Lee back up to her room. The night nurse knows the medication she should have."

"Yes, Doctor."

"Wait!" Buddy called. "Please!"

"Excuse me," Dr. Gross said, stepping back through the door. Without Lee. "But we have to get her upstairs and under a sedative, immediately. Believe me, I'm sorry for this inconvenience."

Buddy sat down on the bed and twisted his face. "What's . . . the matter with her?"

Dr. Gross was silent a moment. "I suppose I have to give you an explanation. That's difficult, because I don't *know*, exactly. Of the three proven telepaths that have been discovered since a concerted effort has been made to study them, Lee is the most powerful. She's a brilliant, incredibly creative child. But her mind has suffered so much trauma—from all the lives telepathy exposes her to—she's become hopelessly suicidal. We're trying to help her. But if she's left alone for any length of time, sometimes weeks, sometimes hours, she'll try to kill herself."

"Then when's she gonna be better?"

Dr. Gross put his hands in his pockets and looked at his sandals. "I'm afraid to cure someone of a mental disturbance, the first thing you have to do is isolate them from the trauma. With Lee that's impossible. We don't even know which part of the brain controls the telepathy, so we couldn't even try lobotomy. We haven't found a drug that affects it yet." He shrugged. "I wish we could help her. But when I'm being objective, I can't see her *ever* getting better. She'll be like this for the rest of her life. The quicker you can forget about her, the less likely you are to hurt her. Good night. Again, I'm very sorry this had to happen."

"G'night." Buddy sat in his bed a little while. Finally he turned off the light and lay down. He had to masturbate three times before he fell asleep. In the morning, though, he still had not forgotten the little black girl who had come to him and awakened . . . so much in him.

The doctors were upset about the bandage and talked of sympathetic ophthalmia. They searched his left cornea for any last bits of metal dust. They kept him in the hospital three more days, adjusting the pressure between his vitreous and aqueous humors to prevent his till now undiscovered tendency toward glaucoma. They told him that the thing that had occasionally blurred the vision in his left eye was a vitreous floater and not to worry about it. Stay home at least two weeks, they said. And wear your eye patch until two days before you go back to work. They gave him a hassle with his workmen's compensation papers too. But he got it straightened out. He'd filled in a date wrong.

He never saw the little girl again.

And the radios and jukeboxes and Scopitones in New York and Buenos Aires, Paris and Istanbul, in Melbourne and Bangkok played the music of Bryan Faust.

The day Bryan Faust was supposed to leave Earth for Venus, Buddy went back to the spaceport. It was three days before he was supposed to report to work, and he still wore the flesh-colored eyepatch.

"Jesus," he said to Bim as they leaned at the railing of the observation deck on the roof of the hangar, "just look at all them people."

Bim spat down at the hot macadam. The liner stood on the takeoff pad under the August sun.

"He's going to sing before he goes," Bim said. "I hope they don't have a riot."

"Sing?"

"See that wooden platform out there and all them loudspeakers? With all those kids, I sure hope they don't have a riot."

"Bim, can I get down onto the field, up near the platform?"

"What for?"

"So I can see him up real close."

"You were the one talking about all the people."

Buddy, holding the rail, worked his thumb on the brass. The muscles in his forearm rolled beneath the tattoo: *To Mars I Would Go for Dolores-Jo*, inscribed on Saturn's rings. "But I *got* to!"

"I don't see why the hell—"

"There's this little nigger girl, Bim—"

"Huh?"

"*Bim!*"

"Okay. Okay. Get into a coverall and go down with the clocker crew. You'll be right up with the reporters. But don't tell anybody I sent you. You know how many people want to get up there? Why you want to get so close for anyway?"

"For a—" He turned in the doorway. "For a friend." He ran down the stairs to the lockers.

Bryan Faust walked across the platform to the microphones. Comets soared over his shoulders and disappeared under his arms. Suns novaed on his chest. Meteors flashed around his elbows. Shirts of polarized cloth with incandescent, shifting designs were now being called Fausts. Others flashed in the crowd. He pushed back his hair, grinned, and behind the police-block hundreds of children screamed. He laughed into the microphone; they quieted. Behind him a bank of electronic instruments glittered. The controls were in the many jeweled rings hanging bright and heavy on his fingers. He raised his hands, flicked his thumbs across the gems, and the instruments, programmed to respond, began the cascading introduction to *Corona*. Bryan Faust sang. Across Kennedy, thousands—Buddy among them—heard.

And on her cot, Lee listened. "Thank you, Buddy," she whispered. "Thank you." And felt a little less like dying.

—*New York*
August 1966

aye, and gomorrah . . .

And came down in Paris:

Where we raced along the Rue de Médicis with Bo and Lou and Muse inside the fence, Kelly and me outside, making faces through the bars, making noise, making the Luxembourg Gardens roar at two in the morning. Then climbed out, and down to the square in front of St. Sulpice where Bo tried to knock me into the fountain.

At which point Kelly noticed what was going on around us, got an ashcan cover, and ran into the pissoir, banging the walls. Five guys scooted out; even a big pissoir only holds four.

A very blond man put his hand on my arm and smiled, "Don't you think, Spacer, that you . . . people should leave?"

I looked at his hand on my blue uniform. *"Est-ce que tu es un frelk?"*

His eyebrows rose, then he shook his head. "Une *frelk,*" he corrected. "No. I am not. Sadly for me. You look as though you may once have been a man. But now . . ." He smiled. "You have nothing for me now. The police." He nodded across the street where I noticed the gendarmerie for the first time. "They don't bother us. You are strangers, though. . . ."

But Muse was already yelling, "Hey, come on! Let's get out of here, huh?" And left.

And went up again.

And came down in Houston:

"Goddamn!" Muse said. "Gemini Flight Control—you mean this is where it all started? Let's get *out* of here, *please!*"

So took a bus out through Pasadena, then the monoline to Galveston, and were going to take it down the Gulf, but Lou found a couple with a pickup truck—

"Glad to give you a ride, Spacers. You people up there on them planets and things, doing all that good work for the government."

—who were going south, them and the baby, so we rode in the back for two hundred and fifty miles of sun and wind.

"You think they're frelks?" Lou asked, elbowing me. "I bet they're frelks. They're just waiting for us give 'em the come-on."

"Cut it out. They're a nice, stupid pair of country kids."

"That don't mean they ain't frelks!"

"You don't trust anybody, do you?"

"No."

And finally a bus again that rattled us through Brownsville and across the border into Matamoros, where we staggered down the steps into the dust and the scorched evening, with a lot of Mexicans and chickens and Texas Gulf shrimp fishermen—who smelled worst— and *we* shouted the loudest. Forty-three whores—I counted—had turned out for the shrimp fishermen, and by the time we had broken two of the windows in the bus station they were all laughing. The shrimp fishermen said they wouldn't buy us no food but would get us drunk if we wanted, 'cause that was the custom with shrimp fishermen. But we yelled, broke another window; then, while I was lying on my back on the telegraph office steps, singing, a woman with dark lips bent over and put her hand on my cheek. "You are very sweet." Her rough hair fell forward. "But the men, they are standing around and watching *you*. And that is taking up *time*. Sadly, their time is our money. Spacer, do you not think you . . . people should leave?"

I grabbed her wrist. "*¡Usted!*" I whispered. "*¿Usted es una frelka?*"

"*Frelko en español.*" She smiled and patted the sunburst that hung from my belt buckle. "Sorry. But you have nothing that . . . would be useful to me. It is too bad, for you look like you were once a woman, no? And I like women, too. . . ."

I rolled off the porch.

"Is this a drag, or is this a drag!" Muse was shouting. "Come *on!* Let's *go!*"

We managed to get back to Houston before dawn, somehow.

And went up.

And came down in Istanbul:

That morning it rained in Istanbul.

At the commissary we drank our tea from pear-shaped glasses, looking out across the Bosphorus. The Princess Islands lay like trash heaps before the prickly city.

"Who knows their way in this town?" Kelly asked.

"Aren't we going around together?" Muse demanded. "I thought we were going around together."

"They held up my check at the purser's office," Kelly explained. "I'm flat broke. I think the purser's got it in for me," and shrugged. "Don't want to, but I'm going to have to hunt up a rich frelk and come on friendly," went back to the tea; *then* noticed how heavy the silence had become. "Aw, come *on,* now! You gape at me like that, and I'll bust every bone in that carefully-conditioned-from-puberty body of yours. Hey you!" meaning me. "Don't give me that holier-than-thou gawk like you never went with no frelk!"

It was starting.

"I'm not gawking," I said and got quietly mad.

The longing, the old longing.

Bo laughed to break tensions. "Say, last time I was in Istanbul—about a year before I joined up with this platoon—I remember we were coming out of Taksim Square down Istiqlal. Just past all the cheap movies we found a little passage lined with flowers. Ahead of us were two other spacers. It's a market in there, and farther down they got fish, and then a courtyard with oranges and candy and sea urchins and cabbages. But flowers in front. Anyway, we noticed something funny about the spacers. It wasn't their uniforms: they were perfect. The haircuts: fine. It wasn't till we heard them talk-ing—They were a man and woman dressed up like spacers, trying *to pick up frelks*! Imagine, queer for frelks!"

"Yeah," Lou said. "I seen that before. There were a lot of them in Rio."

"We beat hell out of them two," Bo concluded. "We got them in a side street and went to *town!*"

Kelly's tea glass clicked on the counter. "From Taksim down Istiqlal till you get to the flowers? Now why didn't you say that's where the frelks were, huh?" A smile on Kelly's face would have made that okay. There was no smile.

"Hell," Lou said, "nobody ever had to tell me where to look. I go out in the street and frelks smell me coming. I can spot 'em halfway along Piccadilly. Don't they have nothing but tea in this place? Where can you get a drink?"

Bo grinned. "Moslem country, remember? But down at the end of the Flower Passage there're a lot of little bars with green doors and marble counters where you can get a liter of beer for about fifteen cents in lira. And there're all these stands selling deep-fat-fried bugs and pig's gut sandwiches—"

"You ever notice how frelks can put it away? I mean liquor, not . . . pig's guts."

And launched off into a lot of appeasing stories. We ended with the one about the frelk some spacer tried to roll who announced: "There are two things I go for. One is spacers; the other is a good fight. . . ."

But they only allay. They cure nothing. Even Muse knew we would spend the day apart, now.

The rain had stopped, so we took the ferry up the Golden Horn. Kelly straight off asked for Taksim Square and Istiqlal and was directed to a dolmush, which we discovered was a taxicab, only it just goes one place and picks up lots and lots of people on the way. And it's cheap.

Lou headed off over Ataturk Bridge to see the sights of New City. Bo decided to find out what the Dolma Boche really was; and when Muse discovered you could go to Asia for fifteen cents—one lira and fifty krush—well, Muse decided to go to Asia.

I turned through the confusion of traffic at the head of the bridge and up past the gray, dripping walls of Old City, beneath the trolley wires. There are times when yelling and helling won't fill the lack. There are times when you must walk by yourself because it hurts so much to be alone.

I walked up a lot of little streets with wet donkeys and wet camels and women in veils; and down a lot of big streets with buses and trash baskets and men in business suits.

Some people stare at spacers; some people don't. Some people stare or don't stare in a way a spacer gets to recognize within a week after coming out of training school at sixteen. I was walking in the park when I caught her watching. She saw me see and looked away.

I ambled down the wet asphalt. She was standing under the arch of a small, empty mosque shell. As I passed she walked out into the courtyard among the cannons.

"Excuse me."

I stopped.

"Do you know whether or not this is the shrine of St. Irene?" Her English was charmingly accented. "I've left my guidebook home."

"Sorry. I'm a tourist too."

"Oh." She smiled. "I am Greek. I thought you might be Turkish because you are so dark."

"American red Indian." I nodded. Her turn to curtsy.

"I see. I have just started at the university here in Istanbul. Your uniform, it tells me that you are—" and in the pause, all speculations resolved—"a spacer."

I was uncomfortable. "Yeah." I put my hands in my pockets, moved my feet around on the soles of my boots, licked my third from the rear left molar—did all the things you do when you're uncomfortable. *You're so* exciting *when you look like that,* a frelk told me once. "Yeah, I am." I said it too sharply, too loudly, and she jumped a little.

So now she knew I knew she knew I knew, and I wondered how we would play out the Proust bit.

"I'm Turkish," she said. "I'm not Greek. I'm not just starting. I'm a graduate in art history here at the university. These little lies one makes for strangers to protect one's ego . . . why? Sometimes I think my ego is very small." That's one strategy.

"How far away do you live?" I asked. "And what's the going rate in Turkish lira?" That's another.

"I can't pay you." She pulled her raincoat around her hips. She was very pretty. "I would like to." She shrugged and smiled. "But I am . . . a poor student. Not a rich one. If you want to turn around and walk away, there will be no hard feelings. I shall only be sad."

I stayed on the path. I thought she'd suggest a price after a little while. She didn't.

And that's another.

I was asking myself, *What do you want the damned money for anyway?* when a breeze upset water from one of the park's great cypresses.

"I think the whole business is unhappy." She wiped drops from her face. There had been a break in her voice and for a moment I looked too closely at the water streaks. "I think it's unhappy that they have to alter you to make you a spacer. If they hadn't, then *we* . . . If spacers had never been, then we could not be . . . the way we are. Did you start out male or female?"

Another shower. I was looking at the ground and droplets went down my collar.

"Male," I said. "It doesn't matter."

"How old are you? Twenty-three, twenty-four?"

"Twenty-three," I lied. It's reflex. I'm twenty-five, but the younger they think you are, the more they pay you. But I didn't *want* her damn money—

"I guessed right then." She nodded. "Most of us are experts on spacers. Do you find that? I suppose we have to be." She looked at me with wide black eyes. At the end of the stare, she blinked rapidly. "You would have been a fine man. But now you are a spacer, building water-conservation units on Mars, programming mining computers on Ganymede, servicing communication relay towers on the moon. The alteration . . . " Frelks are the only people I've ever heard say "the alteration" with so much fascination and regret. "You'd think they'd have found some other solution. They could have found another way than neutering you, turning you into creatures not even androgynous; things that are—"

I put my hand on her shoulder, and she stopped like I'd hit her. She looked to see if anyone was near. Lightly, so lightly then, she raised her hand to mine.

I pulled my hand away. "That are what?"

"They could have found another way." Both hands in her pockets now.

"They could have. Yes. Up beyond the ionosphere, baby, there's too much radiation for those precious gonads to work right anywhere you might want to do something that would keep you there over twenty-four hours, like the moon, or Mars, or the satellites of Jupiter—"

"They could have made protective shields. They could have done more research into biological adjustment—"

"Population Explosion time," I said. "No, they were hunting for any excuse to cut down kids back then—especially deformed ones."

"Ah, yes." She nodded. "We're still fighting our way up from the neo-puritan reaction to the sexual freedom of the twentieth century."

"It was a fine solution." I grinned and put my hand over my crotch. "I'm happy with it." And scratched. I've never known why that's so much more obscene when a spacer does it.

"Stop it," she snapped, moving away.

"What's the matter?"

"Stop it," she repeated. "Don't do that! You're a child."

"But they choose us from children whose sexual responses are hopelessly retarded at puberty."

"And your childish, violent substitutes for love? I suppose that's one of the things that's attractive. Yes, I know you're a child."

"Yeah? What about frelks?"

She thought awhile. "I think we are the sexually retarded ones they miss. Perhaps it was the right solution. You really don't regret you have no sex?"

"We've got you," I said.

"Yes." She looked down. I glanced to see the expression she was hiding. It was a smile. "You have your glorious, soaring life—*and* you have us." Her face came up. She glowed. "You spin in the sky, the world spins under you, and you step from land to land, while we . . ." She turned her head right, left, and her black hair curled and uncurled on the shoulder of her coat. "We have our dull, circled lives, bound in gravity, *worshiping* you!" She looked back at me. "Perverted, yes? In love with a bunch of corpses in free fall!"

Suddenly she hunched her shoulders. "I don't like having a free-fall-sexual-displacement complex."

"That always sounded like too much to say."

She looked away. "I don't like being a frelk. Better?"

"I wouldn't like it either. Be something else."

"You don't choose your perversions. *You* have no perversions at all. *You're* free of the whole business. I love you for that, Spacer. My love starts with the fear of love. Isn't that beautiful? A pervert substitutes something unattainable for 'normal' love: the homosexual, a mirror, the fetishist, a shoe or a watch or a girdle. Those with free-fall-sexual-dis—"

"Frelks."

"Frelks substitute—" she looked at me sharply again—"loose, swinging meat."

"That doesn't offend me."

"I wanted it to."

"Why?"

"You don't have desires. You wouldn't understand."

"Go on."

"I want you because you can't want me. That's the pleasure. If someone really had a sexual reaction to . . . us, we'd be scared away. I wonder how many people there were before there were you, waiting for your creation. We're necrophiles. I'm sure grave robbing has fallen off since you started going up. But you couldn't understand . . ." She paused. "If you did, then I wouldn't be scuffing leaves now and trying to think from whom I could borrow sixty lira." She stepped over the knuckles of a root that had cracked the pavement. "And that, incidentally, is the going rate in Istanbul."

I calculated. "Things still get cheaper as you go east."

"You know," and she let her raincoat fall open, "you're different from the others. You at least *want* to know—"

I said, "If I spat on you for every time you'd said that to a spacer, you'd drown."

"Go back to the moon, loose meat." She closed her eyes. "Swing on up to Mars. There are satellites around Jupiter where you might do some good. Go up and come down in some other city."

"Where do you live?"

"You want to come with me?"

"Give me something," I said. "Give me something—it doesn't have to be worth sixty lira. Give me something that you like, anything of yours that means something to you."

"No!"

"Why not?"

"Because I—"

"—don't want to give up part of that ego. None of you frelks do!"

"You really don't understand that I just don't want to buy you?"

"You have nothing to buy me with."

"You are a child," she said. "I love you."

We reached the gate of the park. She stopped, and we stood time enough for a breeze to rise and die in the grass. "I . . ." she offered tentatively, pointing without taking her hand from her coat pocket. "I live right down there."

"All right," I said. "Let's go."

A gas main had once exploded along this street, she explained to me, a gushing road of fire as far as the docks, overhot and overquick. It had been put out within minutes, no building had fallen, but the charred fascias glittered. "This is sort of an artist and student quarter." We crossed the cobbles. "Yuri Pasha, number fourteen. In case you're ever in Istanbul again." Her door was covered with black scales; the gutter was thick with garbage.

"A lot of artists and professional people are frelks," I said, trying to be inane.

"'So are lots of other people." She walked inside and held the door. "We're just more flamboyant about it."

On the landing hung a portrait of Atatürk. Her room was on the second floor. "Just a moment while I get my key—"

Marsscapes! Moonscapes! On her easel was a six-foot canvas showing the sunrise flaring on a crater's rim! There were copies of the original Observer pictures of the moon pinned to the wall, and pictures of every smooth-faced general in the International Spacer Corps.

On one corner of her desk was a pile of those photo magazines about spacers that you can find in most kiosks all over the world: I've seriously heard people say they were printed for adventurous-minded high school children. They've never seen the Danish ones. She had a few of those too. There was a shelf of art books, art history texts. Above them were six feet of cheap paper-covered space operas: *Sin on Space Station #12, Rocket Rake, Savage Orbit.*

"Arrack?" she asked. "Ouzo, or pernod? You've got your choice. But I may pour them all from the same bottle." She set out glasses on the desk, then opened a waist-high cabinet that turned out to be a refrigerator. She stood up with a tray of lovelies: fruit puddings, Turkish delight, braised meats.

"What's this?"

"Dolmades. Grape leaves filled with rice and pignolis."

"Say it again?"

"Dolmades. Comes from the same Turkish word as 'dolmush.' They both mean 'stuffed.'" She put the tray beside the glasses. "Sit down."

I sat on the studio-couch-that-becomes-bed. Under the brocade I felt the deep, fluid resilience of a glycogel mattress. They've got the idea that it approximates the feeling of free fall.

"Comfortable? Would you excuse me for a moment? I have some friends down the hall. I want to see them for a moment." She winked. "They like spacers."

"Are you going to take up a collection for me?" I asked. "Or do you want them to line up outside the door and wait their turn?"

She sucked a breath. "Actually I was going to suggest both." Suddenly she shook her head. "Oh, what do you want!"

"What will you give me? I want something," I said. "That's why I came. I'm lonely. Maybe I want to find out how far it goes. I don't know yet."

"It goes as far as you will. Me? I study, I read, paint, talk with my friends—" she came over to the bed, by my boots sat down on the floor—"go to the theater, look at spacers who pass me on the street, till one looks back; I am lonely too." She put her head on my knee. "I want something. But," and after a minute neither of us had moved, "you are not the one who will give it to me."

"You're not going to pay me for it," I countered. "You're not, are you?"

On my knee her head shook. After a while she said, all breath and no voice, "Don't you think you . . . should leave?"

"Okay," I said, and stood up.

She sat back on the hem of her coat. She hadn't taken it off yet. I went to the door.

"Incidentally." She folded her hands in her lap. "There is a place in New City you might find what you're looking for, called the Flower Passage—"

I turned toward her, angry. "The frelk hangout? Look, I don't *need* money! I said *anything* would do! I don't want—"

She had begun to shake her head, laughing quietly. Now she lay her cheek on the wrinkled place where I had sat. "Do you persist in misunderstanding? It is a *spacer* hangout. When you leave, I am going to visit my friends and talk about . . . ah, yes, the beautiful one that got away. I thought you might find . . . perhaps someone you know."

With anger, it ended.

"Oh," I said. "Oh, it's a spacer hangout. Yeah. Well, thanks." And went out.

And found the Flower Passage, and Kelly and Lou and Bo and Muse. Kelly was buying beer so we all got drunk, and ate fried fish and fried clams and fried sausage, and Kelly was waving the money around, saying, "You should have seen him! The changes I put that frelk through, you should have *seen* him! Eighty lira is the going rate here, and he gave me a hundred and fifty!" and drank more beer.

And went up.

—*Milford*
September 1966

driftglass

Sometimes I go down to the port, splashing sand with my stiff foot at the end of my stiff leg locked in my stiff hip, with the useless arm a-swinging, to get wet all over again, drink in the dives with cronies ashore, feeling old, broken, sorry for myself, laughing louder and louder. The third of my face that was burned away in the accident was patched with skin grafts from my chest, so what's left of my mouth distorts all loud sounds; sloppy sartorial reconstruction. Also I have a hairy chest. Chest hair does not look like beard hair, and it grows all up under my right eye. And: my beard is red, my chest hair brown, while the thatch curling down over neck and ears is sun-streaked to white here, darkened to bronze there, 'midst general blondness.

By reason of my being a walking (I suppose my gait could be called headlong limping) horror show, plus a general inclination to sulk, I spend most of the time up in the wood and glass and aluminum house on the surf-sloughed point that the Aquatic Corp ceded me along with my pension. Rugs from Turkey there, copper pots, my tenor recorder, which I can no longer play, and my books.

But sometimes, when the gold fog blurs the morning, I go down to the beach and tromp barefoot in the wet edging to the sea, searching for driftglass.

It was foggy that morning, and the sun across the water moiled the mists like a brass ladle. I lurched to the top of the rocks, looked down through the tall grasses into the frothing inlet where she lay, and blinked.

She sat up, long gills closing down her neck and the secondary slits along her back just visible at their tips because of much hair, wet and curling copper, falling there. She saw me. "What are you doing here, huh?" She narrowed blue eyes.

"Looking for driftglass."

"What?"

"There's a piece." I pointed near her and came down the rocks like a crab with one stiff leg.

"Where?" She turned over, half in, half out of the water, the webs of her fingers cupping nodules of black stone.

While the water made cold overtures between my toes, I picked up the milky fragment by her elbow where she wasn't looking. She jumped, because she obviously had thought it was somewhere else.

"See?"

"What . . . what is it?" She raised her cool hand to mine. For a moment the light through the milky gem and the pale film of my own webs pearled the screen of her palms. (Details like that. Yes, they are the important things, the points from which we suspend later pain.) A moment later wet fingers closed to the backs of mine.

"Driftglass," I said. "You know all the Coca-Cola bottles and cut-crystal punch bowls and industrial silicon slag that goes into the sea?"

"I know the Coca-Cola bottles."

"They break, and the tide pulls the pieces back and forth over the sandy bottom, wearing the edges, changing their shape. Sometimes chemicals in the glass react with chemicals in the ocean to change the color. Sometimes veins work their way through in patterns like snowflakes, regular and geometric; others, irregular and angled like coral. When the pieces dry, they're milky. Put them in water and they become transparent again."

"*Ohhh!*" she breathed as the beauty of the blunted triangular fragment in my palm assailed her like perfume. Then she looked at my face, blinking the third, aqueous-filled lid that we use as a correction lens for underwater vision.

She watched the ruin calmly.

Then her hand went to my foot where the webs had been torn

back in the accident. She began to take in who I was. I looked for horror, but saw only a little sadness.

The insignia on her buckle—her stomach was making little jerks the way you always do during the first few minutes when you go from breathing water to air—told me she was a Biological Technician. (Back up at the house there was a similar uniform of simulated scales folded in the bottom drawer of the dresser and the belt insignia said Depth Gauger.) I was wearing some very frayed jeans and a red cotton shirt with no buttons.

She reached for my neck, pushed my collar back from my shoulders and touched the tender slits of my gills, outlining them with cool fingers. "Who are you?" Finally.

"Cal Svenson."

She slid back down in the water. "You're the one who had the terrible . . . but that was years ago! They still talk about it, down . . ." She stopped.

As the sea softens the surface of a piece of glass, so it blurs the souls and sensibilities of the people who toil beneath her. And according to the last report of the Marine Reclamation Division there are to date seven hundred and fifty thousand who have been given gills and webs and sent under the foam where there are no storms, up and down the American coast.

"You live on shore? I mean around here? But so long ago . . ."

"How old are you?"

"Sixteen."

"I was two years older than you when the accident happened."

"You were eighteen?"

"I'm thirty-one now. Which means it happened over a dozen years ago. It *is* a long time."

"They still talk about it."

"I've almost forgotten," I said. "I really have. Say, do you play the recorder?"

"I used to."

"Good! Come up to my place and look at my tenor recorder. And I'll make some tea. Perhaps you can stay for lunch—"

"I have to report back to Marine Headquarters by three. Tork is going over the briefing to lay the cable for the big dive, with Jonni and the crew." She paused, smiled. "But I can catch the undertow and be there in half an hour if I leave by two-thirty."

On the walk up I learned her name was Ariel. She thought the patio was charming, and the mosaic evoked, "Oh, look!" and "Did you do this yourself?" a half-dozen times. (I had done it, in the first lonely years.) She picked out the squid and the whale in battle, the wounded shark and the diver. She told me she didn't get time to read much, but she was impressed by all the books. She listened to me reminisce. She talked a lot to me about her work, husbanding the deep-down creatures they were scaring up. Then she sat on the kitchen stool, playing a Lukas Foss serenade on my recorder, while I put rock salt in the bottom of the broiler tray for two dozen Oysters Rockefeller, and the tea water whistled. I'm a comparatively lonely guy. I like being followed by beautiful young girls.

II

"Hey, Juao!" I bawled across the jetty.

He nodded to me from the center of his nets, sun glistening on polished shoulders, sun lost in rough hair. I walked across to where he sat, sewing like a spider. He pulled another section up over his horny toes, then grinned at me with his mosaic smile: gold, white, black gap below, crooked yellow; white, gold, white. Shoving my bad leg in front I squatted.

"I fished out over the coral where you told me." He filled his cheek with his tongue and nodded. "You come up to the house for a drink, eh?"

"Fine."

"Just . . . a moment more."

There's a certain sort of Brazilian you find along the shore in the fishing villages, old yet ageless. See one of their men and you think he could be fifty, he could be sixty—will probably look the same when he's eighty-five. Such was Juao. We once figured it out. He's seven hours older than I am.

We became friends sometime before the accident when I got tangled in his nets working high lines in the Vorea Current. A lot of guys would have taken their knife and hacked their way out of the situation, ruining fifty-five, sixty dollars' worth of nets. That's an average fisherman's monthly income down here. But I surfaced and sat around in his boat while we untied me. Then, like typical coastal kids, we came in and got plastered. Since I cost him a day's fishing, I've been giving him hints on where to fish ever since. He buys me drinks when I come up with something.

This has been going on for fifteen years. During that time my life has been smashed up and land-bound. In the same time Juao has married off his five sisters, got married himself and had two children. (Oh, those *bolitos* and *teneros asados* that Amalia—her braids swung out, her brown breasts shook so when she turned to laugh—would make for Sunday dinner/supper/Monday breakfast.) I rode with them in the ambulance 'copter all the way into Brasília. In the hospital hall Juao and I stood together, both still barefoot, he tattered with fish scales in his hair, me just tattered, and I held him while he cried and I tried to explain how a world that could take a pubescent child and with a week of operations make an amphibious creature that can exist for a month on either side of the sea's foam-fraught surface could still be helpless before certain rampant endocrine cancers coupled with massive renal deterioration. Juao and I returned to the village alone, by bus, three days before our birthday—back when I was twenty-three and Juao was twenty-three and seven hours old.

"This morning," Juao said. (The shuttle danced in the web at the end of the orange line.) "I got a letter for you to read me. It's about the children. Come on, we go up and drink." The shuttle paused, backtracked twice, and he yanked the knot tight. We walked along the port toward the square. "Do you think the letter says that the children are accepted?"

"If it's from the Aquatic Corp. They just send postcards when they reject someone. The question is, how do *you* feel about it?"

"You are a good man. If they grow up like you, then it will be fine."

"But you're still worried." I'd been prodding Juao to get the kids into the International Aquatic Corp nigh on since I became their godfather. It would mean much time away from the village during their training period—and they might eventually be stationed in any ocean in the world. But two motherless children had not been easy on Juao or his sisters. The Corp would mean education, travel, interesting work, the things that make up one kind of good life. They wouldn't look twice their age when they were thirty; and not too many amphimen look like me.

"Worry is part of life. But the work is dangerous. Did you know there is an amphiman going to try and lay cable down in the Slash?"

I frowned. "Again?"

"Yes. And that is what you tried to do when the sea broke you to pieces and burned the parts, eh?"

"Must you be so damned picturesque?" I asked. "Who's going to beard the lion this time?"

"A young amphiman named Tork. They speak of him down at the docks as a brave man."

"Why the hell are they still trying to lay the cable there? They've gotten by this long without a line through the Slash."

"Because of the fish," Juao said. "You told me why fifteen years ago—"

"Sixteen," I said, "actually. We had a birthday three months back, you and me."

Juao went on as if it made no difference. "The fish are still there, and we fishermen who cannot live below are still here. If the children go for the operations, then there will be less fishermen. But today . . ." He shrugged. "They must either lay the line across the fish paths or down in the Slash." Juao shook his head.

Funny things, the great power cables the Aquatic Corp has been strewing across the ocean floor to bring power to their undersea mines and farms, to run their oil wells—and how many flaming wells have I capped down there—for their herds of whale, and chemical distillation plants. They carry two-hundred-sixty-cycle current. Over certain sections of the ocean floor, or in sections of the water with certain mineral contents, this sets up inductance in the water itself which sometimes—and you will probably get a Nobel prize if you can detail exactly why it isn't always—drives the fish away over areas up to twenty-five and thirty miles, unless the lines are laid in the bottom of those canyons that delve into the ocean floor.

"This Tork thinks of the fishermen. He is a good man too."

I raised my eyebrows—the one that's left, anyway—and tried to remember what my little Undine had said about him that morning. And remembered not much.

"I wish him luck," I said.

"What do you feel about this young man going down into the coral-rimmed jaws to the Slash?"

I thought for a moment. "I think I hate him."

Juao looked up.

"He is an image in a mirror where I look and am forced to regard what I once was," I went on. "I envy him the chance to succeed where I failed, and I can come on just as quaint as you can. I hope he makes it."

Juao twisted his shoulders in a complicated shrug (once I could do that) which is coastal Brazilian for, "I didn't know things had progressed to that point, but seeing that they have, there is little to be done."

"The sea is that sort of mirror," I said.

"Yes." Juao nodded.

Behind us I heard the slapping of sandals on concrete. I turned in time to catch my goddaughter in my good arm. My godson had grabbed hold of the bad one and was swinging on it.

"Tio Cal—?"

"Hey, Tio Cal, what did you bring us?"

"Clara, you will pull him over," Juao reprimanded. "Let go, Fernando!"

And, bless them, they ignored their father.

"What did you bring us?"

"What did you bring us, Tio Cal?"

"If you let me, I'll show you." So they stepped back, dark-eyed and quivering. I watched Juao watching: brown pupils on ivory balls, and in the left eye a vein had broken in a jagged smear. He was loving his children, who would soon be as alien to him as the fish he netted. He was also looking at the terrible thing that was me and wondering what would come to his own spawn. And he was watching the world turn and grow older, clocked by the waves, reflected in that mirror.

It's impossible for me to see what the population explosion and the budding colonies on Luna and Mars and the flowering beneath the ocean really look like from the disrupted cultural mélange of a coastal fishing town. But I come closer than many others, and I know what I don't understand.

I pushed around in my pocket and fetched out the milky fragment I had brought from the beach. "Here. Do you like this one?" And they bent above my webbed and alien fingers.

In the supermarket, which is the biggest building in the village, Juao bought a lot of cake mixes. "That moist, delicate texture," whispered the box when you lifted it from the shelf, "with that deep flavor, deeper than chocolate!"

I'd just read an article about the new vocal packaging in a U.S. magazine that had gotten down last week—so I was prepared and stayed in the fresh vegetable section to avoid temptation. Then we went up to Juao's house. The letter proved to be what I'd expected. The kids had to take the bus to Brasília tomorrow. My godchildren were on their way to becoming fish.

We sat on the front steps and drank and watched the donkeys and the motorbikes and the men in baggy trousers, the women in yellow scarves and bright skirts with wreaths of garlic and sacks of onions. As well, a few people glittered by in the green scales of amphimen uniforms.

Finally Juao got tired and went in to take a nap. Most of my life has been spent on the coast of countries accustomed to siestas, but those first formative ten were passed on a Danish collective farm and the idea never really took. So I stepped over my goddaughter, who had fallen asleep on her fists on the bottom step, and walked back through the town toward the beach.

III

At midnight Ariel came out of the sea, climbed the rocks, and clicked her nails against my glass wall so that droplets ran, pearled by the gibbous moon.

Earlier I had stretched in front of the fireplace on the sheepskin throw to read, then dozed off. The conscientious timer had asked me if there was anything I wanted, and getting no answer had turned off the Dvořák Cello Concerto, which was on its second time around, extinguished the reading lamp, and stopped dropping logs onto the flame so that now, as I woke, the grate was carpeted with coals.

She clicked again, and I raised my head from the cushion. The green uniform, her amber hair—all color was lost under the silver light outside. I lurched across the rug, touched the button, and the glass slid into the floor. The breeze came to my face as the barrier fell.

"What do you want?" I asked. "What time is it, anyway?"

"Tork is on the beach, waiting for you."

The night was warm but windy. Below the rocks silver flakes chased each other in to shore. The tide lay full.

I rubbed my face. "The new boss man? Why didn't you bring him up to the house? What does he want to see me about?"

She touched my arm. "Come. They are all down on the beach."

"Who all?"

"Tork and the others."

She led me across the patio and to the path that wound to the sand. The sea roared in the moonlight. Down the beach people stood around a driftwood fire that whipped the night. Ariel walked beside me.

Two of the fishermen from town were crowding each other on

the bottom of an overturned washtub, playing guitars. The singing, raucous and rhythmic, jarred across the paled sand. Shark's teeth shook on the necklace of an old woman dancing. Others were sitting on an overturned dinghy, eating.

Over one part of the fire on a skillet two feet across, oil frothed through pink islands of shrimp. One woman ladled them in; another ladled them out.

"Tio Cal!"

"Look, Tio Cal is here!"

"Hey, what are you two doing up?" I asked. "Shouldn't you be home in bed?"

"Poppa Juao said we could come. He'll be here, too, soon."

I turned to Ariel. "Why are they all gathering?"

"Because of the laying of the cable tomorrow at dawn."

Someone was running up the beach, waving a bottle in each hand.

"They didn't want to tell you about the party. They thought that it might hurt your pride."

"My what . . . ?"

"If you knew they were making so big a thing of the job you had failed at—"

"But—"

"—and that had hurt you so in failure. They did not want you to be sad. But Tork wants to see you. I said you would not be sad. So I went to bring you down from the rocks."

"Thanks, I guess."

"Tio Cal?"

But the voice was bigger and deeper than a child's.

He sat on a log back from the fire, eating a sweet potato. The flame flickered on his dark cheekbones, in his hair, wet and black. He stood, came to me, held up his hand. I held up mine and we slapped palms. "Good." He was smiling. "Ariel told me you would come. I will lay the power line down through the Slash tomorrow." His uniform scales glittered down his arms. He was very strong. But standing still, he still moved. The light on the cloth told me that.

"I . . ." He paused. I thought of a nervous, happy dancer. "I wanted to talk to you about the cable." I thought of an eagle; I thought of a shark. "And about the . . . accident. If you would."

"Sure," I said. "If there's anything I could tell you that would help."

"See, Tork," Ariel said. "I told you he would talk to you about it."

I could hear his breathing change. "It really doesn't bother you to talk about the accident?"

I shook my head and realized something about that voice. It was a boy's voice that could imitate a man's. Tork was not over nineteen.

"We're going fishing soon," Tork told me. "Will you come?"

"If I'm not in the way."

A bottle went from the woman at the shrimp crate to one of the guitarists, down to Ariel, to me, then to Tork. (The liquor, made in a cave seven miles inland, was almost rum. The too-tight skin across the left side of my mouth makes the manful swig a little difficult to bring off. I got "rum" down my chin.) He drank, wiped his mouth, passed the bottle on and put his hand on my shoulder. "Come down to the water."

We walked away from the fire. Some of the fishermen stared after us. A few of the amphimen glanced, and glanced away.

"Do all the young people of the village call you Tio Cal?"

"No. Only my godchildren. Their father and I have been friends since I was . . . well, younger than you."

"Oh, I thought perhaps it was a nickname. That's why I called you that."

We reached wet sand where orange light cavorted at our feet. The broken shell of a lifeboat rocked in moonlight. Tork sat down on the shell's rim. I sat beside him. The water splashed to our knees.

"There's no other place to lay the power cable?" I asked. "There is no other way to take it except through the Slash?"

"I was going to ask you what you thought of the whole business. But I guess I don't really have to." Tork shrugged and clapped his hands together a few times. "All the projects this side of the bay have grown huge and cry for power. The new operations tax the old lines unmercifully. There was a power failure last July in Cayine down the shelf below the twilight level. The whole underwater village was without light for two days; three amphimen died of overexposure to the cold currents coming up from the depths. If we laid the cables farther up, we chance disrupting our own fishing operations as well as those of the fishermen on shore."

I nodded.

"Cal, what happened to you in the Slash?"

Eager, scared Tork. I was remembering now, not the accident, but the midnight before, pacing the beach, guts clamped with fists of fear and anticipation. Some of the Indians back where they make the liquor still send messages by tying knots in palm fibers. One could have spread my entrails then, or Tork's tonight, to read our respective horospecs.

Juao's mother knew the knot language, but he and his sisters never bothered to learn because they wanted to be modern, and, as children, still confused with modernity the new ignorances, lacking modern knowledge.

"When I was a boy," Tork said, "we would dare each other to walk the boards along the edge of the ferry slip. The sun would be hot and the boards would rock in the water, and if the boats were in and you fell down between the boats and the piling, you could get killed." He shook his head. "The crazy things kids will do. That was back when I was eight or nine, before I became a waterbaby."

"Where was it?"

Tork looked up. "Oh. Manila. I'm Filipino."

The sea licked our knees, and the gunwale sagged under us.

"What happened in the Slash?"

"There's a volcanic flaw near the Slash's base."

"I know."

"And the sea is hypersensitive down there. You don't insult her fashion or her figure. We had an avalanche. The cable broke. The sparks were so hot and bright they made gouts of foam fifty feet high on the surface, so they tell me."

"What caused the avalanche?"

I shrugged. "It could have been just a goddamned coincidence.

There are rock falls down there all the time. It could have been the noise from the machines—though we masked them pretty well. It could have been something to do with the inductance from the smaller power cables. Or maybe somebody just kicked out the wrong stone that was holding everything up."

One webbed hand became a fist, sank into the other, and hung. Calling, "Cal!"

I looked up. Juao, pants rolled to his knees, shirt sailing in the sea wind, stood in the weave of white water. Tork looked up too. The wind lifted his hair from his neck; and the fire roared on the beach.

"They're getting ready to catch a big fish!" Juao called.

Men were already pushing their boats out. Tork clapped my shoulder. "Come, Cal. We fish now." We waded back to the shore.

Juao caught me as I reached dry sand. "You ride in my boat, Cal!"

Someone came by with the acrid flares that hissed. The water slapped around the bottom of the boats as we wobbled into the swell.

Juao vaulted in and took up the oars. Around us green amphimen walked into the sea, struck forward, and were gone.

Juao pulled, leaned, pulled. The moonlight slid down his arms. The fire diminished on the beach.

Then among the boats, there was a splash, an explosion, and the red flare bloomed in the sky: the amphimen had sighted a big fish.

The flare hovered, pulsed once, twice, three times, four times (twenty, forty, sixty, eighty stone they estimated its weight to be), then fell.

Suddenly I shrugged out of my shirt, pulled at my belt buckle. "I'm going over the side, Juao."

He leaned, he pulled, he leaned. "Take the rope."

"Yeah. Sure." It was tied to the back of the boat. I made a loop in the other end, slipped it around my shoulder. I swung my bad leg over the side, flung myself on the black water—

—mother-of-pearl shattered over me. That was the moon, blocked by the shadow of Juao's boat ten feet overhead. I turned below the rippling wounds Juao's oars made stroking the sea.

One hand and one foot with torn webs, I rolled over and looked down. The rope snaked to its end, and I felt Juao's strokes pulling me through the water.

They fanned below with submarine flares. Light undulated on their backs and heels. They circled, they closed, like those deep-sea fish who carry their own illumination. I saw the prey, glistening as it neared a submarine flare.

You chase a fish with one spear among you. And that spear would be Tork's tonight. The rest have ropes to bind him that go up to the fishermen's boats.

There was a sudden confusion of lights below. The spear had been shot!

The fish, long as a tall and short man together, rose through the ropes. He turned toward the depths, trailing his pursuers. But others waited there, tried to loop him. Once I had flung those ropes, treated with tar and lime to dissolve the slime on the fish's body and hold to the beast. The looped ropes caught, and by the movement of the flares, I saw them jerked down their paths. The fish turned, rose again, this time toward me.

He pulled around when one line ran out (and somewhere on the surface the prow of a boat bobbed low) but turned back and came on.

Of a sudden, amphimen were flicking about me as the fray's center drifted by. Tork, his spear dug deep, forward and left of the marlin's dorsal, had hauled himself astride the beast.

The fish tried to shake him, then dropped his tail and rose straight. Everybody started pulling toward the surface. I broke foam and grabbed Juao's gunwale.

Tork and the fish exploded up among the boats. They twisted in air, in moonlight, in froth. The fish danced across the water on its tail, fell.

Juao stood up in the boat and shouted. The other fishermen shouted too, and somebody perched on a prow flung a rope. Someone in the water caught it.

Then fish and Tork and me and a dozen amphimen all went underwater at once.

They dropped in a corona of bubbles. The fish struck the end of another line, and shook himself. Tork was thrown free, but he doubled back.

Then the lines began to haul the beast up again, quivering, whipping, quivering again.

Six lines from six boats had him. For one moment he was still in the submarine moonlight. I could see his wound tossing scarves of blood.

When he (and we) broke surface, he was thrashing again, near Juao's boat. I was holding onto the side when suddenly Tork, glistening, came out of the water beside me and went over into the dinghy.

"Here you go," he said, turning to kneel at the bobbing rim, and pulled me up while Juao leaned against the far side to keep balance.

Wet rope slopped the boards. "Hey, Cal!" and my abdomen did a mini-hiccup, which meant I'd gone from water to air. (In the other direction the transition is unnoticeable.) From fluttering gills, water ran down my back, my shoulders. The only time you really feel them. And Tork laughed, grabbed up the rope, and began to haul.

The fish prised wave from white wave in the white water.

The boats came together. The amphimen had all climbed up. Ariel was across from us, holding a flare that drooled smoke down her arm. She peered by the hip of the fisherman who was standing in front of her.

Juao and Tork were hauling the rope. Behind them I was coiling it with one hand as it came back to me.

The fish came up and was flopped into Ariel's boat, tail out, head up, chewing air. More hics.

I had just finished pulling on my trousers when Tork fell down on the seat behind me and grabbed me around the shoulders with his wet arms. "Look at our fish, Tio Cal! Look!" He gasped air, laughing, his dark face diamonded beside the flares. "Look at our fish there, Cal!"

Juao, grinning white and gold, pulled us back into shore. The fire, the singing, hands beating hands—and my godson had put pebbles in the empty rum bottles and was shaking them to the music—the guitars spiraled around us as we carried the fish up the sand and the men brought the spit.

"Watch it!" Tork said, grasping the pointed end of the great stick that was thicker than his wrist.

We turned the fish over.

"Here, Cal?"

He prodded two fingers into the white flesh six inches back from the bony lip.

"Fine."

Tork jammed the spit in.

We worked it through the body. By the time we carried it to the fire, they had brought more rum.

"Hey, Tork. Are you going to get some sleep before you go down in the morning?" I asked.

He shook his head. "Slept all afternoon." He pointed toward the roasting fish with his elbow. "That's my breakfast."

But when the dancing grew violent a few hours later, just before the fish was to come off the fire, and the kids were pushing the last of the sweet potatoes from the ashes with sticks, I walked back to the lifeboat shell we had sat on earlier. It was three-quarters flooded.

Curled below still water, Tork slept, fist loose before his mouth, the gills at the back of his neck pulsing rhythmically. Only his shoulder and hip made islands in the floated boat.

"Where's Tork?" Ariel asked me at the fire. They were swinging up the sizzling fish.

"Taking a nap."

"Oh, he wanted to cut the fish!"

"He's got a lot of work ahead. Sure you want to wake him?"

"No, I'll let him sleep."

But Tork was walking from the water, brushing his dripping hair back from his forehead.

He grinned at us, then went to carve. I remember him standing on the table, astraddle the meat, arm going up and down with the big knife (details, yes, those are the things you remember), stopping to hand down the portions, then hauling his arm back to cut again.

That night, with music and stomping on the sand and shouting back and forth over the fire, we made more noise than the sea.

IV

The eight-thirty bus was more or less on time.

"I don't think they want to go," Juao's sister said. She was accompanying the children to the Aquatic Corp Headquarters in Brasília.

"They are just tired," Juao said. "They should not have stayed up so late last night. Get on the bus now. Say good-bye to Tio Cal."

"Good-bye." (Fernando.)

"Good-bye." (Clara.)

But kids are never their most creative in that sort of situation. And I suspect that my godchildren may just have been suffering their first (or one of their first) hangovers. They had been very quiet all morning.

I bent down and gave them a clumsy hug. "When you come back on your first weekend off, I'll take you exploring down below at the point. You'll be able to gather your own coral now."

Juao's sister got teary, cuddled the children, cuddled me, Juao, then got on the bus.

Someone was shouting out the bus window for someone at the bus stop not to forget something. They trundled around the square and then toward the highway. We walked back across the street where the café owners were putting out canvas chairs.

"I will miss them," he said, like a long-considered admission.

"You and me both." At the docks near the hydrofoil wharf where the submarine launches went out to the undersea cities, we saw a crowd. "I wonder if they had any trouble laying the—"

A woman screamed in the crowd. She pushed from the others, dropping eggs and onions. She began to pull her hair and shriek. (Remember the skillet of shrimp? She had been the woman ladling them out.) A few people moved to help her.

A clutch of men broke off and ran into a side street. I grabbed a running amphiman, who whirled to face me.

"What in hell is going on?"

For a moment his mouth worked on his words for all the trite world like a beached fish.

"From the explosion . . ." he began. "They just brought them back from the explosion at the Slash!"

I grabbed his other shoulder. "What happened!"

"About two hours ago. They were just a quarter of the way through, when the whole fault gave way. They had a goddamn underwater volcano for half an hour. They're still getting seismic disturbances."

Juao was running toward the launch. I pushed the guy away and limped after him, struck the crowd and jostled through calico, canvas, and green scales.

They were carrying the corpses out of the hatch of the submarine and laying them on a canvas spread across the dock. They still return bodies to the countries of birth for the family to decide the method of burial. When the fault had given, the hot slag that had belched into the steaming sea was mostly molten silicon.

Four of the bodies were only slightly burned here and there; from their bloated faces (one still bled from the ear) I guessed they had died from sonic concussion. But several of the corpses were almost totally encased in dull, black glass.

"Tork—" I kept asking. "Is one of them—?"

It took me forty-five minutes, asking first the guys who were carrying, then going into the launch and asking some guy with a clipboard, and then going back on the dock and into the office to find out that one of the more unrecognizable figures was, yes, Tork.

Juao brought me a glass of buttermilk at the café on the square. He sat still a long time, then finally rubbed away his white mustache, released the chair rung with his toes, put his hands on his knees.

"What are you thinking about?"

"That it's time to go fix nets. Tomorrow morning I will fish." He regarded me a moment. "Where should I fish tomorrow, Cal?"

"Are you wondering about . . . sending the kids off today?"

He shrugged. "Fishermen from this village have drowned. Still it is a village of fishermen. Where should I fish?"

I finished my buttermilk. "The mineral content over the Slash should be high as the devil. Lots of algae will gather tonight. Lots of small fish down deep. Big fish hovering over."

He nodded. "Good. I will take the boat out there tomorrow."

We got up.

"See you, Juao."

I limped back to the beach.

V

The fog had unsheathed the sand by ten. I walked around, poking clumps of weeds with a stick, banging the same stick on my numb leg. When I lurched up to the top of the rocks, I stopped in the still grass. "Ariel?"

She was kneeling in the water, head down, red hair breaking over sealed gills. Her shoulders shook, stopped, shook again.

"Ariel?" I came down over the blistered stones.

She turned away to look at the ocean.

The attachments of children are so important and so brittle. "How long have you been sitting here?"

She looked at me now, the varied waters of her face stilled on drawn cheeks. And her face was exhausted. She shook her head.

Sixteen? Seventeen? Who was the psychologist, back in the seventies, who decided that "adolescents" were just physical and mental adults with no useful work? "You want to come up to the house?"

The head shaking got faster, then stopped.

After a while I said, "I guess they'll be sending Tork's body back to Manila."

"He didn't have a family," she explained. "He'll be buried here, at sea."

"Oh," I said.

And the rough volcanic glass, pulled across the ocean's sands, changing shape, dulling—

"You were—you liked Tork a lot, didn't you? You kids looked like you were pretty fond of each other."

"Yes. He was an awfully nice—" Then she caught my meaning and blinked. "No," she said. "Oh, no. I was—I was engaged to Jonni . . . the brown-haired boy from California? Did you meet him at the party last night? We're both from Los Angeles, but we only met down here. And now . . . they're sending his body back this evening." Her eyes got very wide, then closed.

"I'm sorry."

I'm a clumsy cripple; I trip all over everybody's emotions. In that mirror I guess I'm too busy looking at what might have been.

"I'm sorry, Ariel."

She opened her eyes and began to look around her.

"Come on up to the house and have an avocado. I mean, they have avocados in now—not at the supermarket. But at the old town market on the other side. And they're better than any they grow in California."

She kept looking around.

"None of the amphimen get over there. It's a shame, because soon the market will probably close, and some of their fresh foods are really great. Oil and vinegar is all you need on them." I leaned back on the rocks. "Or a cup of tea?"

"Okay." She remembered to smile. I know the poor kid didn't feel like it. "Thank you. I won't be able to stay long, though."

We walked back up the rocks toward the house, the sea on our left. Just as we reached the patio, she turned and looked back. "Cal?"

"Yes? What is it?"

"Those clouds over there, across the water. Those are the only ones in the sky. Are they from the eruption in the Slash?"

I squinted. "I think so. Come on inside."

—*New York*
November 1966

we, in some strange power's employ, move on a rigorous line

For R. Zelazny

I

*O*nly the dark and her screaming.

First: sparks glint on her feet, and crack and snap, lighting rocks, dirt. Then no screams. She almost falls, whips erect. Silver leggings: Pop-pop-pop. Light laces higher, her arms are waving (trying to tell myself, "But she's dead already—"), and she weaves like a woman of white and silver paper, burning on the housing of the great ribbed cable exposed in the gully we'd torn from the earth.

"Thinking about your promotion?"

"Huh?" I looked up on Scott, who was poking at me with a freckled finger. Freckles, dime-sized and penny-colored, covered face, lips, arms, shoulders, got lost under the gold hair snarling his chest and belly. "What's it feel like to be a section-devil? I've been opting for it two years now." Freckled fingers snapped. "Pass me up and take you!" He leaned back in his hammock, dug beneath his tool belt to scratch himself.

I shook my head. "No, something else. Something that happened a while back. Nothing, really."

Night scoured our windows.

The Gila Monster sped.

Light wiped the panes and slipped away.

Scott suddenly sat up, caught his toes, and frowned. "Sometimes I think I'll spend the rest of my working life, just a silver-suited line-demon, dancing along them damned strings." He pointed with his chin at the cross-section sixteen-foot cable chart. "Come thirty-five, when I want to retire—and it's less than ten years off—what'll I be able to say? I did my job well?" He made a fist around the hammock edge. "I didn't do it well enough to make anything out of it." Hand open and up. "Some big black so-and-so like you comes along and three years later . . . section-devil!"

"You're a better demon than I am, Scott."

"Don't think I don't know it, either." Then Scott laughed. "No, let *me* tell *you*: a good demon doesn't necessarily make a good devil. The skills are different skills. The talents aren't the same. Hell, Blacky, you'd think, as your friend, I'd spare you. Say, when do you check out of this cabin? Gotta get used to somebody else's junk. Will you stay on at the old Monster here?"

"They said something about transferring me to Iguana. What with the red tape, it won't happen for a couple of weeks. I'll probably just give Mabel a hand till then. She gave me a room right over the tread motor. I complained about your snoring, and we agreed it would be an improvement."

That rated a swing; Scott just nodded.

I thought around for something to say and came up with: "You know I'm due an assistant, and I can choose—"

"Hell!" He flung himself back so I could only see his feet. (Underneath the hammock: one white woolen sock [gray toe], magazine, three wrenches.) "I'm no clerk. You have me running computers and keeping track of your confusion, filing reclamation plans and trying to hunt them out again—and all that for a drop in salary—"

"I wouldn't drop your salary."

"I'd go up the wall anyway."

"Knew that's what you'd say."

"Knew you'd make me say it."

"Well," I said, "Mabel asked me to come around to her office."

"Yeah. Sure." Release, relief. "Clever devil, Mabel. Hey. You'll be screening new applicants for whoever is gonna share my room now you been kicked upstairs. See if you can get a girl in here?"

"If I can." I grinned and stepped outside.

Gila Monster guts?

Three-quarters of a mile of corridors (much less than on some luxury ocean liners); two engine rooms to power the adjustable treads that carry us over land and sea; a kitchen, cafeteria, electrical room, navigation offices, office offices, tool repair shop, and cetera. With such in its belly, the Gila Monster crawls through the night (at about a hundred fifty *k*'s cruising speed), sniffing along the great cables (courtesy the Global Power Commission) that net the world, web evening to night, dawn to day, and yesterday to morrow.

"Come in, Blacky," Mabel said at my knock.

She brushed back silver hair from her silver collar (the hair is natural) and closed her folder. "Seems we have a stop coming up just over the Canadian border."

"Pick up Scott's new roommate?"

"Power Cadet Susan Suyaki. Seventeen years old. Graduated third in her class last summer."

"Seventeen? Scott should like that."

"Wish she had some experience. The bright ones come out of school too snooty."

"I didn't."

"You still are."

"Oh, well. Scott prefers them with spirit."

"They're flying her in by helicopter to the site of our next job."

"Which line broke?"

"No break. It's a conversion."

I raised an eyebrow. "A rare experience for Miss Suyaki. I've only been through one, during my first couple of months on Salamander. That was a goodly while ago."

Mabel gave me a super-cynical-over-the-left-cheekbone. "You haven't *been* in the Power Corps a goodly while. You're just brilliant, that's all."

"It was a goodly while for *me*. Not all of us have had your thirty years' experience, ma'am."

"I've always felt experience was vastly overrated as a teacher." She started to clean her nails with a metal rule. "Otherwise, I would never have recommended you for promotion." Mabel is a fine devil.

"Thankee, thankee." I sat and looked at the ceiling map. "A conversion." Musing. "Salamander covered most of Mongolia. A little village in Tibet had to be connected up to the lines. We put cable through some of the damnedest rock. They were having an epidemic of some fever that gave you oozy blisters, and the medical crew was trying to set itself up at the same time. We worked twenty-four hours a day for three days, running lines, putting in outlets, and hooking up equipment. Three days to pull that primitive enclave of skin huts, caves, and lean-tos into the twenty-first century. Nothing resembling a heater in the whole place, and it was snowing when we got there."

Over joined fingertips Mabel bobbed her chin. "And to think, they'd been doddering along like that for the last three thousand years."

"Probably not much more than two hundred. The village had been established by refugees from the Sino-Japanese War. Still, I get your point."

"They were happy when you left?"

"They were happi-*er*," I said. "Still, you look at the maps—you trace cables over the world, and it's pretty hard to think there are still a few places that haven't been converted."

"I'm not as dreamy as you. Every couple of years Gila or Iguana stumbles over a little piece of the planet that's managed to fall through the net. They'll probably be turning them up a hundred years from now. People cling to their backwardness."

"Maybe you're—the border of *Canada*!"

"That is the longest take I've ever seen. Wake up, boy. Here I've been telling everybody how bright you are, recommending you for promotion—"

"Mabel, how can we have a conversion on the border of Canada? You convert villages in upper Anatolia, nameless little islands in the Indian Ocean—Tibet. There's no place you could lay another cable in the Americas. A town converted to Global Power along there?"

Mabel nodded some more. "I don't like conversions. Always something messy. If everything went by the books, you'd think it would be one of our easiest maneuvers."

"You know me. I never go by the books."

She, musing this time: "True, doll. I still don't like 'em."

"The one I was telling you about, in Tibet. We had a bad accident."

Mabel asked what it was with her eyebrows.

"A burning. Middle of the night, when somebody had wandered down into the trough to troubleshoot one of the new connections. She was climbing up on the housing, when the power went on. Some sort of high-amperage short. She went up like the proverbial moth."

Mabel stopped bobbing. "Who was she?"

"My wife."

"Oh." After a moment she said, "Burnings are bad. Hell of a waste of power, if nothing else. I wondered why you chose to room with Scott when you first came on the Gila Monster rather than Jane, Judy, or—"

"Julia was the young lady out for my tired brown body back then."

"You and your wife must have come straight out of the academy together. In your first year? Blacky, that's terrible. . . ."

"We had, that's right, and it was."

"I didn't know." Mabel looked adequately sincere.

"Don't tell me you didn't guess?"

"Don't joke . . . well, joke if you want." Mabel is a fine woman. "A conversion just over the Canadian border." She shook her head. "Blacky, we're going to have a problem, you and I."

"How so, ma'am?"

"Again: you are going to have a problem with me. I am going to have a problem with you."

"Pray, how, gentle lady?"

"You're a section-devil now. I'm a section-devil. You've been one for just under six hours. I've been one for just over sixteen years. But by the books, we are in equal positions of authority."

"Fair maid," I said, "thou art off thy everloving nut."

"You're the one who doesn't go by the books. I do. Power of authority divided between two people doesn't work."

"If it makes you feel any better, I still consider you boss. You're the best boss I ever had too. Besides, I like you."

"Blacky—" she looked up at the skylight where the moon, outside the frame, still lit the tessellations—"there is something going on out there just across the border that I guess I know more about than you. You only know it's a conversion; and where it is, is odd. Let me warn you: you will want to handle it one way. I will want to handle it another."

"So we do it your way."

"Only I'm not so sure my way is best."

"Mabel—"

"Go, swarthy knight. We meet beyond the Canadian borders to do battle." She stood up looking very serious.

"If you say so."

"See you in the morning, Blacky."

I left the office, wondering at knights and days. Oh well, however, anyway: Scott was snoring, so I read until the rush of darkness outside was drifting gray.

II

The dawning sky (working top to bottom):

Sable, azure, gules—

—mountains dexter, sinister a hurst of oak, lots of pines, a few maples. The Gila Monster parked itself astride a foamy brook below a waterfall. I went outside on the balcony and got showered as leaves sprinkled the stainless flank of our great striding beast.

"Hello? Hey, hello!"

"Hi." I waved toward where she was climbing down the— whoops! Into the water to her knee. She squealed, climbed back up the rock, and looked embarrassed.

"Cadet Suyaki?"

"Eh . . . yes, sir." She tried to rub her leg dry. Canadian streams at dawn are cold.

I took off my shirt, made a ball, and flung it to her. "Section-devil Jones." (She caught it.) "Blacky'll do. We're pretty informal around here."

"Oh . . . thank you." She lifted her silver legging, removed her boot to dry a very pretty ankle.

I gave the stairway a kick.

Clank-*chchchchc*-thud!

The steps unfolded, and the metal feet stamped into pine needles. I went down to the bank.

"Waiting long?"

She grinned. "Oh, I just got here."

And beyond the rocks there was a corroborative roar and snapping; a helicopter swung up through the trees.

Cadet Suyaki stood quickly and waved.

Somebody in the cockpit waved back till copper glare wiped him out.

"We saw you getting parked—" She looked down the length of Gila Monster.

I have said, or have I?

Cross an armadillo with a football field. Nurse the offspring on a motherly tank. By puberty: one Gila Monster.

"I'll be working under you?"

"Myself and Mabel Whyman."

She looked at me questioningly.

"Section-Devil Whyman—Mabel—is really in charge. I was just promoted from line-demon yesterday."

"Oh. Congratulations!"

"Hey, Blacky! Is that my new roommate?"

"That," I pointed at Scott, all freckled and golden, leaning over the rail, "is your pardner. You'll be rooming together."

Scott came down the steps, barefoot, denims torn off mid-thigh, tool belt full of calipers, meters, and insulation spools.

"Susan Suyaki," I announced, "Scott Mackelway."

She extended her hand. "I'm glad to meet—"

Scott put a big hand on each of little Miss Suyaki's shoulders. "So am I, honey. So am I."

"We'll be working very closely together, won't we?" asked Susan brightly. "I like that!" She squeezed one of his forearms. "Oh, I think this'll work out very well."

"Sure it will," Scott said. "I'm . . ." Then I saw an open space on his ear pinken. "I sure hope it does."

"You two demons get over to the chameleon nest!"

Scott, holding Sue's hand, pointed up to the balcony. "That's Mabel. Hey, boss! We going anyplace I gotta put my shoes on?"

"Just scouting. Get going."

"We keep the chameleon over the port tread." Scott led Sue down the man-high links of the Monster's chain drive.

Thought: some twenty-four hours by, if Mabel had yelled, "You two demons . . ." the two demons would have been Scott and me.

She came, all silver, down the steps.

"You smile before the joust, Britomart?"

"Blacky, I'm turning into a dirty old woman." At the bottom step, she laid her forefinger on my chest, drew it slowly down my stomach and finally hooked my belt. "You're beautiful. And I'm not smiling; I'm leering."

I put my arm around her shoulder, and we walked the pine needles. She put her hands in her silver pockets. Hip on my thigh, shoulder knocking gently on my side, hair over my arm, she pondered the ferns and the oaks, the rocks and the water, the mountains and the flank of our Gila Monster couchant, the blaze of morning between the branches. "You're a devil. So there are things I can say to you, ostensibly, that would be meaningless to the others." She nodded ahead to where Scott and Sue were just disappearing around the three-meter hub.

"I await thy words most eagerly, Lady."

Mabel gestured at the Monster. "Blacky, do you know what the Monster, and the lines he prowls, really are?"

"I can tell you don't want an answer out of the book from your tone of voice, Miss Rules-and-Regulations."

"They're symbols of a way of life. Global Power Lines keep how many hundreds of thousands of refrigeration units functioning around the equator to facilitate food storage; they've made the Arctic habitable. Cities like New York and Tokyo have cut populations to a third of what they were a century ago. Back then, people used to be afraid they would crowd each other off the planet, would starve from lack of food. Yet the majority of the world was farming less than three percent of the arable land, and living on less than twenty percent of the world's surface. Global Power Lines meant that man could live anyplace on dry land he wanted, and a good number of places under the sea. National boundaries used to be an excuse for war; now they're only cartographical expedients. Riding in the Monster's belly, it's ironic that we are further from this way of life we're helping to maintain than most. But we still benefit."

"Of course."

"Have you ever asked yourself exactly how?"

"Education, leisure time," I suggested, "early and sliding retirements . . ."

Mabel chuckled. "Oh, much more, Blacky. So much more. Men and women work together; our navigator, Faltaux, is one of the finest poets writing in French today, with an international reputation, and is still the best navigator I've ever had. And Julia, who keeps us so well fed and can pilot us quite as competently as I can and is such a lousy painter, works with you and me and Faltaux and Scott on the same Maintenance Station. Or just the fact that you can move out of Scott's room one day and little Miss Suyaki can move in the next with an ease that would have amazed your great-great ancestors in Africa as much as mine in Finland. *That's* what this steel egg-crate means."

"Okay," I said. "I'm moved."

We came around the hub. Scott was heaving up the second door of the chameleon's garage and pointing out to Sue where the jack and the graphite can were kept.

"Some people," Mabel went on as I dropped my arm from her shoulder, "don't particularly like this way of life. Which is why we are about to attempt a conversion here on the Canadian border."

"A conversion?" Sue popped up. "Isn't that when you switch an area or a dwelling to Global—"

At which point Scott swung at Mabel. He caught her upside the head. She yelled and went staggering into the leaves.

I jumped back, and Sue did a thing with her Adam's apple.

Something went *Nnnnnnnnnnn* against the hub, then chattered away through the ferns. Ferns fell.

"Look!" Sue cried.

I was staring at the eight-inch scratch in the Gila Monster's very hard hide, at about the level where Mabel's carotid had been a moment back.

But across the water, scrambling up the rocks, was a yellow-headed kid wearing a little less than Scott.

Sue ran through the weeds and picked up the blade. "Were they trying to *kill* somebody?"

Mabel shrugged. "You're Cadet Suyaki? We're going to explore the conversion site. Dear me, that looks vicious."

"I used to hunt with a bolo," Sue said warily. "At home. But I've never even *seen* one of these . . . ?" Two blades were bolted in a twisted cross, all four prongs sharpened.

"My first too. Hope it's my last." Mabel looked around the clearing. "Am I ever optimistic. Pleased to meet you, Suyaki. Well, come on. Crank up Nelly. And for Pete's sake, let's get *in*."

The chameleon, ten feet long, is mostly transparent plastic, which means you can see sea, sunset, or forest right through.

Scott drove with Mabel beside him.

Me and Sue sat in back.

We found the chewed-up asphalt of an old road and crawled right along up the mountain.

"Where are . . . we going, exactly?" Sue asked.

"Honey," Mabel said, "I'll let you know when we get there." She put the throwing blade in the glove compartment with a grunt. Which does a lot of good with transparent plastic.

III

Sue leaned against the door. "Oh, look! Look down!"

We'd wound high enough and looped back far enough on the abominable road so that you could gaze down through the breaks;

beyond the trees and rocks you could see the Gila Monster. It still looked big.

"Eh . . . look up," suggested Scott and slowed the chameleon. A good-sized tree had come up by the roots and fallen across the road.

The man standing in front of it was very dirty. The kid behind, peering through the Medusa of roots, was the one who had tried to decapitate Mabel.

"What . . . are they?" Sue whispered.

"Scott and Sue, you stay right here and keep the door open so we can get back in fast. Blacky, we go on up."

The man's hair, under the grease, was brass-colored.

Some time ago his left cheek had been opened up, then sewn so clumsily you could see the cross-stitching. The lobe of his left ear was a rag of flesh. His sleeve-ripped shirt hung buttonless and too short to tuck in, even if he'd had a mind to. A second welt plowed an inch furrow through chest hair, wrecked his right nipple, and disappeared under his collar.

As we came up, Mabel took the lead. I overtook her; she gave me a faint-subtle-nasty and stepped ahead again.

He was a hard guy, but the beginning of a gut was showing over the double bar and chain contraption he used to fasten his studded belt. At first I thought he was wearing mismatched shoes: one knee-high, scuffed, and cracked-soled boot. The other foot was bare, a length of black chain around the ankle, two toes, little and middle, gone.

I looked back at his face to see his eyes come up to mine.

Well, I was still sans shirt; back in the chameleon Sue's pants leg was still rolled up. Mabel was the only one of us proofed neat and proper.

He looked at Mabel. He looked at me. He looked at Mabel. Then he bent his head and said, "Rchht-*ah*-pt, what are you doing up here, huh?" That first one produced a yellow oyster about eight inches north of Mabel's boot toe, six south of his bare one. His head came up, the lower lip glistening and hanging away from long, yellow teeth.

"Good morning." I offered my hand. "We're . . . " (He looked at it.) ". . . surveying."

He took his thumb from his torn pocket; we shook. A lot of grease, a lot of callus, it was the hand of a very big man who had bitten his nails since he was a very small boy.

"Yeah? What are you surveying?"

He wore a marvelous ring.

"We're from Global Power Commission."

Take a raw, irregular nugget of gold—

"Figured. I saw your machine down the road."

—a nugget three times the size either taste or expediency might allow a ring—

"We've had reports that the area is underpowered for the number of people living here."

—punch a finger-sized hole, so that most of the irregularities are on one side—

"Them bastards down in Hainesville probably registered a complaint. Well, we don't live in Hainesville. Don't see why it should bother them."

—off center in the golden crater place an opal, big as his—as *my* thumbnail—

"We have to check it out. Inadequate power doesn't do anybody any good."

—put small diamonds in the tips of the three prongs that curved to cage the opal—

"You think so?"

—and in the ledges and folds of bright metal capping his enlarged knuckle, bits of spodumene, pyrope, and spinel, all abstract, all magnificent.

"Look, mister," I said, "the Hainesville report says there are over two dozen people living on this mountain. The power commission doesn't register a *single* outlet."

He slipped his hands into his back pockets. "Don't believe I have seen any, now you mention it."

Mabel said, "The law governs how much power and how many

outlets must be available and accessible to each person. We'll be laying lines up here this afternoon and tomorrow morning. We're not here to make trouble. We don't want to find any."

"What makes you think you might?"

"Well, your friend over there already tried to cut my head off."

He frowned, glanced back through the roots. Suddenly he leaned back over the trunk and took a huge swipe. "Get out of here, Pitt!"

The kid squeaked. The face flashed in the roots (lank hair, a spray of acne across flat cheek and sharp chin), and jangling at her hip was a hank of throwing blades. She disappeared into the woods.

As the man turned, I saw, tattooed on the bowl of his shoulder, a winged dragon, coiled about and gnawing at a swastika.

Mabel ignored the whole thing:

"We'll be finished down the mountain this morning and will start bringing the lines up here this afternoon."

He gave half a nod—lowered his head and didn't bring it up—and that was when it dawned on me we were doing this thing wrong.

"We do want to do this easily," I said. "We're not here to make problems for you."

His hands crawled from his knees back to his waist.

"You can help us by letting people know that. If anyone has any questions about what we're doing, or doesn't understand something, they can come and ask for me. I'm Section-Devil Jones. Just ask for Blacky down at the Gila Monster."

"My name's Roger . . ." followed by something Polish and unpronounceable that began with Z and ended in Y. "If you have problems, you can come to me. Only I ain't saying I can do anything."

Good exit line. But Roger stayed where he was. And Mabel beside me was projecting stark disapproval.

"Where do most of the folks around here live?" I asked, to break the silence.

He nodded up. "On High Haven."

"Is there somebody in charge, a mayor or something like that I could talk to?"

Roger looked at me like he was deciding where I'd break easiest if he hit. "That's why I'm down here talking to you."

"You?" I didn't ask. What I *did* say was: "Then perhaps we could go up and see the community. I'd like to see how many people are up there, perhaps suggest some equipment, determine where things have to be done."

"You want to visit on High?"

"If we might."

He made a fist and scratched his neck with the prongs of his ring. "All right." He gestured back toward the chameleon. "You can't get that any further up the road."

"Will you take us, then?"

He thought awhile. "Sure." Then he let a grin open over the yellow cage of teeth. "Get you back down too." Small victory.

"Just a moment," Mabel said, "while we go back and tell the driver."

We strolled to the chameleon.

"You don't sound very happy with my attempt to make peace."

"Have I said a word?"

"*Just* what I mean. Can you imagine how these people live, Mabel, if Roger there is the head of the Chamber of Commerce?"

"I can imagine."

"He looks as bad as any of those villagers in Tibet. Did you *see* the little girl? This, in the middle of the twenty-first century!"

". . . just over the Canadian border. Scott," Mabel said, "take me and Sue back down to the Monster. If you are not back by noon, Blacky, we will come looking for you."

"Huh? You mean you're not going with me? Look," I told Scott's puzzled frown, "don't worry, I'll be back. Sue, can I have my shirt?"

"Oh, I'm terribly sorry! Here you are. It may be damp—"

"Mabel, if we did go up there together—"

"Blacky, running this operation with two devils admittedly presents problems. Running it with none at all is something else entirely. You're a big devil now. You know what you're doing. I even know. I just think you're crazy."

"*Ma*-bel—"

"On up there with you! And sow as much goodwill as you can. If it avoids one-tenth the problems I know we're going to have in the next twelve hours, I will be eternally grateful."

Then Mabel, looking determined, and Sue and Scott, looking bewildered, climbed into the chameleon.

"Oh." She leaned out the door. "Give this back to them." She handed me the throwing blade. "See you by noon." The chameleon swayed off down the road. I put my shirt on, stuck the blade in my belt, and walked back to Roger.

He glanced at it, and we both thought nasty-nasty-evilness at one another. "Come on." He climbed over the tree. I climbed over after.

Parked behind the trunk was an old twin-turbo pteracycle. Roger lifted it by one black and chrome bat-form wing. The chrome was slightly flaked. With one hand he grasped the steering shaft and twisted the choke ring gently. The other hand passed down the wing with the indifference we use to mask the grosser passions. "Hop on my broomstick and I'll take you up to where the angels make their Haven." He grinned.

And I understood many things.

So:

SMALL ESSAY

on a phenomenon current some fifty years back when the date had three zeroes. (Same time as the first cables were being laid and demons were beginning to sniff about the world in silver armor, doctoring breaks, repairing relays, replacing worn housings. Make the fancy sociological connections, please.) That's when pteracycles first became popular as a means of short- (and sometimes not so short-) range transportation. Then they were suddenly taken up by a particularly odd set of asocials. Calling themselves individualists, they moved in veritable flocks. Dissatisfied with society, they wracked the ages for symbols from the most destructive epochs: skull and bones, fasces, swastika, and guillotine. They were accused of the most malicious and depraved acts, sometimes with cause, sometimes without. They took the generic name of angels (Night's Angels, Red Angels, Hell's Angels, Bloody Angels, one of these lifted from a similar cult popular another half century before. But then most of their mythic accouterments were borrowed). The common sociological explanation: they were a reaction to population decentralization, the last elements of violence in a neutral world. Psychological: well, after all, what does a pteracycle look like?—two round cam-turbines on which you sit between the wings, then this six-foot metal shaft sprouting up between your legs that you steer with (hence the sobriquet "broomstick") and nothing else but goggles between you and the sky. You figure it. Concluding remarks: angels were a product of the turn of the century. But nobody's heard anything serious about them for thirty years. They went out with neon buttons, the common cold, and transparent vinyl jockey shorts. Oh, the teens of *siècle* twenty-one saw some dillies!

The End

I climbed on the backseat. Roger got on the front, toed one of the buttons on the stirrup (for any fancy flying you have to do some pretty fast button-pushing; ergo, the bare foot), twisted the throttle ring, and lots of leaves shot up around my legs. The cycle skidded up the road, bounced twice on cracks, then swerved over the edge. We dropped ten feet before we caught the draft and began the long arc out and up. Roger flew without goggles.

The wind over his shoulder carried a smell I first thought was the machine. Imagine a still that hasn't bathed for three months. He flew *very* well.

"How many people are there in High Haven?" I called.

"What?"

"I said, how many people are there in—"

"About twenty-seven."

We curved away from the mountain, curved back.

The Gila Monster flashed below, was gone behind rocks. The mountain turned, opening a rocky gash.

At the back of the gorge, vaulting the stream that plummeted the mountain's groin, someone had erected a mansion. It was a dated concrete and glass monstrosity from the late twentieth century (pre–power lines). Four terraced stories were cantilevered into the rock. Much of the glass was broken. Places that had once been garden had gone wild with vine and brush. A spectacular metal stairway wound from the artificial pool by the end of the roadway that was probably the same one we'd ridden up with the chameleon, from porch to porch, rust-blotched like a snake's back.

The house still had much stolid grandeur. Racked against a brick balustrade were maybe twenty pteracycles: what better launch than the concrete overhang, railing torn away. One cycle was off the rack. A guy was on his knees before it, the motor in pieces around him. A second, fists on hips, was giving advice.

A third guy shielded his eyes to watch us. A couple of others stopped by the edge of the pool. One was the girl, Pitt, who had been down with Roger before.

"High Haven?"

"What?" Pteracycles are loud.

"Is that High Haven?"

"Yeah!" We glided between the rocks, skimmed foaming boulders, rose toward glass and concrete. Cement rasped beneath the runners, and we jounced to a stop.

A couple of guys stepped from a broken window. A couple more came up the steps. Someone looking from the upper porch disappeared, to return a moment later with five others, another girl among them.

There was a lot of dirt, a lot of hair, a number of earrings. (I counted four more torn ears; I'd avoid fights if I were going to wear my jewelry that permanent.) A kid with much red hair—couldn't quite make a beard yet—straddled the cycle rack. He pushed back the flap of his leather jacket to scratch his bare belly with black-rimmed nails. The dragon on his chest beat its wings about the twisted cross.

I got off the cycle left, Roger right.

Someone said, "Who's that?"

A few of the guys glanced over their shoulders, then stepped aside so we could see.

She stood behind the dawn-splashed hem of glass at the side of the broken wall-window.

"He's from the Global Power Commission." Roger shoved a thumb at me. "They're parked down the mountain."

"You can tell him to go back to hell where he came from."

She wasn't young. She was beautiful though.

"We don't need anything he's selling."

The others mumbled, shuffled.

"Shut it," Roger said. "He s not selling anything."

I stood there feeling uncomfortably silver, but wondering that I'd managed to win over Roger.

"That's Fidessa," he said.

She stepped through the window.

Wide, high facial bones, a dark mouth and darker eyes. I want to describe her hair as amber, but it was an amber so dark only direct sunlight caught its reds. The morning fell full on it; it spread her shoulders. Her hands were floured, and she smeared white on her hips as she came toward me.

"Fidessa?" All right. I'm not opposed to reality imitating art.

"He's okay," Roger said in response to her look.

"Yeah?"

"Yeah. Get out of the way." He shoved her. She nearly collided with one of the men, who just stepped out of the way in time. She still gave the poor guy a withering *noli me tangere* stare. Kept her stuff, too.

"You want to see the place?" Roger said and started in. I followed.

Someone who looked like he was used to it picked up Roger's cycle and walked it to the rack.

Fidessa came up beside us as we stepped into the house.

"How long has this bunch been here?" I asked.

"There's been angels on High for forty years. They come; they go. Most of this bunch has been here all summer."

We crossed a room where vandals, time, and fire had left ravage marks. The backs of the rooms had been cut into the rock. One wall, wood-paneled, had become a palimpsest of scratched names and obscenities: old motors and motor parts, a pile of firewood, rags, and chains.

"We don't want power up here," Fidessa said. "We don't need it." Her voice was belligerent and intense.

"How do you survive?"

"We hunt," Roger said as the three of us turned down a stone stairwell. The walls at the bottom flickered. "There's Hainesville about ten miles from here. Some of us go over there and work when we have to."

"Work it over a little too?" (Roger's mouth tightened.) "When you have to?"

"When we have to."

I could smell meat cooking. And bread.

I glanced at Fidessa's powdered hips. They rocked with her walking: I didn't look away.

"Look." I stopped three steps from the doorway. "About the power installation." Light over my uniform deviled the bottom of my vision.

Roger and Fidessa looked.

"You've got over two dozen people here, and you say there have been people here for forty years? How do you cook? What do you do for heat in winter? Suppose you have medical emergencies? Forget the law. It's made for you; not us."

"Go to hell," Fidessa said and started to turn away. Roger pulled her back by the shoulder.

"I don't care how you live up here," I said because at least Roger was listening. "But you've got winter sitting on your doorstop. You use liquid fuel for your broomsticks. You could have them converted to battery and run them off rechargeable cells for a third the cost."

"Storage cells still give you about a hundred and fifty miles less than a full liquid tank."

Fidessa looked disgusted and started downstairs again. I think

Roger was losing patience because he turned after her. I followed again.

The lower room was filled with fire.

Chains and pulley apparatus hung from the ceiling. Two furnaces were going. Two pit fires had been dug into the floor. The ceiling was licked across with inky tongues. Hot air brushed back and forth across my face; the third brush left it sweaty.

I looked for food.

"This is our forge." Roger picked up a small sledge and rattled it against a sheet of corrugated iron leaning on the wall. "Danny, come out here!"

Barefoot, soot-smeared, the smears varnished with sweat: bellows and hammers had pulled his muscles taut, cut and defined them, so that each sat on his frame apart. Haircut and bath admitted, he would have been a fine-looking kid—twenty, twenty-five? He came forward knuckling his left eye. The right was that strange blue-gray that always seems to be exploding when it turns up (so rarely) in swarthy types like him.

"Hey there! What you doing?" Roger grimaced at me. "He's nearly deaf."

Danny dropped his fist from his face and motioned us into the back.

And I caught my breath.

What he'd been rubbing wasn't an eye at all. Scarred, crusted, then the crust broken and drooling; below his left eyebrow was a leaking sore.

We followed Danny between the fires and anvils to a worktable at the back. Piles of throwing blades (I touched the one in my belt) were at varied stages of completion. On the pitted boards among small hammers, punches, and knives, were some lumps of gold, a small pile of gems, and three ingots of silver. About the jeweler's anvil lay earrings, and a buckle with none of the gems set.

"This is what you're working on now?" Roger picked up the buckle in greasy fingers already weighted with gold.

I bent to see, then pointed from the buckle to Roger's ring, and looked curious. (Why are we always quiet or shouting before the deaf?) Roger nodded.

"Danny does a lot of stuff for us. He's a good machinist too. We're all pretty good turbo mechanics, but Danny here can do real fine stuff. Sometimes we fly him over to Hainesville, and he works there."

"Another source of income?"

"Right."

Just then Pitt came between the flames. She held half a loaf of bread. "Hey, Danny!" in a voice for the deaf, "I brought you some—" saw us and stopped.

Danny looked up, grinned, and circled the girl's shoulder with one arm, took the bread in the other hand, and bit.

His smile reflected off Pitt's.

The elastic fear loosened on her face as she watched the one-eyed smith chewing crust. She was very close to pretty then.

I was glad of that.

Danny turned back to the bench, Pitt's shoulder still tucked under his arm. He fingered the rings, found a small one for her, and she pulled forward with, "Oh . . ." and the gold flickered in her palm. The smile moved about her face like flame. (The throwing blades clinked on her hip.) Silent Danny had the rapt look of somebody whose mind was bouncing off the delight he could give others.

Fidessa said: "Have they got all of the first batch out of the ovens?" She looked at the bread and actually snarled. Then she sucked her teeth, turned, and marched away.

"Say," I asked Pitt, "do you like it up here?"

She dropped the ring, looked at me; then all the little lines of fear snapped back.

I guess Danny hadn't heard me, but he registered Pitt's discomfort. As he looked between us, his expression moved toward bewildered anger.

"Come on." Roger surprised me with a cuff on the shoulder. "Leave the kids alone. Get out of here." I was going to object to being pushed, but I guess Roger just pushed people. We left.

"Hey," Roger said, watching his feet as he walked. "I want to explain something to you." We left the fires. "We don't want any power up here."

"That has come across." I tried to sound as sincere as he did. "But there is the law." Sincerity is my favorite form of belligerence.

Roger stopped in front of the window (unbroken here), put his hands in his back pockets, and watched the stream spit down the gorge.

It was, I realized, the same stream the Gila Monster was parked across a mile below.

"You know I'm new at this job, Blacky," he said after a while. "I've just been archangel a couple of weeks. The only reason I took over the show is because I had some ideas on how to do it better than the guy before me. One of my ideas was to run it with as little trouble as possible."

"Who was running it before?"

"Sam was archangel before I was, and Fidessa was head cherub. They ran the business up here, and they ran it hard."

"Sam?"

"Take a whole lot of mean and pour it into a hide about three times as ugly as mine: Sam. He put out Danny's eye. When we get hold of a couple of cases of liquor, we have some pretty wild times up here. Sam came down to the forge to fool around. He heated up one end of a pipe and started swinging it at people. He liked to see them jump and holler. That's the kind of mean he was. Danny doesn't like people fooling around with his tools and things anyway. Sam got after Pitt, and Danny rushed him. So Sam stuck the hot pipe into Danny's head." Roger flexed his thumbs. "When I saw that, I realized I was going to have to do something. We rumbled about two weeks ago." He laughed and dropped his hands. "There was a battle in Haven that day!"

"What happened?"

He looked at the water. "You know the top porch of Haven? I threw him off the top porch onto the second. Then I came down and hurled him headlong off onto the bottom one." He pointed out the window. "Then I came down and threw him into the river. He limped around until I finally told the guys to take a couple of flaming torches and run him down the rocks where I couldn't see him no more." Behind his back now he twisted his ring. "I can't see him. Maybe he made it to hell . . . or Hainesville."

"Did . . . eh, Fidessa go along with the promotion?"

"Yeah." He brought his hands before him. Light struck and struck in the irregularities of metal. "I don't think I would have tried for the job if she hadn't. She's a lot of woman."

"Kill the king and take the queen."

"I took Fidessa first. Then I had to . . . kill the king. That's the way things go in Haven."

"Roger?"

He didn't look at me.

"Look, you've got a kid back there at the anvil who needs a doctor. You say he's a good part of your bread and butter. And you let him walk around with a face like that? What *are* you trying to do?"

"Sam used to say we were trying to live long enough to show the bastards how mean we could be. I say we're just trying to live."

"Suppose Danny's eye infection decides to spread? I'm not casting moral aspersions just to gum up the works. I'm asking if you're even doing what you want to." (He played with his ring.) "So you've avenged Danny; you won the fair damsel. What about that infection—"

Roger turned on me. His scar twisted on his cheek, and lines of anger webbed his forehead. "You really think we didn't try to get him to a doctor? We took him to Hainesville, then we took him to Kingston, then back to Hainesville, and finally out to Edgeware. We carried that poor screaming half-wit all over the night." He pointed back among the fires. "Danny grew up in an institute, and you get him anywhere near a city when he's scared, and he'll try to run away. We couldn't get him in to a doctor."

"He didn't run away from here when his eye was burned."

"He lives here. He's got a place to do the few things he can do well. He's got a woman. He's got food and people to take care of him. The business with Sam, I don't even think he understood what happened. When you're walking through a forest and a tree falls on you and breaks your leg, you don't run away from the forest.

Danny didn't understand that he was more important in Haven than big Sam with all his orders and bluster and beat-you-to-a-pulp if you look at him wrong: that's why Sam had to hurt him. But you try to explain that to Danny." He gestured at the fire. "*I* understood though." As he gestured, his eye caught on the points and blades of the ring. Again he stopped to twist it. "Danny made this for Sam. I took it off him on the bottom porch."

"I still want to know what's going to happen to Danny."

Roger frowned. "When we couldn't get him into a doctor's office in Edgeware, we finally went into town, woke up the doctor there at two in the morning, made him come outside the town and look at him there. The doc gave him a couple of shots of antibiotics and some salve to put on it, and Pitt makes sure he puts it on every day too. The doc said not to bandage it because it heals better in the air. We're bringing him back to check it next week. What the hell do you think we are?" He didn't sound like he wanted an answer. "You said you wanted to look around. Look. When you're finished, I'll take you back down, and you tell them we don't want no power lines up here!" He shook his jeweled finger at me with the last six words.

I walked around Haven awhile (pondering as I climbed the flickering stair that even the angels in Haven have their own spot of hell), trying to pretend I was enjoying the sun and the breeze, looking over the shoulders of the guys working on their cycles. People stopped talking when I passed. Whenever I turned, somebody looked away. Whenever I looked at one of the upper porches, somebody moved away.

I had been walking twenty long minutes when I finally came into a room to find Fidessa, smiling.

"Hungry?"

She held an apple in one hand and in the other half a loaf of that brown bread, steaming.

"Yeah." I came and sat beside her on the split-log bench.

"Honey?" in a can rusted around the edge with a kitchen knife stuck in it.

"Thanks." I spread some on the bread, and it went running and melting into all those little air bubbles like something in Danny's jewelry furnace. And I hadn't had breakfast. The apple was so crisp and cold it hurt my teeth. And the bread was warm.

"You're being very nice."

"It's too much of a waste of time the other way. You've come up here to look around. All right. What have you seen?"

"Fidessa," I said, after a silent while in which I tried to fit her smile with her last direct communication with me ("Go to hell," it was?) and couldn't. "I am *not* dense. I do *not* disapprove of you people coming up here to live away from the rest of the world. The chains and leather bit is not exactly my thing, but I haven't seen anybody here under sixteen, so you're all old enough to vote: in my book that means run your own lives. I would even say this way of life opens pathways to the more mythic and elemental hooey of mankind. I have heard Roger, and I have been impressed, yea, even moved, by how closely his sense of responsibility resembles my own. I too am new at my job. I *still* don't understand this furor over half a dozen power outlets. We come peacefully; we'll be out in a couple of hours. Leave us the key, go make a lot of noise over some quiet hamlet, and shake up the locals. We'll lock up when we go and stick it under the doormat. You won't even know we've been here."

"Listen, line-demon."

An eighty-seven-year-old granny of mine, who had taken part in the Detroit race riots in nineteen sixty-nine, must have used that same tone to a bright-eyed civil rights worker in the middle of the gunfire who, three years later, became my grandfather: "Listen, white boy . . ." Now I understood what granny had been trying to get across with her anecdote.

"—you don't know what's going on up here. You've wandered around for half an hour, and nobody but me and Roger has said a thing to you. What is it you think you understand?"

"Please, not demon. Devil."

"All you've seen is a cross-section of a process. Do you have any idea what was here five, or fifteen, years ago? Do you know what will be here five years from now? When I came here for the first time, almost ten years back—"

"You and Sam?"

Four thoughts passed behind her face, none of which she articulated.

"When Sam and me first got here, there were as many as a hundred and fifty angels at a time roosting here. Now there's twenty-one."

"Roger said twenty-seven."

"Six left after Sam and Roger rumbled. Roger thinks they're going to come back. Yoggy might. But not the others."

"And in five years?"

Fidessa shook her head. "Don't you understand? You don't have to kill us off. We're dying."

"We're not trying to kill you."

"You are."

"When I get down from here, I'm going to do quite a bit of proselytizing. Devil often speak with"—I took another bite of bread—"honeyed tongue. Might as well use it on Mabel." I brushed crumbs from my shining lap.

She shook her head, smiling sadly. "No." I wish women wouldn't smile sadly at me. "You are kind, handsome, perhaps even good." They always bring that up too. "And you are out to kill us."

I made frustrated noises.

She held up the apple.

I bit; she laughed.

She stopped laughing.

I looked up.

There in the doorway Roger looked a mite puzzled.

I stood. "You want to run me back down the mountain?" I asked with brusque ingenuousness. "I can't promise you anything. But I'm going to see if I can't get Mabel to sort of forget this job and take her silver-plated juggernaut somewhere else."

"You just do . . . this thing," Roger said "Come on."

While Roger was cutting his pteracycle out from the herd, I glanced over the edge.

At the pool, Pitt had coaxed Danny in over his knees. It couldn't have been sixty-five degrees out. But they were splashing and laughing like mud puppies from, oh, some warmer clime.

IV

A Gila Monster rampant?

Watch:

Six hydraulic lifts with cylinders thick as oil drums adjust the suspension up another five feet to allow room for blade work. From the "head," the "plow," slightly larger than the skull of a Triceratops, chuckles down into the dirt, digs down into the dirt. What chuckled before, roars. Plates on the side slide back.

Then Mabel, with most of her office, emerges on a telescoping lift to peer over the demons' shoulders with telephoto television.

The silver crew itself scatters across the pine needles like polished bearings. The monster hunkers backward, dragging the plow (angled and positioned by one of the finest contemporary poets of the French language): a trough two dozen feet wide and deep is opened upon the land. Two mandibles extend now, with six-foot wire brushes that rattle around down there, clearing off the top of the ribbed housing of a sixteen-foot cable. Two demons (Ronny and Ann) guide the brushes, staking worn ribs, metering for shorts in the higher frequency levels. When the silver worm has been bared a hundred feet, side cabinets open, and from over the port treads the crane swings out magnetic grapples.

One of the straightest roads in the world runs from Leningrad to Moscow. The particular czar involved, when asked for his suggestion as to just where the road should run, surprised architects and chancellors by taking a rule and scribing a single line between the cities. "There," he said, or its Russian equivalent. What with Russia being what it was in the mid-eighteenth century, there the road was built.

Except in some of the deeper Pacific trenches and certain annoying Himalayan passes, the major cables and most of the minor ones were laid out much the same way. The only time a cable ever bends sharp enough to see is when a joint is put in. We were putting in a joint.

Inside, demons (Julia, Bill, Frank, Dimitri) are readying the clip, a U of cable fifteen feet from bend to end. On those ends are very complicated couplings. They check those couplings very carefully, because the clip carries all that juice around the gap while the joint is being inserted.

The cranes start to squeal as, up in her tower, Mabel presses the proper button. The clip rises from the monster's guts, swings over the gleaming rib with Scott hanging onto the rope and riding the clip like some infernal surfer.

Frank and Dimitri come barreling from between the tread rollers to join Sue outside, so that the half-circle clips slip over the cable right on the chalk mark. Then Scott slides down to dance on the line with a ratchet, Sue with another. On each end of the clip they drive down the contacts that sink to various depths in the cable.

Frank: "She uses that thing pretty well."

Dimitri: "Maybe they're teaching them something in the academy after all these years?"

Frank: "She's just showing off because she's new—hey, Sue? Do you think she'd go after a neck tourniquet if we sent her?"

The eight-foot prong goes down to center core. Sixty thousand volts there. The seven-foot, six-inch prong goes to the stepper ground. That's a return for a three-wire high-voltage line that boosts you up from the central core to well over three hundred thousand volts. Between those two, you can run all the utilities for a city of a couple or six million. Next prong takes you down to general high-frequency utility power. Then low-frequency same. There's a layer of communications circuits next that lets you plug into a worldwide computer system: I mean if you ever need a worldwide computer. Then the local antennae for radio and TV broadcasts. Then all the check circuits to make sure that all the inner circuits are functioning. Then smaller antennae that broadcast directly to Gila Monster and sibling the findings of the check circuits. And so forth. And so on. For sixteen feet.

Scott's ratchet clicks on the bolt of the final prong (he let Sue beat him—he will say—by one connection), and somebody waves up at Mabel, who has discovered they're a minute and a half behind schedule and worries about these things.

Another crane is lowering the double blade. Teeth ratch, and sparks whiten their uniforms. Demons squint and move back.

Dimitri and Scott are already rolling the connecting disk on the sledge to the rim of the trough. (Hey, Sue! Watch it, honey. This thing only weighs about three hundred pounds.)

("I bet she don't make a hundred and ten.")

A moment later the blade pulls away, and the section of cable is lifted and tracked down the monster, and the whole business slips into the used-blade compartment.

The joint, which has the connections to take taps from the major cable so we can string the lines of power to Haven itself, is rolled and jimmied into place. Ratchets again. This time the whole crew screws the lugs to the housing.

And Mabel sighs and wipes her pale, moist brow, having gotten through the operation without a major blackout anywhere in the civilized world—nothing shorted, casualties nil, injuries same. All that is left is for the U to be removed so that things start flowing again. And there's hardly anything that can go wrong now.

Roger got me back just as they were removing the U. I came jogging down the rocks, waved to people, bopped on up the stairs, and played through the arteries of the beast. I came out on the monster's back, shielding my eyes against the noon.

The shadow of Mabel's office swung over me. I started up the ladder on the side of the lift, and moments later poked my head through the trapdoor.

"Hey, Mabel! Guess what's up on High Haven."

I don't think she was expecting me. She jumped a little. "What?"

"A covey of pteracycle angels, straight from the turn of the century. Tattoos, earrings, leather jackets and all—actually I don't think most of them can afford jackets. They're pretty scroungy."

Mabel frowned. "That's nice."

I hoisted to sitting position. "They're not really bad sorts. Eccentric, yes. I know you just got through connecting things up. But what say we roll up all our extension cords and go someplace else?"

"You are out of your mind." Her frown deepened.

"Naw. Look, they're just trying to do their thing. Let's get out of here."

"Nope."

"They look on this whole business as an attempt to wipe them—why not?"

"Because I want to wipe them out."

"Huh? Now don't tell me you were buzzed by angels when you were a little girl and you've carried feud fodder ever since."

"Told you we were going to argue, Blacky." She turned around in her chair. "The last time I had a conversation, it was a vegetarian cult that had taken refuge in the Rockies. Ate meat only once a year on the eve of the autumnal equinox. I will never forget the look on that kid's face. The first arrow pinned his shirt to the trunk of an oak—"

"Happy Halloween, St. Sebastian. *Ehhh*! But these aren't cannibals," I said, "Mabel."

"The conversion before that was a group of utopian socialists who had set up camp in the Swiss Alps. I don't think I could ever trace a killing directly to them—I'm sorry, I'm not counting the three of my men who got it when the whole business broke out into open fighting. But they made the vegetarians look healthy. The one before that—"

"Mabel—"

"I assume you're interrupting me because you've gotten my point."

"You were talking about ways of life before. Hasn't it occurred to you that there is more than one way of life possible?"

"That is too asinine for me even to bother answering. Get up off the floor."

I got up.

"If we are going to begin our argument with obvious banalities, consider these: hard work does not hurt the human machine. That's

what it is made for. But to work hard simply to remain undernour-
ished, or to have to work harder than you're able so that someone
else can live well while you starve, or to have no work at all and
have to watch yourself and others starve—this is disastrous to the
human machine. Subject any statistically meaningful sample of
people to these situations, and after a couple of generations you will
have wars, civil and sovereign, along with all the neuroses that such
a *Weltanschauung* produces."

"You get an A for obviousness."

"The world being the interrelated mesh that it is, two hundred
million people starving in Asia had an incalculable effect on the
psychology and sociology of the two hundred million overfed, over-
leisured North Americans during the time of our grandparents."

"B for banality."

"Conclusion—"

"For which you automatically get a C."

"—there has not been a war in forty years. There were only six
murders in New York City last year. Nine in Tokyo. The world has
a ninety-seven percent literacy rate. Eighty-four percent of the world
population is at least bilingual. Of all the political and technologi-
cal machinations that have taken place in the last century to cause
this, Global Power Lines were probably the biggest single factor.
Because suddenly people did not have to work to starve. That problem was alleviated, and the present situation has come about in the
time it takes a child to become a grandparent. The generation alive
when Global Power began was given the time to raise an interesting
bunch of neurotics for a second generation, and they had the intelligence and detachment to raise their bunch healthy enough to produce us."

"We've gone about as far as we can go?"

"Don't be snide. My point is simply that in a world where millions were being murdered by wars and hundreds of thousands by
less efficient means, there was *perhaps* some justification for saying
about any given injustice, "What can I do?" But that's not this
world. Perhaps we know too much about our grandparents' world
so that we expect things to be like that. But when the statistics are

what they are today, one boy shot full of arrows to a tree is a very different matter."

"What I saw up there—"

"—bespoke violence, brutality, unwarranted cruelty from one person to another, and if not murder, the potential for murder at every turn. Am I right?"

"But it's a life they've chosen! They have their own sense of honor and responsibility. You wouldn't go see, Mabel. I did. It's not going to harm—"

"Look, Teak-head! Somebody tried to kill *me* this morning with that thing you've still got in your belt!"

"Mabel—!" which exclamation had nothing to do with our argument.

She snatched up the microphone, flicked the button. "Scott, what the hell are you doing!" Her voice, magnified by the loud-speakers, rolled over the plates and dropped among demons.

What Scott Had Done:

He'd climbed on the U to ride it back up into the monster. With most of the prongs ratcheted out, he had taken a connector line (probably saying to Sue first, "Hey, I bet you never seen this before!") and tapped the high voltage and stuck it against the metal housing. There's only a fraction of an ampere there, so it wasn't likely to hurt anything. The high-voltage effect in the housing causes a brush discharge the length of the exposed cable. Very impressive. Three-foot sparks crackling all over, and Scott grinning, and all his hair standing up on end.

A hedge of platinum—

A river of diamonds—

A jeweled snake—

What is dangerous about it and why Mabel was upset is (One) if something does go wrong with that much voltage, it is going to be more than serious. (Two) The U clip's connected to the (Bow!) gig-crane; the gig-crane's connected to the (Poo!) crane-house; the crane-house is anchored to the (Bip!) main chassis itself, and hence the possibility of all sorts of damage.

"Goddamn it, Scott—"

The least dangerous thing that could have gone wrong would have been a random buildup of energies right where Scott had stuck the wire against the housing. Which I guess is what happened because he kept reaching for it and jerking his hand away, like he was being tickled.

Mabel got at the controls and pulled the arm of the rheostat slowly down. She has a blanket ban on all current, and could walk it down to nothing. (All the voltage in the world won't do a thing if there're no amps behind it.) "They know damned well I don't like to waste power!" she snapped. "All right, you silver-plated idiots," she rumbled about the mountain, "get inside. That's enough for today."

She was mad. I didn't pursue the conversation.

B orn out of time, I walked eye-deep in Gila droppings. Then I sat awhile. Then I paced some more. I was supposed to be filling out forms in the navigation office, but most of the time I was wondering if I wouldn't be happier shucking silver for denim to go steel wool the clouds. Why grub about the world with dirty demons when I could be brandishing my resentments against the night winds, beating my broomstick (as it were) across the evening; justifying the ways of angels, if not gods, to . . . only all my resentments were at Mabel.

A break on the balcony from figure flicking.

And leaning on the rail, this, over-looked and -heard:

Sue and Pitt stood together on the rim of the trough.

"Well, I'll tell you," Sue was saying, "I like working here. Two years in the Academy after high school and you learn all about Power Engineering and stuff. It's nice 'cause you do a lot of traveling," Sue went on, rather like the introduction to the Academy Course of Study brochure. Well, it's a good introduction. "By the way," she finished, and by the way she finished, I knew she'd been wondering awhile, "what happened to your friend's eye?"

Pitt hoofed at the dirt. "Aw, he got in a fight and got it hurt real bad."

"Yeah," Sue said. "That's sort of obvious." The two girls looked off into the woods. "He could really come out here. Nobody's going to bother him."

"He's shy," Pitt said. "And he doesn't hear good."

"It's all right if he wants to stay back there."

"It would be nice to travel around in a healer monster," Pitt said. "I'd like that."

"You want to go inside—?"

"Oh, no! Hey, I gotta get back up on High Haven." And Pitt (maybe she'd seen me on the balcony) turned and ran into the trees.

"Good-bye!" Sue called. "Thank your friend for riding me all around the mountain. That was fun." And above the trees I saw a broomstick break small branches.

I went back into the office. Mabel had come in and was sitting on my desk, looking over the forms in which I'd been filling.

I sorted through various subjects I might bring up to avoid arguing with the boss.

"It takes too much energy to sort out something we won't argue about," Mabel said. "Shall we finish up?"

"Fine. Only I haven't had a chance to argue."

"Go on."

"You go on. The only way I'll ever get you is to let you have enough cable to strangle yourself."

She put the forms down. "Take you up on that last bit of obvious banality for the day: suppose we put the outlets and lines in? They certainly don't have to use them if they don't like."

"Oh, Mabel! The whole thing is a matter of principle!"

"I'm not strangling yet."

"Look. You *are* the boss. I've said we'd do it your way. Okay. I mean it. Good night!" Feeling frustrated, but clean and silver, I stalked out.

Frank Faltaux once told me that the French phrase for it is *l'esprit d'escalier*—the spirit of the backstairs. You think of what you *should* have said after you're on the way down. I lay in the hammock in my new room fairly blistering the varnish on the banister.

Evening shuffled leaves outside my window and slid gold poker chips across the pane. After much restlessness, I got up and went outside to kibitz the game.

On the stream bank I toed stones into the water, watched the water sweep out the hollows, and ambled beside the current, the sound of the falls ahead of me; behind, laughing demons sat on the treads drinking beer.

Then somebody called the demons inside, so there was only the evening and water.

And laughter above me . . .

I looked up the falls.

Fidessa sat there, swinging her sneaker heels against the rock.

"Hello?" I asked.

She nodded and looked like a woman with a secret. She jumped down and started over the rocks.

"Hey, watch it. Don't slip in the—"

She didn't.

"Blacky!"

"Eh . . . what can I do for you?"

"Nothing!" with her bright brown eyes. "Do you want to come to a party?"

"Huh?"

"Up on High Haven."

Thought: that the cables had not gone up there this afternoon had been mistaken for a victory on my part.

"You know I haven't won any battles down here, yet." Oh, equivocatious *yet*. I scratched my neck and did other things that project indecision. "It's very nice of you and Roger to ask me."

"Actually, *I'm* asking you. In fact"—conspiratorial look—"why don't you bring one of your girls along?" For a whole second I thought it was a non-ulterior invitation. "Roger might be a little peeved if he thought I just came down to drag you by yourself up to an angel blast."

Tall, very dark, and handsome, I've had a fair amount of this kind of treatment at the hands of various ladies even in this enlightened age.

So it doesn't bother me at all. "Sure. Love to come."

My ulterior was a chance to drag Mabel out to see my side. (As devils stalked the angels' porches . . . I slew the thought.) Then again, I was still feeling pretty belligerent. Hell, who wants to take your debate rival to a party?

I looked back at the monster. Sue sat at the top of the steps reading. "Hey!"

She looked up. I made come-here motions. She put down the book and came.

"What's Scott doing?"

"Sleeping."

One of the reasons Scott will never be a devil is that he can sleep anywhere, anytime. A devil must be able to worry all night, then be unable to sleep because he's so excited about the solution that arrived with the dawn. "Want to go to a party?"

"Sure."

"Fidessa's invited us up to High Haven. You'll have a chance to see your friend Pitt again."

She came into the scope of my arm and settled her head on my shoulder, frowning. "Pitt's a funny kid." The passing wrinkles on a seventeen-year-old girl's face are charming. "But I like her." She looked up, took hold of my thumb, and asked, "When are we going?"

"Now," Fidessa said.

We climbed.

"Ever fly a broomstick?" Fidessa asked.

"I used to fly my wife back and forth to classes when I was at the academy," I admitted. (Interesting I've managed to put that fact out of this telling so long. Contemplate that awhile.) "Want me to drive?"

With me at the steering shaft, Sue behind me chinning my scapula, and Fidessa behind her, we did a mildly clumsy takeoff, then a lovely spiral—"Over there," Fidessa called—around the mountain's backbone and swung up toward the gorge.

"Oh, I love riding these things!" Sue was saying. "It's like a roller coaster. Only more so!"

That was *not* a comment on my flying. We fell into the rocky mouth. (One doesn't forget how to ride a bicycle, either.) Our landing on the high porch was better than Roger's.

I found out where they did the cooking I'd smelled that morning. Fidessa led us up through the trees above the house. (Roast meat . . .) Coming through the brush, hand in hand with Sue, I saw our late cadet wrinkle her nose, frown: "Barbecued pork?"

They had dug a shallow pit. On the crusted, gleaming grill a pig, splayed over coals, looked up cross-eyed. His ears were charred. The lips curled back from tooth and gap-tooth. He smelled great.

"Hey," Roger called across the pit. "You come up here this evening? Good!" He saluted with a beer can. "You come for the party?"

"I guess so."

Someone came scrabbling up the rock carrying a cardboard crate. It was the redheaded kid with the dragon on his chest. "Hey, Roger, you need some lemons? I was over in Hainesville, and I swiped this whole goddamn box of lemons—"

Someone grabbed him by the collar of his leather jacket with both hands and yanked it down over his shoulders; he staggered. The crate hit the edge of the pit. Lemons bounced and rolled.

"Goddamnit, cut that out—"

Half a dozen fell through the grate. Somebody kicked the carton, and another half-dozen rolled down the slope.

"Hey—"

Half a minute into a free-for-all, two cans of beer came across. I caught them and looked up to see Roger, by the cooler, laughing. I twisted the tops off (there was a time, I believe, when such a toss would have wreaked havoc with the beer—progress), handed one to Sue, saluted.

Fidessa had maneuvered behind Roger. And was laughing too.

Sue drank, scowled. "Say, where is Pitt?"

"Down at the house."

She flashed bright teeth at me. I nodded.

"Call me when food's on." She pulled away, skirting tussling angels, and hopped down the rocks.

Where does the mountain go when it goes higher than Haven?

Not knowing, I left the revelers and mounted among the brush and boulders. Wind snagged on pines and reached me limping. I looked down the gorge, surveyed the crowded roofs of Haven, sat for a while on a log, and was peaceful.

I heard feet on leaves behind, but didn't look. Fingers on my eyes—and Fidessa laughing. I caught one wrist and pulled her around. The laugh stilled on her face. She, amused, and I, curious, watched each other watch each other.

"Why," I asked, "have you become so friendly?"

Her high-cheeked face grew pensive. "Maybe it's because I know a better thing when I see it."

"Better?"

"Comparative of *good*." She sat beside me. "I've never understood how power is meted out in this world. When two people clash, the more powerful wins. I was very young when I met Sam. I stayed with him because I thought he was powerful. Does that sound naive?"

"At first, yes. Not when you think about it."

"He insisted on living in a way totally at odds with society. That takes . . . power."

I nodded.

"I still don't know whether he lost it at the end. Maybe Roger simply had more. But I made my decision before they rumbled. And I ended up on the right side."

"You're not stupid."

"No, I'm not. But there's another clash coming. I think I know who will win."

"I don't."

She looked at her lap. "Also, I'm not so young anymore. I'm tired of being on the side of the angels. My world is falling apart, Blacky. I've got Roger; I understand why Sam lost, but I don't understand why Roger won. In the coming battle, you'll win and Roger will lose. That I don't understand at all."

"Is this a request for me in my silver long johns, to take you away from all this?"

She frowned. "Go back down to Haven. Talk to Roger."

"On the eve of the war, the opposing generals meet together. They explain how war would be the worst thing for all concerned. Yet all creation knows they'll go to war."

Her eyes inquired.

"I'm quoting."

"Go down and talk to Roger."

I got up and walked back through the woods. I had been walking five minutes when:

"Blacky?"

I stopped by an oak whose roots clutched a great rock. When trees get too big in terrain like this, there is very little for them to hold, and they eventually fall.

"I thought I saw you wander off up here."

"Roger," I said, "things don't look so good down at the Gila Monster."

He fell into step beside me. "You can't stop the lines from coming up here?" He twisted the great ring on his scarred finger.

"The law says that a certain amount of power must be available for a given number of people. Look. Even if we put the lines up, why do you have to use them? I don't understand why this business is so threatening to you."

"You don't?"

"Like I said, I sympathize . . ."

His hands went into his pockets. It was dark enough here among the trees so that, though light flaked above the leaves, I couldn't see his expression.

His tone of voice surprised me: "You don't understand what's going on up here, do you? Fidessa said you didn't." It was fatigue. "I thought you . . ." and then his mind went somewhere else. "These power lines. Do you know what holds these guys here? I don't. I do know it's weaker than you think."

"Fidessa says they've been drifting away."

"I'm not out to make any man do what he don't want. Neither was Sam. That's the power he had; and I have. Their freedom was our power. You put them lines up, and they'll use them. Maybe not at first. But they will. You beat us long enough, and we go down!"

Beyond the trees I could see the barbecue pit. "Maybe you're just going to have to let it go."

He shook his shadowed face. "I haven't had it long, so it shouldn't be so hard to lose it. But no."

"Roger, you're not losing anything. When the lines go up here, just ignore—"

"I'm talking about power. *My* power."

"How?"

"They know what's going on." Roger motioned to include the rest of the angels in Haven. "They know it's a contest. And I am going to lose. Would it be better if I came on like Sam? He'd have tried to break your head. Then he'd have tried to bust your tinfoil eggcrate apart with broomsticks. Probably got himself and most of the rest of us in the hoosegow."

"He would have."

"Have you ever lost something important to you, Blacky, something so important you couldn't start to tell anybody else how important it was? It went. You watched it go. And then it was all gone."

"Yes."

"Yeah? What?"

"Wife of mine."

"She leave you for somebody else?"

"She was burned to death on an exposed power cable, one night—in Tibet. I watched. And then she was . . . gone."

"You and me," Roger said after a moment, "we're a lot alike, you know?" I saw his head drop. "I wonder what it would be like to lose Fidessa . . . too."

"Why do you ask?"

Broad shoulders shrugged. "Sometimes the way a woman acts, you get to feel . . . Sam knew. But it's stupid, huh? You think that's stupid, Blacky?"

Leaves crashed under feet behind us. We turned.

"Fidessa . . . ?" Roger said.

She stopped in the half-dark. I knew she was surprised to over-take us.

Roger looked at me. He looked at her. "What were you doing up there?"

"Just sitting," she said before I did.

We stood a moment more in the darkness above Haven. Then Roger turned, beat back branches and strode into the clearing. I fol-lowed.

The pig had been cut. Most of one ham had been sliced. But Roger yanked up the bone and turned to me. "This is a party, hey, Blacky!" His scarred face broke on laughter. "Here! Have some party!" He thrust the hot bone into my hands. It burned me.

But Roger, arm around somebody's shoulder, lurched through the carousers. Someone pushed a beer at me. The hock, where I'd dropped it on pine needles, blackened beneath the boots of angels.

I did get food after a fashion. And a good deal to drink.

I remember stopping on the upper porch of Haven, leaning on what was left of the rail.

Sue was sitting down by the pool. Stooped but glistening from the heat of the forge, Danny stood beside her.

Then behind me:

"You gonna fly? You gonna fly the moon off the sky? I can see three stars up there! Who's gonna put 'em out?" Roger balanced on the cycle rack, feet wide, fist shaking at the night. "I'm gonna fly! Fly till my stick pokes a hole in the dark! Gods, you hear that? We're coming at you! We're gonna beat you to death with broom-sticks and roar the meteors down before we're done. . . ."

They shouted around him. A cycle coughed. Two more.

Roger leaped down as the first broomstick pulled from the rack, and everybody fell back. It swerved across the porch, launched over the edge, rose against the branches, above the branches, spreading dark wings.

"You gonna fly with me?"

I began a shrug.

His hand hit my neck and stopped it. "There are gods up there we gotta look at. You gonna stare 'em down with me?"

Smoke and pills had been going around as well as beer.

"Gods are nothing but low blood sugar," I said. "St. Augustine, Peyote Indians . . . you know how it works—"

He turned his hand so the back was against my neck. "Fly!" And if he'd taken his hand away fast, that ring would have hooked out an inch of jugular.

Three more broomsticks took off.

"Okay, why not?"

He turned to swing his cycle from the rack.

I mounted behind him. Concrete rasped. We went over the edge, and the bottom fell out of my belly again. Branches clawed at us, branches missed.

Higher than Haven.

Higher than the mountain that is higher than Haven.

Wind pushed my head back, and I stared up at the night. Angels passed overhead.

"Hey!" Roger bellowed, turning half around so I could hear. "You ever done any skysweeping?"

"No!" I insisted.

Roger nodded for me to look.

Maybe a hundred yards ahead and up, an angel turned wings over the moon, aimed down, and—his elbows jerked sharply in as he twisted the throttle rings—turned off both turbos.

The broomstick swept down the night.

And down.

And down.

Finally I thought I would lose him in the carpet of green-black over the mountain. And for a while he was lost. Then:

A tiny flame, and tiny wings, momentarily illuminated, pulled from the tortuous dive. As small as he was, I could *see* the wings bend from the strain. He was close enough to the treetops so that for a moment the texture of the leaves was visible in a speeding pool of light. (How many angels *can* dance on the head of a pin?) He was *so* tiny. . . .

"What the hell is our altitude anyway?" I called to Roger.

Roger leaned back on the shaft, and we were going up again.

"Where are we going?"

"High enough to get a good sweep on."

"With two people on the cycle?" I demanded.

And we went up.

And there were no angels above us anymore.

And the only thing higher than us was the moon.

There is a man in the moon.

And he leers.

We reached the top of our arc. Then Roger's elbows struck his sides.

My tummy again. Odd feeling: the vibrations on your seat and on your foot stirrups aren't there. Neither is the roar of the turbos.

It is a very quiet trip down.

Even the sound of the wind on the wings behind you is carried away too fast to count. There is only the mountain in front of you. Which is down.

And down.

And down.

Finally I grabbed Roger's shoulder, leaped forward and yelled in his ear, "I hope you're having fun!"

Two broomsticks zoomed apart to let us through.

Roger looked back at me. "Hey, what were you and my woman doing up in the woods?" With the turbos off you don't have to yell.

"Picking mushrooms."

"When there's a power struggle, I don't like to lose."

"You like mushrooms?" I asked. "I'll give you a whole goddamn basket just as soon as we set runners on Haven."

"I wouldn't joke if I was sitting as far from the throttle ring as you are."

"Roger—"

"You can tell things from the way a woman acts, Blacky. I've done a lot of looking, at you, at Fidessa, even at that little girl you brought up to Haven this evening. Take her and Pitt. I bet they're about the same age. Pitt don't stand up too well against her. I don't mean looks either. I'm talking about the chance of surviving they'd have if you just stuck them down someplace. I'm thirty-three years old, Blacky. You?"

"Eh . . . thirty-one."

"We don't check out too well either."

"How about giving it a chance?"

"You're hurting my shoulder."

My hand snapped back to the grip. There was a palm print in sweat on the denim.

Roger shook his head. "I'd dig to see you spread all over that mountain."

"If you don't pull out, you'll never get the opportunity."

"Shit . . ." Roger said. His elbows went out from his side.

The broomstick vibrated.

Branches stopped coming at us quite so fast. (I could see separate branches!) The force of the turn almost tore me off. I told you before, you could see the wings bend? You can hear them too. Things squeaked and creaked in the roar.

Then, at last, we were rising gently once more.

I looked up.

I breathed.

The night was loud and cool and wonderful.

Miniature above us now, another angel swept down across the moon. He plummeted toward us as we rode up the wind.

Roger noticed before I did.

"Hey, the kid's in trouble!"

Instead of holding his arms hugged to his sides, the kid worked them in and out as though he were trying to twist something loose.

"His rings are frozen!" Roger exclaimed.

Others had realized the trouble and circled in to follow him down. He came fast and wobbling—passed us!

His face was all teeth and eyes as he fought the stick. The dragon writhed on his naked chest. It was the redhead in the unzipped leather jacket.

The flock swooped to follow.

The kid was below us. Roger gunned his cycle straight down to catch up, wrenched out again, and the kid passed us once more.

The kid had partial control of one wing. It didn't help because whenever he'd shift the free aileron, he'd just bank off in another direction at the same slope.

Branches again . . .

Then something unfroze in the rogue cycle. His slope suddenly leveled, and there was fire from the turbos.

For three seconds I thought he was going to make it.

Fire raked the treetops for thirty feet; we swooped over a widening path of flame. And nothing at the end of it.

A minute later we found a clearing. Angels settled like mad leaves. We started running through the trees.

He wasn't dead.

He was screaming.

He'd been flung twenty feet from his broomstick through small branches and twigs, both legs and one arm broken. Most of his clothes had been torn off. A lot of skin too.

Roger forgot me, got very efficient, got Red into a stretcher between two broomsticks, and got to Hainesville, fast. Red was only crying when the doctor finally put him to sleep.

We took off from the leafy suburban streets and rose toward the porches of Haven.

The gorge was a serpent of silver.

The moon glazed the windows of Haven.

Somebody had already come back to bring the news.

"You want a beer?" Roger asked.

"No thanks. Have you seen the little girl who came up here with me? I think it's about time we got back."

But he had already started away. There was *still* a party going on.

I went into the house, up some stairs, didn't find Sue, so went down some others. I was halfway down the flickering steps to the forge when I heard a shriek.

Then Sue flashed through the doorway, ran up the steps, and crashed into me. I caught her just as one-eyed Danny swung round the doorjamb. Then Pitt was behind him, scrabbling past him in the narrow well, the throwing blade in her hand halfway through a swing.

And stopped.

"Why doesn't someone tell me what the hell is going on?" I proposed. "You put yours away, and I'll put away mine." Remember that throwing blade I had tucked under my belt? It was in *my* hand now. Pitt and I lowered our arms together.

"Oh, Blacky, let's get *out* of here!" Sue whispered.

"Okay," I said.

We backed up the steps. Then we ducked from the door and came out on the porch. Sue still leaned on my shoulder. When she got her breath back, she said: "They're nuts!"

"What happened?"

"I don't know, I mean . . ." She stood up now. "Dan was talking to me and showing me around the forge. And he makes all that beautiful jewelry. He was trying to fool around, but I mean, really—with that eye? And I was trying to cool him anyway, when Pitt came in. . . ." She looked at the porch. "That boy who fell . . . they got him to the doctor?"

I nodded.

"It was the redheaded one, wasn't it? I hope he's all right." Sue shook her head. "He gave me a lemon."

Fidessa appeared at my shoulder. "You want to go down?"

"Yeah."

"Take that cycle. The owner's passed out inside. Somebody'll bring him down tomorrow to pick it up."

"Thanks."

Glass shattered. Somebody had thrown something through one of Haven's remaining windows.

The party was getting out of hand at the far end of the porch. Still point in the wheeling throng, Roger watched us.

Fidessa looked a moment, then pushed my shoulder. "Go on."

We dropped over white water, careening down the gorge.

V

Scott opened an eye and frowned a freckled frown over the edge of his hammock. "Where . . . [obscured by yawn] . . . been?"

"To a party. Don't worry. I brought her back safe and sound."

Scott scrubbed his nose with his fist. "Fun?"

"Sociologically fascinating, I'm sure."

"Yeah?" He pushed up on his elbow. "Whyn't you wake me?" He looked back at Sue, who sat quietly on her hammock.

"We shook you for fifteen minutes, but you kept trying to punch me."

"I did?" He rubbed his nose again. "I did not!"

"Don't worry about it. Go to sleep. G'night, Sue."

In my room I drifted off to the *whirr* of broomsticks remembered.

Then—was it half an hour later?—I came awake to a real turbo. A cycle came near the Monster's roof.

Runners . . .

Correction: landed on.

I donned silver and went outside on the long terrace. I looked to my left up at the roof.

Thuds down the terrace to the right—

Danny recovered from his leap. His good eye blinked rapidly. The other was a fistful of wet shadow.

"What are you doing here?" I asked too quietly for him to have heard. Then I looked up at the curved wall. Fidessa slid down. Danny steadied her.

"Would you mind telling me what brings you two here this hour of the morning?"

After five silent seconds I thought she was playing a joke. I spent another paranoid three thinking I was about to be victim to a cunning nefariousness.

But she was terrified.

"Blacky—"

"Hey, what's the matter, girl?"

"I . . ." She shook her head. "Roger . . ." Shook it again.

"Come inside and sit down."

She took Danny's arm. "Go in! Go in, Danny . . . please!" She looked about the sky.

Stolid and uncomprehending, Danny went forward. Inside, I saw a bruise on his cheek that hadn't been there before, and he was favoring one leg. He sat on the hammock, left fist wrapped in his right hand.

Fidessa stood, turned, walked, stopped.

"What's the matter? What happened on High Haven?"

"We're leaving." She watched for my reaction.

"Tell me what happened."

She put her hands in her pockets, took them out again. "Roger got after Danny."

"What?"

We regarded the silent smith. He blinked and smiled.

"Roger got crazy after you left."

"Drunk?"

"Crazy! He took everybody down to the forge, and they started to break up the place. . . . He made them stop after a little while. But then he talked about killing Danny. He said that Sam was right. And then he told me he was going to kill me."

"It sounds like a bad joke."

"It wasn't . . ." I watched her struggle to find words to tell me what it was.

"So you two got scared and left?"

"I wasn't scared then." Her voice retreated to shortness. She glanced up. "I'm scared now."

Swinging gently, Danny put one foot on top of the other and rubbed his toes with the ball of his other foot.

"So you brought Danny along?"

"He was running away. After the fracas down in the forge, he was taking off into the woods. I told him to come with me."

"Clever of you to come here."

She looked angry, then anger lost focus and became fear again.

"We didn't know anywhere else to go." Her hands closed and broke like wings. "I came here first because I . . . wanted to warn you."

"Of what?"

"Roger—I think him and the rest of the angels are going to try and rumble with you here."

"What . . . ?"

She nodded.

"This has suddenly gotten serious. Let's go talk to Boss Lady." I opened the door to the corridor. "You too."

Danny looked up surprised, unfolded his hands and feet.

"Yeah, you!"

Mabel was exercising her devilish talents:

Ashtray filled with the detritus of a pack of cigarettes, papers all over everything; she had one pencil behind her ear and was chewing on another. It was three in the morning.

We filed into the office, me first, Fidessa, then Danny.

"Blacky? Oh, hello—good *Lord*!" (That was Danny's eye.)

"Hi, Mabel. How's the midnight oil?"

"If you strain it through white bread, reduce it over a slow Bunsen, and recondense the fumes in a copper coil, I hear you have something that can get you high." She frowned at Danny, realized she was frowning, smiled. "What happened to that boy's face?"

"Meet Fidessa and Danny, from High Haven. They've just run away and stopped off to tell us that we may be under attack shortly by angels who are none too happy about the lines and outlets we're putting up tomorrow."

Mabel looked over the apex of her fingertips. "This has gotten serious," she echoed. Mabel looked tired. "The Gila Monster is a traveling maintenance station, not a mobile fortress. How have your goodwill efforts been going?"

I was going to throw up my hands—

"If Blacky hadn't been up there," Fidessa said, "talking with Roger like he did, they'd have been down here yesterday afternoon instead."

I projected her an astral kiss.

"What about him?" She nodded at Danny. "What happened to—"

"Where the hell," Scott demanded, swinging through the door like a dappled griffon, "did you take that poor kid, anyway?"

"What kid?"

"Sue! You said you went to a party. That's not what I'd call it!"

"What are you talking about?"

"She's got two bruises on her leg as big as my hand and one on her shoulder even bigger. She said some one-eyed bastard tried to rape—"

Then he frowned at Danny, who smiled back quizzically.

"She told me," I said, "that he tried to get fresh with her—"

"With a foot and a half of two-by-four? She told *me* she didn't want to tell *you*—" his mottled finger swung at me—"what *really* happened, so *you* wouldn't be hard on them!"

"Look, I haven't been trying to gloss over anything I saw on—"

At which point Mabel stood.

Silence.

You-know-what were passing.

Something clanged on the skylight: cracks shot the pane, though it didn't shatter. We jumped, and Scott hiccoughed. Lying on top of the glass was a four-pronged blade.

I reached over Mabel's desk and threw a switch by her thumb.

Fidessa: "What . . . ?"

"Floodlights," I said. "They can see us, lights or no. This way we can see them—if they get within fifty meters." We used the lights for night work. "I'm going to take us up where we can look at what's going on," I told Mabel.

She stepped back so I could take the controls.

When the cabin jerked, Danny's smile gave out. Fidessa patted his arm.

The cabin rose.

"I hope you know what you're . . . ." Scott began.

Mabel told him to shut up with a very small movement of the chin.

Outside the window, broomsticks scratched like matches behind the trees.

Water whispered white down the falls. The near leaves shook neon scales. And the cable arched the dark like a flayed rib.

Wingforms fell and swept the rocks, shadowed the water. I saw three land.

"That's Roger!"

At the window Fidessa stood at my left, Mabel at my right.

Roger's broomstick played along the still unburied cable, came down in a diminishing pool of shadow directly on the line. I heard runners scrape the housing. Half a dozen or more angels had landed on either side of the trough.

At the far end of the exposed line up near the rocks, he dismounted and let his broomstick fall on its side. He started slowly to walk the ribbing.

"What do they want?" Scott asked.

"I'm going to go and see," I said. (Mabel turned sharply.) "You've got peeper-mikes in here." The better to overhear scheming demons: if they'd been on, Mabel would have been able to foresee Scott's little prank of the afternoon. "Hey! You remember Scott's little prank this afternoon? You can duplicate it from here, can't you?"

"A high-voltage brush discharged from the housing. Sure I can—"

"It'll look so much more impressive at night! I'm going out there to talk to Roger on the cable. If anything goes wrong, I'll yell. You start the sparks. Nobody will get hurt, but it should scare enough hell out of them to give me a chance to get out of harm's way." I flipped on the peeper-mike and started for the trapdoor. An introductory burst of static cleared to angel mumblings.

Mabel stopped me with a hand on my shoulder. "Blacky, I can make a brush discharge from in here. I can also burn anybody on that line—"

I looked at her. I breathed deeply. Then I pulled away and dropped through to the Gila Monster's roof. I sprinted over the plated hull, reached the "head" between two of the floods, and gazed down. "Roger!"

He stopped and squinted up into the light. "—Blacky?"

"What are you doing here?"

Before he answered, I kicked the latch of the crane housing and climbed down onto the two-foot grapple. I was going to yell back at Mabel, but she was watching. The crane began to hum, and swung forward with me riding, out and down.

When I came close to the cable, I dropped (floodlights splashing my shoulders); I got my balance on the curved ribbing. "Roger?"

"Yeah?"

"What are you doing down here?"

On the dirt piled beside the cable the other angels stood. I walked forward.

"What are you doing? Come on: it's the third time I've asked you." When the wire is sixteen feet in diameter, a tightrope act isn't that hard. Still . . .

Roger took a step, and I stopped. "You're not going to put up those cables, Blacky."

He looked awful. Since I'd seen him last he'd been in a fight. I couldn't tell if he'd won or lost.

"Roger, go back up on High Haven."

His shoulders sagged; he kept swallowing. Throwing blades clinked at his belt.

"You think you've won, Blacky."

"Roger—"

"You haven't. We won't let you. We won't." He looked at the angels around us. "IS THAT RIGHT!" I started at his bellow.

They were silent. He turned back and whispered. "We won't . . ."

My shadow reached his feet. His lay out behind him on the ribbing.

"You came down here to make trouble, Roger. What's it going to get you?"

"A chance to see you squirm."

"You've done that once this evening."

"That was before . . ." He looked down at his belt. My stomach tightened. ". . . Fidessa left. She ran away from me." Hung on his cheek scar, confusion curtained his features.

"I know." I glanced over my shoulder where the office swayed above the monster. In the window were four silhouettes: two women and two men.

"She's up . . . ?" The curtain pulled back to reveal rage. "She came down here—to you?"

"To *us*. Have you got that distinction through your bony head?"

"Who's up there with her?" He squinted beyond the floodlights. "Danny?"

"That's right."

"Why?"

"She said he was running away anyway."

"I don't have to ask you; I know why."

"They're listening to us. *You* can ask them if you want."

Roger scowled, threw back his head. "Danny! What you running away from me for? Come on with us, now."

No answer.

"You gonna leave Haven and Pitt and everything?"

No answer.

"Fidessa!"

Yes . . . Roger?

Her voice, so firm in person, was almost lost in the electronic welter.

"Danny really wants to run down here with the devils?"

He . . . does, Roger.

"Danny!"

No answer.

"I know you can hear me! You make him hear me, Fidessa! Don't you remember, Danny . . . ?"

No answer.

"Danny, you come out of there if you want and go on back with me. After what you did to that girl, I had to give you a beatin'. That's all. It wasn't as bad as how Sam did you when you stole that money from us. But an eye is too harsh. And I'm archangel now. Come on back."

As Roger's discomfort grew to fill the silence, the kindest thing I could think was that, just as Danny had been unable to comprehend Sam's brutalities, so he could ignore Roger's generosities.

"Fidessa?"

Roger?

"You coming back up to High Haven with me." Neither question mark nor exclamation point defines that timbre.

No, Roger.

When Roger turned to me, it looked like the bones in his head had all broken and were just tossed in the bag of his face.

"And you . . . you're putting up them cables tomorrow?"

"That's right."

Roger's hand went out from his side; started forward. Things came apart. He struck at me.

"Mabel, *now!*"

When he hit at me again, he hit through fire.

The line grew white stars. We crashed, crackling. I staggered, lost my balance, found it again.

Beyond the glitter I saw the angels draw back. The discharge was scaring everybody but Roger.

We grappled. Sparks tangled his lank hair, flickered in his eyes, on his teeth; we locked in the fire. He tried to force me off the cable. "I'm gonna . . . break . . . you!"

We broke.

I ducked by, and whirled to face him, backing away. Even though the other angels had scattered, Roger had realized the fireworks were show.

He pulled at his belt.

"I'll stop you!"

Then the blade was a glinting cross above his shoulder.

"Roger, even if you do, that's not going to stop—"

"I'll kill you!"

The blade spun down the line.

I ducked and it missed.

"Roger, stop it! Put that blade—" I ducked again, but the next one caught my forearm. Blood ran inside my sleeve. . . . "Roger! You'll get burned!"

"You better *hurry!*" The third blade spun out with the last word.

I leaped to the side of the trough, rolled over on my back—saw him crouch with the force of the next blade, now dug into the dirt where my belly had been.

I had already worked the blade from my own belt. As I flung it (I knew it was going wild, but it would make Roger pause), I shrieked with all rage and frustration playing my voice: "*Burn* him!"

The next blade was above his head.

Off balance on my back, there was no way I could have avoided it. Then:

Sparks fell back into the housing.

From the corner of my eye, I'd seen Mabel, in the office window, move to the rheostat.

Roger stiffened.

He wove back; snapped up screaming. His arm flailed the blade around his head.

Then the scream was exhausted.

The first flame flickered on his denims.

His ankle chain flared cherry and smoked against his skin.

The blade burned in his hand.

Broomsticks growled over the sky as angels beat retreat. I rolled to my stomach, coughing with rage, and tried to crawl up (the smell of roast meat . . .), but I only got halfway to the top before my arm gave. I went flat and started to slide down the dirt toward the line. My mouth filled with earth. I tried to swim up the slope, but kept slipping down. Then my feet struck the ribbing.

I just curled up against the cable, shaking, and the only thing going through my mind: Mabel doesn't like to waste power.

VI

Gules, azure, sable—

(Working bottom to top.)

"You sure you feel all right?"

I touched the bandage beneath torn silver. "Mabel, your concern is sweet. Don't overdo it."

She looked across the chill falls.

"You want to check out Haven before we go to work?"

Her eyes were red from fatigue. "Yeah."

"Okay. There's still a broomstick—aw, come on."

Just then the chameleon swung up the roadway with Scott, properly uniformed now, driving. He leaned out. "Hey, I got Danny down to town. Doctor looked at his eye." He shrugged.

"Put it away and go to bed."

"For twenty minutes?"

"More like a half an hour."

"Better than nothing." Scott scratched his head. "I had a good talk with Danny. No, don't worry. He's still alive."

"What did you say?"

"Just rest assured I said it. And he heard it." He swung the door closed, grinned through it, and drove off toward the hub.

A way of life.

Mabel and I went up on the monster's roof. Fidessa and Danny had left it there. Mabel hesitated again before climbing on.

"You can't get the chameleon up that road," I told her.

The turbos hummed, and we rose above the trees.

We circled the mountain twice. As Haven came into view, I said: "Power, Mabel. How do you delegate it so that it works for you? How do you set it up so that it doesn't turn against itself and cause chaos?"

"You just watch where you're flying."

High Haven was empty of angels. The rack was overturned, and there were no broomsticks about. In the forge the fires were out. We walked up the metal stairway through beer cans and broken glass. At the barbecue pit I kicked a lemon from the ashes.

"The devils gain Haven only to find the angels fled."

"Sure as hell looks like it," I muttered.

On the top porch Mabel said, "Let's go back down to the Gila Monster."

"You figure out where you're going to put in your outlets?"

"Everyone seems to have decided the place is too hot and split."

She looked at her bright toe. "So if there's nobody living up here, there's no reason to run power up here—by law. Maybe Roger's won after all."

"Now wait a minute—"

"I've been doing a lot of thinking this morning, Blacky."

"So have I."

"Then give a lady the benefit of your ponderings."

"We've just killed somebody. And with the world statistics being what they are . . ."

Mabel brushed back white hair. "Self-defense and all that. I still wonder whether I like myself as much this morning as I did yesterday."

"You're not putting lines up?"

"I am not."

"Now, wait. Just because—"

"Not because of that. Because of nothing to do with angels. Because of what angels have taught me about me. There's nobody up here anymore. I go by the books."

"All right. Let's go back then."

I didn't feel particularly good. But I understood: you have to respect somebody who forces you to accept his values. And in that situation, the less you agree, the more you have to respect.

We flew back down the mountain.

I landed a little clumsily fifty yards up the stream.

"You liked that?"

Mabel sighed deeply, and grinned at me a little. "I guess I'm just not made for this sort of thing. Coming inside?"

I squinted. "You go on. I'll be there in a few minutes."

She cocked her silver brows high as though she understood something I didn't, but grinned again. Then she started away.

What I really wanted to do was take another ride. I also wanted to get the whole thing out of my mind: well, there were a lot more forms to be filled in. Big choice, but it fixed me squarely at the brink of indecision. I stood there toeing stones into the water.

Sound behind me in the leaves made me turn.

Fidessa, tugging at the pteracycle, one leg over the seat, cringed when she saw me. "It's *mine!*" she insisted with all the hostility of the first time we'd met.

I'd already jerked my hand back, when I realized she meant the broomstick. "Oh," I said. "Yeah, sure. You go on and take it. I've done my high-flying for the week."

But she was looking at me strangely. She opened her mouth, closed it. Suddenly she hissed, "You're a monster! You're a monster, Blacky; and the terrible thing is you'll never understand why!"

My reflex was to put my hand behind me again. But that was silly, so I didn't. "You think I'm some sort of ghoul? I'm not trying to steal anything that isn't mine. I tried to give it back to Danny, but he wouldn't take—" I reached down to pull it off my finger.

Then I saw Fidessa's eyes drop and realized with guilt and astonishment that she hadn't even *seen* the ring—till now.

I opened my mouth. Excuses and apologies and expressions of chagrin blundered together on my tongue. Nothing came out.

"Monster!" she whispered once more. And the smile of triumph with the whisper made the backs of my thighs and shoulders erupt in gooseflesh.

Fidessa laughed and threw about her black-red hair. Laughing, she twisted at the throttle. The laugh became a growl. The growl became a roar. She jerked back on the rod, and the broomstick leaped, like a raging thing. Bits of the forest swirled up thirty feet. She leaned (I thought) dangerously to the side, spun round, and lifted off. Her high wing sliced branch ends and showered me with twigs and more torn green.

I brushed at my face and stepped back as, beyond the leaves, she rose and rose and rose, like Old Meg, like ageless Mab, like an airborne witch of Endor.

Some history here:

I was transferred at the end of the week to Iguana. Six months later word came over the line that Mabel had retired. So Global Power lost another good devil. Iguana lumbers and clanks mainly about Drake's Passage, sniffing around in Antarctica and Cape Horn.

Often I sit late in the office, remembering, while the cold south winds scour the skylight—

Okay, so I failed to tell you something:

About when I went to look at Roger's body.

He had fallen by the line. We were going to let the Gila Monster bury him when it buried the cable.

I'd thought the ring might have melted. But that hand had hardly blistered.

I took it off him and climbed out of the trough. As I came over the mound, between the brush and the tree trunks, something moved.

"Pitt?"

She darted forward, changed her mind, and ducked back.

"Do you . . . want to take this back to Danny?" I held it out.

She started forward again, saw what I held. A gasp, and she turned, fled into the woods.

I put it on.

Just then Sue, all sleepy-eyed and smiling, stepped onto the balcony and yawned, "Hello, Blacky."

"Hi. How do you feel?"

"Fine. Isn't it a perfectly lovely—?" She flexed her arm. "Sore shoulder." (I frowned.) "Nothing so bad I can't [sigh] work."

"That's good."

"Blacky, what was the commotion last night? I woke up a couple of times, saw lights on. Did Mabel send everybody back to work?"

"It wasn't anything, honey. You just stay away from the trough until we cover it up. We had some trouble there last night."

"Why? *Isn't* it a perfectly lovely—?"

"That's an order."

"Oh. Yes, sir."

She looked surprised but didn't question. I went inside to get Mabel to get things ready to leave.

I kept it.

I didn't take it off.

I wore it.

For years.

I still do.

And often, almost as often as I think about that winter in Tibet, I recall the October mountains near the Canadian border where the sun sings cantos of mutability and angels fear to tread now; where still, today, the wind unwinds, the trees re-leave themselves in spring, and the foaming gorge disgorges.

—Rifton
November 1967

cage of brass

Describe the darkness inside Brass? It was too complete to fix with words. He shunted and shuttled through the black until he stopped in one of the cells, was lowered by the mechanical hands into the glycerine coffin, and the lid fell like a feather falling on a mound of feathers. That darkness? Perhaps you could hint at it with a lack of words. Perhaps you could hint at it by saying that once the voices came, there was nothing else:

"Hey!"

". . . aaaaaaah . . ."

"Hey! What's your monicker, buddy-boy?"

"I don't tink he wake up yet."

"Shut up! Hey, come on and give with something besides the grumbly-grunts!"

". . . aaah . . . wha . . . ?"

"He's comin' roun' now."

". . . who are . . . ?"

"I'm Hawk, grunter. And that's—"

"I'm Pig. Hawk wants 'a know what they got ya for."

"Oh. I . . . my name . . ."

"That's it, baby. Give Hawk what he wants. Hawk always gets what he wants."

" 'S'right. You tell 'im, Hawk."

". . . Cage. Jason Cage."

"Who'd you cross, Cage, to get stored down here in the sub-basement with the likes of us?"

"I . . . look, leave me alone!"

"No!"

"I don't . . . I just want to be left—"

"I'll make Pig do his hollering act. Baby, that'll drive you battier than you feel now. Go on, Pig. Holler!"

"'Aloooah—glogalogologologa—Rh*eeeeeeee*shiminy! Biminy! Whiminy! Zapologologola—"

". . . all *right*!"

"You don't get left alone, Mister Jason Cage. I been here a year now with nothing but Pig to babble with. And they burned out half his brain before they dumped him down here. No, you ain't going to be left alone. You talk to me!"

"Hawk wants 'a know what they got you here in Brass for."

"And you're going to *tell* Hawk why they got you here in Brass. You hear that, Mister half-asleep Cage?"

"(breath) . . . (breath) . . . I guess you fellows don't get too many newspapers down here."

"Never read no newspapers even when I weren't here (chuckle)."

"Shut up, Pig! Come on. Spill, Cage."

"I don't want to talk about—"

"Talk!"

"I'll tell ya all 'bout me if ya tell me 'bout you. Ya gotta talk, Mister Cage. I heard jus' 'bout all there is to hear about Hawk. An' there ain't much left to hear 'bout me. Please, Mister Cage—"

"Shut it, Pig. Cage: talk, I said."

"All . . . right. All right. But it hurts."

"Hurt, Cage."

"They ain't put us in Brass to make us happy—"

"There's a world out there. What world do you come from, Hawk?"

"A place called Krags, from a city called Ruption, where the streets are cracks down to the hot core of the planet and lava broils up with sulfur and brim."

"Yeah, yeah, you told me all about Ruption, where the green and yellow smoke twists up between the balconies of the rich men's palaces in the charred evening—"

"Shut up, Pig. Go on, Cage."

"Don't shut up, Pig. What about you?"

"You wanna know where I'm from, Mister Cage?"

"He's from a world called Alba, Cage."

"Yeah, Alba, an' a city called Dusk. Dusk is in the mountains, where we got caves cut way down in the ice, and sunset and dawn flame in the fog and make the ice dance like diamonds."

"I've heard it, Pig. Let Cage talk."

"Well I come from a world called . . . Earth."

"Earth?"

"Be quiet, Pig!"

"From a city called Venice. At least that's where I was arrested, where I was tried, and where I was sentenced to spend the rest of my life in Brass. Venice? There the ocean comes and makes streets between the great palazzos and crowded slums strung with clotheslines, where the motorboats stop on the market street, decks spread with cabbages and tomatoes and persimmons and mussels and artichokes and clams and lobsters. Where the visitors and the architectural students and the bankers and the artists stroll down the tiled trapezoid of the Piazza, move among the pink columns of the Doge's Palace, come and walk down the waterfront and gaze into the canaletti where the Bridge of Sighs arches between the Doge's Palace and the old dungeon. Where the students will see you wandering by yourself with the park on one side and the sea on the other, and run up to you and slap your back and tell you to come with them, and drag you back to the vaporetto that hums down the Grand Canal, singing and joking with the girls, while I try to point out to Bruno the historic bits of architecture that have fascinated men of Earth since Ruskin. Then storm down the alley to the Mensa, rollick over the Ponte Academia, its boards brown and hung with moss underneath, pass the little wine shops, then upstairs, where you pound on the doors to make the cooks let you in and then everybody is eating and singing, and Bruno is telling you that it is all right, not to worry, and you cannot be sad anymore because it is Venice. . . ."

"Hey, wa' 'sa matter, Mister Cage?"

"Go on, Cage."

"Have either of you ever seen Brass from the outside?"

"Sure as hell can't see it from the inside."

"Shut up, Pig. No."

"It's on a plane of rock and snow. Even the clouds are scrawny. They shroud the nights and let the stars peek down on Brass itself. And it just sits there and doesn't look back."

"Nobody's ever supposed to have seen Brass, Mr. Cage."

"Yeah, how'da ya know what it looks like?"

"I've seen a picture. I've seen many things I'm not supposed to have seen, Pig. I was an architectural student, you see."

"On Earth?"

"In Venice?"

"That's right. I was once allowed access to the plans. I got a chance to see where all the corridors go and where they come from."

"You did?"

"I could tell you where every brick and block in Hagia Sofia is placed and mortared. I could tell you how they put together the optical-illusory temple of Ancqor on the world of Keplar down to the last mirror. And I know every blind corridor and twist and turn and gate and time lock and drainage conduit in Brass."

"You do?"

"Hey, you mean you know how you could get out of here?"

"Venice . . ."

"Hey, Hawk. Maybe Cage knows how to get us out of here!"

"Shut up, Pig. Keep talking, Cage."

"Venice, that's so far away now; no more nights in the wine shop while Giamba throws his knife to cut the sausages hanging from the rafters; those nights where we drank the wine from the south and the wine from the north to see which was sweeter. They are gone. Bruno is gone. And so is the beautiful lazy-eyed girl who destroyed it all: Bruno, me and the beautiful girl called—"

"Cage!"

"—Sapphire!"

"Cage, listen to me!"

"Yeah, you better listen to Hawk!"

"Sapphire is gone. . . ."

"Can you tell us how come these three coffins can talk to one another? I been in one coffin before this one. I cried and screamed and whimpered like a dog there. But this is the first one where I ever heard anyone answer. All the answer I got was Pig. But it was more than before. What is it, some kind of whispering chamber-effect?"

"Why we three can . . . hear?"

"Yeah, can you tell Hawk an' me that? I been in two before this one an' I ain't never heard no voices."

"The tri-nexus . . . yes, that must be it. The prisoners in Brass are stored in glycerine coffins that feed and wash them and minister to any medical needs and keep them from hurting themselves . . . too badly. You can hurt yourself just to the point of death, then the coffin knocks you out with drugs and makes you get better. You can get out of it to exercise once a day, in the dark, in a little stone cubicle—"

"Yeah, yeah. We know all that, Cage. But why the parly-parly in these three coffins?"

"At the tri-nexus—that's at the very bottom of the prison, three chambers come together around the old drainage pipes. Hollow metal pipes instead of stone between these three chambers. A new drainage system was put in a hundred and fifty years ago. If the pipes were filled up with waste and things, then you couldn't hear. But the new system goes somewhere else. Now that the pipes are empty, these three coffins in the lowest level have . . . well, you can hear . . . through the drains."

"What about getting out, Mister Cage? Hawk and me sure would like to get out of this."

"Quiet, Pig."

". . . the drains . . . of the city, emptying along the canal, into the water, the bits of paper, the leaves, the filth of animals and humans floating in the water along the back canals of the city . . . "

"What's 'a matter with 'im, Hawk?"

"Just listen, Pig."

". . . alone, wandering alone in the back alleys of the city, the sky running like purple waters between the narrow rooftops, the water beside me like dirty blood, arteries laid open between crumbling stones. Oh, it's a terrible city, beautiful with its wells and its rusted railings, and its rickety porches hanging over the water, its shop windows alive with the glass of Murano, its children dark-eyed and dark-haired with skin like dirty soap, a city of beauty, a city of lone-liness. . . ."

"Cage, we're alone. Here in Brass, you hear about it all the time, the prison without guards. It's all automatic. All the coffin changing, the feeding, it all goes on without guards. Now you say you know how Brass is laid out. How can we believe all that?"

"I know. I knew the stones of the city better than Ruskin, better than Persey. I knew the crack in the rock where Napoleon laid his pick to the Ponte San Marco, and I know the workings of the locks in the dungeon by which the Doge could flood the lower chambers of the prison when he had to be rid of vast numbers of political prisoners without question; I knew the passage by which Titian's *Assumption of the Virgin* was smuggled from St. Mark's to the cellar of Di Trevi the wool merchant, or the foundations for the gate by which Marion visited Angiolina before their betrothal. I have walked down the staircase of the palace as did Byron and Shelley, and like them I found the secret entrance into the Palazzo Scarlotti where the nightly debauches are still being carried on by the decadent sons of the sons of Fottia, in the mirrored halls, in the tapestried pavilions. All the city was open to me, and I was profoundly alone."

"What's he talkin', Hawk?"

"Shhh . . ."

"And into the aloneness, into the Venetian evening, came Sapphire. Hawk, Pig, have you ever seen a woman?"

"Pig, who was the most beautiful woman you ever saw?"

"Huh? Well, there was Jody-b, and when I us'ta bring in my haul back in the caves of Dusk, she'd laugh and wallop me and wrestle me for the best piece, and the others would stand around the fire, hoopin' and hollering, and bettin' on which of us, she or me, would win—"

"I knew a woman in Ruption. She walked in the burning streets of the city, and the flames fell back into the earth around her. Her name was Lanza, and when she dropped her fire-colored hair across my face, her fire-colored mouth on mine—"

"Neither of you have known Sapphire. Neither of you have

known a woman. She was the daughter of an Ambassador to Earth from the thirteenth planet of Sirius. You come from Krags and Alba? She had summered on one and wintered on the other and found them dull, tawdry, productive of incomparable ennui. And she had come to Venice. I saw her three times in one afternoon. Venice is a small city, and if you are wandering the streets, you will pass other wanderers may times; first on the steps of the bridge at Ferovia, while women with their husbands carried their baby carriages across the steps, and lottery vendors hurried by, their sticks streaming with tickets. Again, at the Rialto, I saw her as they were closing the stalls along the bridge, and she stopped to examine a flask, then replaced it and looked over the balustrade into the water; the third time, when I dared speak to her, was on a little back canal, where she had stopped on the tiny Ponte Diavolo, leaning on the rail, while the sunset gilded the swells of the water that flapped at the rotten, rusty stones. I came upon her just as she was offering a piece of something to one of the cats. I ran to her, struck her hand away, and when she drew back, frightened and surprised, I explained that the wild cats that roamed the city were vicious, many of them diseased, and that with so much fishing in the city they could fend for themselves. First she looked offended, then just annoyed, but at last she laughed and agreed to go with me when I invited her back to the university, begged her to come, explained how much fun the students were, how delightful the city could be with good companionship, till at last she smiled and exclaimed, "Why, you poor, lonely man. Of course I'll come with you," and she came, while I told her all about the prizes I'd won, and the buildings I'd planned, and the papers I'd written; and when we reached the Grand Canal, I helped her onto the vaporetto; and as we plowed the water between the gorgeous facades, I pointed out to her the Ca' D'oro, the Scholas, and the great merchant palazzos that towered into the evening behind the colored landing poles, their reflections shimmering until the public-boat's ripples shattered them. And when we went up to the students' dining room, oh, they were so friendly with us, and Bruno came all the way over to invite us to the party he was giving that night. "I couldn't find you earlier or I would have invited you before," he explained. And that night we drank wine and danced on the balcony, and the breeze lifted Sapphire's scarf and hung it over the moon for a moment so that her face was in shadow, and I held her hand, and she smiled in shadow, and below the water carried flecks of silver down toward a bridge. And then the scarf dropped again. . . ."

"Hey, Hawk! He's stopped talkin'."

"Cage? Hey, come on, Cage."

"W-w-why . . ."

"That's right. Go on, Cage."

"Why do . . . men commit crimes? You voices in the darkness, why do men commit crimes in the first place?"

"I guess I jus' did it 'cause I was hungry. It gets cold at Dusk. I got hungry, and stealin' was easier than workin'. Only I got caught. Which would'a been okay, only I got hungry again an' stole some more. 'Bout the fifth time or so, after I'd beat up on a couple of patrolmen, and two of them died, they just threw their hands up and threw me in Brass. You say why do people—"

"I say why is this, Cage. The streets of Ruption are filled with hot fires and hot men; there is revenge; there is pride; there is the writhing hate for the workings of a decadent world that curses us with morality. That's why I ran my gang of marauders and looters through the coffers of the city, battled the flying patrolmen from the roofs of the palace, watching my men fall around me, laughing as the floodlights swept the roof and I shook my fist at the sky that blazed with the fires of their jets bright as the fires of the streets, firing back, till I was the only one left—"

"No . . . Hawk. That's not it, Pig. Or perhaps that's what it is with some men. But with me it was so much more, so *much* more. It was later in the evening, when again I went on the balcony, to clear my head. I was light-headed from joy and wine, and as I gazed on the water, the lights reeled before me, my knees gave and I fell with my face pressed to the cold stone rail, looking over the red-tiled roofs of the city, bleached now by the lowering moon. For a moment I thought my exaltation was to be replaced by sickness. I pushed myself up, turned back to stagger between the glass doors, with the curtains shaking in the breeze. Wine bottles had spilled on the rug. Giamba lay on the couch, his hair awry, his shirt wet with his own bile. The plates of hors d'oeuvres were half empty, and even those that were not had been used for ashtrays. The only light in the room was from the stub of a candle in one still-upright bottle. The moon reached in white fingers and brushed away the shadows. I staggered forward. They were all gone, I thought at first. Then, in the doorway of Bruno's room I saw them.

"Blades of pain shot into my head, tried to unfix my eyes! I swallowed what rose in my throat, swallowed what rose again! Muscles all over my body began to shake. Then something came out—I thought it would be a scream, but it was laughter.

"Bruno raised his face from her neck, frowned. Then asked blearily, 'Are you going now—'

"'Oh, yes,' I told him. 'But the two of you must come with me. The night is just beginning. Come, come, I will show you a really good time.' She looked at me, as drunk as he, and I knew that for a moment she did not even remember who I was. Oh, I was maniacal with my laughter. I hustled Bruno, protesting, into his jacket; and as I wrapped her scarf again and again about her shoulders, I suddenly felt her start, pull away from me, but I pretended not to notice, chattered on cheerily, and almost pushed them out into the hallway, where Bruno asked, 'Now what party would anybody in Venice invite you to?' Only I just laughed, and soon we were out on the little walkway beside the canal.

"'This way! This way,' and they followed me down beside the canaletti, then out to the Campanile, up the arch of the Academy Bridge, and across the broad end of the Strada Nova, into the tiny alley that has no name. We crossed another of the city's thousand bridges (there aren't really a thousand; only six hundred and eighty-two) and hurried beneath the covered waterway. It let us out two small streets from the clutter of steps rising to the Ferovia side of the Rialto. But we moved off down to a little blue-tiled walkway, then pushed through a gate and hurried down an alley where the lights were out. I started to climb the low wall.

"'Where are we . . .' she began. But Bruno *shhhhhed* and laughed.

'I've been a student in the city almost a year, and I still don't know. But Jason knows every gutter and alley of the place. He's getting us there by a shortcut.' Then he growled, 'I hope we get where you're going soon.' But I just hurried them along. I remember she said once, '. . . But there's no rail to the canal here—' but by then I was working loose the grate. 'In here, in here . . .' Again Bruno explained for me, 'Jason likes to pull surprises on people. He's always crawling up from somebody's cellar. Venice is a city of intrigue, you know. . . .' But by then, by then our breaths were echoing in the dark passage. Our feet clacked, and she had begun half-crying noises. But again I just urged them on faster. 'Don't worry,' Bruno assured her, but his voice was almost as unsteady as hers. 'Jason doesn't get all these prizes each year for nothing. He's got an absolute sense of spatial relations. He *can't* get lost.' We passed under a grating which let half a dozen blades of moonlight through the fog and down beside the underground bridge we were crossing. She caught her breath. There was no rail here either. I told them to watch out for the steps. We left the moonlight, and in another fifteen minutes we were there. I closed a door behind us and let out my breath. 'We're here,' I told them. 'Come on, Bruno, I need your help.' I moved along the wall, the blueprints almost visible before my eyes. Four steps, five. 'Duck your head, Bruno!' and, 'Here. Give me a hand.' I guided him to the great bar across the wheel. 'Now, bear down on this with me.' He took the bar. 'Will this get us into the party? I don't hear any—' I stopped him. 'This way to the cellar. Come on, lean on it.' At first I thought the ancient lock wouldn't budge. My toes came up off the dusty stone. Then I felt Bruno lend his weight, and—it gave! Metal ground. I heard the weights fall. Then a rush of water. I heard her say, 'What was that? Bruno, Jason?' And then she let out a cry. Water splashed about my feet. 'Hey!' Bruno said, 'what's all this?' I backed away from the lock, and began to laugh. 'We're in the dungeon, the Duke's dungeon, on the lowest level, where he had the water locks! You remember, Bruno? Where he could open the floodgates to drown his prisoners?'

"'Hey, if this is some kind of joke, Jason, it's not funny!' I heard her splashing toward us now. 'How do we get out of here? Which way do we go? It's all pitch-dark.' Then she cried out and stumbled. Because the water was rushing so hard now, it was difficult to stand. It had already reached our knees. I just started to back away. They splashed after me. She came near us, then hit her head on the overhang of stone, and fell. Bruno tried to help her; then, all at once, he was raging. He dived for me, caught me. 'Look, you're going to drown too if you think you're going to drown us.' She was splashing toward us, just screaming. I tried to pull away, but both of them got me. We fell in the water. Her scarf, I remember, was wet between my fingers. I just stayed under, swam down, which they weren't expecting and . . . got away. With the currents, it was hard to judge the distances accurately, but I surfaced once more, took a breath, then dove beneath the low wall, already underwater, clawed my way under the stone, then at last shot up to the surface, pulled myself up the steps. The water was halfway up the stairs. I could hear them screaming behind the rocks. When I stood, the water was all the way up to my chest. . . . They found me, wandering across the Piazza, in front of the Byzantine facade of St. Mark's, passing through the shadows of the four great bronze horses thrown from the basilica's roof. I was soaking wet—and was dragging her wet scarf behind me."

"By all the gods of Alba—"

"By the single god of Krags—"

"By whatever gods are left on Earth, I tell you I laughed like a demon! They found me. They found me, and I told them. The alarms had already gone off. But, by then, it was too late. The Doges were very efficient. Very . . . Because she was the daughter of an ambassador from another world, it became an interworld offense. So instead of incarcerating me in the city, they sent me here, here to the interworlds' prison called Brass. . . ."

"Hey, Hawk, he ain't talkin' no more!"

"Cage? Look, Jason Cage, you say you know the architecture of Brass as well as you knew the setup of that dungeon in . . . whatever-its-name-was? Come on, now! Talk."

"I know. I know them all. I know the floor plan for the Shining

Mosque in Iran. I know the structure of cellars in the Museum of Life at Beta-Centauri. If Daedalus had ever left plans for the Labyrinth, had I seen them once, I would have needed no thread. . . ."

"Then what about Brass, Cage? How about where we are now? Do you think you could get us out of here?"

"Here at the . . . tri-nexus? Very near, there are the . . . yes, the tunnels that the original workmen used to enter and leave the structure, when they built the thing, all those years ago. But . . . but they are sealed off. Leave, you say? But how can I leave? I am guilty. My heart is all crusted with the metal of guilt. I am here . . . to suffer. Yes! Even if I were to leave, guilt is a prison around my heart."

"Hey, Hawk, I think he really *has* gone nuts."

"Listen, Cage. Where we are, here at this tri-nexus, is there any way you know of to get into that tunnel?"

"You . . . you want to get out? But . . . but . . . I killed them. I'm guilty. I deserve—"

"Look, Cage!"

"My crimes make all the worlds guilty."

"Come on, Mister Cage. We wanna get out."

"Talk, Cage. Talk more."

"She was . . . she was beautiful as water, as fire, as fog—"

"Talk about Brass!"

"Brass? Yes, Brass . . . the prison, the prison with the three chambers near the workmen's tunnel. The keystones, perhaps. Yes, they wouldn't be set."

"What are you talking about, Cage? Make it so I can see it, clear as Venice."

"These three cells we're in. They come together around the drainage system like three fat slices of cake with their points together. The walls would be where the knife goes—"

"And the drain is where you'd put the candle for a one-year-old's birthday?"

"That's right. And the stones in the joining walls, near the tip, they can't be mortared in. They weigh perhaps three hundred pounds apiece."

"Three hundred pounds? One person couldn't move that, Hawk."

"But two could, Pig."

"And each covers a drop-shaft into the workers' tunnel that winds and turns and rises to the rocks outside. . . ."

"If you pushed from your side, Pig, then I pulled from the other . . ."

"What about him?"

"Cage, we can move our stone out, and then move yours—"

"No. No, this is where I stop."

"Hawk, the lid is starting to open for exercise period. Come on, let's get that stone."

"Cage, you won't be able to move your stone by yourself. You better let us help you. Once we go, you'll be here forever."

"No! No . . . I belong here. I must stay here . . . I must . . . I have to stay and be part of the great tower of Brass, like one of its very rocks, become part of the bedrock itself. I can hear, hear you now, hear the stone scraping against the stone. You grunt. You pant. But it moves, slowly. Yes, I hear it moving, like the great lock in the dungeon of the Doge, scraping, scraping. There! You've got it now . . . Pig? What tasks of knavery had you bent those shoulders to on Alba? Hawk, what did you pit your strength against to strain such force into being at Krags? Pig . . . ? Hawk . . . ? Hawk . . . ? Pig—! I can't hear you anymore. Have you . . . gone? Pig? Hawk . . . ?"

Describe the silence inside Brass?

Now it too was complete. Perhaps you could hint at it by a lack of words. Perhaps you could hint at it by saying once the voices left, there was . . . nothing.

—*New York*
December 1967

high weir

"What do you know!" Smith, from the top of the ladder.

"What is it?" Jones, at the bottom.

And Rimkin thought desperately: Boiled potatoes! My God, boiled potatoes! If I took toothpicks and stuck them in boiled potatoes, then stuck one on top of the other, made heads, arms, legs—like little snowmen—they would look just like these men in space suits on Mars.

"Concaved!" Smith called down. "You know those religious pictures they used to have back home, in the little store windows, where the eyes followed you down the street? The faces were carved in reverse relief like this."

"Those faces aren't carved in reverse relief!" Mak, right next to Rimkin, shouted up. "I can see that from here."

"Not the whole face," Smith said. "Just the eyes. That's why they had that funny effect when we were coming across the sand."

Mak, Rimkin thought. Mak. Mak. What distinguishes that man besides the *k* in his name?

"They are handsome up there." That from Hodges. "A whole year of speculation over whether those little bits of purple stone were carved or natural—and suddenly here it all is, right on High Weir. The answer. Look at it: it means intelligence. It means culture. It means an advanced culture at least on the level of the ancient Greeks, too. Do you realize the spaces between these temple columns lead to a whole new branch of anthropology?"

"We don't know that this thing's a temple," Mak grunted.

"A whole new complex of studies!" Hodges reiterated. "We're all of us Sir Arthur Evans unearthing the great staircase of Knossos. We're Schliemanns digging up the treasures of Atreus."

I don't know where any of them are, Rimkin thought. Their voices come through the rubber-ringed grills inside my helmet. All these boiled-potato figures against the grainy rust; that one there who I think is Hodges; the sun blinds out the faceplate. And, for all I know, behind the plastic is a grotesquerie as deformed as those domed heads along the architrave above us. . . .

"Hey, Rimkin, you're the linguist. Why aren't you poking around for something that looks like writing?"

"Huh . . .?" And as he said it, without hearing their laughter, he knew that inside their onion helmets they were smiling and shaking their heads. Jones said:

"Here we are on Mars, and Rimky is *still* in another world. Is there any writing or hen-scratching up there where you are, Smith?"

"Nothing up here. But look at the surface of this eye, the way it's carved out!"

"What about it?"

Then Jimmi—Rimkin could always tell Jimmi because her suit was a head and a half shorter than any of the others—climbed up the rough stone foundation blocks and, with a beautiful "Martian lope" and a wake of russet dust, crossed the flooring, then turned back. "Look!" He could always tell her voice, no matter the static and distortion of the radios (short range; no fidelity). "Here's one that fell!"

"Here!" Rimkin said. "Let me see." They mustn't think he wasn't interested.

Her soft voice said in his ear: "I can't very well move it. You'll have to come up here, Rimky."

But he was already climbing. "Yes, yes. Of course. I'm coming." And there was the sound of somebody trying not to snicker, position concealed by lack of stereo.

The carving had fallen. And it had cracked on the stone flags.

He walked up to Jimmi. The top of her helmet came to the middle of his upper arm.

"It's so funny," she said with that oddness to her laughter the radio couldn't mask. "It looks just like a Martian."

"What?"

She looked up at him, small brown face behind the white frame. The movements of her laughter were displaced from the sound in his ear. "Just look." She turned back. "The great, high forehead, the big beady eyes, and hardly any chin. Wouldn't you have guessed? Martians would turn out to look just like a nineteen-fifties s-f film."

"Maybe . . ." A third of the face had fallen away. The crack went through the left eye. What remained of the mouth leered with prune-puckered lips. "Maybe it's all a joke. Perhaps some of the military people from Bellona came here and set this whole thing up like an elaborate stage set. Just to play a joke on us. They *would*, you know! This is absurd, just the five of us taking the skimmer on a routine scouting trip across High Weir plateau, not sixty-five miles from the base, and coming across—"

"—across a structure as big as the Parthenon? Hell, bigger than the Temple of Zeus!" Hodges exploded. "Come off it, Rimky! You can't just sneak off in the morning and erect an entire stone ruin. Not one like this."

"Yes, but it's so—"

"Hey! You people!" Again, the voice came from Smith. "Somebody come up here and take a look at the eyes. Are they the same stone as the rest of the building, just very highly polished? Or are they some different material set in? I can't tell from here."

Jimmi bent awkwardly and ran her glove over the broken surface. She who is dark and slender and the definition of all grace, Rimkin thought, muffled against the blazing ruin beneath deep turquoise skies.

"It's an inset, Dr. Smith." She made a blunted gesture, and Rimkin bent to see.

The eyes were cylinders of translucent material perhaps nine inches in diameter and a foot long. They were set flush into the face, the front surfaces ground to shimmering concavities.

"Lots of them are different colors," Mak noted.

Rimkin himself had noticed that the great row of eyes gave off an almost Day-Glo quality, from across the dunes; up close, they were mottled.

"What are they made of?" Hodges asked.

"The building's that Marsite stuff," Jones said. The light, purplish rock "marsite" had been found as soon as the military base in Bellona had grown larger than a single bubble-hut. Rimkin, there with the Inter-Nal University group, had spent much time looking at the worn fragments, playing after-dinner games with the military men (who barely tolerated the contingent of scholars) speculating as to whether they were carved or natural. The purple shards could have been Martian third cousins to the Venus of Wellendorf, or they could have simply been eroded fragments tossed for millennia by the waterless waves.

"What are the eyes made of?" Hodges demanded. "Semi-precious stone? Is it something smelted, or synthetic? That opens up a whole world of possibilities about the culture."

"I can chip some off this broken one to take back—"

"Rimkin! No!" Hodges shouted, and in a moment the bumpy air suit had scrambled over the foundation. Hodges swayed on bloated feet. "Rimkin . . . look, wake up! We've just had the first incontrovertible proof that there is—or at any rate at one time there was—intelligent life beside us in the universe. In the solar system! And you want to start chipping. Sometimes you come on like one of those brass-decked thick skulls back at the base!"

"Oh, Hodges, cut it out!" Jimmi snapped. "Leave him alone. It's bad enough trying to put up with those thick skulls you're talking about. If we start this sort of bickering—"

"Stop trying to protect him, Jimmi," Hodges countered. "All right, perhaps he's a brilliant linguist in a library cubicle. But he's absolute deadweight on this expedition. He spends all his time either completely uninterested in what's going on, or worse, making absurd suggestions like breaking up the most important archaeological discovery in human history with a sledgehammer!"

"I wasn't going to break up—"

Then: "Oh my—God . . . No! This is—"

And Rimkin thought: Which one is it? Jesus, with all this distortion, I can't tell what direction the voices are coming from. I can place any accent on Earth, but I can't even recognize their individual voices anymore! Which one?

Hodges turned around. "What is it?"

Jones, still down on the sand, called up, "What is it, Dr. Smith? What's happening up there?"

"This is just . . . no . . . this is amazing!"

They were all going to the base of the column against which the ladder was leaning. So Rimkin went too.

The white-suited figure on the top rung was peering into one of the eyes with a flashlight.

"Dr. Smith, are you all right?"

"Yes, yes. I'm fine. Please, just wait! But this . . . "

"That's a low-power laser-beam he's looking in there with," someone began.

"He said be quiet," from someone else.

I can hear five people breathing in my ears, Rimkin thought. What could he be looking at? "Dr. Smith," Rimkin called.

"Shhhh!"

Rimkin went on doggedly. "Can you describe what you're looking at?"

"Yes, I . . . think so. It's—Mars. Only, the way it must have been. A city, the city around this building. Roads. Machines that move, and a horizon full of man-made—buildings? Perhaps they're buildings. The picture moves—and the streets are full of creatures, like the statues. No, they're different. Some hurry . . . some go slowly . . . this whole plateau, all of High Weir must have been some incredible acropolis for a mammoth, cosmopolitan community. Wait! They're unveiling some sort of statue. Now, they're presenting one of them to the people. Maybe a priest. Or a sacrifice—"

After moments of silence, Mak said. "What pictures are you talking about?"

"It's like looking through a window onto what must have been here . . . on this plateau perhaps hundreds of thousands of years ago. As soon as I shine my laser-light into the concaved surface, I'm suddenly looking out on three-dimensional moving scenes, just as real . . . just as strange . . ."

Mak turned to Hodges. "Is it some sort of animated diorama?"

"It's got to be some kind of hologram. A moving hologram!" At the top of the ladder, Dr. Smith finally looked down. "You've got to come up here and see this! I just wanted to look at the inside of the eye on this carving closely. I thought with the laser-light I might detect crystalline structures, perhaps get a clue to what the eyes were made from. But I saw pictures!" He started down the ladder. "You've all just got to go up there and take a look!" Smith's indrawn breath roared in Rimkin's ear. "It's the most amazing thing I've ever seen."

"Still think somebody came by and built this today just to get us off on a wild-goose chase, eh, Rimkin?" Hodges chided. "Let me go up and look. I've got my own beam, Dr. Smith." Hodges started up the rungs as Smith reached the bottom.

Frowning behind his faceplate, Rimkin took out his own flash. For a moment he fondled the tube; then he went back over the rusty sand tongues and purple stone to where the head had fallen. He looked at the whole eye. He looked at the broken one. He did not know what perversity made him crouch before the latter. He flicked on his laser-beam.

It took half an hour for Mak, Hodges, Jimmi, and Jones to climb the ladder, watch for two or three minutes, then climb down. They were gathering to go back to the skimmer when Jimmi saw Rimkin. She loped over to him.

She laughed when she saw what he was doing. "Now aren't we a bunch of dopes! Some of us could have looked at this one down here. Come on, we're going back now."

Rimkin switched off his beam, but still crouched before the tilted visage.

"Oh, come on, Rimky. They're starting back already."

Rimkin drew breath, then stood slowly. "All right." They started across the dressed stone flooring. The sand, fine as dust, spewed about their white boots like powdered blood.

II

The commons room of the skimmer was a traveling fragment of classical academia. The celitex walls looked depressingly like walnut paneling. Above the brass-fixtured folding desk surfaces, the microfilms were stacked behind Naugahyde spines lettered in gold leaf. There was a mantelpiece above the heating nook. Glowing plates shot pale flickerings across the fur throws. The whole construct, with its balcony library cubicles (and a bust of Richard Nielson, president of Inter-Nal University, on his pedestal at the turn of the stairwell) was a half-serious joke of Dr. Edward Jones. But the university people, by and large, were terribly appreciative of the extravagant facade, after a couple of weeks in the unsympathetic straits of the military back at Bellona Base.

Mak sat on the hassock, rolling the sleeves of his wool shirt over his truck-driver forearms. He had headed the Yugoslavian expedition that had unearthed Gevgeli Man. Mak's boulderlike build (and what forehead he had was hidden by a falling thatch of Sahara-colored hair) had brought the jokes in the anthropology department to new nadirs: "This is Dr. Mak Hargus, the Gevgeli Man . . . eh, man . . ."

Mak raised the periscope of his briar from his shirt pocket. "Tell me about holograms. I've seen them, of course, the three-dimensional images and all. But how do they work? And how did the ancient Martians store all those pictures that just pop up under laser-light?"

Ling Wong Smith dropped his fists into the baggy pocket of his corduroy jacket. He and Mak gazed over the ferns in the windowbox. Outside the triplex pane, across the dusty bruise of High Weir, the dark columns—twelve whole, seven broken—sketched the incredible culture they had viewed in the polished eyes along the carved lintel.

Jimmi pushed her dark braid back from her shoulder and leaned on the banister to look.

Ling Wong Smith turned away. "It's basically a matter of information storage, Mak." He lowered himself to the arm of the easy chair, meshed his long fingers and bent forward so that his straight black hair slipped forward.

"The Martians certainly stored one hell of a lot of information in those eyes," Hodges commented, coming jerkily down the stairs on her crutches. She was large, almost as large (and soft) as Mak was large (and hard). She had a spectacular record in cultural anthropology, and combined a sort of braying energy, enthusiastic idealism, and a quite real sensitivity (she had been a cripple since birth), with which she had managed to stagger through all sorts of bizarre cultures in East Africa, Anatolia, and Southern Cambodia to emerge with thorough and cohesive accounts of religions, mores, and manners. Her space suit was a prosthetic miracle that enabled her to move as easily as anyone while she wore it. But outside it, she still used aluminum crutches.

From his go game with Jones in the corner, Rimkin watched her lurch down the stairs. She must think they're a psychological advantage, he decided.

"Go on, Ling. Now tell us all about holograms." She picked up one crutch and waved it at the Chinese psychologist, only just avoiding the venerable Nielson.

"Information storage," Smith repeated. "Basically it's a photograph, taken without a lens, but with perfectly parallel beams of light—the sort you get in laser-light. The only scattering is that which comes from the irregularities of the surface of the object being recorded. The final plate looks like a blotchy configuration of grays—or mud if it's in color. But when you shine the parallel beams of a laser-light on this plate, you get a three-dimensional, full-color image hanging over the plate—"

"—that you can walk around," Mak finished.

"You can walk around up to a hundred and eighty degrees," Smith amended. "It's just a completely different way of storing information from the regular photographic method. And it is far more efficient."

Jones said softly, from across the gaming board, "It's your move, Rimky."

"Oh." Rimkin picked up another black oval from his pot between his first two fingers and hesitated above the grid, dotted with white and black. Bits of information. He tried to encompass the areas of territory mapped below him, but they kept breaking up into small corner battles. "There." He clicked his stone to the board.

Jones frowned. "Sure you don't want to take that move back?"

"No. No, I don't."

"You can, you know," Jones went on, affable. "This isn't chess. The rules are that you can take a move back if you—"

"I know that," Rimkin said loudly. "Don't you think I know that? I want to go—" he looked around and saw the other watching—"there!" The click of his stone had been very loud.

"All right." Jones's stone ticked the board. "Double atari." But Rimkin was looking past Jones's small, heart-shaped, Nigerian face, to the others in the room, thinking, How can I tell them apart? They all just blend with one another. The room is round, their faces are round, stuck on little round bodies. Suddenly he closed his eyes. If they started talking, I know I wouldn't be able to tell any of them apart. How is one supposed to know? How?

And if I opened my eyes?

"Your move, Rimkin," Jones said. "I've got two of your stones in atari."

Rimkin opened his eyes on the grid of black and white. "Oh," he said, and tried to strangle up a laugh. "Yes. That was a pretty silly move after all, wasn't it?"

III

Such an absurd move; he lay in his bunk with his eyes closed and his lips open over his teeth in a leer, trying to think of a better one. He hadn't slept in two nights. An hour like this . . . maybe it was only a few minutes, but it seemed like an hour . . . and he sat up.

He swung the reading machine over his bed and rolled it to the closing of the *Tractatus*. He'd been rereading it the afternoon the skimmer had left Bellona: *Wovon man nicht sprechen kann . . .* He pushed the machine aside and ran his hand under his undershirt. The skimmer would not leave till the morning. They should return to Bellona that night and report their discovery to Those Who Were in Charge of Such Things. But the university people (especially the anthropology department) treasured their brief freedom. One more examination of the site tomorrow, a few cursory readings and measurements . . .

Rimkin walked barefoot into the hall. It must have only been a few minutes, because strips of light from reading machines underlined three doors. Which room belonged to whom? He knew, and yet somehow there seemed no way to know . . .

Down at the portal, he put his air suit on over his underwear. The plastic ring-forms felt odd against his thighs and arms without the usual padding. He stepped into the lock.

Outside, sharp stars dropped frostlights. The sand was filled with great, slopping puddles of ink. Cold, cold outside. The little motor humming in the vicinity of his chin kept the silicone circulating between the double thickness of his faceplate to avoid frosting. He stepped. And stepped. The desert sucked his boots.

The others? It was not even that he disliked them. He was infinitely confused by them. Dune and shadow received him. As he walked, he looked up. One bright star was . . . moving. If he stood still, he could follow the movement distinctly. Phobos? Demos? He knew it was one of the two tiny Martian moons. But for the life of him, Rimkin could not remember whether it was Fear or Terror that coursed the frozen jewelry of the Martian night.

He saw the ruin.

He tried to blank the struggling anxieties that squirmed into the edges of his consciousness. Seven hundred and fifty-odd vitally important enzyme reactions are occurring constantly in the human body. Were any one of them to break down for even two/three minutes, the body would die. So, just to fix the free fear that ranged his mind, he worried about one of these seven hundred and fifty-odd complex reactions suddenly coming to a halt; until he lost the subject of his worry in the coils of sand. And fear moved free above him, tangible as the slender columns, the sculpted architrave.

He looked up at the faces, obscured by darkness. The eyes caught and grayed the starlight, and regarded him. Rimkin began to paw under the flap of his pack for his flash. He found it after much too much time—he had forgotten what he was looking for twice—and rotated the dispersal grid to break up the laser-beam into ordinary light.

He played the beam over the stones. They were gray, now. He wondered if the purple were actually only a reflection from the desert. No, it was just the weakness of his beam. He walked along the sand to the place where the foundation could be mounted. He started to climb, once more aware of the inside of his suit against bare skin. The heating was working adequately, but the plastic and metal textures were so odd. He wanted to take the suit off and place his hand on the stone, then grew terrified that he might; because the Martian night was almost a hundred degrees below freezing.

Rimkin stood on the edge of the foundation and fanned his light toward the fallen head. He approached across the sandy blocks. The smaller fragment of face lay like a saucer. Its half-eye had cracks all through. Rimkin squatted before the major portion of the face, leaned toward the fractured orb. He raised his flash, twisted back the dispersal-grid so that the bright, singular beam fell on the broken circle; flicker, and flicker, image and image. The fragmented orb began to weep the sights of ages.

Dawn comes quickly on worlds with thin atmospheres. It climbed the dunes behind Rimkin and laid its blazing hands on his shoulders. And the mechanism of his suit began to hum and twitter about him to prepare for the two-hundred-degree rise that would occur in the next twenty minutes.

"Rimkin . . .?"

Who was breathing in his ear?

"Rimkin, are you up there?"

The voices had been calling for some time. But with just a sound coming out of a machine by your ear, how was he supposed to know what they were?

"Rimky, there you are! What are you doing? Have you been here all morning?"

He turned around—and fell over.

"Rimkin!"

He had been in one position for almost nine hours, and every muscle, once moved, was in agony. In the pain fogging his vision like heat, he watched the boiled potato, jogging toward him in a cloud of fiery dust.

Through his gasps he kept on trying to get out: "Why . . . who are . . . which . . . who are—"

"It's me, Evelyn."

Evelyn, he thought. Who was Evelyn? "Who . . ."

She reached him. "Evelyn Hodges, who did you think it was? Are you hurt? Has something gone wrong with your suit? Oh I *knew* I should have brought Mak out here with me. The outside temperature is about ten degrees Fahrenheit right now. But in fifteen minutes it'll be ninety or more. I can't get you back to the ship by myself."

"No—No." Rimkin shook his head. "All right. My suit. I'm just—"

"What is it, then?"

The pain was incredible, but for a moment he was in control enough to get out: "I'm just stiff . . . I was in one position for so long. I just . . . just forgot."

"How long is a long time?" Hodges demanded.

"Almost all night, I guess." His arms weren't so bad. He pushed himself up and propped himself against the stone.

Hodges bent down, picked up the flash (a feat she could only do with her specially constructed suit) and turned it around. "You've been looking at the pretty pictures?"

Rimkin nodded. "Eh . . . yes."

She made a sound that had something of confusion, something of frustration. "You just be glad I came looking for you!" She squatted beside him, and after much maneuvering, got herself seated. "I can never sleep past five-thirty in the morning anyway, and I got to thinking that perhaps I'd let myself get carried away a couple of times with you. You know, back at the base, with all those ribbons and brass flapping around, saying all those stupid things, we've all been under a bit of pressure. Early this morning I was in the hall, saw the light from your reading machine, and thought you might be up. I peeped in, because the door was open, but you weren't in bed. I figured you must be in the library; but the doors down to the port were open and your suit was gone—well, this is the only thing worth going out to look at. You've been here since last night?"

"Yes. I have."

"Rimky," Hodges said after a few moments, "we're all oddballs in our way. You're really not all that strange when you start looking at the rest of us. Maybe you're just a little less used to fitting your angles into other people's spaces. But I have been doing some thinking. And I have a feeling I've put my finger on the reason you were so . . . well, preoccupied all last evening. Give me a listen and tell me if I'm right."

She rocked a couple of times beside him to settle inside her blimp. "Yesterday I said something about the Martians having at least reached the level of the Greeks. But that was before we discovered the moving hologram records. That at least brings their technology—or one facet of it, at any rate—to a level comparable to the middle of the twentieth century. Or even well beyond. We still can't embed a moving hologramic image into a crystal that just starts to play back automatically under laser-light. Now if they were all that advanced, then there should be scads of written evidence around here. If not things like books, then at least carved in the stone. But there isn't a scratch, not a dated cornerstone, no mayor's name carved over the doorway. Hell, there're at least mason's marks on the blocks in the Khufu Pyramid. Now you're our semanticist, Rimky, and it must be pretty important to you that there be some evidence of a Martian language. But the fact that there isn't any immediately visible about a structure this imposing, coupled with the fact that they obviously stored so much *visually* . . ." Her voice hung on the word as a card player's fingers might linger on a daring discard. "Well, there's a good possibility, Rimky, that they just weren't a verbal race, and they somehow managed to achieve this level of technology without ever employing written communication, sort of the same way the Incas and Mayas reached their cultural level and still managed totally to bypass the invention of the wheel. If that *is* the case, Rimky, that makes you sort of useless on this expedition. I could see that getting to you, upsetting you."

He could tell she was waiting for some great reaction of relief, now that a truth had outed. How did she expect to detect it? Perhaps the change in breathing would come through the suit phones. He tried to remember who she was. But there were all seven hundred and fifty-odd enzyme reactions to think about, to make sure that one of them didn't suddenly stop . . .

"You know," she was going on (Hodges? Yes it *was* the Hodges woman), "I'm really the useless one on the expedition. You know what my talent is? I'm the one who can make friends with all sorts of Eskimos and jungle bunnies. And then there were the mountain cannibals in the Caucasus who wanted to make me their queen." She laughed metallically. "They certainly did. I don't care if I never see another piece of decayed yak butter again as long as I live. Rimky, I'm here just in case we run into a tribe of *live* Martians." She looked out across the barren copper. After a few more moments she said, "I think you'd pretty well agree there's a good deal more chance you'll find Martian writing than I'll find the models for those carvings up there, wandering around in nomadic tribes. And what's more, it *does* get under my skin. I guess, being on edge like that, I've occasionally said some things, some of them to you, I'd have best held in. If you've got a skill or a discipline, you want to use it. You don't want to drag it halfway across the solar system because there's a one-in-a-thousand chance somebody might just want a minute of your time." She patted his forearm. "Am I anywhere near it?"

Rimkin thought: Live Martians? If I were a live Martian, then I wouldn't have to worry about the seven hundred and fifty enzyme reactions that keep the human body alive. But then, there'd be others, different ones, even more complicated, even more dangerous, because they have to function over a much wider temperature range. Am I a Martian? Am I one of those strange creatures I watched in the beam of my flash, walking the strange alleys with the garnet-colored walls, driving their beasts, and greeting one another with incomprehensible gestures? But this woman, which one is she? "Where's Jimmi . . . ?" Rimkin asked.

He heard Hodges start to say something; then she decided not to, and began the complicated maneuver of her prostheses to stand. "Can you walk, Rimkin? I think I'd better get you back to the skimmer."

"The skimmer . . . ? Oh, yes. Of course. It's time to go back to the skimmer, isn't it?"

He ached. All over his body, he ached. But he managed to stand, thinking: Why does it hurt so? Perhaps it's one of the seven hundred reactions, starting to fail, and I'm going to . . .

"Let's hurry up," Hodges urged. "If you've been out here all night, you're probably on the third time through your air. I bet it's stale as an old laundry bag in there."

Rimkin started slowly across the stones. But Hodges paused. Suddenly she bent down before the cracked visage and shone Rimkin's laser on the broken iris: She looked for the whole minute it took Rimkin to reach the edge. She made puzzled *"mmmmm"* sounds twice.

When she joined him to climb down to the sand, she was frowning behind the white frame of her helmet. And a couple of times she made stranger faces.

IV

The process of getting Rimkin to bed pretty well finished getting everybody else up. When Dr. Jones wanted to give him a sedative, Rimkin went into a long and fairly coherent discussion about the drug's causing possible upset in his enzymal chemistry, which the others listened to seriously until suddenly he started to cry. At last he let Jimmi give him the injection. And while the pretty Micronesian qualitative analyst stroked his forehead, he fell asleep.

Mak, in his weight allowance for Equipment Vital to the Facilitation of Your Specialized Functions, had secreted a Westphalian ham and a gallon of good Slivowitz, contending that breakfast was pointless without a hefty slice of the one and at least a pony of the other. But he was willing to share; the ritual of breakfast was left to his episcopacy. Anyway, he had the best luck among them beating dehydrated eggs back into shape. Now, in the small area under the steps where such things were done, he was clanking and fuming like a rum-and-maple dragon.

Smith came down the stairs.

A skillet cover rang on the pan rim. Mak grunted. "I didn't realize he was that bad, Ling."

Jones folded the gaming board; the pattern of white and black fell apart. He slid the pebbles into the pot, and pushed the stud on the pot base. "I guess none of us did." The pot began to vibrate. The white stones were substantially less dense than the black ones, so, after a good shaking, ended up on top. "Do you think Mars is just too much for him?" Dr. Jones had already noticed that the separation process took longer on this lightweight planet than at home.

"Naw." Mak ducked from under the stairs with his platter of ham and eggs. The steam rose and mixed with the pipe smoke. "This must have been building for months, maybe all his life, if Freud's progeny are to be trusted."

He leaned over hefty Miss Hodges and set the platter down. Then he frowned at her. "You look oddly pensive, ma'am."

Hodges, using her aluminum stalks, pushed herself around from the table so she could see Smith, who was at the bottom of the stairs. "What happens if you cut—or break—a hologram plate in half, Ling?"

"I guess you get half the image," Jimmi said. She was sitting on an upper step. Richard Nielson was staring directly at the top of her head.

"If I sit down at the table before the rest of you," Mak said, ducking under the steps for the coffeepot, "you're only going to get half your breakfast."

Smith, Jones, and Jimmi took their chairs. Mak set the steaming enameled pot (it too was from Yugoslavia, and had come with Equipment Vital) on the coffee tile, sat down and took four pieces of toast.

"Actually you don't." Ling passed the egg platter to Hodges. "If you think of it as a method of information storage, you'll understand. You take the ordinary hologram plate, cut it in half, and then shine a laser-beam on it, and you get the complete, three-dimensional image hanging there, full-size. Only it's slightly out of focus, blurry, a little less distinct." He folded a sliver of ham with blackened edges and skewered it to some toast. "And if you cut it again, the image just goes a bit more out of focus. Try and imagine a photograph and a hologram of the same object side by side. Every dot of light-sensitive emulsion on each is a bit of information about the object. But the information dots on the photographic plate only relate to one point of a two-dimensional reduction. The information dots on the hologram plate relate to the entire, solid, three-dimensional object. So you see, it's vastly more efficient and far more complete. Theoretically, even a square millimeter cut from a hologram will have something to tell you about the whole object."

"Does that 'theoretical' *mean* something," Mak asked, between burblings of his briar, "or is it just rhetoric?"

"Well," Ling said, "there is a point of diminishing returns. From what I've said, it would seem that most information storage is essentially photographic; writing, tape, punch cards—"

"But those are all linear," Dr. Jones objected.

"Photographic in that there's a one-to-one relation between each datum and each unintegrated fact—"

"Think of a photograph as composed of the lines of a television picture," Jimmi said, hastily swallowing eggs and toast. "A photograph can be reduced to linear terms too."

"That's right," Ling said.

"Diminishing returns . . ." Hodges prompted.

"Oh, yes. It's simply this: if you only have a relatively small number of addresses—cybernetics term for the places your data are going to go—" he explained to Jimmi's puzzled look, "then you're often better off with photographic or linear storage. That's because you need so many bits of hologramic information before the image starts to clear enough to be—"

"—anything but a menacing shadow, a ghost, a specter of itself, a vague outline filled with the unknown and too insubstantial to contain it."

Everyone looked at Hodges.

"What *are* you talking about, Evelyn?"

"Rimkin." She gestured with her brandy glass to keep Mak from filling it to the brim. "Poor, crazy Rimky."

"Oh, he isn't crazy," Jones insisted. "He may be having a nervous breakdown on us, which is too bad. But he's a brilliant, brilliant man. He *did* end up beating me at go last night. Sometimes I'm just afraid these sorts of situations are merely occupational hazards."

"True, Jonesy." She smiled ruefully and sipped. "And that's all I meant by crazy."

"You brought this whole business up in the first place, about the broken holograms," Ling said. "Why, Evelyn?"

The inflamed light of the morning desert jeweled the glass in her puffy fingers. "Do you remember the head that had fallen from the frieze? It was cracked so that one of the eyes had broken in half. When I found him this morning, he'd been out all night with his laser-beam looking at the images in the broken eye." She put her glass on the table.

After a while, Dr. Smith asked, "Did you take a look?"

Evelyn Hodges nodded.

"Well?" Mak asked.

"Just what you said, Ling. The images were whole. But they were slightly blurred, out of focus. I think there was something off with the timing too. That's all."

Mak leaned forward, made disgusted sounds, and began to batter his ashes over the detritus of crusts and butter on his plate. "Let's go out and finish up those measurements." He poked the stem in his pocket. The periscope dropped. "If he was up all night, that shot should keep him asleep till this evening."

V

It didn't.

Rimkin woke fighting the drug after they had been gone twenty minutes.

And he still didn't know where he was. Not where he should be, certainly. Because his head hurt; it felt as though the side had been broken away. His whole body was sore. He lurched from the bed and tried to focus on the table—but every object on it had a halo, like the superimpositions from special-effect sequences in old color films.

Jimmi was sitting on the bottom step, reading. She had chosen (a little unwillingly) to stay with the patient.

Crash!

She looked up.

Richard Nielson was trundling down the steps toward her. And at the top, stood naked Rimkin. Jimmi leapt away as the bust struck the reader she had dropped on the steps.

"Rimky, are you . . . ?"

He came down the steps, three of them slowly, seven of them fast, the last two slowly. Then, while she was debating whether to try and restrain him physically, he was gone through the double doors to the lockers. She ran toward them—the two brass handles swung up and clicked. She crashed against them. But behind the veneer that looked like walnut was ribbed steel.

Inside the locker Rimkin fumbled the catches of his air suit and thought: Hot. Hot outside. Twice he dropped the contraption on the grilled floor. Boiled . . . boiled *something*. An Earthman would boil out there on the desert without a suit. But why was he worrying? He wasn't sure who or what he might be. But the streets with their shaggy pennants, and their elegant citizens walking their shambling beasts with blood-colored eyes; they were waiting for him there in the hot city, the dusty city, with high, Marsite facades from which the carven heads gazed down on dry gutters.

He didn't need a suit, of course. But the lock-release switch was inside the suit, and it wouldn't work unless the suit was sealed. He picked up the white, slippery material again. Sealing the suit was almost habit; and the habits must have been working, because the skimmer door was opening now. Through his faceplate he could almost see the great city of High Weir stretching away to the temple. But slightly out of focus, indistinct . . . How was he supposed to know which were the shapes of time-cast dust and which were the intelligent creations of the amazing culture of his people, his planet? He brushed his arm around his faceplate—but that didn't do any good.

He walked down the blazing, alien street.

And the street sucked his boots.

He was going to take off his air suit soon. Yes. Because there was no need for it in such a brilliant city. But wait just a few minutes, because things were still too unfocused, too amorphous. And sand, from when he'd brushed his arm across his faceplate, kept trickling down the plastic. Nor were the figures in front of him Martians. He didn't think they were Martians. They were white and bulbous and were busy about the shards of purple stone, doing things to the slim columns that rose to prick the Martian noon.

"Who are you?" he said.

Two of them turned around.

"Rimkin . . . !"

"I don't know who you are," he told them.

"Hey, what's he doing out here?"

"I'm a Martian," Rimkin told them. "You're nothing but . . . that's right, potatoes!" He tried to laugh, but it came out crying because his head hurt very badly, and he was dopey from whatever they had given him that morning.

"We've got to get him back to the skimmer! Come on, Rimky."

"I'm going to take off my air suit," he said. "Because I'm a Martian and you—"

But then they were all around him. And they kept holding his hands down, which was easy because he was weak from the drug. And the carved heads, the gleaming eyes, melted behind his tears.

"Rimkin! Rimkin! Are you out there? Evelyn, Mak, Rimkin's out there someplace!"

"We've got him, Jimmi! It's all right. We're bringing him back to the skimmer."

"Who are you? I can't tell who you are!"

"Oh, Rimky, are you all right?"

"I'm a Martian. I can take off my space suit—"

"No, you don't, fellow. Keep your hands down."

"I think you're all crazy, you know? I'm a Martian, but you're all talking to somebody who isn't even here!"

"Rimkin, go on back with them and don't give them any trouble. For me, for Jimmi. They just want to help."

"I don't even know you. Why do I have to come back? This is my city. These are my buildings, my house. It's just not clear anymore. And it hurts."

"Keep your hands down. Come on—"

"Jimmi, are you all right? How did he get out? He didn't hurt you, did he?"

"I guess the sedative wasn't strong enough. He surprised me, and managed to lock me in the study. I just found Evelyn's emergency keys in her room a minute ago so I could get down to the controls and radio you. What are we going to do with him?"

"I'm going to go to Mars. I can take off my space suit. I'm a Martian. I'm a Martian—"

"He doesn't seem to be dangerous. They'll get him back to Earth, fill him full of calming drugs, and in six months he'll probably be good as new. I wouldn't be surprised to find out he goes into this sort of thing periodically. I spent a couple of weeks in a hospital drying out once."

"Why can't I take off my suit? I'm a Martian—"

"Rimky, remember all those enzyme reactions you were going on at us about this morning when you didn't want to take your shot? You open your suit, and the temperature out here will work so much havoc with them you won't have time to blink. You'll also fry."

"But which ones? How can I tell which ones will . . ."

"Evelyn, I can't hit him over the head. I'll crack his helmet."

"I know, I know, Mak. We'll get him back. Oh, this is so terrible! What causes something like this to happen to a perfectly fine—more than fine mind, Ling?"

"Don't hit me over the head. Don't . . . I'm a Martian. And it hurts."

"We won't hurt you, Rimky."

"Evelyn, we're out here exploring the ruins of new civilizations on other planets and we still don't know. We know much of it's chemical, and we can do something about a lot of it, but we still don't . . . Holograms, Evelyn . . ."

"What, Ling?"

"Nobody's ever been able to figure out how the brain stores information. We know the mind remembers everything it sees, hears, feels, smells, as well as all sorts of cross-referencing. People have just always assumed that it must be basically a photographic process, all the separate bits of data stored in the juncture of each individual synapse. But suppose, Evelyn, the brain stores hologramically. Then madness would be some emotional or chemical situation that blocked off access to large parts of the cerebral hologram."

"Then large parts of the world would just lose their sharpness, their focus . . ."

"Like Rimkin here?"

"Now *keep* your hands *away* from your suit catch!"

"Come on, Rimkin. Once we get you home, you'll be all right."

"It won't hurt anymore?"

"That's right. Try to relax."

As they reached the lock, Rimkin turned to one of the white, inflated figures and his voice grew tearful. "Aren't I . . . aren't I really a Martian?"

Two white hands patted the shoulders of his air suit. "You're George Arthur Rimkin, Associate Professor of Semantics at Inter-

Nal University, a very brilliant man who has been under a lot of pressure recently."

Rimkin looked out over beautiful rifts and dells, shapes that could have been sand dunes, that could have been the amazing structures of the great Martian city of High Weir, that could have been . . . He was crying again. "It hurts so much," he said quietly, "how am I supposed to tell?"

—*New York*
May 1968

time considered as a helix of semi-precious stones

Lay ordinate and abscissa on the century. Now cut me a quadrant. Third quadrant if you please. I was born in 'fifty. Here it's 'seventy-five.

At sixteen they let me leave the orphanage. Dragging the name they'd hung me with (Harold Clancy Everet, and me a mere lad—how many monickers have I had since; but don't worry, you'll recognize my smoke) over the hills of East Vermont, I came to a decision:

Me and Pa Michaels, who had belligerently given me a job at the request of *The Official* looking *Document* with which the orphanage sends you packing, were running Pa Michaels' dairy farm, i.e., thirteen thousand three hundred sixty-two piebald Guernseys all asleep in their stainless coffins, nourished and drugged by pink liquid flowing in clear plastic veins (stuff is sticky and messes up your hands), exercised with electric pulsers that make their muscles quiver, them not half-awake, and the milk just a-pouring down into stainless cisterns. Anyway. The Decision (as I stood there in the fields one afternoon like the Man with the Hoe, exhausted with three hard hours of physical labor, contemplating the machinery of the universe through the fog of fatigue): With all of Earth, and Mars, and the Outer Satellites filled up with people and what-all, there had to be something more than this. I decided to get some.

So I stole a couple of Pa's credit cards, one of his helicopters, and a bottle of white lightning the geezer made himself, and took off. Ever try to land a stolen helicopter on the roof of the Pan Am building, drunk? Jail, schmail, and some hard knocks later I had attained to wisdom. But remember this o best beloved: I have done three honest hours on a dairy farm less then ten years back. And nobody but nobody has ever called me Harold Clancy Everet again.

Hank Culafroy Eckles (redheaded, a bit vague, six-foot-two) strolled out of the baggage room at the spaceport, carrying a lot of things that weren't his in a small briefcase.

Beside him the Business Man was saying, "You young fellows today upset me. Go back to Bellona, I say. Just because you got into trouble with that little blonde you were telling me about is no reason to leap worlds, come on all glum. Even quit your job!"

Hank stops and grins weakly: "Well . . ."

"Now I admit, you have your real needs, which maybe we older folks don't understand, but you have to show some responsibility toward . . ." He notices Hank has stopped in front of a door marked MEN. "Oh. Well. Eh." He grins strongly. "I've enjoyed meeting you, Hank. It's always nice when you meet somebody worth talking to on these damned crossings. So long."

Out same door, ten minutes later, comes Harmony C. Eventide, six-foot even (one of the false heels was cracked, so I stuck both of them under a lot of paper towels), brown hair (not even my hairdresser knows for sure), oh so dapper and of his time, attired in the bad taste that is oh so tasteful, a sort of man with whom no Business Men would start a conversation. Took the regulation 'copter from the port over to the Pan Am building (Yeah. Really. Drunk), came out of Grand Central Station, and strode along Forty-Second toward Eighth Avenue, with a lot of things that weren't mine in a small briefcase.

The evening is carved from light.

Crossed the plastiplex pavements of the Great White Way—I think it makes people look weird, all that white light under their chins—and skirted the crowds coming up in elevators from the subway, the sub-subway, and the sub-sub-sub (eighteen and first week out of jail, I hung around here, snatching stuff from people—but daintily, daintily, so they never knew they'd been snatched), bulled my way through a crowd of giggling, goo-chewing schoolgirls with flashing lights in their hair, all very embarrassed at wearing transparent plastic blouses which had just been made legal again (I hear the breast has been scene [as opposed to obscene] on and off since the seventeenth century) so I stared appreciatively; they giggled some more. I thought, Christ, when I was that age, I was on a goddamn dairy farm, and took the thought no further.

The ribbon of news lights looping the triangular structure of Communication, Inc., explained in Basic English how Senator Regina Abolafia was preparing to begin her investigation of Organized Crime in the City. Days I'm so happy I'm disorganized I couldn't begin to tell.

Near Ninth Avenue I took my briefcase into a long, crowded bar. I hadn't been in New York for two years, but on my last trip through ofttimes a man used to hang out here who had real talent for getting rid of things that weren't mine profitably, safely, fast. No idea what the chances were I'd find him. I pushed among a lot of guys drinking beer. Here and there were a number of well-escorted old bags wearing last month's latest. Scarfs of smoke gentled through the noise. I don't like such places. Those there younger than me were all morphadine heads or feebleminded. Those older only wished more younger ones would come. I pried my way to the bar and tried to get the attention of one of the little men in white coats.

The lack of noise behind me made me glance back.

She wore a sheath of veiling closed at the neck and wrists with huge brass pins (oh so tastefully on the border of taste); her left arm was bare, her right covered with chiffon like wine. She had it down a lot better than I did. But such an ostentatious demonstration of one's understanding of the finer points was absolutely out of place in a place like this. People were making a great show of not noticing.

She pointed to her wrist, blood-colored nail indexing a yellow-orange fragment in the brass claw of her wristlet. "Do you know what this is, Mr. Eldrich?" she asked; at the same time the veil across her face cleared, and her eyes were ice; her brows, black.

Three thoughts: (One) She is a lady of fashion, because coming in from Bellona I'd read the Delta coverage of the "fading fabrics" whose hue and opacity were controlled by cunning jewels at the wrist. (Two) During my last trip through, when I was younger and Harry Calamine Eldrich, I didn't do anything *too* illegal (though one loses track of these things); still I didn't believe I could be dragged off to the calaboose for anything more than thirty days under that name. (Three) The stone she pointed to . . .

". . . Jasper?" I asked.

She waited for me to say more; I waited for her to give me reason to let on I knew what she was waiting for. (When I was in jail, Henry James was my favorite author. He really was.)

"Jasper," she confirmed.

"—Jasper . . ." I reopened the ambiguity she had tried so hard to dispel.

". . . Jasper—" But she was already faltering, suspecting I suspected her certainty to be ill-founded.

"Okay, Jasper." But from her face I knew she had seen in my face a look that had finally revealed I knew she knew I knew.

"Just whom have you got me confused with, ma'am?"

Jasper, this month, is the Word.

Jasper is the pass/code/warning that the Singers of the Cities (who last month sang "Opal" from their divine injuries; and on Mars I'd heard the Word and used it thrice, along with devious imitations, to fix possession of what was not rightfully my own; and even there I pondered Singers and their wounds) relay by word of mouth for that loose and roguish fraternity with which I have been involved (in various guises) these nine years. It goes out new every thirty days; and within hours every brother knows it, throughout six worlds and worldlets. Usually it's grunted at you by some blood-soaked bastard staggering into your arms from a dark doorway; hissed at you as you pass a shadowed alley; scrawled on a paper scrap pressed into your palm by some nasty-grimy moving too fast through the crowd. And this month, it was: Jasper.

Here are some alternate translations:

Help!

or

I need help!

or

I can help you!

or

You are being watched!

or

They're not watching now, so *move*!

Final point of syntax: If the Word is used properly, you should never have to think twice about what it means in a given situation. Fine point of usage: Never trust anyone who uses it improperly.

I waited for her to finish waiting.

She opened a wallet in front of me. "Chief of Special Services Department Maudline Hinkle," she read without looking at what it said below the silver badge.

"You have that very well," I said, "Maud." Then I frowned. "Hinkle?"

"Me."

"I know you're not going to believe this, Maud. You look like a woman who has no patience with her mistakes. But my name is Eventide. Not Eldrich. Harmony C. Eventide. And isn't it lucky for all and sundry that the Word changes tonight?" Passed the way it is, the Word is no big secret to the cops. But I've met policemen up to a week after change date who were not privy.

"Well, then: Harmony. I want to talk to you."

I raised an eyebrow.

She raised one back and said, "Look, if you want to be called Henrietta, it's all right by me. But you listen."

"What do you want to talk about?"

"Crime, Mr. . . . ?"

"Eventide. I'm going to call you Maud, so you might as well call me Harmony. It really *is* my name."

Maud smiled. She wasn't a young woman. I think she even had a few years on Business Man. But she used makeup better than he did. "I probably know more about crime than you do," she said. "In fact I wouldn't be surprised if you hadn't even heard of my branch of the police department. What does Special Services mean to you?"

"That's right, I've never heard of it."

"You've been more or less avoiding the Regular Service with alacrity for the past seven years."

"Oh, Maud, really—"

"Special Services is reserved for people whose nuisance value has suddenly taken a sharp rise . . . a sharp enough rise to make our little lights start blinking."

"Surely I haven't done anything so dreadful that—"

"We don't look at what you do. A computer does that for us. We simply keep checking the first derivative of the graphed-out curve that bears your number. Your slope is rising sharply."

"Not even the dignity of a name—"

"We're the most efficient department in the Police Organization. Take it as bragging if you wish. Or just a piece of information."

"Well, well, well," I said. "Have a drink?" The little man in the white coat left us two, looked puzzled at Maud's finery, then went to do something else.

"Thanks." She downed half her glass like someone stauncher than that wrist would indicate. "It doesn't pay to go after most criminals. Take your big-time racketeers, Farnesworth, the Hawk, Blavatskia. Take your little snatch-purses, small-time pushers, housebreakers, or vice-impresarios. Both at the top and the bottom of the scale, their incomes are pretty stable. They don't really upset the social boat. Regular Services handles them both. They think they do a good job. We're not going to argue. But say a little pusher starts to become a big-time pusher; a medium-sized vice-impresario sets his sights on becoming a full-fledged racketeer; that's when you get problems with socially unpleasant repercussions. That's when Special Services arrive. We have a couple of techniques that work remarkably well."

"You're going to tell me about them, aren't you?"

"They work better that way," she said. "One of them is holo-gramic information storage. Do you know what happens when you cut a hologram plate in half?"

"The three-dimensional image is . . . cut in half?"

She shook her head. "You get the whole image, only fuzzier, slightly out of focus."

"Now I didn't know that."

"And if you cut it in half again, it just gets fuzzier still. But even if you have a square centimeter of the original hologram, you still have the whole image—unrecognizable but complete."

I mumbled some appreciative *m*'s.

"Each pinpoint of photographic emulsion on a hologram plate, unlike a photograph, gives information about the entire scene being hologrammed. By analogy, hologramic information storage simply means that each bit of information we have—about you, let us say—relates to your entire career, your overall situation, the com-plete set of tensions between you and your environment. Specific facts about specific misdemeanors or felonies we leave to Regular Services. As soon as we have enough of our kind of data, our method is vastly more efficient for keeping track—even predict-ing—where you are or what you may be up to."

"Fascinating," I said. "One of the most amazing paranoid syn-dromes I've ever run up against. I mean just starting a conversation with someone in a bar. Often, in a hospital situation, I've encoun-tered stranger—"

"In your past," she said matter-of-factly, "I see cows and heli-copters. In your not too distant future, there are helicopters and hawks."

"And tell me, oh Good Witch of the West, just how—" Then I got all upset inside. Because nobody is supposed to know about that stint with Pa Michaels save thee and me. Even the Regular Ser-vice, who pulled me, out of my head, from that whirlybird bounc-ing toward the edge of the Pan Am, never got that one from me. I'd eaten the credit cards when I saw them waiting, and the serial num-bers had been filed off everything that could have had a serial num-ber on it by someone more competent than I: good Mister Michaels had boasted to me, my first lonely, drunken night at the farm, how he'd gotten the thing in hot from New Hampshire.

"But why—" it appalls me the clichés to which anxiety will drive us—"are you telling me all this?"

She smiled, and her smile faded behind her veil. "Information is only meaningful when shared," said a voice that was hers from the place of her face.

"Hey, look, I—"

"You may be coming into quite a bit of money soon. If I can calculate right, I will have a helicopter full of the city's finest arriving to take you away as you accept it into your hot little hands. That is a piece of information . . ." She stepped back. Someone stepped between us.

"Hey, Maud—"

"You can do whatever you want with it."

The bar was crowded enough so that to move quickly was to make enemies. I don't know—I lost her and made enemies. Some weird characters there: with greasy hair that hung in spikes, and three of them had dragons tattooed on their scrawny shoulders, still another with an eye patch, and yet another raked nails black with pitch at my cheek (we're two minutes into a vicious free-for-all, case you missed the transition. I did) and some of the women were screaming. I hit and ducked, and then the tenor of the brouhaha changed. Somebody sang "Jasper!" the way she is supposed to be sung. And it meant the heat (the ordinary, bungling Regular Service I had been eluding these seven years) were on their way. The brawl spilled into the street. I got between two nasty-grimies who were doing things appropriate with one another, but made the edge of the crowd with no more wounds than could be racked up to shaving. The fight had broken into sections. I left one and ran into another that, I realized a moment later, was merely a ring of people standing around somebody who had apparently gotten really messed.

Someone was holding people back.

Somebody else was turning him over.

Curled up in a puddle of blood was the little guy I hadn't seen in two years who used to be so good at getting rid of things not mine.

Trying not to hit people with my briefcase, I ducked between the hub and the bub. When I saw my first ordinary policeman, I tried very hard to look like somebody who had just stepped up to see what the rumpus was.

It worked.

I turned down Ninth Avenue and got three steps into an inconspicuous but rapid lope—

"Hey, wait! Wait up there . . ."

I recognized the voice (after two years, coming at me just like that, I recognized it) but kept going.

"Wait. It's me, Hawk!"

And I stopped.

You haven't heard his name before in this story; Maud mentioned *the* Hawk, who is a multimillionaire racketeer basing his operations on a part of Mars I've never been to (though he has his claws sunk to the spurs in illegalities throughout the system) and somebody else entirely.

I took three steps back toward the doorway.

A boy's laugh there: "Oh, man. You look like you just did something you shouldn't."

"Hawk?" I asked the shadow.

He was still the age when two years' absence means an inch or so taller.

"You're still hanging around here?" I asked.

"Sometimes."

He was an amazing kid.

"Look, Hawk, I got to get out of here." I glanced back at the rumpus.

"Get." He stepped down. "Can I come, too?"

Funny. "Yeah." It makes me feel very funny, him asking that. "Come on."

By the streetlamp half a block down, I saw his hair was still pale as split pine. He could have been a nasty-grimy: very dirty black denim jacket, no shirt beneath; very ripe pair of black jeans—

I mean in the dark you could tell. He went barefoot; and the only way you can tell on a dark street someone's been going barefoot for days in New York is to know already. As we reached the corner, he grinned up at me under the streetlamp and shrugged his jacket together over the welts and furrows marring his chest and belly. His eyes were very green. Do you recognize him? If by some failure of information dispersal throughout the worlds and worldlets you haven't, walking beside me beside the Hudson was Hawk the Singer.

"Hey, how long have you been back?"

"A few hours," I told him.

"What'd you bring?"

"Really want to know?"

He shoved his hands into his pockets and cocked his head. "Sure."

I made the sound of an adult exasperated by a child. "All right." We had been walking the waterfront for a block now; there was nobody about. "Sit down." So he straddled the beam along the siding, one filthy foot dangling above the flashing black Hudson. I sat in front of him and ran my thumb around the edge of the briefcase.

Hawk hunched his shoulders and leaned. "Hey . . ." He flashed green questioning at me. "Can I touch?"

I shrugged. "Go ahead."

He grubbed among them with fingers that were all knuckle and bitten nail. He picked two up, put them down, picked up three others. "Hey!" he whispered. "How much are all these worth?"

"About ten times more than I hope to get. I have to get rid of them fast."

He glanced down past his toes. "You could always throw them in the river."

"Don't be dense. I was looking for a guy who used to hang around that bar. He was pretty efficient." And half the Hudson away a water-bound foil skimmed above the foam. On her deck were parked a dozen helicopters—being ferried up to the Patrol Field near Verazzano, no doubt. For moments I looked back and forth between the boy and the transport, getting all paranoid about Maud. But the boat *mmmm*ed into the darkness. "My man got a little cut up this evening."

Hawk put the tips of his fingers in his pockets and shifted his position.

"Which leaves me uptight. I didn't think he'd take them all, but at least he could have turned me on to some other people who might."

"I'm going to a party later on this evening—" he paused to gnaw on the wreck of his little fingernail—"where you might be able to sell them. Alexis Spinnel is having a party for Regina Abolafia at Tower Top."

"Tower Top . . . ?" It had been a while since I palled around with Hawk. Hell's Kitchen at ten; Tower Top at midnight—

"I'm just going because Edna Silem will be there."

Edna Silem is New York's eldest Singer.

Senator Abolafia's name had ribboned above me in lights once that evening. And somewhere among the endless magazines I'd perused coming in from Mars, I remembered Alexis Spinnel's name sharing a paragraph with an awful lot of money.

"I'd like to see Edna again," I said offhandedly. "But she wouldn't remember me." Folk like Spinnel and his social ilk have a little game, I'd discovered during the first leg of my acquaintance with Hawk. He who can get the most Singers of the City under one roof wins. There are five Singers of New York (a tie for second place with Lux on Iapetus). Tokyo leads with seven. "It's a two-Singer party?"

"More likely four . . . if I go."

The inaugural ball for the mayor gets four.

I raised the appropriate eyebrow.

"I have to pick up the Word from Edna. It changes tonight."

"All right," I said. "I don't know what you have in mind, but I'm game." I closed the case.

We walked back toward Times Square. When we got to Eighth Avenue and the first of the plastiplex, Hawk stopped. "Wait a minute," he said. Then he buttoned his jacket up to his neck. "Okay."

Strolling through the streets of New York with a Singer (two years back I'd spent much time wondering if that was wise for a man of my profession) is probably the best camouflage possible for a man of my profession. Think of the last time you glimpsed your favorite Tri-D star turning the corner of Fifty-seventh. Now be honest. Would you really recognize the little guy in the tweed jacket half a pace behind him?

Half the people we passed in Times Square recognized him. With his youth, funereal garb, black feet and ash-pale hair, he was easily the most colorful of Singers. Smiles; narrowed eyes; very few actually pointed or stared.

"Just exactly who is going to be there who might be able to take this stuff off my hands?"

"Well, Alexis prides himself on being something of an adventurer. They might just take his fancy. And he can give you more than you can get peddling them in the street."

"You'll tell him they're all hot?"

"It will probably make the idea that much more intriguing. He's a creep."

"You say so, friend."

We went down into the sub-sub. The man at the change booth started to take Hawk's coin, then looked up. He began three or four words that were unintelligible inside his grin, then just gestured us through.

"Oh," Hawk said, "thank you," with ingenuous surprise, as though this were the first, delightful time such a thing had happened. (Two years ago he had told me sagely, "As soon as I start looking like I expect it, it'll stop happening." I was still impressed by the way he wore his notoriety. The time I'd met Edna Silem, and I'd mentioned this, she said with the same ingenuousness, "But that's what we're chosen for.")

In the bright car we sat on the long seat. Hawk's hands were beside him; one foot rested on the other. Down from us a gaggle of bright-bloused goo-chewers giggled and pointed and tried not to be noticed at it. Hawk didn't look at all, and I tried not to be noticed looking.

Dark patterns rushed the window.

Things below the gray floor hummed.

Once a lurch.

Leaning once, we came out of the ground.

Outside, the city tried on its thousand sequins, then threw them away behind the trees of Ft. Tryon. Suddenly the windows across from us grew bright scales. Behind them girders reeled by. We got out on the platform under a light rain. The sign said TWELVE TOW-ERS STATION.

By the time we reached the street, however, the shower had stopped. Leaves above the wall shed water down the brick. "If I'd known I was bringing someone, I'd have had Alex send a car for us. I told him it was fifty-fifty I'd come."

"Are you sure it's all right for me to tag along then?"

"Didn't you come up here with me once before?"

"I've even been up here once before that," I said. "Do you still think it's . . ."

He gave me a withering look. Well; Spinnel would be delighted to have Hawk even if he dragged along a whole gang of real nasty-grimies—Singers are famous for that sort of thing. With one more or less presentable thief, Spinnel was getting off light. Beside us rocks broke away into the city. Behind the gate to our left the gardens rolled up toward the first of the towers. The twelve immense luxury apartment buildings menaced the lower clouds.

"Hawk the Singer," Hawk the Singer said into the speaker at the side of the gate. *Clang* and tic-tic-tic and *Clang*. We walked up to the path to the doors and doors of glass.

A cluster of men and women in evening dress were coming out. Three tiers of doors away they saw us. You could see them frowning at the guttersnipe who'd somehow gotten into the lobby (for a moment I thought one of them was Maud because she wore a sheath of the fading fabric, but she turned; beneath her veil her face was dark as roasted coffee); one of the men recognized him, said something to the others. When they passed us, they were smiling. Hawk paid about as much attention to them as he had to the girls on the subway. But when they'd passed, he said, "One of those guys was looking at you."

"Yeah. I saw."

"Do you know why?"

"He was trying to figure out whether we'd met before."

"Had you?"

I nodded. "Right about where I met you, only back when I'd just gotten out of jail. I told you I'd been here once before."

"Oh."

Blue carpet covered three-quarters of the lobby. A great pool filled the rest in which a row of twelve-foot trellises stood, crowned with flaming braziers. The lobby itself was three stories high, domed and mirror-tiled.

Twisting smoke curled toward the ornate grill. Broken reflections sagged and recovered on the walls.

The elevator door folded about us its foil petals. There was the distinct feeling of not moving while seventy-five stories shucked down around us.

We got out on the landscaped roof garden. A very tanned, very blond man wearing an apricot jumpsuit, from the collar of which emerged a black turtleneck dicky, came down the rocks (artificial) between the ferns (real) growing along the stream (real water; phony current).

"Hello! Hello!" Pause. "I'm terribly glad you decided to come after all." Pause. "For a while I thought you weren't going to make it." The Pauses were to allow Hawk to introduce me. I was dressed so that Spinnel had no way of telling whether I was a miscellaneous Nobel laureate that Hawk happened to have been dining with, or a varlet whose manners and morals were even lower than mine happen to be.

"Shall I take your jacket?" Alexis offered.

Which meant he didn't know Hawk as well as he would like people to think. But I guess he was sensitive enough to realize from the little cold things that happened in the boy's face that he should forget his offer.

He nodded to me, smiling—about all he could do—and we strolled toward the gathering.

Edna Silem was sitting on a transparent inflated hassock. She leaned forward, holding her drink in both hands, arguing politics with the people sitting on the grass before her. She was the first person I recognized (hair of tarnished silver; voice of scrap brass). Jutting from the cuffs of her mannish suit, her wrinkled hands about her goblet, shaking with the intensity of her pronouncements, were heavy with stones and silver. As I ran my eyes back to Hawk, I saw half a dozen whose names/faces sold magazines, music, sent people to the theater (the drama critic for *Delta*, wouldn't you know), and even the mathematician from Princeton I'd read about a few months ago who'd come up with the "quasar/quark" explanation.

There was one woman my eyes kept returning to. On glance three I recognized her as the New Fascistas' most promising candidate for president, Senator Abolafia. Her arms were folded, and she was listening intently to the discussion that had narrowed to Edna and an overly gregarious younger man whose eyes were puffy from what could have been the recent acquisition of contact lenses.

"But don't you feel, Mrs. Silem, that—"

"You must remember when you make predictions like that—"

"Mrs. Silem, I've seen statistics that—"

"You *must* remember—" her voice tensed, lowered till the silence between the words was as rich as the voice was sparse and metallic—"that if everything, *everything* were known, statistical estimates would be unnecessary. The science of probability gives mathematical expression to our ignorance, not to our wisdom," which I was thinking was an interesting second installment to Maud's lecture, when Edna looked up and exclaimed, "Why, Hawk!"

Everyone turned.

"I *am* glad to see you. Lewis, Ann," she called: there were two other Singers there already (he dark, she pale, both tree-slender; their faces made you think of pools without drain or tribute come upon in the forest, clear and very still; husband and wife, they had been made Singers together the day before their marriage six years ago), "he hasn't deserted us after all!" Edna stood, extended her arm over the heads of the people sitting, and barked across her knuckles as though her voice were a pool cue. "Hawk, there are people here arguing with me who don't know nearly as much as you about the subject. You'd be on my side, now wouldn't you—"

"Mrs. Silem, I didn't mean to—" from the floor.

Then her arms swung six degrees, her fingers, eyes, and mouth opened. "You!" Me. "My dear, if there's anyone I never expected to see here! Why it's been almost two years, hasn't it?" Bless Edna; the place where she and Hawk and I had spent a long, beery evening together had more resembled that bar than Tower Top. "Where have you been keeping yourself?"

"Mars, mostly," I admitted. "Actually I just came back today." It's so much fun to be able to say things like that in a place like this.

"Hawk—both of you—" (which meant either she had forgotten my name, or she remembered me well enough not to abuse it—) "come over here and help me drink up Alexis' good liquor." I tried not to grin as we walked toward her. If she remembered anything, she certainly recalled my line of business and must have been enjoying this as much as I was.

Relief spread Alexis' face: he knew now I was *someone* if not *which* someone I was.

As we passed Lewis and Ann, Hawk gave the two Singers one of his luminous grins. They returned shadowed smiles. Lewis nodded. Ann made a move to touch his arm, but left the motion unconcluded; and the company noted the interchange.

Having found out what we wanted, Alex was preparing large glasses of it over crushed ice when the puffy-eyed gentleman stepped up for a refill. "But, Mrs. Silem, then what do you feel validly opposes such political abuses?"

Regina Abolafia wore a white silk suit. Nails, lips, and hair were one copper color; and on her breast was a worked copper pin. It's always fascinated me to watch people used to being the center thrust to the side. She swirled her glass, listening.

"I oppose them," Edna said. "Hawk opposes them. Lewis and Ann oppose them. We, ultimately, are what you have." And her voice had taken on that authoritative resonance only Singers can assume.

Then Hawk's laugh snarled through the conversational fabric. We turned.

He'd sat cross-legged near the hedge. "Look . . ." he whispered.

Now people's gazes followed his. He was looking at Lewis and Ann. She, tall and blond, he, dark and taller, were standing very quietly, a little nervously, eyes closed (Lewis' lips were apart).

"Oh," whispered someone who should have known better, "they're going to . . ."

I watched Hawk because I'd never had a chance to observe one Singer at another's performance. He put the soles of his feet together, grasped his toes, and leaned forward, veins making blue rivers on his neck. The top button of his jacket had come loose. Two scar ends showed over his collarbone. Maybe nobody noticed but me.

I saw Edna put her glass down with a look of beaming anticipatory pride. Alex, who had pressed the autobar (odd how automation has become the upper crust's way of flaunting the labor surplus) for more crushed ice, looked up, saw what was about to happen, and pushed the cutoff button. The autobar hummed to silence. A breeze (artificial or real, I couldn't tell you) came by, and the trees gave us a final *shush*.

One at a time, then in duet, then singly again, Lewis and Ann sang.

Singers are people who look at things, then go and tell people what they've seen. What makes them Singers is their ability to make people listen. That is the most magnificent oversimplification I can give. Eighty-six-year-old El Posado in Rio de Janeiro saw a block of tenements collapse, ran to the Avenida del Sol and began improvising, in rhyme and meter (not all that hard in rhyme-rich Portuguese), tears runneling his dusty cheeks, his voice clashing with the palm swards above the sunny street. Hundreds of people stopped to listen; a hundred more; and another hundred. And they told hundreds more what they had heard. Three hours later, hundreds from among them had arrived at the scene with blankets, food, money, shovels, and more incredibly, the willingness and ability to organize themselves and work within that organization. No Tri-D report of a disaster has ever produced that sort of reaction. El Posado is historically considered the first Singer. The second was Miriamne in the roofed city of Lux, who for thirty years walked through the metal streets, singing the glories of the rings of Saturn—the colonists can't look at them without aid because of the ultraviolet the rings set up. But Miriamne, with her strange cataracts, each dawn walked to the edge of the city, looked, saw, and came back to sing of what she saw. All of which would have meant nothing except that during the days she did not sing—through illness, or once she was on a visit to another city to which her fame had spread—the Lux Stock Exchange would go down, the number of violent crimes rise. Nobody could explain it. All they could do was proclaim her Singer. Why did the institution of Singers come about, springing up in just about every urban center throughout the system? Some have speculated that it was a spontaneous reaction to the mass media which blanket our lives. While Tri-D and radio and newstapes disperse information all over the worlds, they also spread a sense of alienation from first-hand experience. (How many people still go to sports events or a political rally with their little receivers plugged into their ears to let them know that what they see is really happening?) The first Singers were proclaimed by the people around them. Then, there was a period where anyone could proclaim himself a Singer who wanted to, and people either responded to him or laughed him into oblivion. But by the time I was left on the doorstep of somebody who didn't want me, most cities had more or less established an unofficial quota. When a position is left open today, the remaining Singers choose who is going to fill it. The required talents are poetic, theatrical, as well as a certain charisma that is generated in the tensions between the personality and the publicity web a Singer is immediately snared in. Before he became a Singer, Hawk had gained something of a prodigious reputation with a book of poems published when he was fifteen. He was touring universities and giving readings, but the reputation was still small enough so that he was amazed that I had ever heard of him, that evening we encountered in Central Park. (I had just spent a pleasant thirty days as a guest of the city, and it's amazing what you find in the Tombs Library.) It was a few weeks after his sixteenth birthday. His Singership was to be announced in four days, though he had been informed already. We sat by the lake till dawn while he weighed and pondered and agonized over the coming responsibility. Two years later, he's still the youngest Singer in six worlds by half a dozen years. Before becoming a Singer, a person need not have been a poet, but most are either that or actors. But the roster through the system includes a longshoreman, two university professors, an heiress to the Silitax millions (Tack it down with Silitax), and at least two persons of such dubious background that the ever-hungry-for-sensation Publicity Machine itself has agreed not to let any of it past the copy editors. But wherever their origins, these diverse and flamboyant living myths sang of love, of death, of the changing of seasons, social classes, governments, and the palace guard. They sang before large crowds, small crowds, to an individual laborer coming home from the city's docks, on slum street corners, in club cars of commuter trains, in the elegant gardens atop Twelve Towers, to Alex Spinnel's select soirée. But it has been illegal to reproduce the "Songs" of the Singers by mechanical means (including publishing the lyrics) since the institution arose, and I respect the law, I do, as only a man in my profession can. I offer the explanation then in place of Lewis' and Ann's song.

They finished, opened their eyes, stared about with expressions that could have been embarrassment, could have been contempt.

Hawk was leaning forward with a look of rapt approval. Edna was smiling politely. I had the sort of grin on my face that breaks out when you've been vastly moved and vastly pleased. Lewis and Ann had sung superbly.

Alex began to breathe again, glancing around to see what state everybody else was in, saw, and pressed the autobar, which began to hum and crush ice. No clapping, but the appreciative sounds began;

people were nodding, commenting, whispering. Regina Abolafia went over to Lewis to say something. I tried to listen until Alex shoved a glass into my elbow.

"Oh, I'm sorry . . ."

I transferred my briefcase to the other hand and took the drink, smiling. When Senator Abolafia left the two Singers, they were holding hands and looking at one another a little sheepishly. They sat down again.

The party drifted in conversational groups through the gardens, through the groves. Overhead clouds the color of old chamois folded and unfolded across the moon.

For a while I stood alone in a circle of trees, listening to the music: a de Lassus two-part canon programmed for audio-generators. Recalled: an article in one of last week's large-circulation literaries, stating that it was the only way to remove the feel of the bar lines imposed by five centuries of meter on modern musicians. For another two weeks this would be acceptable entertainment. The trees circled a rock pool; but no water. Below the plastic surface, abstract lights wove and threaded in a shifting lumia.

"Excuse me . . . ?"

I turned to see Alexis, who had no drink now or idea what to do with his hands. He *was* nervous.

". . . but our young friend has told me you have something I might be interested in."

I started to lift my briefcase, but Alexis' hand came down from his ear (it had gone by belt to hair to collar already) to halt me. Nouveau riche.

"That's all right. I don't need to see them yet. In fact, I'd rather not. I have something to propose to you. I would certainly be interested in what you have if they are, indeed, as Hawk has described them. But I have a guest here who would be even more curious."

That sounded odd.

"I know that sounds odd," Alexis assessed, "but I thought you might be interested simply because of the finances involved. I am an eccentric collector who would offer you a price concomitant with what I would use them for: eccentric conversation pieces—and because of the nature of the purchase I would have to limit severely the people with whom I could converse."

I nodded.

"My guest, however, would have a great deal more use for them."

"Could you tell me who this guest is?"

"I asked Hawk, finally, who you were, and he led me to believe I was on the verge of a grave social indiscretion. It would be equally indiscreet to reveal my guest's name to you." He smiled. "But indiscretion is the better part of the fuel that keeps the social machine turning. Mr. Harvey Cadwaliter-Erickson . . ." He smiled knowingly.

I have *never* been Harvey Cadwaliter-Erickson, but Hawk was always an inventive child. Then a second thought went by, viz., the tungsten magnates, the Cadwaliter-Ericksons of Tythis on Triton. Hawk was not only inventive, he was as brilliant as all the magazines and newspapers are always saying he is.

"I assume your second indiscretion will be to tell me who this mysterious guest is?"

"Well," Alex said with the smile of the canary-fattened cat, "Hawk agreed with me that *the* Hawk might well be curious as to what you have in there," (he pointed) "as indeed he is."

I frowned. Then I thought lots of small, rapid thoughts I'll articulate in due time. "*The* Hawk?"

Alex nodded.

I don't think I was actually scowling. "Would you send our young friend up here for a moment?"

"If you'd like." Alex bowed, turned. Perhaps a minute later, Hawk came up over the rocks and through the trees, grinning. When I didn't grin back, he stopped.

"*Mmmm* . . ." I began.

His head cocked.

I scratched my chin with a knuckle. ". . . Hawk," I said, "are you aware of a department of the police called Special Services?"

"I've heard of them."

"They've suddenly gotten very interested in me."

"Gee," he said with honest amazement. "They're supposed to be pretty effective."

"*Mmmm,*" I reiterated.

"Say," Hawk announced, "how do you like that? My namesake is here tonight. Wouldn't you know."

"Alex doesn't miss a trick. Have you any idea *why* he's here?"

"Probably trying to make some deal with Abolafia. Her investigation starts tomorrow."

"Oh." I thought over some of those things I had thought before. "Do you know a Maud Hinkle?"

Hawk's puzzled look said "no" pretty convincingly.

"She bills herself as one of the upper echelon in the arcane organization of which I spoke."

"Yeah?"

"She ended our interview earlier this evening with a little homily about hawks and helicopters. I took our subsequent encounter as a fillip of coincidence. But now I discover that the evening has confirmed her intimations of plurality." I shook my head. "Hawk, I am suddenly catapulted into a paranoid world where the walls not only have ears, but probably eyes and long, claw-tipped fingers. Anyone about me—yea, even very you—could turn out to be a spy. I suspect every sewer grating and second-story window conceals binoculars, a tommy gun, or worse. What I just can't figure out is how these insidious forces, ubiquitous and omnipresent though they be, induced you to lure me into this intricate and diabolical—"

"Oh, cut it out!" He shook back his hair. "I didn't lure—"

"Perhaps not consciously, but Special Services has Hologramic Information Storage, and their methods are insidious and cruel—"

"I said cut it out!" And all sorts of hard little things happened again. "Do you think I'd—" Then he realized how scared I was, I guess. "Look, the Hawk isn't some small-time snatch-purse. He lives in just as paranoid a world as you're in now, only all the time. If he's here, you can be sure there are just as many of his men—eyes and ears and fingers—as there are of Maud Hickenlooper's."

"Hinkle."

"Anyway, it works both ways. No Singer's going to—Look, do you really think *I* would—"

And even though I knew all those hard little things were scabs over pain, I said, "Yes."

"You did something for me once, and I—"

"I gave you some more welts. That's all."

All the scabs pulled off.

"Hawk," I said. "Let me see."

He took a breath. Then he began to open the brass buttons. The flaps of his jacket fell back. The lumia colored his chest with pastel shiftings.

I felt my face wrinkle. I didn't want to look away. I drew a hissing breath instead, which was just as bad.

He looked up. "There're a lot more than when you were here last, aren't there?"

"You're going to kill yourself, Hawk."

He shrugged.

"I can't even tell which are the ones I put there anymore."

He started to point them out.

"Oh, come on," I said too sharply. And for the length of three breaths, he grew more and more uncomfortable till I saw him start to reach for the bottom button. "Boy," I said, trying to keep despair out of my voice, "why do you do it?" and ended up keeping out everything. There is nothing more despairing than a voice empty.

He shrugged, saw I didn't want that, and for a moment anger flickered in his green eyes. I didn't want that either. So he said: "Look . . . you touch a person softly, gently, and maybe you even do it with love. And, well, I guess a piece of information goes on up to the brain where something interprets it as pleasure. Maybe something up there in my head interprets the information in a way you would say is all wrong. . . ."

I shook my head. "You're a Singer. Singers are supposed to be eccentric, sure; but—"

Now he was shaking his head. Then the anger opened up. And I saw an expression move from all those spots that had communicated pain through the rest of his features and vanish without ever becoming a word. Once more he looked down at the wounds that webbed his thin body.

"Button it up, boy. I'm sorry I said anything."

Halfway up the lapels, his hands stopped. "You really think I'd turn you in?"

"Button it up."

He did. Then he said, "Oh." And then, "You know, it's midnight."

"So?"

"Edna just gave me the new Word."

"Which is?"

"Agate."

I nodded.

Hawk finished closing his collar. "What are you thinking about?"

"Cows."

"Cows?" Hawk asked. "What about them?"

"You ever been on a dairy farm?"

He shook his head.

"To get the most milk, you keep the cows practically in suspended animation. They're fed intravenously from a big tank that pipes nutrients out and down, branching into smaller and smaller pipes until it gets to all those high-yield semi-corpses."

"I've seen pictures."

"People."

". . . . and cows?"

"You've given me the Word. And now it begins to funnel down, branching out, with me telling others and them telling still others, till by midnight tomorrow . . ."

"I'll go get the—"

"Hawk?"

He turned back. "What?"

"You say you don't think I'm going to be the victim of any hanky-panky with the mysterious forces that know more than we. Okay, that's your opinion. But as soon as I get rid of this stuff, I'm going to make the most distracting exit you've ever seen."

Two little lines bit down Hawk's forehead. "Are you sure I haven't seen this one before?"

"As a matter of fact I think you have." Now I grinned.

"Oh," Hawk said, then made a sound that had the structure of laughter but was all breath. "I'll get the Hawk."

He ducked out between the trees.

I glanced up at the lozenges of moonlight in the leaves.

I looked down at my briefcase.

Up between the rocks, stepping around the long grass, came the Hawk. He wore a gray evening suit over a gray silk turtleneck. Above his craggy face, his head was completely shaved.

"Mr. Cadwaliter-Erickson?" He held out his hand.

I shook: small sharp bones in loose skin. "Does one call you Mr. . . . ?"

"Arty."

"Arty the Hawk?" I tried to look like I wasn't giving his gray attire the once-over.

He smiled. "Arty the Hawk. Yeah. I picked that name up when I was younger than our friend down there. Alex says you got . . . well, some things that are not exactly yours. That don't belong to you."

I nodded.

"Show them to me."

"You were told what—"

He brushed away the end of my sentence. "Come on, let me see."

He extended his hand, smiling affably as a bank clerk. I ran my thumb around the pressure-zip. The cover went *tsk*. "Tell me," I said, looking up at his head, lowered now to see what I had, "what does one do about Special Services? They seem to be after me."

The head came up. Surprise changed slowly to a craggy leer. "Why, Mr. Cadwaliter-Erickson!" He gave me the up and down openly. "Keep your income steady. Keep it steady, that's one thing you can do."

"If you buy these for anything like what they're worth, that's going to be a little difficult."

"I would imagine. I could always give you less money—"

The cover went *tsk* again.

"—or, barring that, you could try to use your head and outwit them."

"You must have outwitted them at one time or another. You may be on an even keel now, but you had to get there from somewhere else."

Arty the Hawk's nod was downright sly. "I guess you've had a run-in with Maud. Well, I suppose congratulations are in order. And condolences. I always like to do what's in order."

"You seem to know how to take care of yourself. I mean I notice you're not out there mingling with the guests."

"There are two parties going on here tonight," Arty said. "Where do you think Alex disappears off to every five minutes?"

I frowned.

"That lumia down in the rocks—" he pointed toward my feet— "is a mandala of shifting hues on our ceiling. Alex—" he chuckled— "goes scuttling off under the rocks where there is a pavilion of Oriental splendor—"

"And a separate guest list at the door?"

"Regina is on both. I'm on both. So's the kid, Edna, Lewis, Ann—"

"Am I supposed to know all this?"

"Well, you came with a person on both lists. I just thought . . ." The Hawk paused.

I was coming on wrong. But a quick change artist learns fairly quick that the verisimilitude factor in imitating someone up the scale is your confidence in your unalienable right to come on wrong. "I'll tell you," I said. "How about exchanging these—" I held out the briefcase—"for some information."

"You want to know how to stay out of Maud's clutches?" He shook his head. "It would be pretty stupid of me to tell you, even if I could. Besides, you've got your family fortunes to fall back on." He beat the front of his shirt with his thumb. "Believe me, boy. Arty the Hawk didn't have that. I didn't have anything like that." His hands dropped into his pockets. "Let's see what you got."

I opened the case again.

The Hawk looked for a while. After a few moments he picked a couple up, turned them around, put them back down, put his hands back in his pockets. "I'll give you sixty thousand for them, approved credit tablets."

"What about the information I wanted?"

"I wouldn't tell you a thing." The Hawk smiled. "I wouldn't tell you the time of day."

There are very few successful thieves in this world. Still less on the other five. The will to steal is an impulse toward the absurd and tasteless. (The talents are poetic, theatrical, a certain reverse charisma . . .) But it is a will, as the will to order, power, love.

"All right," I said.

Somewhere overhead I heard a faint humming.

Arty looked at me fondly. He reached under the lapel of his jacket and took out a handful of credit tablets—the scarlet-banded tablets whose slips were ten thousand apiece. He pulled off one. Two. Three. Four.

"You can deposit this much safely—"

"Why do you think Maud is after me?"

Five. Six.

"Fine," I said.

"How about throwing in the briefcase?" Arty asked.

"Ask Alex for a paper bag. If you want, I can send them—"

"Give them here."

The humming was coming closer.

I held up the open case. Arty went in with both hands. He shoved them into his coat pockets, his pants pockets; the gray cloth was distended by angular bulges. He looked left, right. "Thanks," he said. "Thanks." Then he turned and hurried down the slope with all sorts of things in his pockets that weren't his now.

I looked up through the leaves for the noise, but I couldn't see anything.

I stooped down now and laid my case out. I pulled open the back compartment where I kept the things that did belong to me and rummaged hurriedly through.

———

Alex was just offering Puffy-eyes another Scotch, while the gentleman was saying, "Has anyone seen Mrs. Silem? What's that humming overhead—?" when a large woman wrapped in a veil of fading fabric tottered across the rocks, screaming.

Her hands were clawing at her covered face.

Alex sloshed soda over his sleeve, and the man said, "Oh, my God! Who's that?"

"No!" the woman shrieked. "Oh, no! Help me!" waving her wrinkled fingers, brilliant with rings.

"Don't you recognize her?" That was Hawk whispering confidentially to someone else. "It's Henrietta, Countess of Effingham."

And Alex, overhearing, went hurrying to her assistance. The Countess ducked between two cacti, however, and disappeared into the high grass. But the entire party followed. They were beating about the underbrush when a balding gentleman in a black tux, bow tie, and cummerbund coughed and said in a very worried voice, "Excuse me, Mr. Spinnel?"

Alex whirled.

"Mr. Spinnel, my mother . . ."

"Who are *you*?" The interruption upset Alex terribly.

The gentleman drew himself up to announce: "The Honorable Clement Effingham," and his pants leg shook for all the world as if he had started to click his heels. But articulation failed. The expression melted on his face. "Oh, I . . . my mother, Mr. Spinnel. We were downstairs at the other half of your party when she got very . . . excited. She ran up here—oh, I *told* her not to! I knew you'd be upset. But you must help me!" and then looked up.

The others looked, too.

The helicopter blacked the moon, rocking and settling below its hazy twin parasols.

"Oh, please . . ." the gentleman said. "You look over there! Perhaps she's gone back down. I've got to—" looking quickly both ways—"find her." He hurried in one direction while everyone else hurried in others.

The humming was suddenly syncopated with a crash. Roaring now, as plastic fragments from the transparent roof chattered down through the branches, clattered on the rocks . . .

I made it into the elevator and had already thumbed the edge of my briefcase clasp, when Hawk dove between the unfolding foils. The electric eye began to swing them open. I hit DOOR CLOSE full fist.

The boy staggered, banged shoulders on two walls, then got back breath and balance. "Hey, there's police getting out of that helicopter!"

"Hand-picked by Maud Hinkle herself, no doubt." I pulled the other tuft of white hair from my temple. It went into the case on top of the plastiderm gloves (wrinkled, thick blue veins, long carnelian nails) that had been Henrietta's hands, lying in the chiffon folds of her sari.

Then there was the downward tug of stopping. The Honorable Clement was still half on my face when the door opened.

Gray and gray, with an absolutely dismal expression, the Hawk swung through the doors. Behind him people were dancing in an elaborate pavilion festooned with Oriental magnificence (and a mandala of shifting hues on the ceiling). Arty beat me to DOOR CLOSE. Then he gave me an odd look.

I just sighed and finished peeling off Clem.

"The police are up there . . . ?" the Hawk reiterated.

"Arty," I said, buckling my pants, "it certainly looks that way." The car gained momentum. "You look almost as upset as Alex." I shrugged the tux jacket down my arms, turning the sleeves inside out, pulled one wrist free, and jerked off the white starched dicky with the black bow tie and stuffed it into the briefcase with all my other dickies; swung the coat around and slipped on Howard Calvin Evingston's good gray herringbone. Howard (like Hank) is a redhead (but not as curly).

The Hawk raised his bare brows when I peeled off Clement's bald pate and shook out my hair.

"I noticed you aren't carrying around all those bulky things in your pockets anymore."

"Oh, those have been taken care of," he said gruffly. "They're all right."

"Arty," I said, adjusting my voice down to Howard's security-provoking, ingenuous baritone, "it must have been my unabashed conceit that made me think that those Regular Service police were here just for me—"

The Hawk actually snarled. "They wouldn't be that unhappy if they got me, too."

And from his corner Hawk demanded, "You've got security here with you, don't you, Arty?"

"So what?"

"There's one way you can get out of this," Hawk hissed at me. His jacket had come half-open down his wrecked chest. "That's if Arty takes you out with him."

"Brilliant idea," I concluded. "You want a couple of thousand back for the service?"

The idea didn't amuse him. "I don't want anything from you." He turned to Hawk. "I need something from you, kid. Not him. Look, I wasn't prepared for Maud. If you want me to get your friend out, then you've got to do something for me."

The boy looked confused.

I thought I saw smugness on Arty's face, but the expression resolved into concern. "You've got to figure out some way to fill the lobby up with people, and fast."

I was going to ask why, but then I didn't know the extent of Arty's security. I was going to ask how, but the floor pushed up at my feet and the door swung open. "If you can't do it," the Hawk growled to Hawk, "none of us will get out of here. None of us!"

I had no idea what the kid was going to do, but when I started to follow him out into the lobby, the Hawk grabbed my arm and hissed, "Stay here, you idiot!"

I stepped back. Arty was leaning on DOOR OPEN.

Hawk sprinted toward the pool. And splashed in.

He reached the braziers on their twelve-foot tripods and began to climb.

"He's going to hurt himself!" the Hawk whispered.

"Yeah," I said, but I don't think my cynicism got through. Below the great dish of fire, Hawk was fiddling. Then something under there came loose. Something else went *Clang!* And something else spurted out across the water. The fire raced along it and hit the pool, churning and roaring like hell.

A black arrow with a golden head: Hawk dove.

I bit the inside of my cheek as the alarm sounded. Four people in uniforms were coming across the blue carpet. Another group were crossing in the other direction, saw the flames, and one of the women screamed. I let out my breath, thinking carpet and walls and ceilings would be flameproof. But I kept losing focus on the idea before the sixty-odd infernal feet.

Hawk surfaced on the edge of the pool in the only clear spot left, rolled over onto the carpet, clutching his face. And rolled. And rolled. Then, came to his feet.

Another elevator spilled out a load of passengers who gaped and gasped. A crew came through the doors now with fire-fighting equipment. The alarm was still sounding.

Hawk turned to look at the dozen-odd people in the lobby. Water puddled the carpet about his drenched and shiny pants legs. Flame turned the drops on his cheek and hair to flickering copper and blood.

He banged his fists against his wet thighs, took a deep breath, and against the roar and the bells and the whispering, he Sang.

Two people ducked back into the two elevators. From a doorway half a dozen more emerged. The elevators returned half a minute later with a dozen people each. I realized the message was going through the building, there's a Singer Singing in the lobby.

The lobby filled. The flames growled, the firefighters stood around shuffling, and Hawk, feet apart on the blue rug by the burning pool, Sang, and Sang of a bar off Times Square full of thieves, morphadine-heads, brawlers, drunkards, women too old to trade what they still held out for barter, and trade just too nasty-grimy; where earlier in the evening a brawl had broken out, and an old man had been critically hurt in the fray.

Arty tugged at my sleeve.

"What . . . ?"

"Come on," he hissed.

The elevator door closed behind us.

We ambled through the attentive listeners, stopping to watch, stopping to hear. I couldn't really do Hawk justice. A lot of that slow amble I spent wondering what sort of security Arty had:

Standing behind a couple in bathrobes who were squinting into the heat, I decided it was all very simple. Arty wanted simply to drift away through a crowd, so he'd conveniently gotten Hawk to manufacture one.

To get to the door we had to pass through practically a cordon of Regular Service policemen, who I don't think had anything to do with what might have been going on in the roof garden; they'd simply collected to see the fire and stayed for the Song. When Arty tapped one on the shoulder—"Excuse me please"—to get by, the policeman glanced at him, glanced away, then did a Mack Sennet double-take. But another policeman caught the whole interchange, touched the first on the arm, and gave him a frantic little head-shake. Then both men turned very deliberately back to watch the Singer. While the earthquake in my chest stilled, I decided that the Hawk's security complex of agents and counteragents, maneuvering and machinating through the flaming lobby, must be of such finesse and intricacy that to attempt understanding was to condemn oneself to total paranoia.

Arty opened the final door.

I stepped from the last of the air-conditioning into the night.

We hurried down the ramp.

"Hey, Arty . . ."

"You go that way." He pointed down the street. "I go this way."

"Eh . . . what's that way?" I pointed in my direction.

"Twelve Towers sub-sub-subway station. Look. I've got you out of there. Believe me, you're safe for the time being. Now go take a train someplace interesting. Good-bye. Go on now." Then Arty the Hawk put his fists in his pockets and hurried up the street.

I started down, keeping near the wall, expecting someone to get me with a blow-dart from a passing car, a deathray from the shrubbery.

I reached the sub.

And still nothing had happened.

Agate gave way to Malachite:

Tourmaline:

Beryl (during which month I turned twenty-six):

Porphyry:

Sapphire (that month I took the ten thousand I hadn't frittered away and invested it in The Glacier, a perfectly legitimate ice cream palace on Triton—the first and only ice cream palace on Triton—which took off like fireworks; all investors were returned eight hundred percent, no kidding. Two weeks later I'd lost half of those earnings on another set of preposterous illegalities and was feeling quite depressed, but The Glacier kept pulling them in. The new Word came by):

Cinnabar:

Turquoise:

Tiger's Eye:

Hector Calhoun Eisenhower finally buckled down and spent three months learning how to be a respectable member of the upper-middle-class underworld. That's a novel in itself. High finance; corporate law; how to hire help: Whew! But the complexities of life have always intrigued me. I got through it. The basic rule is still the same: Observe carefully; imitate effectively.

Garnet:

Topaz (I whispered that word on the roof of the Trans-Satellite Power Station, and caused my hirelings to commit two murders. And you know? I didn't feel a thing):

Taafite:

We were nearing the end of Taafite. I'd come back to Triton on strictly Glacial business. A bright pleasant morning it was: the business went fine. I decided to take off the afternoon and go sight-seeing in the Torrents.

". . . two hundred and thirty meters high," the guide announced, and everyone around me leaned on the rail and gazed up through the plastic corridor at the cliffs of frozen methane that soared through Neptune's cold green glare.

"Just a few yards down the catwalk, ladies and gentlemen, you can catch your first glimpse of the Well of This World, where over a million years ago, a mysterious force science still cannot explain caused twenty-five square miles of frozen methane to liquefy for no more than a few hours during which time a whirlpool twice the depth of Earth's Grand Canyon was caught for the ages when the temperature dropped once more to . . ."

People were moving down the corridor when I saw her smiling. My hair was black and nappy, and my skin was chestnut dark today.

I was just feeling overconfident, I guess, so I kept standing around next to her. I even contemplated coming on. Then she broke the whole thing up by suddenly turning to me and saying perfectly deadpan: "Why, if it isn't Hamlet Caliban Enobarbus!"

Old reflexes realigned my features to couple the frown of confusion with the smile of indulgence. *Pardon me, but I think you must have mistaken* . . . No, I didn't say it. "Maud," I said, "have you come here to tell me that my time has come?"

She wore several shades of blue with a large blue brooch at her shoulder, obviously glass. Still, I realized as I looked about the other tourists, she was more inconspicuous amidst their finery than I was. "No," she said. "Actually I'm on vacation. Just like you."

"No kidding?" We had dropped behind the crowd. "You are kidding."

"Special Services of Earth, while we cooperate with Special Services on other worlds, has no official jurisdiction on Triton. And since you came here with money, and most of your recorded gain in income has been through The Glacier, while Regular Services on Triton might be glad to get you, Special Services is not after you as yet." She smiled. "I haven't been to The Glacier. It would really be nice to say I'd been taken there by one of the owners. Could we go for a soda, do you think?"

The swirled sides of the Well of This World dropped away in opalescent grandeur. Tourists gazed, and the guide went on about indices of refraction, angles of incline.

"I don't think you trust me," Maud said.

My look said she was right.

"Have you ever been involved with narcotics?" she asked suddenly.

I frowned.

"No, I'm serious. I want to try and explain something . . . a point of information that may make both our lives easier."

"Peripherally," I said. "I'm sure you've got down all the information in your dossiers."

"I was involved with them a good deal more than peripherally for several years," Maud said. "Before I got into Special Services, I was in the Narcotics Division of the regular force. And the people we dealt with twenty-four hours a day were drug users, drug pushers. To catch the big ones we had to make friends with the little ones. To catch the bigger ones, we had to make friends with the big. We had to keep the same hours they kept, talk the same language, for months at a time live on the same streets, in the same buildings." She stepped back from the rail to let a youngster ahead. "I had to be sent away to take the morphadine detoxification cure twice while I was on the narc squad. And I had a better record than most."

"What's your point?"

"Just this. You and I are traveling in the same circles now, if only because of our respective chosen professions. You'd be surprised how many people we already know in common. Don't be shocked when we run into each other crossing Sovereign Plaza in Bellona one day, then two weeks later wind up at the same restaurant for lunch at Lux on Iapetus. Though the circles we move in cover worlds, they *are* the same—and not that big."

"Come on." I don't think I sounded happy. "Let me treat you to that ice cream." We started back down the walkway.

"You know," Maud said, "if you do stay out of Special Services' hands here and on Earth long enough, eventually you'll be up there with a huge income growing on a steady slope. It might be a few years, but it's possible. There's no reason now for us to be *personal* enemies. You just may, someday, reach that point where Special Services loses interest in you as quarry. Oh, we'd still see each other, run into each other. We get a great deal of our information from people up there. We're in a position to help you, too, you see."

"You've been casting holograms again."

She shrugged. Her face looked positively ghostly under the pale planet. She said, when we reached the artificial lights of the city, "I did meet two friends of yours recently, Lewis and Ann."

"The Singers?"

Maud nodded.

"Oh, I don't really know them well."

"They seem to know a lot about you. Perhaps through that other Singer, Hawk."

"Oh," I said again. "Did they say how he was?"

"I read that he was recovering about two months back. But nothing since then."

"That's about all I know, too," I said.

"The only time I've ever seen him," Maud said, "was right after I pulled him out."

Arty and I had gotten out of the lobby before Hawk actually finished. The next day on the newstapes I learned that when his Song was over, Hawk shrugged out of his jacket, dropped his pants, and walked back into the pool.

The firefighter crew suddenly woke up. People began running around and screaming. He'd been rescued, seventy percent of his body covered with second- and third-degree burns. I'd been industriously trying not to think about it.

"*You* pulled him out?"

"Yes. I was in the helicopter that landed on the roof," Maud said. "I thought you'd be impressed to see me."

"Oh," I said. "How did you get to pull him out?"

"Once you got going, Arty's security managed to jam the eleva-

tor service above the seventy-first floor, so we didn't get to the lobby
till after you were out of the building. That's when Hawk tried to—"

"But it was you who actually saved him, though?"

"The firemen in that neighborhood hadn't had a fire in twelve
years! I don't think they even know how to operate the equipment.
I had my boys foam the pool, then I waded in and dragged him—"

"Oh," I said again. I had been trying hard, almost succeeding,
these eleven months. I wasn't there when it happened. It wasn't my
affair. Maud was saying:

"We thought we might have gotten a lead on you from him, but
when I got him to the shore, he was completely out, just a mass of
open, running—"

"I should have known the Special Services uses Singers, too," I
said. "Everyone else does. The Word changes today, doesn't it?
Lewis and Ann didn't pass on what the new one is?"

"I saw them yesterday, and the Word doesn't change for another
eight hours. Besides, they wouldn't tell *me*, anyway." She glanced at
me and frowned. "They really wouldn't."

"Let's go have those ice-cream sodas," I said. "We'll make small
talk and listen carefully to each other while we affect an air of non-
chalance. You will try to pick up things that will make it easier to
catch me. I will listen for things you let slip that might make it easier for me to avoid you."

"*Um-hm.*" She nodded.

"Why did you contact me in that bar, anyway?"

Eyes of ice: "I told you, we simply travel in the same circles.
We're quite likely to be in the same bar on the same night."

"I guess that's just one of the things I'm not supposed to understand, huh?"

Her smile was appropriately ambiguous. I didn't push it.

It was a very dull afternoon. I couldn't repeat one exchange
from the nonsense we babbled over the cherry-peaked mountains of
whipped cream. We both exerted so much energy to keep up the

appearance of being amused, I doubt either one of us could see our way to picking up anything meaningful—if anything meaningful was said.

She left. I brooded some more on the charred phoenix.

The Steward of The Glacier called me into the kitchen to ask about a shipment of contraband milk (The Glacier makes all its own ice cream) that I had been able to wangle on my last trip to Earth (it's amazing how little progress there has been in dairy farming over the last ten years; it was depressingly easy to hornswoggle that bumbling Vermonter) and under the white lights and great plastic churning vats, while I tried to get things straightened out, he made some comment about the Heist Cream Emperor; that didn't do *any* good.

By the time the evening crowd got there, and the moog was making music, the crystal walls were blazing; and the floor show—a new addition that week—had been cajoled into going on anyway (a trunk of costumes had gotten lost in shipment [or swiped, but I wasn't about to tell *them* that]), and wandering through the tables I, personally, had caught a very grimy little girl, obviously out of her head on morph, trying to pick up a customer's pocketbook from the back of his chair—I just caught her by the wrist, made her let go, and led her to the door daintily, while she blinked at me with dilated eyes and the customer never even knew—and the floor show, having decided what the hell, were doing their act *au naturel,* and everyone was having just a high old time, I was feeling really bad.

I went outside, sat on the wide steps, and growled when I had to move aside to let people in or out. About the seventy-fifth growl, the person I growled at stopped and boomed down at me, "I thought I'd find you, if I looked hard enough! I mean if I really looked."

I looked at the hand that was flapping at my shoulder, followed the arm up to a black turtleneck where there was a beefy, bald, grinning head. "Arty," I said, "what are . . . ?" But he was still flapping and laughing with impervious *gemütlichkeit.*

"You wouldn't believe the time I had getting a picture of you, boy. Had to bribe one out of the Triton Special Services Department. That quick change bit: great gimmick. Just great!" The Hawk sat down next to me and dropped his hand on my knee. "Wonderful place you got here. I like it, like it a lot." Small bones in veined dough. "But not enough to make you an offer on it yet. You're learning fast there, though. I can tell you're learning fast. I'm going to be proud to be able to say I was the one who gave you your first big break." Arty's hand came away, and he began to knead it into the other. "If you're going to move into the big time, you have to have at least one foot planted firmly on the right side of the law. The whole idea is to make yourself indispensable to the good people. Once that's done, a good crook has the keys to all the treasure houses in the system. But I'm not telling you anything you don't already know."

"Arty," I said, "do you think the two of us should be seen together here . . . ?"

The Hawk held his hand above his lap and joggled it with a deprecating motion. "Nobody can get a picture of us. I got my men all around. I never go anywhere in public without my security. Heard you've been looking into the security business yourself," which was true. "Good idea. Very good. I like the way you're handling yourself."

"Thanks. Arty, I'm not feeling too hot this evening. I came out here to get some air. . . ."

Arty's hand fluttered again. "Don't worry, I won't hang around. You're right. We shouldn't be seen. Just passing by and wanted to say hello. Just hello." He got up. "That's all." He started down the steps.

"Arty?"

He looked back.

"Sometime soon you will come back; and that time you will want to buy out my share of The Glacier, because I'll have gotten too big; and I won't want to sell because I'll think I'm big enough to fight you. So we'll be enemies for a while. You'll try to kill me. I'll try to kill you."

On his face, first the frown of confusion, then the indulgent smile. "I see you've caught on to the idea of hologramic information. Very good. Good. It's the only way to outwit Maud. Make sure all your information relates to the whole scope of the situation. It's the only way to outwit me, too." He smiled, started to turn, but thought of something else. "If you can fight me off long enough and keep growing, keep your security in tiptop shape, eventually, we'll get to the point where it'll be worth both our whiles to work together again. If you can just hold out, we'll be friends again. Someday. You just watch. Just wait."

"Thanks for telling me."

The Hawk looked at his watch. "Well. Good-bye." I thought he was going to leave finally. But he glanced up again. "Have you got the new Word?"

"That's right," I said. "It went out tonight. What is it?"

The Hawk waited till the people coming down the steps were gone. He looked hastily about, then leaned toward me with hands cupped at his mouth, rasped, "Pyrite," and winked hugely. "I just got it from a gal who got it direct from Colette," (one of the three Singers of Triton). Arty turned, jounced down the steps, and shouldered his way into the crowds passing on the strip.

I sat there mulling through the year till I had to get up and walk. All walking does to my depressive moods is add the reinforcing rhythm of paranoia. By the time I was coming back, I had worked out a dilly of a delusional system: The Hawk had already begun to weave some security-ridden plot about me, which ended when we were all trapped in some dead-end alley, and trying to get aid I called out, "Pyrite!" which would turn out not to be the Word at all but served to identify me for the man in the dark gloves with the gun/grenade/gas.

There was a cafeteria on the corner. In the light from the window, clustered over the wreck by the curb was a bunch of nasty-grimies (à la Triton: chains around the wrist, bumblebee tattoo on cheek, high-heel boots on those who could afford them). Straddling the smashed headlight was the little morph-head I had ejected earlier from The Glacier.

On a whim I went up to her. "Hey . . . ?"

She looked at me from under hair like trampled straw, eyes all pupil.

"You get the new Word yet?"

She rubbed her nose, already scratch red. "Pyrite," she said. "It just came down about an hour ago."

"Who told you?"

She considered my question. "I got it from a guy, who says he got it from a guy, who came in this evening from New York, who picked it up there from a Singer named Hawk."

The three grimies nearest made a point of not looking at me. Those farther away let themselves glance.

"Oh," I said. "Oh. Thanks."

Occam's Razor, along with any real information on how security works, hones away most such paranoia. Pyrite. At a certain level in my line of work, paranoia's just an occupational disease. At least I was certain that Arty (and Maud) probably suffered from it as much as I did.

The lights were out on The Glacier's marquee. Then I remembered what I had left inside and ran up the stairs.

The door was locked. I pounded on the glass a couple of times, but everyone had gone home. And the thing that made it worse was that I could *see* it sitting on the counter of the coat-check alcove under the orange bulb. The steward had probably put it there, thinking I might arrive before everybody left. Tomorrow at noon Ho Chi Eng had to pick up his reservation for the Marigold Suite on the Interplanetary Liner *The Platinum Swan,* which left at one-thirty for Bellona. And there behind the glass doors of The Glacier, it waited with the proper wig, as well as the epicanthic folds that would halve Mr. Eng's sloe eyes of jet.

I actually thought of breaking in. But the more practical solution was to get the hotel to wake me at nine and come in with the cleaning man. I turned around and started down the steps; and the thought struck me, and made me terribly sad, so that I blinked and smiled just from reflex; it was probably just as well to leave it there till morning, because there was nothing in it that wasn't mine anyway.

—Milford
July 1968

omegahelm

Bloody lace lazied on the bay.

Pink clouds filigreed the sky.

The great red sun, at the world's rim, worked its changes on the green sea below her, the coppery east beyond her, the marbled rocks she climbed on.

Squinting, she turned to face it.

Model her flat, sunlit features in dark terra-cotta around eyes green as that sea. Dry. Then, with a ball-peen hammer, shatter it from behind—only the instant between impact and the first cracks erupting through, catch a picture from the front.

There was that about her face.

Her hands seemed to have too many knuckles, on forearms corded with too many small muscles, too many big veins. The left—how could five fingers hold all those rings? Three big iron ones; four bigger ones of bronze; some were narrow and copper; three, of silver (on different fingers), were set with shards of different jades; two, of bright aluminum (on the same), bore both agates and opals. The gold one on her thumb was cast in a lizard's head, big as a dyll nut and gnawing a milky stone. Her left hand was hooked, by that lizard-headed thumb, over the webbed belt slanting her hip. To one side her pelvic blade stuck above the leather. (Her wrist seemed to have an extra knob of bone.) Her right, rough from crafts, weathered, from worlds away, with large knuckles and no rings, hung, like planking, askew.

A strong body. Still, you were more aware of the bone in it. Leaves beside her—metallic spikes—chittered with the breeze. Red roots tangled the clay like thread. Her bare breasts, flattened now with sixty years on her long rib cage, shifted.

She looked to sea.

A sliver of ivory, thin as a nail paring, widened, puddling the water with light. The moon, called Pretania-IV, was rising.

Brush five meters below her moved. Gylda's face appeared between branches: black, nervous, inquisitive, and young.

Splotched color on Gylda's boot by the ferns: colors shifted. Gylda stepped onto the path, trying to smile, brushing one hand down her multicolored trousers. She took three steps on the dust, soft soles whispering.

Pretania-light spread the water.

"They called me from Omegahelm," Vondramach said, "to say you had officially handed in your resignation."

"Just before I left Omegahelm to come here—" Gylda's hand halted on her trouser hip—"they told me you had officially accepted it."

"Then this is just a personal farewell, a good-bye between two women, two friends, who have had a very profitable association over the last four years." Vondramach held out her ringless hand.

"Five years." Gylda climbed, looking between it and the green eyes.

"Has it been that long?"

"Five and a half years. I remember, because it was just a week before my twenty-fourth birthday. That would make it a little *over* five and a half, actually. You could say it was closer to six."

Vondramach laughed. "You are always so tactful about correcting me. Sometimes I've made mistakes on purpose, just to see how you'll manage it. But then, sometimes, I simply . . . make mistakes. I don't like making mistakes." She looked out at the sea. "But I appreciate tact."

"I know we've discussed my leaving before." Gylda gained the ledge. "But I wasn't sure how you'd feel when I actually did it."

"I am a powerful woman. You are not. And I could feel very badly, couldn't I? Well, you have killed many people for me. You have saved many others. And I have some worlds I would not have had if you—and others—had not done your jobs quite so efficiently. I am sad to lose you. But I am grateful for what you have accomplished. You were a very good spy. Those are my feelings. And I shall act on them." (That in Vondra's face never put people at their ease, though many people, Gylda knew, were attracted to it even while it disturbed.) "I have always felt it necessary to make my feelings very clear. There has been too much confusion, pain—and death—when I have not. But you know that. I want to give you something, Gylda. Where are you going, now? What are you going to do?"

"I want to return to my world. You remember? It's called Velm. It circles a sun called Iiriani. Just below a range of mountains to the south, there's a furniture cooperative where I can take a primary job in design. My tact—as you call it—I'd like to apply in counseling. But there're numerous secondary jobs available in the area I want to live. There may even be a city soon. And I'm going to bring up children."

"Yes. That is what you told me you would eventually want to do, back when I first met you. You are consistent. And consistency is a virtue—one I have always striven for myself. Very well. I shall give you—" Vondra glanced at the disk of the sun, a third below the horizon now—"a home for your children. It shall be . . . oh! large as Omegahelm itself, and—"

Gylda's laugh began nervously but broke full. "Vondra! Omegahelm? What would I . . . ?" She shook her head. "You'll really give me an administrative office building the size of a small town, large enough to run the affairs of half a dozen worlds, as a home for—?"

"—and where, in Omegahelm, I have information banks," Vondra went on, "and historical archives and computer chains, your home will have the artworks of . . . well, the best of your own world certainly. And you'll select a dozen or so artists that you've encountered on others in your travels during your service with me, and I shall see that representative collections of their best productions are shipped to you, collections that scholars will come to study for years. Oh, it will be the size of Omegahelm, but its details will be created especially for you by my finest architects. Its technology will be advanced—of a domestic design, of course. And—of course—I shall make sure that it is ecologically feasible for the area in which you—" The dark expression halted: the myriad movements that had composed it all stilled. In stasis, the emotion those features projected was astonishingly different.

"The nicest thing about Omegahelm," Gylda said, with a light yet measured tone, "is that it's eight hundred kilometers away." Her tone dropped, while the intensity with which she observed Vondra's face increased. "Here, with you, I'm glad to be . . . free of it." Gylda raised her hand to her sternum. On a thin chain around her neck hung an inch-long gold bar, at one end a cluster of gem-tipped wires. Before, it had been hard to see. The red light burnished one of her dark arms. Pretania-IV's first glow silvered the other. Gylda closed her fist on the hanging trinket. "I wore this the day you first met me, Vondra."

"And I laughed at it," Vondramach said, no laughter anywhere in her flat, dry voice. "And you took it off, for five, almost six years."

"But you've accepted my resignation. Since I am no longer in your service, I thought I might wear it again." Gylda shrugged. "I thought you might laugh at it again."

"I strive for consistency. I do not always achieve it." Vondramach reached across to move her large, heavily ringed hand around and down her elbow. "Nor are you always so tactful."

"Tact is only honesty with compassion," Gylda said. "You are very powerful. I am very honest. I thought about it. And I decided it would have been dishonest of me not to wear my cyhnk today."

"You like to believe that honesty is a kind of power, don't you?" Vondra said. "Many people who have neither power nor tact feel that way. Well, it isn't. Or rather, I can no longer tell whether it is or isn't anymore. Real power—which is what I do have and what I know about—puts a strange horizon around a world. It gives things a strange perspective. Once, when I was very, very young, I used to think how enjoyable it would be to have a great deal of money. It must be twenty years at least since I first realized—one afternoon while I was having my annual financial conference with my monetary advisers for my several worlds—that, back when I was forty, I used to have such meetings once a week. But as other, truly important, matters grew pressing and my power grew from holdings on two worlds to complete control of three, those meetings dropped to once a month. By the time I had become outright controller of nine worlds, they had dropped to once a year: the part of my power measurable in money was such a minuscule percentage of the whole that it could command no more of my time. Indeed, I realized that day, even these meetings could be dispensed with, if I desired it, for they were now just a gesture, more for my advisers' sake than for mine."

"You have abolished money as a mode of exchange on several of your worlds now," Gylda commented. "I suppose when you have enough money on other worlds to do that, then money more or less takes care of itself."

"Those worlds are much better off for the abolition," Vondra said. "And yet I have not been able to abolish . . . that." Her thick, jeweled thumb flicked toward the cyhnk between Gylda's breasts. "Neither on any world—nor from my friend and most trusted employee."

"It is only a sygn, Vondra," Gylda said, as one repeats the obvious to one who has rejected it long ago. "A signifier, they used to say, whose meaning—whose signified—shifts from place to place, world to world, person to person. On my world, in the very small part of it where I want to live, for me, it means home, the futures fanning out from it, the children I hope to raise, the society I want to see beside them, the connections and reconnections they will form between me and that society, the nurture stream I hope to set bubbling through the sands of the Velmian deserts—I've made up my mind to live in the southern part of my world. The last time I was there, when I visited the northern geosectors, I saw all sorts of unpleasant incidents between the colonizing humans and the native race—"

"A sygn whose meaning changes from world to world, person to person." Vondra shook her head. "No consistency. And you wonder how anyone who deals with the kind of power I do must object to it so strongly?" She closed her fingers on Gylda's wrist, pulled Gylda's hand from the talisman. Stones and metals slipped roughly down the breasts' inner slopes. At Vondra's hip, bare fingers made a fist.

On the black skin, the gem-chips were splattered wine. The last fragment of the sun, secanted by the sea, rouged the rocks. The bar looked bloody.

"For you it means a desired way of life." And the last of the sun was down, leaving only moon-blush on the water. The sky behind Vondra was dark blue. She released Gylda's wrist. "Why won't you say it: what you want is a family." Under Pretania-IV, the water had lost its jade. The waves below them were like lead, tangled with red foam, as the clays around them were tangled with roots.

"On the world I am returning to, in the section where I'm going, they call it a nurture stream. Why not use the terms of one's own world? 'Family?' I have no idea what a family is."

"You are being disingenuous. You know as well as I do: A family is a mother, a father, and a son," Vondra said, with the voice one used to inculcate the obvious. "It is the basic human mode of replication. Any sex can substitute for any part of it. Any part of it can be omitted. But that is the basic template in which omissions, replications, and substitutions must take place."

"And I grew up in a clone camp on a world that needed to increase its population drastically and quickly. You spent your childhood in a birth-defect experimental control group on an L-5 station circling a moon, Vondra. Neither one of us has ever known a family directly, though we had happy enough childhoods. Yet you work for the concept of the family; you support the idea of the family on a dozen worlds. And those who support the idea of the family have always supported you. It's a meaning, a tradition, an institution, with its form and history, to which its adherents refuse to fix a sygn, a title, a name, because once you fix a sygn to it, you say, the meaning starts to slip, change, adjust to its changing context, while the very people who change it are always appealing to that sygn to justify it. You lose just that consistency you have striven so hard for, while the actual change becomes invisible." Gylda smiled—which was only visible from a muscle's movement at the silhouette of her jaw. "You see, I know the argument well."

"Yes. And despite that argument, you still follow an institution that proposes a signifier, the cyhnk you wear, with no fixed meaning."

"I told you, Vondra. I believe in and follow what the sygn—what the cyhnk—means on *my* world. That's why I was wearing it when you met me. That's why, in my travels to other worlds in your service, whether they were worlds that believed in the sygn or the family, I could easily take it off. But now I am going back; and so I've put it back on."

"And you don't see how much its meaning has changed in the interim?" Vondramach's expression had not changed; but there were certain blanks among those shadowed features that those close to her had learned to read as irony. "Before it made me laugh. Now it does not. What does that change mean to you? Come, woman."

In the breeze silver spikes hissed.

"It means you have changed your feelings—" The cyhnk's gems were a Pleiades between Gylda's breasts—"or you are being more honest about feelings you have had all along."

Vondra looked over the flat of moss-mottled rock they'd reached. "Come, sit with me." She squatted.

Gylda sat beside her, her shoulder a warm half-inch away from Vondramach's bare arm, the sole of her boot close enough to Vondramach's to feel the grasses bunched between them.

Vondra stared out at the water, with its red detritus of light, that had, moments back, dropped full into evening. Now she sat too, putting her hands behind her on the rock. "Once," Vondra said, stretching out one leg and turning the foot first in, then out, "I made a child."

Quickly and softly, Gylda said: "You are a powerful woman. Perhaps the most powerful in the universe. There are very few things you have not done, Vondramach."

"Fiddle," Vondra said. "If I didn't have a very real sense of just how much bigger than I am the universe is, I would never be able to wield the power in it that I do. You have talked to me of raising children. I want to talk to you of the reality of such a situation, and under the most ideal conditions that power can provide. Father, mother, son? We know that one parent can be dispensed with. A son? Well, somehow it never occurred to me to make a male. And since the family is a natural form, I followed my natural instincts. And I made a child . . . a child who was to be a great artist, a great sculptor. At the time I had an interest in sculpture. Therefore, I decided to encode my child with all we can abstract of spatial knowledge and material textures, as well as the last three thousand years' history of the plastic arts, inscribed on her memetosomes. But since mine was, as it must be in everything these days, a passing interest, I preset, by polynucleatidal sequence, her life span at seven minutes. She would grow from youth, through majority, to old age in that breadth—I should say breath—of time." Vondra's ringed and unringed fingers spread on the warm, damp stone.

Listening, Gylda hunched her shoulders.

"I stood at the observation glass and watched the womb doors open. She rolled onto the nursery pad, where I had left all the tools and materials she might need—chisels, mallets, clay, and trowels, as well as a mechanical duplicator that could be programmed for any sort of distortion. Her prostheses had been affixed prenatally; their fittings would expand as she grew. Wet and patched with shreds of her caul, she immediately began to flail about, gulping, and pushing herself up, and falling, her arms flexing, visibly strengthening as I watched, her eyes gaining focus, her boneless head on its thickly veined neck pulsing and shaking, her blowhole sucking in the warm gases that vaporized from the needle-valve carrying the nutrients, the hormones, and the enzymes I had not bothered to provide her with genetically. She had already begun to trickle that yellow mucilage—the waste of the great metabolic rate her body, never more than thirty pounds, was undergoing. Her artificial locomoters goosenecked about; for a moment I thought their suction cups would not adhere to the pad's black plastic surface—she would be a cripple! But no, they caught; she could move, could drag herself forward, could position herself in front of the tools, clays, wood, wire, fiberglass, and stone; squint at them, nudge them, caress them—which she did, now, with greater and greater avidity. At a minute and thirty seconds she underwent puberty: the fleshy bag at her belly flooded, swelled to a translucent balloon, veins and capillaries quivering on the membrane. Perhaps a minute before she reached her full strength, she turned her head toward me—my face was pressed against the viewing glass: beside my cheeks my fingers spread." In grass, Vondramach's fingers, ringed and bare, closed. "She stared with those immense green eyes . . . her inheritance from me. They were much more intelligent eyes than yours or mine. Her cerebral capacity, all of it functioning immediately on birth, was nine times that of an ordinary human. She stretched one jointed plastic claw toward me, and . . . I suppose she shrieked. Did her brief, gigantic intellect, in that loose, wet head, for a moment consider our relationship? Her mouth opened over soft, toothless gums. What came through the speaker was a liquid hiss. The mechanical appendage, swaying at me, accidentally hit against a hunk of clay I had left for her. She turned to it, stared at it, pondered it. But already that claw had picked up a stray gobbet and was absently kneading it into a tiny sphere. Suddenly she dropped it, plunged two other arms into the soft stuff, pulled loose a single hunk, and regarded the broken landscape on the parted surface— that was her first sculptural work. Quickly she transferred it to the metal shelf I had provided for her finished projects, anchoring it to one of the onyx bases there, and, for moments more, examined it, turned it on its base, studying it from all sides. No one will ever be sure what it spoke to her, during the process of its creation, or what she felt in contemplating its achievement. Over the next minute and a half she produced six more of these early, experimental works, each consisting of the random surface of a clay shard broken from the main mass—actually she made nine. But two did not please her, and she ground them back into the parent lump. Immediately she had finished these, she turned to the duplicator, whose operation, as well as the operation of the rest of the tools, she knew by memetosome imprint. Quickly she made reproductions of, first I believe it was, a chisel I had left her, in fine-grained marble; then, a small mallet molded of a fiberglass compound; then a clay knife, which she reproduced in bronze. The finished sculptures, which she ranged on the shelf, were the duplicated copies mounted beside the original tools: chisel with chisel, knife with knife, mallet with mallet, so that copy and original must both be observed at once. In this way, as she employed each sculptural tool, she exhausted its possible use. But already the duplicator was at work on the next project she had set it to. For as she finished at the shelf, the duplicator stage rose through the electrostatic rings. On it, in pale, translucent stone, was a replica of her own dwarfed, overmuscled body—the bulged eyes, the engorged bladder, the thickened neck, and all half-dozen prostheses. At first I was bewildered by this trite reproduction and wondered what she intended it for. But as I watched, she . . . hurled herself upon it! She drew back. She hurled herself again! And again! My fingers grew clammy on the glass. My throat dried. My daughter flung herself onto her effigy once more. This time her bladder ruptured, splashing over the stone. Those glands which, in you and me, secrete digestive juices, I had genetically altered in her to produce far more powerful acids. She was equipped to release them in a tiny, hard stream through a small sphincter at her bladder's base, for direct carving or polishing. But she had chosen to use them this way—and to perish. The statue burned and smoked and blistered down one side. Immolated, she hugged herself against it, locomotors pushing and slipping against the nursing pad; and slipping more. One of her own small callused hands fell from the marble shoulder. She turned her head weakly, once more stared at me, green eyes cataracted and blistered now from her own splattered vitriol. She died, creating that final, awesome work . . . oh, perhaps two minutes before age would have taken her anyway, and she would have grown too weak to more than mull through the achievements of her youth and maturity."

Gylda watched the back of Vondramach's neck, while she hugged her own knees.

"My daughter's works are among the most precious things I own. I keep them in a case in my rooms in Omegahelm: seven shards of broken clay, mounted on onyx; the half-dozen replicas of tools mounted with their models; and the marble figure of a humped and bug-eyed matoid, with face and limbs deformed even further by spilled acids. And—oh, yes—her single, charming piece of juvenilia I recovered: she had tossed aside the clay bit she had absently rolled into an almost perfect sphere. Over the years I have spent many hours contemplating them, hours that amount to many times the life it took to produce them. In their austere way, they are all beautiful pieces. But I tell you, I am still haunted by her shriek, her jointed arm stretched toward me, her immense, her wise, her suffering eyes one color with my own. And I have sworn never to bear a daughter like that again." The breeze returned. Vondramach turned toward Gylda. Leaves between the rocks below hissed.

"You've supported the concept of the family on more than a dozen worlds." All Gylda's features were dark. "And I know that much of your early support came from family supporters. I'd always wondered why you yourself never had—" Then Gylda snarled.

Vondra did not move.

Gylda's face was still dark. But the gasping, choking grunt told how violently that face twisted. Gylda pushed away, backing across the rock. As her head moved, Pretania-IV light caught her features: pain!

Pain too startling even to let her scream; so she choked and gagged and snarled, scrambling backward, managing somehow to get her knees under her. She tore at her neck.

The cyhnk chain broke.

Gasping, she flung it from her.

Vondra laughed.

Lying on the moss, the bar and wires glowed orange-pink. Crossing it was a thin blur of smoke. Tangerine brightened to white. Burning, the dark moss smelled like mint.

Gylda rubbed near the spot between her breasts where the totem had hung. The spot itself, burned and blistering, was still too painful to touch. Her gasps had in them the wreckage of the cry she still refused full voice.

"I'm laughing," Vondra said, as she stood up, "at your cyhnk—at your stupid sygn—for the same reason I laughed at it when I first met you."

On the ground the glowing metal darkened to red; red faded toward black.

"Did you know the reason I first laughed six years ago? It was because I could have done what I just did. When I met you, I chose not to. This time, I chose otherwise. Such choices are the way it is with power—even silly little powers such as that one. It's a trick I can do with an inductance field from one of my rings. But the power, you see, was always there. As was the laughter. Consistency. Go back to Omegahelm, and from there to your own world. And you will find, in your southern desert, near your furniture cooperative, a new home being built for you, its basements sunk as many stories beneath the scrumbly soil, and its upper courts raised as many stories above it, as Omegahelm's courts and basements."

Breathing hard, Gylda stepped across the rock, watching the laughing woman with Pretania-light glittering on her hand. Suddenly Gylda bent, snatched up something from the moss, turned, and stalked down toward the high brush.

"And by all means, wear your cyhnk! Though I laugh, I have no objections—to what it symbolizes. On your world. In the south. By your furniture cooperative. Where a new Omegahelm rises to meet you—no *bigger* than Omegahelm! Yes! It *shall* be bigger! And I say it will be even more suited to your experiments in childrearing than Omegahelm was for mine. And may you be more successful than I was! Oh, yes! And do wear your cyhnk! Wear it as a sygn of my generosity and my power! And my friendship. I have no objection to such sygns. Though I laugh . . . !" Vondramach took a breath, and another, and a third.

She stood awhile—not alone: she had not traveled alone for years, though the majority of what accompanied her was mechanical, much of it miniature, and most of it out of sight. Vondra watched Pretania-IV flicker on the night sea. Then, as Gylda had done minutes before, she walked down the rocks to begin the brief journey back to Omegahelm.

—London
October 1973

among the blobs

(1) "I'm terribly sorry, ma'am. I'm sorry." He swayed, one arm raised, torso stalled in the torque of its own turning. His name was Joe. To one side of his back was, not a pain nor even a feeling, but rather a sensational ghost, an unformed blob, where she had lurched against his army jacket, or he had backed into her tweed. "Are you all right?" She probably couldn't hear because of the subway car's roar. "You okay?"

"Yes." (Was she confused a little, a little bewildered?) "That's all right." Swaying by the pole, her fuchsia scarf pulled through something gold, amoeboid, and splattered with ruby glass, she looked like one of the black Miss Subways. He had no idea if she were five years older or five years younger than he. Joe turned, because after all, all he'd done was bump her a little; or she'd bumped him. But I could have smiled, he thought, reaching for and missing and then getting the next hanger. He knew his smile was good. (2) And Bat D—, in a rocket of luciprene-6 with vytrol fittings, careened at ballistic speeds through interstellar night. Flakes had fallen off the black, letting in light: stars. Bat was dubious and alert, with the belly feeling that is both anxiety and enthusiasm. His would be the first human encounter with the Blob—which had been reported flûtchülát-ing (a form of communication? digestion? play?) in sector E-3. Till this report Bat D—, of the blazing death-laser, slayer of twenty-seven seven-foot Uranites, hero of the Kpt rebellion on Fomalhaut-G, had poohed the existence of Blobs, but the closer his luciprene hull swooped toward Galactic Council, the more indubitable seemed the Blob's particular order of ontological resolution—what an earlier, less vulgar epoch would have called her "reality." (3) And Joe, on the Broadway Local, headed for Forty-Second, wearing a Pendleton that didn't look it because his friend Joe—another Joe—had been in with his truck the day before yesterday, and the two of them had worked on the transmission six hours up at the Dyckman Street garage.

One train door stuck.

Army jacket open, Joe hammered up the concrete steps to the station concourse, loped under pipes and fluorescent fixtures, passed the rack of phone booths, the doughnut emporium. Another twenty-five steps and the florist concession pressed dull plants against glass; then down past the stall of Latin records, across from the hot-dog-pasteles, piña-colada-Coca-Cola-cuchifrito counter, and toward the BMT.

Joe had been moving all this time through the late rush-hour crowds, which crowds we have not mentioned till now because he was just about to separate himself from them. Joe thought of these crowds as a Blob, to which he was by and large indifferent.

Neither the Blob nor Joe's indifference, however, were impregnable to analysis. There were the men, of whom he was vaguely resentful, because if he stood too close to one in the crush, or sat too close to one on a subway seat—too much body contact—they might suspect he was not a heterosexual lustful-panting-monster, and the grapevine had it they could get hostile toward the other kind. There were the women, of whom he was vaguely resentful, because, since everyone knew all men were heterosexual lustful-panting-monsters, if he bumped one or brushed one (not to mention stood too near or sat too close), he had to apologize, be appallingly polite, and generally come on far more deferentially than any normal human should be expected to to establish that, indeed, he was *not* a heterosexual lustful-panting-monster. At twenty-six, actually, he knew how to deal with the men: stand or sit where you want and fuck 'em. They could move. The women, however, confused him a little, bewildered him. And women were a subject about which the grapevine was distressingly un- (if not ill-) informed. Resentment, however vague, is not pleasant; hence the indifference in which he traveled.

At the blue and white column, Joe swung left toward the john.

The wooden gate—not, this time, "Closed for Cleaning"—was wedged back, askew on its hinges. Some time ago they'd painted the tiled entrance hall blue. Hand-sized paint flakes had fallen away. The antiseptic with which the place was flushed every other day had blistered what paint remained. Sometimes it left fumes so strong you couldn't stay inside long enough to take an honest leak.

In front of five of the ten porcelain urinals—most of the brass flush-treadles lay without tension on the red-tiled floor—(4) half the Galactic Council was in attendance. It was a highly formalized gathering. Members came and went according to an arcane protocol Bat D— still did not understand. Each member entered the High and Icy Hall (here and there still crossed with traces of unbreathable fumes) to linger, silently and intently for an arbitrary while, before what looked to Bat D— for all the world like something from a book on Twentieth-Century toilet fixtures.

The members of the Council were laboring to express the Blob.

The Blob was not impregnable to analysis: it was a largely mucusoid emulsion contained in a selectively permeable membrane within which drifted a nucleus, various nucleoli, vacuoles, ribosomes, mitochondria, and chloroplasts, the whole a symbiotic intrusion of eukaryotic and prokaryotic cells from a less vulgar moment in the pluroma when all was closer than it is today to organic soup, to inorganic matter.

The Council members, minds on high matters, manipulated their computers.

The Blob was, appropriately, near Betelgeuse.

And Betelgeuse was in E-3. (5) Joe lingered at the next-to-the-end urinal. He had a thing for older guys with big, heavily veined cocks and small hands with overlong nails; and the guy to his left, at the end urinal (Pushing sixty? But that was all right), was probably a librarian. He wore a dumb-silly coat with a fur collar you couldn't button up. Or a designer. The black portfolio leaned on the wall behind them. But that was all right.

A bum lurched through the door (probably not as old as this guy beside him with those long, long nails the color of aluminum in winterlight. In his own too wide, too horny hand, at the memory only a second old—rather than at what was beside him—Joe hardened), mustache full of mucus, missing a lot of hair over one ear, missing shirt buttons; and the breast pocket gone. His pants leg was ripped, knee to cuff, showing a shin like soap. The bum looked around: "Aw, Jesus Christ, nothin' in here but a bunch of . . . I mean ever'body in here is one of them fuckin' . . . Hey you there, I bet you're one of . . ."

To Joe's right, two members of the Galactic Council glanced at each other, smiled. One shook his head. Hands down before white porcelain, busy with calculations, they manipulated and manipulated.

Wilson, the deaf-mute hustler, fists pouched in his frayed windbreaker, came bopping in. Joe knew him because Wilson had once tried to score from Joe, who had bought him a cup of coffee at the hot dog counter across the concourse and explained to him—Joe had two aunts who had been born deaf and with whom he had stayed for a year in Portland when he was ten, which is how he knew the deaf-and-dumb sign language—that at this particular spot there was just too much of it walking around for free to make it worth a working man's time. Wilson came around the bum ("Hey, you ain't interested in these fuckin' faggots, huh . . . ?"), surveyed the Council Members at their stalls, and left.

"Shit . . . !" The bum turned, started out, stumbled into the jamb. An incoming Member—a subway worker Joe had seen here a few times before—steadied him:

"Hey, watch it, old man."

The worker moved the bum out to arm's length and looked down to see a dripping cuff; and the shin was wet. Not having made it to a stall, the bum lurched out, leaving sneaker piss-prints on the chalky floor.

Joe turned back to the man beside him: gray hair, Vandyke beard, glasses. They exchanged glances, anxious, enthusiastic, eye to lens, lens to groin. That crank (Joe had grown up in Seattle), those nails: Joe felt the warmth of orgasm heating the backs of his knees. (6) The salmon light of Betelgeuse slanted through the clear wall of Sumpter VII, the Fort named—jokingly—by the first generation of galactic anthropologists, how many years ago now . . . ? And where were they today: reduced to inert jelly during the tragic Kpt. Now, this Blob . . . ? Bat D— walked across reddened tiles of luciprene-57 past the Fort's transparent north facade, that looked out across the magnetic sands webbed with molten ammonia runulets worming the hyperborean chill, toward the sheer range called Chroma—because of the pink, fuchsia, and vermilion clays streaking its silver slopes. Warily, Bat turned from the window-wall to round a partition studded with ruby vytrol—

She quivered there within the high, luminous geometries of Sumpter VII, contracting her gargantuan bulk inward from those bloated pseudopods into which her viscid soap-collared stuffs had spread. Nucleoli and vacuoles and just plain bubbles puckered her membrane. She could sense him, Bat could tell. Languorously, she heaved herself forward.

Bat D—'s thumb snapped open the cover of his Naugahyde holster. He tugged loose his death-laser, its handle of black ivory worked into rare scrimshaw by the Little Folk of Antares-10, its symmetrically veined and partitioned barrel molded of clear lucite casting resin by Jonas and Barboli of Fenton, Pennsylvania. Carefully, Bat raised the gun.

The Blob said: "Burble, burble . . . burble." She flattened her amoeboid volume slightly, then heaved again.

Bat fired—and a pseudopod, a little charred, smoking a little, dropped from the ceiling and knocked the death-laser fifteen feet to crack the partition. Ruby vytrol chattered to the floor, glittered on the tiles.

Bat D—, terrified and exuberant, stepped back. The Blob, enraged, hurled herself. Bat D— shrieked and flung up his arms. She smacked him, knee to chin, with a strange and violet warmth that flattened him to the ground. She rolled across him, was in him at every orifice—ears, urethra, anus, mouth, nostrils. She was without him. She was within him. She rolled through him. She flowed around him.

While he lay, gloriously stalled within her circling torque, with her within him within her, the Blob said: "Honey, what's *with* this shit resenting strange niggers on the subway? *That* sort of double-think earns you no popcorn coupons from the Big Movie Theater in the sky. Try to imagine an older, less vulgar epoch. Just be your sweet self—you *have* a lovely smile. But Lord, this luciprene is getting to me. Tastes like old airplane glue!"

For a moment Bat D— thought he would really die. But the Blob withdrew. Letting a howl that resembled nothing so much as the Twentieth-Century war-whoop of Sheena, Queen of the Jungle, she flung herself at Fort Sumpter VII's north wall.

It shattered.

Eyes still tight, Bat heard fragments thud outward on the sand, clatter inward to the floor.

Moments later when, panting and weak, he pulled himself erect beside the jagged pane—already frosting with ammonia from the hyperborean chill—the Blob, a football field away, was flûtchülát-ing (a method of transportation? reproduction? art?) across the black sands, making her erratic path between runulets, toward the Chroma's ceramic and silver. (7) Joe leaned his forehead on the tile above the urinal, taking deep breaths.

The man beside him zipped his fly, squeezed Joe's jacketed elbow (with that *fine* hand), and whispered: "You know, fellow, you really get into it, don't you?" (One of the Council's feyer members had actually applauded. Another had gotten scared and run.) "You're too much. . . . Maybe I'll see you in here again sometime . . . ?"

Without lifting his head, Joe grinned; and nodded—because when, on the odd Thursday you found somebody that much what you were into, it took a minute to get it back together. Faint pain pulsed in his spleen—he'd come that hard. He stuffed himself back in his fly, took another breath, looked up—

The man, and his portfolio, were gone.

On the urinal edge, semen trailed the glaze.

Joe shouldered out between two more arriving members (the blue door was marked E-3) and nearly bumped the incoming policeman. Joe grinned at the cop, nodded; automatically, the cop smiled, nodded back—then apparently remembered himself and frowned.

But Joe was already making it down the concrete ramp to the RR—when two high-school girls collided with him from behind. As he turned, "I'm sorry!" started up behind his teeth, but he chewed and chomped it into, "Hello . . ." And smiled.

One girl giggled over her packages. The other, with more packages, blinked.

After a moment the blinking one said, hesitantly: "Oh . . . excuse me."

"That's okay," Joe said. "What *are* all those?"

The packages were part of an exhibit they were setting up at the Brooklyn Public Library on the history of Puerto Rico. They talked about it through three trains. When they did say good-bye, all three of them were grinning a lot—grinning too much, Joe decided once he was in the car.

Well, old habits die hard. So kill a little harder. Interesting kids, Joe thought. Maybe he should check out the exhibit. Perhaps next Wednesday, after he'd finished standing around at Unemployment. And he would be at the Fourteenth Street john in ten minutes—unless he stopped in at Twenty-third, which, the grapevine had it, was sort of kicky this month.

—*New York*
February 1976

tapestry

They noticed that virginity was needed,
To trap the unicorn in every case,
But not that, of those virgins who succeeded,
A high percentage had an ugly face.

—Auden, *The Quest*

Imagine one loose thread pulled violently—huntsmen, virgins, hounds, hedge sparrows, hawks, and that leering Varlet will snarl, distort, mangle, and tear apart. The bone of the tapestry is coarse linen, lined and backed with something resembling canvas. And all the faces and hands of all the hundred figures throughout the seven tapestries are woven in a distorted way. Examine the hand of that man with his sleeve fallen halfway down his forearm. What is it? Thread, silk, nothing living, only gray and white stitching.

The panel there is incomplete. Note the torn edges. How much smaller it is! But it was once as big as the others. Extrapolate the threads, pull them together, and watch the Virgin woven into her virginity again. The Unicorn is white, the only animal displayed with his sex recognizable, whereas hounds, foxes, and the tight-crotched and doubleted hunters all seem to be placed in conveniently decent positions—or castrated. Extend the torn cloth, continue the intertwining of flower and vine that makes the background. Who has captured whom? Has the pale, imprisoned girl seduced this godhorse, or has—by all the laws of logic—the horse seduced her? The rest of the tapestry is gone. We do not know. Europa and the white bull—the godhead metamorphosed into a virile animal, whose virility is thread and silk and brocade. The witch who left us instructions on how to catch Unicorns failed to mention whether the Virgin was good for more than one throw.

There is blood in every tapestry but the first.

A wild boar is goring a hound. The Unicorn is pierced through the side in his corral, and the Virgin . . . is no longer a Virgin. The leering Varlet from the castle is slain in a hunting accident.

Notice that there is no water in any of the tapestries except through the artificial means of a fountain. No rivulet, no seascape in the distance, no dew or rain in any scene. And the fountain is not on a panel which shows blood, signifying that this is not a Christian allegory. Or is, at any rate, only supposed to look like one to the uninitiate. Blood as a Christian symbol must always be accompanied by water: Christ's pierced side, and the rains that followed; the water transubstantiated into blood at the Last Supper is only given its power through the water with which Christ washed the feet of the disciples. No, the women who designed these tapestries wove into them something other than religious mysteries, but, to avoid heresy, gave it a seeming religious cast by the Unicorn with the pierced side: the Christ crucified. Without the sea, the order of rivers, the royalty of waves, there is no true religious dignity. The Jordan, the Ganges, the Euphrates, or the Styx, the river through the Vale of Tempe, or the Boreal streams around Ultima Thule: and there is a lake at Nemi.

There is no hint of the sea here, and so something else is intended. Look at the fragmentary tapestry again. What was woven into the missing part? Take time and wind it in gold, red, and turquoise filaments. Wind those into woods' flowers, make elders and beech trees, oaks and yews with purplish bark. This fragment purportedly showed the Virgin luring the Unicorn to the trap. How? Take time, take twenty minutes, and weave it into a tapestry. Oh, she must have stood at least that long in the forest, waiting, uncomfortably, her corset too tight and the brocade of her paneled skirt caught with bits of leaves. She bites at a hangnail on her thumb, starts as a jay or a lapwing utters its condensed shriek. The forest floor beneath the embroidered flowers is damp and moistens her thin soles. She has sweated in the heavy dress, even though the air is cool, and she fears her underarms will smell through her perfume. Halfheartedly she looks for mint to chew but cannot find it in the profusion of weeds and undergrowth.

A sound. She whirls her head and stops it, jaw-jarring hard, transfixing the darkness beyond the trees; and her hair shakes in its coiffure beneath the veil of her conical cap. The leaves shiver in front of her, and the fear she feels twists in her stomach, a squirming knot of little animals she'd never known nested there. Her train ruffles, and the breeze ruffling it moves leaves from a stretch of dirty white: the shoulder of the beast. He'd been sleeping all afternoon in a damp bower where the greenery had mostly fallen off the trees, and he had rubbed the grass down to a frizzle with his thrashing-around nights. The Unicorn has not bathed in four months, and issues an unpleasant, horsey smell. Rising, he pokes his head into the thicket, the horn cleaving blossoms and quivering. The Virgin sees immediately that its spirals are not really regular at all. Obviously he has not taken care of it because it is tarnished and chipped. His eyes are large, brown, and the whites, which show just at the back and front of the almond-shaped aperture of his eye sockets, are bloodshot. Mucus has strung down from them, as on a lapdog who has not had its eyes washed with boric acid. The black labia of his nostrils expand.

The Virgin is disgusted.

So is the Unicorn: although he finds the smell of her sweating flesh attractive, the medicinal pungency of alcohol and ambergris, the rancid hair oil, sweetened with dead flowers, revolt him. But he is still sleepy, and comes nearer. His hooves are muddy, she notes. Men who don't wash their feet, at least before getting into bed, have always annoyed her—as a concept; she *is* a virgin and only knows about such things through reading. His horn should be polished. She takes a step nearer and stops when he snorts; snot flies in globules and strings. Then he winks a nostril at her and whinnies. The Virgin is fascinated by his vulgarity. Her stomach feels a little weak—but she is fascinated. Staring at the mess on his nose, she is about to abandon the whole silly thing and make her way back to the castle as best she can, when suddenly the animal bends his head and wipes it off on the grass, leaving the blades darker, shiny, broken. Well, it's off his face. As he raises his head, the Virgin takes one more step.

The Unicorn is encouraged and leaps forward.

The Virgin shrieks, tries to run backward, trips over the end of her train, and sprawls, spread-eagled, the wind knocked out of her; her cap has come off; she can feel her hairdo gone loose; and the silly Unicorn is leering down at her with the oddest grin she can possibly picture on the teeth of a horse. Gingerly she tries to roll over but the beast is standing on her dress. She glances through his forelegs and sees that his stomach is almost hairless, pink-skinned like the belly of a rat, incredibly dirty. The whole area of his sex is matted and muddy and gives the impression of something profoundly useless. The only way it could have possibly gotten in that condition, she thinks, is from masturbating on a muddy log.

He neighs at her, and her face is splattered with drops of saliva. Goddamn it, she thinks. Violently she rolls aside—the dress rips beneath his muddy hoof. Then she screams, because the Unicorn has bent down and flicked her back to her back with his horn, ripping her bodice and opening a cut from an inch over her nipple to above her collarbone, and tearing a shoulder ligament. It hurts like hell. "You cut that out," she cries. Tears whirl into her eyes, making them burn. There's blood on her fingers.

Again she pulls; the dress rips more, but the Unicorn jumps back, perhaps afraid of the blood. The Virgin manages to get to her feet, holding her skirt up with one hand and her bodice closed with the other. The Unicorn backs away, walks in a circle (his rectum is matted with dung halfway down his thighs, and his tail is burred with nettles and wood-lice), paws the ground. Again he faces her, coming toward her with watered thighs and the silver of his hooves visible in flakes through dried mud. The green boughs dip and whisper oppressively, and the sun suddenly scatters gold coins over his back that slip off, one by one, as he walks forward. She walks backward, terrified and bleeding.

Her back comes up against bark.

With rubies in his eyes he brings his head toward hers, and the flies crawling in his ear shimmer like green glass in the stained marble trumpet. His nose, wet velvet, pushes her neck, and he moves his shoulder and foreleg against her, and her hand is on the rough pelt, shivering in the decision whether to push him away, or to press him closer as her father has instructed. He whispers to her in a voice like sand ground into crumpled leaves. Among hoarse gasps and neighings, she hears: "You fool! You fool! I'm only a myth in Unicorn's clothing, but I'll rip you to bloody pieces. . . !" Pressure hardens into a bent knee on her belly. Protests get all snarled up with what is in her throat. She breaks away, trips, regains her footing, flees. . . .

Something turns forest to cathedral in her head. As she stumbles, the labyrinth of trees becomes halls, galleries, carved stone, a haphazard cloister of apseways and narthex posts in which is suddenly raised the image of a crucifixion of someone not her. Vines petrify before her into classical friezes. And his feet on the sod sound like metal balls flung at granite. Like mad hags and tree wraiths, leaves whip her on, whip her shoulder where the dress is torn; twigs like spread fingers slap her forehead and catch her hair as she ducks beneath a low limb, which is for her the buttress flying by the choir columns of oak. He is close to her, a rhythm of hooves syncopated with limb snappings, skittering rocks, and the battering of leaves on her forelegs. She will run, and the pain builds burning in her chest; and she will canter, while terror solidifies into rotten logs in the path, flailing black branches, and the raking cries of seven rooks, circling; and she will. . . .

—New York
September 1960

prismatica

Homage à James Thurber

I

Once there was a poor man named Amos. He had nothing but his red hair, fast fingers, quick feet, and quicker wits. One gray evening when the rain rumbled in the clouds, about to fall, he came down the cobbled street toward Mariners' Tavern to play jackstraws with Billy Belay, the sailor with a wooden leg and a mouth full of stories that he chewed around and spit out all evening. Billy Belay would talk and drink and laugh and sometimes sing. Amos would sit quietly and listen—and always win at jackstraws.

But this evening as Amos came into the tavern, Billy was quiet; and so was everyone else. Even Hidalga, the woman who owned the tavern and took no man's jabbering seriously, was leaning her elbows on the counter and listening with opened mouth.

The only man talking was tall, thin, and gray. He wore a gray cape, gray gloves, gray boots, and his hair was gray. His voice sounded to Amos like wind over mouse fur, or sand ground into old velvet. The only thing about him not gray was a large black trunk beside him, high as his shoulder. Several rough and grimy sailors with cutlasses sat at his table—they were so dirty they were no color at all!

". . . and so," the soft gray voice went on, "I need someone clever and brave enough to help my nearest and dearest friend and me. It will be well worth someone's while."

"Who is your friend?" asked Amos. Though he had not heard the beginning of the story, the whole tavern seemed far too quiet for a Saturday night.

The gray man turned and raised a gray eyebrow. "There is my

friend, my nearest and dearest." He pointed to the trunk. From it came a low, muggy *Ulmphf*.

All the mouths that were hanging open about the tavern closed.

"What sort of help does he need?" asked Amos. "A doctor?"

The gray eyes widened, and all the mouths opened once more.

"You are talking of my nearest and dearest friend," said the gray man, softly.

From across the room Billy Belay tried to make a sign for Amos to be quiet, but the gray man turned around, and the finger Billy had put to his lips went quickly into his mouth as if he were picking his teeth.

"Friendship is a rare thing these days," said Amos. "What sort of help do you and your friend need?"

"The question is: would you be willing to give it?" said the gray man.

"And the answer is: if it is worth my while," said Amos, who really could think quite quickly.

"Would it be worth all the pearls you could put in your pockets, all the gold you could carry in one hand, all the diamonds you could lift in the other, and all the emeralds you could haul up from a well in a brass kettle?"

"That is not much for true friendship," said Amos.

"If you saw a man living through the happiest moment of his life would it be worth it then?"

"Perhaps it would," Amos admitted.

"Then you'll help my friend and me?"

"For all the pearls I can put in my pockets, all the gold I can carry in one hand, all the diamonds I can lift in the other, all the emeralds I can haul up from a well in a brass kettle, *and* a chance to see a man living through the happiest moment of his life—I'll help you!"

Billy Belay put his head down on the table and began to cry. Hidalga buried her face in her hands. All the other people in the tavern turned away and began to look rather gray themselves.

"Then come with me," said the gray man, and the rough sailors with cutlasses rose about him and hoisted the trunk to their grimy shoulders—*Onvbpmf* came from the trunk—and the gray man flung out his cape, grabbed Amos by the hand, and ran out into the street.

In the sky the clouds swirled and bumped each other, trying to upset the rain.

Halfway down the cobbled street the gray man cried, "Halt!"

Everyone halted and set the trunk down on the cobblestones.

The gray man went over and picked up a tangerine-colored alley cat that had been searching for fish heads in a garbage pail. "Open the trunk," he said. One of the sailors took an iron key from his belt and opened the lock on the top of the box. The gray man took out his thin sword of gray steel and pried up the lid ever so slightly. Then he tossed the cat inside.

Immediately he let the lid drop, and the sailor with the iron key locked the lock on the top. From inside came the mew of a cat that ended with a deep, depressing *Elmblmpf*.

"I think," said Amos, who after all thought quickly and was quick to tell what he thought, "that everything is not quite right in there."

"Be quiet and help me," said the thin gray man, "or I shall put *you* in the trunk with my nearest and dearest."

For a moment Amos was just a little afraid.

II

Then they were on a ship, and all the boards were gray from having gone so long without paint. The gray man took Amos into his cabin, and they sat down on opposite sides of a table.

"Now," said the gray man, "here is a map."

"Where did you get it?" asked Amos.

"I stole it from my worse and worst enemy."

"What is it a map of?" Amos asked. He knew you should ask as many questions as possible when there were so many things you didn't know.

"It is a map of many places and many treasures, and I need someone to help me find them."

"Are these treasures the pearls and gold and diamonds and emeralds you told me about?"

"Nonsense," said the gray man. "I have more emeralds and diamonds and gold and pearls than I know what to do with," and he opened a closet door.

Amos stood blinking as jewels by the thousands fell out on the floor, glittering and gleaming, red, green, and yellow.

"Help me push them back in the closet," said the gray man. "They're so bright that if I look at them too long, I get a headache."

So they pushed the jewels back and leaned against the closet door till it closed. Then they returned to the map.

"Then what *are* the treasures?" Amos asked, full of curiosity.

"The treasure is happiness, for me and my nearest and dearest friend."

"How do you intend to find it?"

"In a mirror," said the gray man. "In three mirrors—or rather, one mirror broken in three pieces."

"A broken mirror is bad luck," said Amos. "Who broke it?"

"A wizard so great and so old and so terrible that you and I need never worry about him."

"Does this map tell where the pieces are hidden?"

"Exactly," said the gray man. "Look, we are here."

"How can you tell?"

"The map says so," said the gray man. And sure enough, in large letters one corner of the map was marked: HERE.

"Perhaps somewhere nearer than you think, up this one, and two leagues short of over there, the pieces are hidden."

"Your greatest happiness will be to look into this mirror?"

"It will be the greatest happiness for myself and for my nearest and dearest friend."

"Very well," said Amos. "When do we start?"

"When the dawn is foggy and the sun is hidden and the air is gray as gray can be."

"Very well," said Amos a second time. "Until then, I shall walk around and explore your ship."

"That will be tomorrow at four o'clock in the morning," said the gray man. "So don't stay up too late."

"Very well," said Amos a third time.

As Amos was about to leave, the gray man picked up a ruby that had fallen from the closet and not been put back. On the side of the trunk, which now sat in the corner, was a small triangular door that Amos had not seen. The gray man pulled it open, tossed in the ruby, and slammed it quickly: *Orghmflbfe.*

III

Outside, the clouds hung so low the top of the ship's tallest mast threatened to prick one open. The wind tossed about in Amos's red hair and scurried in and out of his rags.

Sitting on the railing of the ship a sailor was splicing a rope.

"Good evening," said Amos. "I'm exploring the ship, and I have very little time. I have to be up at four o'clock in the morning. So can you tell me what I must be sure to avoid because it would be so silly and uninteresting that I would learn nothing from it?"

The sailor frowned awhile, then said, "There is nothing at all interesting in the ship's brig."

"Thank you very much," said Amos and walked on till he came to another sailor whose feet were awash in soap suds. The sailor was pushing a mop back and forth so hard that Amos decided he was trying to scrub the last bit of color off the gray boards. "Good evening to you too," said Amos. "I'm exploring the ship, and I have very little time since I'm to be up at four o'clock in the morning. I was told to avoid the brig. So could you point it out to me? I don't want to wander into it by accident."

The sailor leaned his chin on his mop handle awhile, then said, "If you want to avoid it, don't go down the second hatchway behind the wheelhouse."

"Thank you very much," said Amos and hurried off to the wheelhouse. When he found the second hatchway, he went down very quickly and was just about to go to the barred cell when he saw the grimy sailor with the iron key—who must be the jailer as well, thought Amos.

"Good evening," Amos said. "How are you?"

"I'm fine, and how is yourself, and what are you doing down here?"

"I'm standing here, trying to be friendly," said Amos. "I was told there was nothing of interest down here. And since it is so dull, I thought I would keep you company."

The sailor fingered his key awhile, then said, "That is kind of you, I suppose."

"Yes, it is," said Amos. "What do they keep here that is so uninteresting everyone tells me to avoid it?"

"This is the ship's brig, and we keep prisoners here. What else should we keep?"

"That's a good question," said Amos. "What *do* you keep?"

The jailer fingered his key again, then said, "Nothing of interest at all."

Just then, behind the bars, Amos saw the pile of grubby gray blankets move. A corner fell away, and he saw just the edge of something as red as his own bright hair.

"I suppose, then," said Amos, "I've done well to avoid coming here." And he turned around and left.

But that night, as the rain poured over the deck and the drum-drum-drumming of heavy drops lulled everyone on the ship to sleep, Amos hurried over the slippery boards under the dripping eaves of the wheelhouse to the second hatchway, and went down. The lamps were low, the jailer was huddled asleep in a corner on a piece of gray canvas, but Amos went immediately to the bars and looked through.

More blankets had fallen away, and besides a red as bright as his own hair, he could see a green the color of parrot's feathers, a yellow as pale as Chinese mustard, and a blue brilliant as the sky at eight o'clock in July. Have you ever watched someone asleep under a pile of blankets? You can see the blankets move up and down, up and down with breathing. That's how Amos knew this was a person. "*Pssst,*" he said. "You colorful but uninteresting person, wake up and talk to me."

Then all the blankets fell away, and a man with more colors on him than Amos had ever seen sat up rubbing his eyes. His sleeves were green silk with blue and purple trimming. His cape was crimson with orange design. His shirt was gold with rainbow checks, and one boot was white and the other was black.

"Who are you?" asked the parti-colored prisoner.

"I am Amos, and I am here to see what makes you so uninteresting that everyone tells me to avoid you and covers you up with blankets."

"I am Jack, the Prince of the Far Rainbow, and I am a prisoner here."

"Neither one of those facts is so incredible compared to some of the things in this world," said Amos. "Why are you the Prince of the Far Rainbow, and why are you a prisoner?"

"Ah," said Jack, "the second question is easy to answer, but the first is not so simple. I am a prisoner here because a skinny gray man stole a map from me and put me in the brig so I could not get it back from him. But why am I the Prince of the Far Rainbow? That is exactly the question asked me a year ago today by a wizard so great and so old and so terrible that you and I need never worry about him. I answered him, 'I am Prince because my father is King, and everyone knows I should be.' Then the wizard asked me, 'Why should you be Prince and not one of a dozen others? Are you fit to rule? Can you judge fairly? Can you resist temptation?' I had no idea what he meant, and again I answered, 'I am Prince because my father is King.' The wizard took a mirror and held it before me. 'What do you see?' he asked. 'I see myself, just as I should, the Prince of the Far Rainbow,' said I. Then the wizard grew furious and struck the mirror into three pieces and cried, 'Not until you look into this mirror whole again will you be Prince of the Far Rainbow, for a woman worthy of a prince is trapped behind the glass, and not till she is free can you rule in your own land.' There was an explosion, and when I woke up, I was without my crown, lying dressed as you see me now in a green meadow. In my pocket was a map that told me where all the pieces were hidden. Only it did not show me how to get back to the Far Rainbow. And still I do not know how to get home."

"I see, I see," said Amos. "How did the skinny gray man steal it from you, and what does he want with it?"

"Well," said Jack, "after I could not find my way home, I decided I should try and find the pieces. So I began to search. The first person I met was the thin gray man, and with him was his large black trunk in which, he said, was his nearest and dearest friend. He said if I would work for him and carry his trunk, he would pay me a great deal of money with which I could buy a ship and continue my search. He told me that he himself would very much like to see a woman worthy of a prince. 'Especially,' he said, 'such a colorful prince as you.' I carried his trunk for many months, and at last he paid me a great deal of money with which I bought a ship. But then the skinny gray man stole my map, stole my ship, and put me here in the brig, and told me that he and his nearest and dearest friend would find the mirror all for themselves."

"What could he want with a woman worthy of a prince such as you?" asked Amos.

"I don't even like to think about it," said Jack. "Once he asked me to unzip the leather flap at the end of the trunk and stick my head in to see how his nearest and dearest friend was getting along. But I would not because I had seen him catch a beautiful blue bird with red feathers round its neck and stick it through the same zipper, and all there was was an uncomfortable sound from the trunk, something like *Orulmhf*."

"Oh, yes," said Amos. "I know that sound. I do not like to think what he would do with a woman worthy of a prince such as you either." Yet Amos found himself thinking of it. "His lack of friendship for you certainly doesn't speak well of his friendship for his nearest and dearest."

Jack nodded.

"Why doesn't he get the mirror himself, instead of asking me?" Amos wanted to know.

"Did you look at where the pieces were hidden?" asked Jack.

"I remember that one is two leagues short of over there, the second is up this one, and the third is somewhere nearer than you think."

"That's right," said Jack. "And nearer than you think is a great, gray, dull, tangled, boggy, and baleful swamp. The first piece is at the bottom of a luminous pool in the center. But it is so gray there that the gray man would blend completely in with the scenery and never get out again. Up this one is a mountain so high that the North Wind lives in a cave there. The second piece of the mirror is on the highest peak of that mountain. But it is so windy, and the gray man is so thin, he would be blown away before he was halfway to the top. Two leagues short of over there, where the third piece is, there stretches a garden of violent colors and rich perfumes where black butterflies glisten on the rims of pink marble fountains, and bright vines weave in and about. The only thing white in the garden is a silver-white unicorn who guards the last piece of the mirror. Perhaps the gray man could get that piece himself, but he will not want to, I know, for lots of bright colors give him a headache."

"Then it says something for his endurance that he was able to put up with your glittering clothes for so long," said Amos. "Anyway, I don't think it's fair of our gray friend to get your mirror with your map. You should at least have a chance at it. Let me see. The first place we are going is somewhere nearer than you think."

"In the swamp, then," said Jack.

"Would you like to come with me," asked Amos, "and get the piece yourself?"

"Of course," said Jack. "But how?"

"I have a plan," said Amos, who could think very quickly when he had to. "Simply do as I say." Amos began to whisper through the bars. Behind them the jailer snored on his piece of canvas.

IV

At four o'clock the next morning when the dawn was foggy and the sun was hidden and the air was as gray as gray could be, the ship pulled up to the shore of a great, gray, dull, tangled, boggy, and baleful swamp.

"In the center of the swamp," said the gray man, pointing over the ship's railing, "is a luminous pool. At the bottom of the pool is a piece of mirror. Can you be back with it by lunch?"

"I think so," said Amos. "But that *is* terribly gray. I might blend into the scenery so completely I could never get out again."

"With your red hair?" asked the gray man.

"My red hair," said Amos, "is only on the top of my head. My clothes are ragged and dirty and will probably turn gray in no time with all this mist. Are there any bright-colored clothes on the ship, glittering with gold and gleaming with silk?"

"There is my closet full of jewels," said the gray man. "Wear as many as you want."

"They would weigh me down," said Amos, "and I could not be back for lunch. No, I need a suit of clothes that is bright and brilliant enough to keep me from losing myself in all that. For if I *do* lose myself, *you* will never have your mirror."

So the gray man turned to one of his sailors and said, "You know where you can get him such a suit."

As the man started to go, Amos said, "It seems a shame to take someone's clothes away, especially since I might not come back anyway. Give my rags to whoever owns the suit to keep for me until I return." Amos jumped out of his rags and handed them to the sailor, who trotted off toward the wheelhouse. Minutes later he was back with a bright costume: the sleeves were green silk with blue and purple trimming, the cape was crimson with orange design, the shirt was gold with rainbow checks, and sitting on top of it all was one white boot and one black.

"These are what I need," said Amos, putting on the clothes quickly, for he was beginning to get chilly standing in his underwear. Then he climbed over the edge of the boat into the swamp. He was so bright and colorful that nobody saw the figure in dirty rags run quickly behind them to the far end of the ship and also climb over into the swamp. Had the figure been Amos—it was wearing Amos' rags—the red hair might have attracted some attention, but Jack's hair, for all his colorful costume, was a very ordinary brown.

The gray man looked after Amos until he disappeared. Then he put his hand on his forehead, which was beginning to throb a little, and leaned against the black trunk, which had been carried to the deck.

Glumphvmr came from the trunk.

"Oh, my nearest and dearest friend," said the gray man, "I had almost forgotten you. Forgive me." He took from his pocket an envelope, and from the envelope he took a large, fluttering moth. "This flew in my window last night," he said. The wings were pale blue, with brown bands on the edges, and the undersides were flecked with spots of gold. He pushed in a long metal flap at the side of the trunk, very like a mail slot, and slid the moth inside.

Fuffle came from the trunk; the gray man smiled.

In the swamp, Amos waited until the prince had found him. "Did you have any trouble?" Amos asked.

"Not at all," laughed Jack. "They didn't even notice that the jailer was gone." For what they had done last night, after we left them, was to take the jailer's key, free the prince, and tie up the jailer and put him in the cell under all the gray blankets. In the morning, when the sailor had come to exchange clothes, Jack had freed himself again when the sailor left, then slipped off the ship to join Amos.

"Now let us find your luminous pool," said Amos, "so we can be back by lunch."

Together they started through the marsh and muck. "You know," said Amos, stopping once to look at a gray spiderweb that spread from the limb of a tree above them to a vine creeping on the ground, "this place isn't so gray after all. Look closely."

And in each drop of water on each strand of the web, the light was broken up as if through a tiny prism into blues and yellows and reds. As they looked, Jack sighed. "These are the colors of the Far Rainbow," he said.

Jack said no more, but Amos felt sorry for him. They went quickly now toward the center of the swamp.

"No, it isn't completely gray," said Jack. On a stump beside them a green-gray lizard blinked a red eye at them, a golden hornet buzzed above their heads, and a snake that was gray on top rolled out of their way and showed an orange belly.

"And look at that!" cried Amos.

Ahead through the tall gray tree trunks, silvery light rose in the mist.

"The luminous pool!" cried the prince, and they ran forward.

Sure enough, they found themselves on the edge of a round, silvery pool. Across from them, large frogs croaked, and one or two bubbles broke the surface. Together Amos and Jack looked into the water.

Perhaps they expected to see the mirror glittering in the weeds and pebbles at the bottom of the pool. Perhaps they expected their own reflections. But they saw neither. Instead, the face of a beautiful girl looked up at them from below the surface.

Jack and Amos frowned. The girl laughed. And the water bubbled.

"Who are you?" asked Amos.

In return, from the bubbles they heard, "Who are you?"

"I am Jack, Prince of the Far Rainbow," said Jack, "and this is Amos."

"I am a woman worthy of a prince," said the face in the water, "and my name is Lea."

Now Amos asked, "Why are you worthy of a prince? And how did you get where you are?"

"Ah," said Lea, "the second question is easy to answer, but the first is not so simple. For that is the same question asked me a year and a day ago by a wizard so great and so old and so terrible that you and I need never worry about him."

"What did you say to him?" asked Jack.

"I told him I could speak all the languages of men, that I was brave and strong and beautiful, and could govern beside any man. He said I was proud, and that my pride was good. But then he saw how I looked in mirrors at my own face, and he said that I was vain, and my vanity was bad, and that it would keep me apart from the prince I was worthy of. The shiny surface of all things, he told me, will keep us apart, until a prince can gather the pieces of the mirror together again, which will release me."

"Then I am the prince to save you," said Jack.

"Are you indeed?" asked Lea, smiling. "A piece of the mirror I am trapped in lies at the bottom of this pool. Once I myself dived from a rock into the blue ocean to retrieve the pearl of white fire that my mother had dropped into the sea and that I wear on my forehead now. That was the deepest dive ever heard of by man or woman, and this pool is ten feet deeper than that. Will you still try?"

"I will try and perhaps die trying," said Jack, "but I can do no more and no less." Then Jack filled his lungs and dove headlong into the pool.

Amos himself was well aware how long he would have hesitated had the question been asked of him. As the seconds passed, he began to fear for Jack's life, and wished he had had a chance to figure some other way to get the mirror out. One minute passed. Perhaps they could have tricked the girl into bringing it up herself. Two minutes—they could have tied a string to the leg of a frog and sent him down to do the searching. Three minutes—there was not a bubble on the water, and Amos surprised himself by deciding the only thing to do was to jump in and at least try to save the prince—

There was a splash at his feet!

Jack's head emerged. A moment later his hand holding the large fragment of a mirror broke surface.

Amos was so delighted he jumped up and down. The prince swam to shore, and Amos helped him out. Then they leaned the mirror against a tree and rested for a while. "It's well I wore these rags of yours," said Jack, "and not my own clothes, for the weeds would have caught in my cloak and the boots would have pulled me down and I would have never come up. Thank you, Amos."

"It's a very little thing to thank me for," Amos said. "But we had better start back if we want to be at the ship in time for lunch."

So they started back and by noon had nearly reached the ship. The prince left the mirror with Amos and darted on ahead to get back to the cell. Then Amos walked out to the boat with the broken glass.

"Well," he called up to the thin gray man, who sat on the top of the trunk, waiting, "here is your mirror from the bottom of the luminous pool."

The gray man was so happy he jumped from the trunk, turned a cartwheel, then fell to wheezing and coughing and had to be slapped on the back several times by the sailors.

"Good for you," he said when Amos had climbed onto the deck and given him the glass. "Now come have lunch with me, but for heaven's sake get out of that circus tent before I get another headache."

So Amos took off the prince's clothes, and a sailor took them to the brig and returned with Amos's rags. When Amos had dressed and was about to go in with the gray man to lunch, his sleeve brushed the gray man's arm. The gray man stopped and frowned so deeply his face became almost black. "These clothes are wet, but the ones you wore were dry. . . ."

"So they are," said Amos. "What do you make of that?"

The gray man scowled and contemplated and cogitated, but could not make anything of it. At last he said, "Never mind. Come and eat."

The sailors carried the black trunk below with them, and Amos and his host ate a heavy and hearty meal. The gray man speared all the radishes from the salad on his knife and flipped them into a funnel he had stuck in a round opening in the trunk: *Fulrmp, Melrulf, Ulfmphgrumf!*

V

"When do I go after the next piece?" Amos asked when they had finished.

"Tomorrow evening when the sunset is golden and the sky is turquoise and the rocks are stained red in the setting sun," said the gray man. "I shall watch the whole proceedings with sunglasses."

"I think that's a good idea," said Amos. "You won't get such a headache."

That night Amos again went to the brig. No one had missed the jailer yet. So there was no guard at all.

"How is our friend doing?" Amos asked the prince, pointing to the bundle of blankets in the corner.

"Well enough," said Jack. "I gave him food and water when they brought me some. I think he's asleep now."

"Good," said Amos. "So one-third of your magic mirror has been found. Tomorrow evening I go off for the second piece. Would you like to come with me?"

"I certainly would," said Jack. "But tomorrow evening it will not be so easy, for there will be no mist to hide me."

"Then we'll work it so you won't have to hide," said Amos. "If I remember you right, the second piece is on the top of a windy mountain so high the North Wind lives in a cave there."

"That's right," said Jack.

"Very well then, I have a plan." Again Amos began to whisper through the bars. Jack smiled and nodded.

They sailed all that night and all the next day. Toward evening they pulled into a rocky shore where a few hundred yards away a mountain rose high and higher into clear twilight.

The sailors gathered on the deck of the ship just as the sun began to set, and the gray man put one gray gloved hand on Amos' shoulder and pointed to the mountain with his other. "There, among the windy peaks, is the cave of the North Wind. Even higher, on the highest and windiest peak, is the second fragment of the mirror. It is a long, dangerous, and treacherous climb. Shall I expect you back for breakfast?"

"Certainly," said Amos. "Fried eggs, if you please, once over lightly, and plenty of hot sausages."

"I will tell the cook," said the gray man.

"Good," said Amos. "Oh, but one more thing. You say it is windy there. I shall need a good supply of rope, then, and perhaps you can spare a man to go with me. A rope is not much good if there is a person only on one end. If I have someone with me, I can hold him if he blows off, and he can do the same for me." Amos turned to the sailors. "What about that man there? He has a rope and is well muffled against the wind."

"Take whom you like," said the gray man, "so long as you bring back my mirror." The well-muffled sailor with the coil of rope on his shoulder stepped forward with Amos.

Had the gray man not been wearing his sunglasses against the sunset, he might have noticed something familiar about the sailor, who kept looking at the mountain and would not look back. But as it was, he suspected nothing.

Amos and the well-muffled sailor climbed down onto the rocks, which the sun had stained red, and started toward the mountain.

Once the gray man raised his glasses as he watched them go but lowered them quickly, for it was the most golden hour of the sunset. The sun sank, and he could not see them anymore. Even so, he stood at the rail a long time till a sound in the darkness roused him from his reverie: *Blmvghm!*

Amos and Jack climbed long and hard through the evening. When darkness fell, at first they thought they would have to stop, but the clear stars made a mist over the jagged rocks, and a little later the moon rose. After that it was easier going. Shortly the wind began. First a breeze tugged at their collars. Then rougher gusts nipped their fingers. At last buffets of wind flattened them against the rock one moment, then tried to jerk them loose the next. The rope was very useful indeed, and neither one complained. They simply went on climbing, steadily through the hours. Once Jack paused a moment to look back over his shoulder at the silver sea below and said something that Amos couldn't hear.

"What did you say?" cried Amos above the howl.

"I said," the prince cried back, "look at the moon!"

Now Amos looked over his shoulder too and saw that the white disk was going slowly down.

They began again, climbing faster than ever, but in another hour the bottom of the moon had already sunk below the edge of the ocean. At last they gained a fair-sized ledge where the wind was not so strong. Above, there seemed no way to go any higher.

Jack gazed out at the moon and sighed. "If it were daylight, I wonder if I could see all the way to the Far Rainbow from here."

"You might," said Amos. But though his heart was with Jack, he still felt good spirits were important to keep up. "We might see it a lot more clearly from the top, you know." But as he said it, the last light of the moon winked out. Now even the stars were gone, and the blackness about them was complete. Then, as they turned to seek shelter in the rising wind, Amos cried, "There's a light!"

"Where's a light?" cried Jack.

"Glowing behind those rocks," cried Amos.

An orange glimmer outlined the top of a craggy boulder. They hurried toward it over the crumbly ledge. When they climbed the rock, they saw that the light came from behind another wall of stone farther away, and they scrambled toward it, pebbles and bits of ice rolling under their hands. Behind the wall the light was even stronger above another ridge. They did their best to climb it without falling who-knows-how-many hundreds of feet to the mountain's foot. At last they pulled themselves onto the ledge and leaned against the side, panting. Far ahead of them, orange flames flickered brightly and there was light enough to see each other's faces. For all the cold wind their foreheads were shiny with the sweat.

"Come on," said Amos, "just a little way. . . ."

And from half a dozen directions they heard: *Come on, just a little . . . just a little way . . . little way . . .*

They stared at each other and Jack jumped up. "Why, we must be in the cave of . . ."

And echoing back they heard: *. . . must be in the cave . . . in the cave of . . . cave of . . .*

". . . the North Wind," whispered Amos.

They started forward again toward the fires. It was so dim and the cave was so big that even with the light they could not see the ceiling or the far wall. The fires themselves burned in huge scooped-out stone basins. They must have been put there for a warning, because just beyond them the floor of the cave dropped away and there was only rolling black.

"I wonder if she's at home," whispered Jack.

Then, before them, was a rushing and a rumbling and a roiling; and from the blackness a voice said, "I am the North Wind, and I am very much at home."

A blast of air sent the fires reeling in the basins, and the sailor's cap that Jack wore flew back into the dark.

"Are you really the North Wind?" Amos asked.

"Yes, I am really the North Wind," came the thunderous voice. "Now you tell me who you are before I blow you into little pieces and scatter them over the whole wide world."

"I am Amos, and this is Jack, Prince of the Far Rainbow," said Amos. "We wandered into your cave by accident and meant nothing improper. But the moon went down, so we had to stop climbing, and we saw your light."

"Where were you climbing to?"

Now Jack said, "To the top of the mountain where there is a piece of a mirror."

"Yes," said the North Wind, "there is a mirror there. A wizard so great and so old and so terrible that you and I never need worry about him placed it there a year and a day ago. I blew him there myself in return for a favor he did me a million years past, for it was he who made this cave for me by artful and devious magic."

"We have come to take the mirror back," said Jack.

The North Wind laughed so loudly that Amos and the prince had to hold onto the walls to keep from blowing away. "It is so high and so cold up there that you will never reach it," said the Wind. "Even the wizard had to ask my help to put it there."

"Then," called Amos, "you could help us get there too?"

The North Wind was silent a whole minute. Then she asked, "Why should I? The wizard built my cave for me. What have you done to deserve such help?"

"Nothing yet," said Amos. "But we can help you if you help us."

"How can you help me?" asked the Wind.

"Well," said Amos, "like this. You say you are really the North Wind. How can you prove it?"

"How can you prove you are really you?" returned the Wind.

"Easily," said Amos. "I have red hair, I have freckles, I am five feet, four inches tall, and I have brown eyes. All you need do is to go to Hidalga who owns the Mariners' Tavern and ask her who has red hair, is so tall, with such eyes, and she will tell you, 'It is my own darling Amos.' And Hidalga's word should be proof enough for anybody. Now, what do *you* look like?"

"What do I look like?" demanded the North Wind.

"Yes, describe yourself to me."

"I'm big and I'm cold and I'm blustery—"

"That's what you *feel* like," said Amos. "Not what you look like. I want to know how I would recognize you if I saw you walking quietly down the street toward me when you were not working."

"I'm freezing and I'm icy and I'm chilling—"

"Again, that's not what you look like; it's what you feel like."

The North Wind rumbled to herself for a while and at last confessed: "But no one has seen the wind."

"So I'd heard," said Amos. "But haven't you ever looked into a mirror?"

"Alas," sighed the North Wind, "mirrors are always kept inside people's houses where I am never invited. So I never had a chance to look in one. Besides, I have been too busy."

"Well," said Amos, "if you help get us to the top of the mountain, we will let you look into the fragment of the mirror." Then he added, "Which is more than your friend the wizard did, apparently." Jack gave Amos a little kick, for it is not a good thing to insult a wizard so great and so old and so terrible as all that, even if you and I *don't* have to worry about him.

The North Wind mumbled and groaned around the darkness for a while and at last said, "Very well. Climb on my shoulders, and I shall carry you up to the highest peak of this mountain. When I have looked into your mirror, I will carry you down again to where you may descend the rest of the way by yourselves."

Amos and Jack were happy as they had ever been, and the North Wind roared to the edge of the ledge, and they climbed on her back, one on each shoulder. They held themselves tight by her long, thick hair, and the Wind's great wings filled the cave with such a roaring that the fires, had they not been maintained by magic, would have been blown out. The sound of the great wing feathers clashing against one another was like steel against bronze.

The North Wind rose up in her cave and sped toward the opening that was so high they could not see the top and so wide they could not see the far wall, and her leaf-matted hair brushed the ceiling, and her long, ragged toenails scraped the floor, and the tips of her wings sent boulders crashing from either side as she leapt into the black.

They circled so high they cleared the clouds, and once again the stars were like diamonds dusting the velvet night. She flew so long that at last the sun began to shoot spears of gold across the horizon; and when the ball of the sun had rolled halfway over the edge of the sea, she settled one foot on a crag to the left, her other foot on the pinnacle to the right, and bent down and, with her great hard hand, set them on the tallest peak in the middle.

"Now where is the mirror?" asked Amos, looking around.

The dawning sun splashed the snow and ice with silver.

"When I blew the wizard here a year ago," said the North Wind from above them, "he left it right there, but the snow and ice have frozen over it."

Amos and the prince began to brush the snow from a lump on the ground, and beneath the white covering was pure and glittering ice. It was a very large lump, nearly as large as the black trunk of the skinny gray man.

"It must be in the center of this chunk of ice," said Jack. As they stared at the shiny, frozen hunk, something moved inside it, and they saw it was the form of the lovely Lea, who had appeared to them in the pool.

She smiled at them and said, "I am glad you have come for the second piece of the mirror, but it is buried in this frozen shard of ice. Once, when I was a girl, I chopped through a chunk of ice to get to an earring my sister had dropped the night before in a winter dance. That block of ice was the coldest and hardest ice any man or woman had ever seen. This block is ten degrees colder. Can you chop through it?"

"I can try," said Jack, "or perhaps die trying. But I can do no more and no less." And he took up the small pickax they had used to help them climb the mountain.

"Will you be finished before breakfast time?" asked Amos, glancing at the sun.

"Of course before breakfast," said the prince, and fell to chopping. The ice chips flew around him, and he worked up such a sweat that in all the cold he still had to take off his shirt. He worked so hard that in one hour he had laid open the chunk, and there, sticking out, was the broken fragment of mirror. Tired but smiling, the prince lifted it from the ice and handed it to Amos. Then he went to pick up his shirt and coat.

"All right, North Wind," cried Amos. "Take a look at yourself."

"Stand so that the sun is in your eyes," said the North Wind, towering over Amos, "because I do not want anyone else to see before I have."

So Amos and Jack stood with the sun in their eyes, and the great blustering North Wind squatted down to look at herself in the mirror. She must have been pleased with what she saw, because she gave a long, loud laugh that nearly blew them from the peak. She leapt a mile into the air, turned over three times, then swooped down upon them, grabbing them up and setting them on her shoulders. Amos and Jack clung to her long, thick hair as the Wind began to fly down the mountain. The Wind cried out in a windy voice: "Now I shall tell all the leaves and whisper to all the waves who I am and what I look like, so they can chatter about it among themselves in autumn and rise and doff their caps to me before a winter storm." The North Wind was happier than she had ever been since the wizard first made her cave.

It gets light on the top of a mountain well before it does at the foot, and this mountain was so high that when they reached the bottom the sun was nowhere in sight, and they had a good half hour until breakfast.

"You run along and get back in your cell," said Amos, "and when I have given you enough time, I shall return and eat my eggs and sausages."

So the prince ran down the rocks to the shore and snuck onto the ship, and Amos waited for the sun to come up. When it did, he started back.

VI

But, at the boat, all had not gone according to Amos' plan during the night. The gray man, still puzzling over Amos' wet clothes—and at last he'd begun to inquire whom Amos had solicited from the sailors to go with him—had gone to the brig himself.

In the brig he saw immediately that there was no jailer—then that there was no prisoner! Furious, he rushed into the cell and began to tear apart the blankets in the corner. Out of the blankets rolled the jailer, bound, gagged, and dressed in the costume of the Prince of the Far Rainbow. For it was the jailer's clothes that Jack had worn when he had gone with Amos to the mountain.

When the gag came off, the story came out, and the part of the story the jailer had slept through, the gray man could guess for himself. So he untied the jailer and called the sailors and made plans for Amos' and the prince's return. The last thing the gray man did was take the beautiful costume back to his cabin where the black trunk waited.

When Amos came up to the ship with the mirror under his arm, he called, "Here's your mirror. Where are my eggs and sausages?"

"Sizzling hot in the pan," said the gray man, lifting his sunglasses. "Where is the sailor you took to help you?"

"Alas," said Amos, "he was blown away by the wind." He climbed up the ladder and handed the gray man the mirror. "Now we only have a third to go, if I remember right. When do I start looking for that?"

"This afternoon when the sun is its highest and hottest," said the gray man.

"Don't I get a chance to rest?" asked Amos. "I have been climbing up and down mountains all night."

"You may take a nap," said the gray man. "But come and have breakfast first." The gray man put his arm around Amos' shoulder and took him down to his cabin where the cook brought them a big, steaming platter of sausages and eggs.

"You have done very well," said the gray man, pointing to the wall where he had hung the first two pieces of the mirror together. Now they could make out what the shape of the third would be. "And if you get the last one, you will have done very well indeed."

"I can almost feel the weight of those diamonds and emeralds and gold and pearls right now," said Amos.

"Can you really?" asked the gray man. He pulled a piece of green silk from his pocket, went to the black box, and stuffed it into a small square door: *Orlmnb!*

"Where is the third mirror hidden?" asked Amos.

"Two leagues short of over there is a garden of violent colors and rich perfume, where black butterflies glisten on the rims of pink marble fountains, and the only thing white in it is a silver-white unicorn who guards the third piece of the mirror."

"Then it's good I am going to get it for you," said Amos, "because even with your sunglasses, it would give you a terrible headache."

"Curses," said the gray man, "but you're right." He took from his pocket a strip of crimson cloth with orange design, went to the trunk, and lowered it through a small round hole in the top. As the last of it dropped from sight, the trunk went *Mlpbgrm!*

"I am very anxious to see you at the happiest moment of your life," said Amos. "But you still haven't told me what you and your nearest and dearest friend expect to find in the mirror."

"Haven't I?" said the gray man. He reached under the table and took out a white leather boot, went to the trunk, lifted the lid, and tossed it in.

Org! This sound was not from the trunk; it was Amos swallowing his last piece of sausage much too fast. He and the gray man looked at one another, and neither said anything. The only sound was from the trunk: *Grublmeumplefrmp . . . hic!*

"Well," said Amos at last, "I think I'll go outside and walk around the deck a bit."

"Nonsense," said the gray man, smoothing his gray gloves over his wrists. "If you're going to be up this afternoon, you'd better go to sleep right now."

"Believe me, a little air would make me sleep much better."

"Believe *me*," said the gray man, "I have put a little something in your eggs and sausages that will make you sleep much better than all the air in the world."

Suddenly Amos felt his eyes grow heavy, his head grow light, and he slipped down in his chair.

When Amos woke up, he was lying on the floor of the ship's brig inside the cell, and Jack, in his underwear—for the sailors had jumped on him when he came back in the morning and given the jailer back his clothes—was trying to wake him up.

"What happened to you?" Amos asked, and Jack told him.

"What happened to you?" asked Jack, and Amos told *him*.

"Then we have been found out, and all is lost," said the prince. "For it is noon already, and the sun is at its highest and hottest. The boat has docked two leagues short of over there, and the gray man must be about to go for the third mirror piece himself."

"May his head split into a thousand shards," said Amos, "with the pain."

"Pipe down in there," said the jailer. "I'm trying to sleep." And he spread out his piece of gray canvas and lay down.

Outside the water lapped at the ship, and after a moment Jack said, "A river runs by the castle of the Far Rainbow, and when you go down into the garden, you can hear the water against the wall just like that."

"Now don't be sad," said Amos. "We need all our wits about us."

From somewhere there was the sound of knocking.

"Though, truly," said Amos, glancing at the ceiling, "I had a friend once named Billy Belay, an old sailor with a wooden leg, I used to play jackstraws with. When he would go upstairs to his room in the Mariner's Tavern, you could hear him walking overhead just like that."

That knocking came again.

"Only that isn't above us," said Jack. "It's below."

They looked at the floor. Then Jack got down on his hands and knees and looked under the cot. "There's a trapdoor there," he whispered to Amos, "and somebody's knocking."

"A trapdoor in the *bottom* of a ship?" asked Amos.

"We won't question it," Jack said; "we'll just open it."

They grabbed the ring and pulled the door back. Through the opening there was only the green surface of the water. Then, below the surface, Lea appeared.

"What are you doing here?" whispered Amos.

"I've come to help you," she said. "You have gotten two-thirds of the broken mirror. Now you must get the last piece."

"How did you get here?" asked Jack.

"Only the shiny surface of things keeps us apart," said Lea.

"Now if you dive through here, you can swim out from under the boat."

"And once we get out from under the boat," said Amos, "we can climb back in."

"Why should we do that?" asked Jack.

"I have a plan," said Amos.

"But will it work even if the gray man is already in the garden of violent colors and rich perfumes, walking past the pink marble fountains where the black butterflies glisten on their rims?" asked Jack.

"It will work as long as the silver-white unicorn guards the fragment of the mirror," said Amos, "and the gray man doesn't have his hands on it. Now dive."

The prince dove, and Amos dove after him.

"Will you pipe down in there," called the jailer without opening his eyes.

In the garden the gray man, with sunglasses tightly over his eyes and an umbrella above his head, was indeed walking through violent colors and rich perfumes, past pink marble fountains where black butterflies glistened. It was hot. He was dripping with perspiration. His head was in agony.

The gray man had walked a long time. Even through his dark glasses he could make out the green and red blossoms, the purple fruit on the branches, the orange melons on the vines. The most annoying things of all, however, were the swarms of golden gnats that buzzed about him. He would beat them away with the umbrella, but they came right back.

After what seemed a long, long trek, he saw a flicker of silver-white. Coming closer, he saw it was a unicorn. It stood in the little clearing, blinking. Just behind the unicorn was the last piece of the mirror.

"Well, it's about time," said the gray man and began walking toward it. But as soon as he stepped into the clearing, the unicorn snorted and struck his front feet against the ground, one after the other.

"I'll just get it quickly without any fuss," said the gray man. But when he stepped forward, the unicorn also stepped forward and the gray man found the sharp point of the unicorn's horn against the gray cloth of his shirt—right where it covered his belly button.

"I'll have to go around it then," said the gray man. But when he moved to the right, the unicorn moved to the right. When he moved to the left, the unicorn did the same.

From the mirror there was a laugh.

The gray man peered across the unicorn's shoulder, and in the piece of glass he saw not his own reflection but the face of a young woman. "I'm afraid," she said cheerfully, "that you shall never be able to pick up the mirror unless the unicorn lets you, for it was placed here by a wizard so great and so old and so terrible that you and I need never worry about him."

"Then what must I do to make this stubborn animal let me by? Tell me quickly because I am in a hurry and have a headache."

"You must prove yourself worthy," said Lea.

"How do I do that?"

"You must show how clever you are," said Lea. "When I was free of this mirror, my teacher, in order to see how well I had learned my lessons, asked me three questions. I answered all three, and these three questions were harder than any questions ever heard by man or woman. I am going to ask you three questions that are ten times as hard, and if you answer them correctly, you may pick up the mirror."

"Ask me," said the gray man.

"First," said Lea, "who is standing just behind your left shoulder?"

The gray man looked back over his shoulder, but all he saw were the bright colors of the garden. "Nobody," he said.

"Second," said Lea, "who is standing just behind your right shoulder?"

The gray man looked back the other way and nearly took off his sunglasses. Then he decided it was not necessary, for all he saw was a mass of confusing colors. "Nobody," he said.

"Third," said Lea, "what are they going to do to you?"

"There is nobody there, and they are going to do nothing," said the gray man.

"You have gotten all three questions wrong," said Lea sadly.

Then somebody grabbed the gray man by the right arm, somebody grabbed him by the left, and they pulled him down on his back, rolled him over on his stomach, and tied his hands behind him. One picked him up by the shoulders and the other by the feet, and they only paused long enough to get the mirror from the clearing, which the unicorn let them have gladly, for there was no doubt that *they* could have answered Lea's questions.

One of the two was Amos, wearing the top half of the costume of the Prince of the Far Rainbow, minus a little green patch from the sleeve and a strip from the crimson cape: he had stood behind some bushes so the gray man could not see his less colorful pants. The other was Prince Jack himself, wearing the bottom of the costume, minus the white leather boot: he had stood behind a low-hanging branch so the gray man had not been able to see him from the waist up.

With the mirror safe—nor did they forget the gray man's umbrella and sunglasses—they carried him back to the ship. Amos' plan had worked: they had managed to climb back on the ship, and, since all the sailors, without the gray man there to prod them, had taken a nap at noon, they had gotten the costume from the gray man's cabin without being seen and had gone after him into the garden.

But here luck turned against them, for no sooner had they reached the shore when the sailors descended on them. The jailer had at last woken up and, finding his captives gone, had organized a searching party, which set out just as Amos and the prince reached the boat.

"Crisscross, cross, and double-cross!" cried the gray man triumphantly as once more Amos and Jack were led to the brig.

The trapdoor had been nailed firmly shut this time, and even Amos could not think of a plan.

"Cast off for the grayest and gloomiest island on the map," cried the gray man.

"Cast off!" cried the sailors.

"And do not disturb me till we get there," said the skinny gray man. "I have had a bad day today, and my head is killing me."

The gray man took the third piece of mirror to his cabin, but he was too ill to fit the fragments together. So he put the last piece on top of the trunk, swallowed several aspirins, and lay down.

VII

On the grayest, gloomiest island on the map is a large, gray, gloomy castle. Stone steps lead up from the shore to the castle entrance. This was the skinny gray man's gloomy gray home. On the following gray afternoon, the ship pulled up to the bottom of the steps, and the gray man, leading two bound figures, walked up to the door.

Later, in the castle hall, Amos and the prince stood bound by the back wall. The gray man chuckled to himself as he hung up the two-thirds completed mirror. The final third was on the table.

"At last it is about to happen," said the gray man. "But first, Amos, you must have your reward for helping me so much." He led Amos, still tied, to a small door in the wall. "In there is my jewel garden. I have more jewels than any man in the world. *Ugh!* They give me a headache. Go quickly, take your reward, and when you come back, I shall show you a man living through the happiest moment of his life. Then I will put you *and* your jewels into the trunk with my nearest and dearest friend."

With the tip of his thin gray sword he cut Amos' ropes, thrusting him into the jewel garden and closing the small door firmly behind him.

It was a sad Amos who wandered through those bright piles of precious gems that glittered and gleamed about. The walls were much too high to climb and they went all the way around. Being a clever man, Amos knew there were some situations in which it was a waste of wit to try and figure a way out. So, sadly, he picked up a small wheelbarrow lying on top of a hill of rubies and began to fill his pockets with pearls. When he had hauled up a cauldron full of gold from the well in the middle of the garden, he put all his reward in the wheelbarrow, went back to the small door, and knocked.

The door opened, and, with the wheelbarrow, Amos was yanked through and bound again. The gray man marched him back to the prince's side and wheeled the barrow to the middle of the room.

"In just a moment," said the thin gray man, "you will see a man living through the happiest moment of his life. But first I must make sure my nearest and dearest friend can see, too." He went to the large black trunk, which seemed even blacker and larger, and stood it on end. With his great iron key he opened it almost halfway, so that it faced the mirror. But from where Amos and Jack were, they could not see into it at all.

The gray man took the last mirror piece, went to the wall, and fitted it in place, saying, "The one thing I have always wanted more than anything else, for myself, for my nearest and dearest friend, is a woman worthy of a prince."

Immediately there was thunder, and light shot from the restored glass. The gray man stepped back.

From the mirror stepped the beautiful and worthy Lea.

"Oh, happiness!" laughed the thin gray man. "She is gray too!"

For Lea was cloaked in gray from head to foot. But almost before the words were out, she loosed her gray cloak, and it fell about her feet.

"Oh, horrors!" cried the thin gray man, and stepped back again.

Under her cloak she wore a scarlet cape with flaming rubies that glittered in the lightning. Now she loosed her scarlet cape, and that too fell to the floor.

"Oh, misery!" screamed the gray man, and stepped back once more.

For beneath her scarlet cape was a veil of green satin, and topazes flashed yellow along the hem. Now she threw the veil back from her shoulders.

"Oh, ultimate depression!" shrieked the thin gray man, and stepped back again, for the dress beneath the veil was silver with trimmings of gold, and her bodice was blue silk set with sapphires.

The last step took the thin gray man right into the open trunk. He cried out, stumbled, the trunk overturned on its side, and the lid fell to with a clap.

There wasn't any sound at all.

"I had rather hoped we might have avoided that," said Lea, as she came over to untie Jack and Amos. "But there is nothing we can do now. I can never thank you enough for gathering the mirror and releasing me."

"Nor can we thank you," said Amos, "for helping us do it."

"Now," said Jack, rubbing his wrists, "I can look at myself again and see why I am Prince of the Far Rainbow."

He and Lea walked to the mirror and looked at their reflections.

"Why," said Jack, "I am a prince because I am worthy to be a prince, and with me is a woman worthy to be a princess."

In the gilded frame now was no longer their reflection, but a rolling land of green and yellow meadows, with red and white houses, and far off a golden castle against a blue sky.

"That's the land of the Far Rainbow!" cried Jack. "We could almost step through into it!" And he began to go forward.

"What about me?" cried Amos. "How do I get home?"

"The same way we do," said Lea. "When we are gone, look into the mirror and you will see your home too."

"And that?" asked Amos, pointing to the trunk.

"What about it?" said Jack.

"Well, what's in it?"

"Look and see," said Lea.

"I'm afraid to," said Amos. "It has said such dreadful and terrible things."

"You, afraid?" asked Jack. "You, who rescued me three times from the brig, braved the gray swamp, and rode the back of the North Wind!"

But Lea inquired gently, "What did it say? I have studied the languages of men, and perhaps I can help. What did it say?"

"Oh, awful things," said Amos, "like *onvbpmf* and *elmblmpf* and *orghmflbfe*."

"That means," said Lea, " 'I was put in this trunk by a wizard so great and so old and so terrible that you and I need never worry about him.'"

"And it said *glumphvmr* and *fuffle* and *fulrmp,*" Amos told her.

"That means," said Lea, "'I was put here to be the nearest and dearest friend to all those grim, gray people who cheat everybody they meet and who can enjoy nothing colorful in the world.'"

"Then it said *orlmnb* and *mlpbgrm* and *gruglmeumplefrmp—hic!*"

"Loosely translated," said Lea: "'One's duty is often a difficult thing to do with the cheerfulness, good nature, and diligence that others expect of us; nevertheless . . .'"

"And when the thin gray man fell into the trunk," said Amos, "it didn't make any sound at all."

"Which," said Lea, "can be stated as: 'I've done it.' Roughly speaking."

"Go see what's in the trunk," said Jack. "It's probably not so terrible after all."

"If you say so," said Amos. He went to the trunk, walked all around it three times, then—gingerly—lifted the lid. He didn't see anything, so he lifted it farther. When he still didn't see anything, he opened it all the way. "Why, there's nothing in—" he began. But something caught his eye at the bottom of the trunk. He reached in and picked it up.

It was a short, triangular bar of glass.

"A prism!" said Amos. "Isn't that amazing. I mean, can you actually *believe* . . ."

But Amos was alone in the castle hall. Jack and Lea had already left. Amos ran to the mirror just in time to see them walking away across the green and yellow meadows to the golden castle. Lea leaned her head on Jack's shoulder, and the prince turned to kiss her raven hair, and Amos thought: "Now there are *two* people living through the happiest moment of their lives."

Then the picture changed, and Amos was looking down a seaside, cobbled street, wet with rain. A storm had just ended. The clouds were breaking apart. Down the block the sign on the Mariners' Tavern swung in the breeze.

Amos ran to get his wheelbarrow, put the prism on top, and wheeled it to the mirror. Then, just in case, he went back and locked the trunk.

Someone opened the door of the Mariners' Tavern and called in, "Why is everybody so glum this evening when there's a beautiful rainbow looped across the world?"

"It's Amos!" cried Hidalga, running from behind the counter.

"It *is* Amos!" cried Billy Belay, thumping after her on his wooden leg.

Everyone else in the tavern came running out too. Sure enough it was Amos, and sure enough a rainbow looped above them to the far horizon.

"Where have you been?" cried Hidalga. "We all thought you were dead."

"You wouldn't believe me if I told you," said Amos, "for you are always saying you take no man's jabbering seriously."

"Any man who can walk out of a tavern one night with nothing and come back in a week with that—" and she pointed to the wheelbarrow full of gold and jewels—"is a man to be taken seriously."

"Then marry me," said Amos, "for I always thought you had uncommonly good sense in matters of whom to believe and whom not to. Your last words have proved you worthy of my opinion."

"I certainly shall," said Hidalga, "for I always thought you an uncommonly clever man. Your return with this wheelbarrow has proved *you* worthy of *my* opinion."

"I thought you were dead, too," said Billy Belay, "after you ran out of here with that thin gray man and his big black trunk. He told us terrible stories of the places he intended to go. But you just up and went with him without having heard anything except the reward."

"There are times," said Amos, "when it is better to know only the reward and not the dangers."

"And this was obviously such a time," said Hidalga, "for you are back now, and we are to be married."

"Well, come in, then," said Billy, "and play me a game of jack-straws, and you can tell us all about it."

They went back into the tavern, wheeling the barrow before them.

"What is this?" asked Hidalga as they stepped inside. She picked up the glass prism from the top of the barrow.

"That," said Amos, "is the other end of the far rainbow."

"The other end of the rainbow?" asked Hidalga.

"Over there," said Amos, pointing back out the door, "is that end. And over there is that end," and he pointed out the front window, "and right here is the *other* end."

Then he showed her how a white light shining through it would break apart and fill her hands with all the colors she could think of.

"Isn't that amazing," said Hidalga. "I mean, can you actually *believe* . . ."

"That's just what I said," Amos told her, and they were both very happy, for they were both clever enough to know that when a husband and wife agree about such things, it means a long and happy marriage is ahead.

—New York
1961

ruins

Lightning cracked a whip on the dark, scarring it with light. Clikit ran for the opening, ducked, fell, and landed in dust. Outside, rain began with heavy drops, fast and full. He shook his head, kneeled back, and brushed pale hair from his forehead. Taut, poised, he tried to sense odors and breezes the way, he fancied, an animal might.

There was the smell of wet dirt.

The air was hot and still.

Blinking, he rubbed rough hands over his cheeks, pulling them away when the pain in his upper jaw above that cracked back tooth shot through his head. A faint light came around corners. Clikit kneaded one ragged shoulder. Dimly he could see a broken column and smashed plaster.

Behind him, the summer torrent roared.

He stood, trying to shake off fear, and walked forward. Over the roar came a clap like breaking stone. He crouched, tendons pulling at the backs of his knees. Stone kept crumbling. Beneath the ball of his foot he could feel sand and tiny pebbles—he had lost one sandal hours ago. He stepped again and felt the flooring beneath his bare foot become tile. The strap on his other sandal was almost worn through. He knew he would not have it long—unless he stopped to break the leather at the weak spot and retie it. Clikit reached the wall and peered around cautiously for light.

In a broken frame above, a blue window let in Tyrian radiance. The luminous panes were held with strips of lead that outlined a screaming crow.

Clikit tensed. But over the fear he smiled. So, he had taken refuge in one of the ruined temples of Kirke, eastern god of Myetra. Well, at least he was traveling in the right direction. It was Myetra he had set out for, uncountable days, if not weeks, ago.

In a corner the ceiling had fallen. Water filmed the wall, with lime streaks at the edge. A puddle spread the tile, building up, spilling a hand's breadth, building again, inching through blue light. As he looked down at the expanding reflection of the ruined ceiling, he pondered the light's origin, for—save the lightning—it was black outside.

He walked to the wall's broken end, looked behind for the source—and sucked in his breath.

Centered on white sand a bronze brazier burned with unflickering flame. Heaped about its ornate feet were rubies, gold chains, damascened blades set with emeralds, silver proof, crowns clotted with sapphires and amethysts. Every muscle in Clikit's body began to shake. Each atom of his feral soul quivered against its neighbor. He would have run forward, scooped up handfuls of the gems, and fled into the wild wet night, but he saw the figure in the far door.

It was a woman.

Through white veils he could see the ruby points of her breasts, then the lift of her hip as she walked out onto the sand, leaving fine footprints.

Her hair was black. Her eyes were blue. "Who are you, stranger?" And her face . . .

"I'm Clikit . . . and I'm a thief, Lady! Yes, I steal for a living. I admit it! But I'm not a very *good* thief. I mean a very bad one. . . ." Something in the expression that hugged her high cheekbones, that balanced over her lightly cleft chin made him want to tell her everything about himself. "But you don't have to be afraid of me, Lady. No, really! Who are—?"

"I am a priestess of Kirke. What do you wish here, Clikit?"

"I was . . ." Dusty and ragged, Clikit drew himself up to his full four-feet-eleven-inches. "I was admiring your jewels there."

She laughed. And the laugh made Clikit marvel at how a mouth could shape itself to such a delicate sound. A smile broke on his own stubbled face, that was all wonder and confusion and unknowing imitation. She said: "Those jewels are nothing to the real treasure of this temple." She gestured toward them with a slim hand, the nails so carefully filed and polished they made Clikit want to hide his own broad, blunt fingers back under his filthy cloak.

Clikit's eyes darted about between the fortune piled before him (and beside him! and behind him!) and the woman who spoke so slightingly of it. Her ebon hair, though the light from the brazier was steady, danced with inner blues.

"Where are you from?" she asked. "Where are you going? And would you like to see the real treasure of the temple?"

"I am only a poor thief, Lady. But I haven't stolen anything for days, I haven't! I live out of the pockets of the rich who stroll the markets of Voydrir, or from what I can find not tied down on the docks of Lehryard, or from what is left out in the gardens of the affluent suburbs in Jawahlo. But recently, though, I've heard of the wealth of Myetra. I only thought I would journey to see for myself. . . ."

"You are very near Myetra, little thief." Absently she raised one hand, thumb and forefinger just touching, as if she held something as fine as the translucent stuffs that clothed her.

And dirty Clikit thought: It is my life she holds, my happiness, my future—all I ever wanted or all I could ever want.

"You must be tired," she went on, dropping her hand. "You have come a long way. I will give you food, rest; moreover, I shall display for you our real treasure. Would you like that?"

Clikit's back teeth almost always pained him, and he had noticed just that morning that another of his front ones (next to the space left from the one that had fallen out by itself a month ago) was loose enough to move with his tongue. He set his jaw hard, swallowed, and opened his mouth again. "That's . . . kind of you," he said, laying two fingers against his knotted jaw muscle, eyes tearing with the pain. "I hope I have the talents to appreciate it."

"Then follow. . . ." She turned away with a smile he desperately wanted to see again—to see whether it was a taunting one at him, or a glorious one for him. What he remembered of it, as he trotted after her, had lain in the maddeningly ambiguous between.

Then he glanced down at her footprints. Fear shivered in him.

Alabaster toe and pink heel had peeked at him from under her shift. But the prints on the white sand were not of a fleshed foot. He stared at the drawn lines—was it some great bird's claw? No, it was bone! A skeleton's print!

Stooping over the clawlike impression, Clikit thought quickly and futilely. If he went to search along the walls for pebbles and stones and fallen chunks of plaster, she would surely see. At once he swept up one, another, and a third handful of sand into his cloak; then he stood, gathering the edges together, twisting the cloak into a club—which he thrust behind him. At another arch the woman turned, motioning him to follow: he was shaking so much he didn't see if she smiled or not. Clikit hurried forward, hands at his back, clutching the sandy weight.

As he crossed the high threshold, he wondered what good such a bludgeon would do if she were really a ghost or a witch.

Another brazier lit the hall they entered with blue flame. He went on quickly, deciding that at least he must try. But as he reached her, without stopping she looked over her shoulder. "The real treasure of this temple is not its jewels. They are as worthless as the sands that strew the tile. Before the true prize hidden in these halls, you will hardly think of them. . . ." Her expression had no smile in it at all. Rather, it was intense entreaty. The blue light made her eyes luminous. "Tell me, Clikit—tell me, little thief—what would you like more than all the jewels in the world?" At a turn in the passage, the light took on a reddish cast. "What would you like more than money, good food, fine clothes, a castle with slaves. . . ."

Clikit managed a gappy grin. "There's very little I prefer over good food, Lady!"—one of his most frequent prevarications. There were few foods he could chew without commencing minutes of agony, and it had been that way so long that the whole notion of eating was, for him, now irritating, inevitable, and awful.

A hint of that smile: "Are you really so hungry, Clikit . . . ?"

True. With the coming of his fear, his appetite, always unwelcome, had gone. "I'm hungry enough to eat a bear," he lied, clutching the sand-filled cloak. She looked away. . . .

He was about to swing—but she turned through another arch, looking back.

Clikit stumbled after. His knees felt as though the joints had come strangely loose. In this odd yellow light her face looked older. The lines of character were more like lines of age.

"The treasure—the real treasure—of this temple is something eternal, deadly and deathless, something that many have sought, that few have ever found."

"Eh . . . what is it?"

"Love," she said, and the smile, a moment before he could decide its motivation, crumbled on her face into laughter. Again she turned from him. Again he remembered he ought to bring his bundle of sand up over his own balding head and down on the back of hers—but she was descending narrow steps. "Follow me down."

And she was, again, just too far ahead. . . .

Tripods on the landings flared green, then red, then white—all with that unmoving glow. The descent, long and turning and long again, was hypnotic.

She moved out into an amber-lit hall. "This way . . ."

"What do you mean—love?" Clikit thought to call after her.

When she looked back, Clikit wondered: Was it this light, or did her skin simply keep its yellowish hue from the light they had passed through above?

"I mean something that few signify by the word, though it hides behind all that men seek when they pursue it. I mean a state that is eternal, unchangeable, imperturbable, even by death. . . ." Her last word did not really end. Its suspiration, rather, became one with the sound of rain hissing through a broken roof in some upper corridor.

Now! thought Clikit. Now! Or I shall never find my way out! But she turned through another arch, and again his resolve fled. She was near him. She was away from him. She was facing him. She faced away. Clikit stumbled through a narrow tunnel low of ceiling and almost lightless. Then there was green, somewhere . . .

A flood of green light . . .

Again she turned. "What would you do with such a treasure?

Think of it, all around you, within you, without you, like a touch that at first seemed so painful you thought it would sear the flesh from your bones but that soon, you realized, after years and years of it, was the first you had ever known of an existence without pain. . . ."

The green light made her look . . . older, much older. The smile had become a caricature. Where, before, her lips had parted faintly, now they shriveled from her teeth.

"Imagine," and her voice made him think of sand ground in old cloth, "a union with a woman so all-knowing she can make your mind sink toward perfect fulfillment, perfect peace. Imagine drifting together down the halls of night, toward the shadowy heart of time, where pure fire will cradle you in its dark arms, where life is a memory of evil at once not even a memory. . . ." She turned away, her hair over her gaunt shoulders like black threads over stone. "She will lead you down halls of sorrow, where there is no human hunger, no human hurt, only the endless desolation of a single cry, without source or cessation. She will be your beginning and your end; and you will share an intimacy more perfect than the mind or body can endure. . . ."

Clikit remembered the burden clutched behind him. Was it lighter? He felt lighter. His brain floated in his skull, now and again bumping against the portals of perception at eye or ear. And they were turning. She was turning.

". . . leading toward perfect comprehension in the heart of chaos, a woman so old she need never consider pain, or concision, or life . . ."

The word pierced him like a mouse fang.

Clikit pulled his cloak from behind him and swung it up over his shoulder with cramped forearms. But at that instant she turned to face him. Face? . . . No face! In blue light black sockets gaped from bald bone. Tattered veils dropped from empty ribs. She reached for him, gently taking an edge of his rags between small bone and bone. Empty?

His waving cloak was empty! The sand had all trickled through some hole in the cloth.

Struggling to the surface of his senses, Clikit whirled, pulled away, and fled along the hall. Laughter skittered after him, glancing from the damp rock about him.

"Come back, my little thief. You will never escape. I have almost wrapped my fingers around your heart. You have come too far . . . too far into the center—" Turning a corner, Clikit staggered into a tripod that overturned, clattering. The steady light began to flicker. "You will come back to me. . . ." He threw himself against the wall, and, because for some reason his legs would not move the way he wanted, he pulled himself along the rocks with his hands. And there was rain or laughter.

And the flickering dimmed.

A tall old woman found him huddled beside her shack door next day at dawn.

Wet and shivering, he sat, clutching his bare toes with thick, grubby fingers, now and again muttering about his sandal strap—it had broken somewhere along a stone corridor. From under a dirty, thinning tangle like cornsilk, his gray gaze moved slowly about the yard.

First she told him to go away, sharply, several times. Then she bit her lower lip and just looked down at him awhile. Finally, she went back into the shack—and came out, minutes later, with a red crock bowl of broth. After he drank it, his talk grew more coherent. Once, when he stopped suddenly, after a whole dozen sentences that had actually made a sort of sense to her, she ventured:

"The ruins of Kirke's temple are an evil place. There are stories of lascivious priestesses walled up within the basement catacombs as punishment for their lusts. But that was hundreds of years ago. Nothing's there now but mice and spiders."

Clikit gazed down into the bowl between his thumbs.

"The old temple has been in ruin for over a century," the woman went on. "This far out of the city, there's no one to keep it up. Really, we tell the children to stay away. But every year or so some youngster falls through some unseen hole or weak spot into some crypt, to break an arm or leg." Then she asked: "If you really wandered so far in, how did you find your way out?"

"The sand . . ." Clikit turned the crock, searching among the bits of barley and kale still on its bottom. "As I was stumbling through those corridors, I saw the trail of sand that had dribbled through my cloak. I made my way along the sandy line—sometimes I fell, sometimes I thought I had lost it—until I staggered into the room where I had first seen the . . ." His pale eyes lifted. ". . . the jewels!"

For the first time the old woman actually laughed. "Well, it's too bad you didn't stop and pick up some of that 'worthless treasure' on your way. But I suppose you were too happy just to have reached open air."

"But I did!" The little man tugged his ragged cloak around into his lap, pulling and prodding at the knots in it. "I did gather some. . . ." One knot came loose. "See . . . !" He pulled loose another.

"See what?" The tall woman bent closer as Clikit poked in the folds.

In the creases was much fine sand. "But I—" Clikit pulled the cloth apart over his lap. More sand broke out and crumbled away as he ran his fingers over it. "I stopped long enough to put a handful of the smaller stones in. Of course, I could take nothing large. Nothing large at all. But there were diamonds, sapphires, and four or five gold lockets set with pearls. One of them had a great black one, right in . . ." He looked up again. ". . . the middle . . ."

"No, it's not a good place, those ruins." Frowning, the woman bent closer. "Not a good place at all. I'd never go there, not by myself on a stormy summer night."

"But I *did* have them," Clikit repeated. "How did they—? Where did they—?"

"Perhaps—" The woman started to stand but stopped, because of a twinge along her back; she grimaced—"your jewels trickled through the same hole by which you lost your sand."

The man suddenly grasped her wrist with short, thick fingers. "Please, take me into your house, Lady! You've given me food. If

you could just give me a place to sleep for a while as well? I'm wet.
And dirty. Let me stay with you long enough to dry. Let me sleep a
bit, by your stove. Maybe some more soup? Perhaps you—or one of
your neighbors—has an old cloak. One without so many holes?
Please, Lady, let me come inside—"

"No." The woman pulled her hand away smartly, stood slowly.
"No. I've given you what I can. It's time for you to be off."

Inside the tall old woman's shack, on a clean cloth over a hard-
wood table, lay sharp, small knives for cutting away inflamed gum,
picks for cracking away the deposits that built up on teeth around
the roots, and tiny files—some flat, some circular—for cleaning out
the rotten spots that sometimes pitted the enamel, for the woman's
position in that hamlet was akin to a dentist's, an art at which,
given the primitive times, she was very skilled. But her knives and
picks and files were valuable, and she had already decided this
strange little man was probably a wandering thief fallen on hard
times—if not an outright bandit.

A kind woman, she was, yes; but not a fool. "You go on, now,"
she said. "I don't want you to come in. Just go."

"If you let me stay with you a bit, I could go back. To the temple.
I'd get the jewels. And I'd give you some. Lots of them. I would!"

"I've given you something to eat." She folded her arms. "Now
go on, I said. Did you hear me?"

Clikit pushed himself to his feet and started away—not like
someone who'd been refused a request, the woman noted, but like
someone who'd never made one.

She watched the barefooted little man hobble unsteadily over a
stretch of path made mud by rain. As a girl, the old woman had
been teased unmercifully by the other children for her height, and
she wondered now if anyone had ever teased him for his shortness.
A wretch like that, a bandit? she thought. Him? "You'll be in
Myetra in half a day if you stay on the main road," she called. "And
keep away from those ruins. They're not a good place at all. . . ."
She started to call something else. But then, if only from his smile
and the smell, when she'd bent over his cloak, those teeth, she
knew, were beyond even *her* art.

She watched him a minute longer. He did not turn back. In the trees behind her shack a crow cawed three times, then flapped up and off through the branches. She picked up the red bowl, overturned on the wet grass, and stepped across the sand, drying in the sun, to go back inside and wait for whichever of the townsfolk would be the first of the day's clients.

—New York
1962

dog in a fisherman's net

After the storm, Panos spread the nets on the concrete, while his younger brother moved the iced crates from deck to dock. Spyro cuffed him to let him know he was finished. Panos grunted, the warm long sound a bear makes when satisfied. *"Ya!"* he called as Spyro started back to the boat. "Take her behind the spit. And rope the nets to the rail this time. I'll mend these dry ones."

"Ne," Spyro yelled above the clashing boats and vaulted to the deck.

Loosed, the line spun from the piling as the boat rocked backward. Panos worked his toes on the jetty's crumbling edge.

Beneath the ghost lights sheeting half the sky, two more boats bucked through the froth that lazed on the water. A wave slapped stone and flung drops higher than his head. Gold fell from cloudings east, and Panos squinted.

When he walked to the center of the net, Panos' knees jabbed from his pants. There were drops like tears on his face, jewels on his hair and sweater.

With bowed legs resting on the heels, Panos sat now and pulled up a ruined section into his lap, hooking the meshes out with his toes to keep it straight. The knife with which he cut the broken threads clean had been whet an hour that morning while he'd waited to go out. With orange thread on a bone shuttle, he retied the running diamonds.

When the fishing boats slammed in, he only looped the knots more quickly, not looking up. Shouting; dogs circling toward the dock; water—the shuttle danced in the webbing. Behind him a truck from the obsidian mines growled. The three o'clock freighter would be late because of the storm. Panos heard a handful of stones chuckle over the sideboards. Near, a running dog—

At the tug under the seat of his pants, Panos looked back over his shoulder. Legs flipped up, a pink mouth choked off a howl, and corks jumped on net wings.

The dog barked, tried to shake off the string, fell, kicked. Panos, roaring, whirled to his knees and grabbed. His own feet snagged and he stumbled. Sinkers rasped concrete. The dog bounded, was dragged back. Panos caught one leg and lost balance. When he jerked his hand back from the teeth, his fingers carried harsh threads across his own face. As he tried to roll from the yelping animal, his hand went out, stopped in string, then worse, went through. Threads chattered.

Men from the boats and the truck ran up. The one with the stick—behind orange strings, Panos saw him hesitate—struck at the dog's head. Netting strained under a cracked boot with toes showing. Netting tore.

He tried to push the men away. They were making it worse. Again the stick, but this time it went on to strike the bony point of Panos' shoulder. Fur twisted on his chest, and a hind foot pawed his cheek.

Someone else was pushing the men aside, and Panos saw Costa, all hair and grooved muscle, drop to his knees and raise a piece of concrete. The road-mender's arm was tarred to the elbow. The rock fell; Panos jerked; and something jabbed his neck—

The knife! Its blade, snagged in the net, had pierced him, hard. Costa struck the dog again, and the barking stopped. Someone kicked at the limp, sticky thing, but when Panos pulled away, somehow the point slipped in another surprising inch. Panos opened his lips to scream—and his mouth flooded with something salty, salty as the sea.

Costa, wielding the clotted rock, pushed back the men. They were shouting. "Hey, Paniyotis!"

From another, "*Ya!* Move back there!"

And, "Open the net! Slowly, slowly! *Ne!* The bitch has torn it enough—"

The last words were stones in a pool of silence.

Two crossed themselves. Two more the same. Costa backed against the waiter who had come out from *Alexi*'s, jumped, and in confusion flung the rock to the water. Behind them another boat clattered, and from the head of the dock Spyro shouted: "*Ya,* somebody take this box!"

No one turned.

Spyro cursed and jumped to the jetty. "Stop gossiping and give me a hand." He stopped beside the stubby piling and lowered the boxes himself, jerking his scarred fingers out in time. At the multiple crash, the top box nearly fell, but he caught it. "What are you staring at there?"

The men blinked at him. Costa whispered, "Your brother . . ."

Three men clenched their jaws so that their cheeks hollowed suddenly.

"What about him?" Spyro pushed the box in place. Then he frowned. "The storm blew the mackerel into our net. Has your catch been poor?"

"Spyro, your brother—" Costa stretched his hand out. Crimson slicked the tar.

"A dog," the waiter from *Alexi*'s began. "A dog got in the net. We only tried to help—"

"He was tearing the strings, Spyro."

"You know the sound of tearing nets is like the Lady's laughter at moondown."

Spyro screamed. Later, he would say, "I did not see what was tied in the torn cords. I felt it. I felt death in it. It yanked my hands up, snatched my face down and shook me by the tongue. Death stuck two fingers in my eyes. I saw nothing. I felt." They picked him up, first trying to protect themselves, then trying to keep Spyro himself from hurt. Had he reached the body, he would have hugged his own life back into it.

They took him into the café, holding him around the shoulders, holding his arms, his waist, as many as possible touching him with their live hands to protect him from the dead thing, Paniyotis.

Costa told Katina, the girl who served in the café, in two grunted sentences what had happened. She smashed her fingertips against her mouth to stop a sound, kneaded her lips, and stepped back against the whitewashed wall.

"So easy to die," said an old man, swinging his beads into his fist and silencing them for the first time that day. "So hard to grieve."

Katina started to run out, but someone grabbed her arm. "Give us coffee. And if you must run, bring a big bowl of soup back from *Alexi*'s. But first give the poor boy brandy."

With no father or brothers to set dowry, obliged to work, and therefore with no marriage possibilities, her feelings were given little care. She bit her lower lip, went to the liquor shelf and took down the Metaxa. One man called for ouzo, but another punched his arm. "Sheep! You have brandy with the grieving man, or you take only coffee."

All those crowding Spyro's table urged him to drink from their glasses as well as his own. He took only one sip from Costa's.

"Panos has had bad luck this whole year. First the falling house wall, then his poor sister who must be married at once—"

Costa hissed for silence. "Don't weigh yesterday's problems, Grandfather. Today's are heavy enough."

"And tomorrow's may be heavier," returned the old man, and began to drop his beads again.

Spyro stood up.

When he looked around, the four men who had crossed themselves at the dock raised their hands, palms up, to shield his glance.

"Gotsi! Gotsi!" insisted Costa—Sit down! Sit down!—"Katina, bring him another brandy!"

But the girl had gone.

Spyro walked to the door and saw them look at each other to see who would stop him. Before their decision, he was outside.

Two steps, three steps across the stone apron: nobody called. Unsure why, he walked back to the dock. In the confusion he recalled someone going to see that the body was taken care of, but the net still lay over the stain.

A black-shawled woman whispered something to the men unloading.

When they saw him look, their hands jumped before their eyes. Then the men stooped quickly to their boxes. Spyro turned.

Katina stood at the dock's head. Her oiled braid looped across the shoulder of her green sweater. The glance of a grieving man brings grief, he thought, and waited for her to raise her hand or look away. He saw fear in her face, but she did not try to cover it. There was something else, to which he could not fit a name. Words growled up from his belly, but stumbled once in his mouth so that he could only blurt, hoarsely, "It was my brother!"

A memory began to beat behind his eyes, hammering out Katina's face. It came by piece and patch. Then, with urgent vividness, it flooded:

Panos had borrowed a shotgun. They had saved a month for cartridges. Spyro had wrapped rags around his feet, Panos had borrowed rubber boots, and they had gone hunting in the central mountains of the island, taking turns with the gun. That afternoon they brought home six rabbits to Piope.

She jumped when they came in, and the box of seashells she had been looking through scattered on the floor. Laughing and crying, she said she had been terrified all day that one brother would accidentally shoot the other.

"Do you worry every time we go out on the boats each morning one of us will drown?" Panos grinned.

She looked at the shells over the packed dirt, then took the rabbits with an amused glance (where hints of something very deep and very frightening as well as frightened always shone in her black, tear-bright eyes), then came back from the stone sink, brushing her light hair from her forehead. There was a scar high on her right temple from the time, as a little girl, some boys threw rocks at her when she tried to play with them.

Both Spyro's and his brother's hair was black.

Piope's hair—it looked like sun in a copper cauldron filled with oil—had upset their mother terribly. She had used calimari ink to darken it and made Piope wear a kerchief every time she went outside to keep the sun from lightening it more. Now Piope's emotions fell like half-lights about the house. Things from outside brought her easily to tears or laughter, so most of the time she stayed indoors, either at housework, or playing with the shells her brothers brought her.

The broiled rabbit was tender and full-flavored, crisp with its slight fat, and juicy. Spyro was so after Panos to go again he could hardly keep his feet under him on the sloppy deck. Finally Panos took him up as far as the limestone bluffs where, beside a bush of paddle catcus leaves, they found a waist-high cypress sapling with half-exposed roots clawing the white earth. With twigs pegged to the ground, and fishing lines, Panos built a snare.

They left the sapling quivering in the autumn wind, bent double. In the morning the sapling was straight, and the dangling hare, hind foot snapped and bloody, was half-dead from exhaustion.

After that they had a rabbit nearly every other day. Then Spyro found a second sapling, and sometimes they had two at once. That was when the house wall fell.

They were coming back from the bluff, two bloody-footed hares at Spyro's waist, when confusion met them at the edge of the town. In the mountain they hadn't even felt the tremor, but along the shore it had been more severe, and the radio said that windows had been broken in Athens. But only two houses had suffered in the island's harbor town. One was a half-completed structure being built by old Austinos.

The other was theirs. The side wall was rubble. The roof sagged like cloth, raveled at the edges with dried seaweed and cracked mud. Piope, her face sore from spent hysteria, blinked in the painful sun, as she paused in her hunt among the stone for broken shells. When somebody tried to talk to her, she cried again, shaking her scarfed head, and ran behind the gnarled almond tree if they persisted.

When Spyro reached the yard through his chattering neighbors, fear filled his mouth like rocks. The shattered familiar, the safety of his birthplace broken, tried to force up questions, but rock sealed his throat. *Panos, what must we do?* But he was as incapable of speech as Piope.

Unasked, Panos answered.

He pulled the rabbits from Spyro's belt, went into the house, and came out with the rafia-covered wine jar that had escaped under the sink. "Costa," he said, "don't get too drunk this evening." He handed the jar to the tarry workman. "You will have to help us tomorrow."

A bony seven-year-old, in a pair of men's army pants ripped off above the knees and bound with rusty bailing cable over his hollow belly, stared across his knuckles. "Take these to your aunt." Panos held out the rabbits. "Perhaps they won't fill you for long, but they'll fatten the worms in your gut some." The boy's scaly eyelids widened. Then he snatched the rabbits and fled.

Spyro got his voice back. "Our house falls in, and you give away everything that remains to us?"

"A few little presents," Panos said, squeezing the back of Spyro's neck. "Are you hungry for wine and broiled rabbit?"

Spyro squinted into the house. "This makes me sicker than any storm. I couldn't hold food."

"Well then?" Panos picked out a shell from under fallen mortar and thumbed the plaster crumbs away. "We only have a little on this island, and still She snatches it away. Though the good Father prays to Kyrios Jesus for us, it may be as the herders say."

"You think because Kyrios Jesus was buried in a stone tomb instead of soil, his body cannot make the land prosper?"

Panos shrugged. "Even with all the cactus and bramble, there are still oranges, olives, and tomatoes enough. I only mean that when the Lady shows Her caprice to one of us, that man must busy his mind thinking of others, or his own misery will paralyze him. What are you crying about Piope?" He handed his sister the shell and pulled her to him while she stood holding it. "The widow Mardoupas has gone to pick up olives for oil this morning. It would take more than an earthquake to stop her fingers. That wise woman's stories made you laugh when you were a little girl. Go help her now, and perhaps you will come home in the evening laughing, even to this." He nodded back down the road. "Come," he said to Spyro.

The donkey trail they walked was walled with granite and red marble. Burros, carrying brush and vegetables between the harbor town of Adamás and the Old City, the Plaka, kept the runnel blotched with dried or steaming lumps over the yellow dirt. The land, brown two months ago in summer, rose now in green terraces on both sides. They turned for a while up the asphalt road till it left the shadow of the bluffs for the sun, and the hot macadam stung through their calluses and forced them to the chalk ditch at the road's edge, where they were quickly dusted white to the knees.

They crossed a grape arbor where the jointed vines lay like crabs on the cracked ground; then up another walled path that wound higher, till the wind at the crest slapped the backs of their necks and brushed their hair forward.

Halfway down they met some twenty goats, driven by a herder with a skinny face and most of his nails rotten from injuries scrabbling after his charges. He spoke with the half-incomprehensible, singsong speech of the old mountains. His gray eyes glittered behind pale hair that beat down his forehead in the wind. He knew a lot of stories, some filthy, most funny, as well as all the old tales. Spyro had spent much time wondering, as had most fishermen, at the light-haired, light-eyed inlanders with their priestless churches where goats were killed; who came into Adamás or the Plaka to drink only at September's equinox, when the men boasted openly in the cafés of sexual intercourse with other men, women, and their beasts. They kept their boys for work and sent their girls to the Plaka gymnasium, and left the handling of money to the women as well, saying that reading, writing, and numbers were a sort of magic, and magic was Her province.

Reaching under his chamois vest to scratch, the herder grimaced. "My sister can write the name of every man in the family, as well as put down a story you tell her one day so that she can give you back the same words in a month's time—and she is not yet fifteen."

Spyro had been to the Plaka gymnasium for a year and had seen a few of the brown-haired mountain girls. "What was your sister's name?"

Curiosity impelled the question, but the herder jabbed him with a wrinkled fist, and though he joked, his tone held alarm. "If She would not tell Her name to any man, why should I tell the name of a woman of my family to you?"

The goats clicked out across the red and orange clays that streaked the hillside. The highest peak of the island heaved from beneath the Plaka, topped with an abandoned monastery, like a jawbone in the clear, late light. Left, terraces lowered to the sea.

When Panos turned onto the stone channel that dropped toward the ruins beside the Old City, the herder laughed. "You go now to where She sleeps. Be quiet, or She may wake."

Panos only grinned at the little fellow once, but Spyro kept glancing back to where the goatherd bobbed on with his flock as he drove them back to town.

At last Spyro sat with his brother on the tower foundation, the old Roman amphitheater above and to the left, the water below. The bay curving away should have been a haven for fish, deep and undisturbed by freighters. But no Christian fisherman brought his boat here. Sometimes herders came to drop handlines from the rocks, but those fishermen who chanced the bay—and at the Orthodox Father's urging, each year a few would try—always returned with tales of snagged nets, or groundings where no rocks should be. Far along the coast, at the craggy brim of the island, smoke trickled from the mines.

Panos hugged in his knees, pulling chalky feet across the stone.

"Why?" ventured Spyro at last. "Why did we come here?"

His brother gestured with his chin. "Why do you think?"

As the sun at the horizon slit sky from water, pale gold bled on the waves. The evening was bruised with copper sores.

"It is beautiful."

"Yes."

"But still, why did we come?"

"We have had a misfortune. First we have given a little to our neighbors. Now we must give a little to—to the gods."

"To Kyrios Jesus, you mean?"

Though Paniyotis' eyes were black, they shone a moment like a herder's. "If it please you."

"Then why do you come to where She sleeps to pray to Kyrios Jesus—"

"I said nothing about prayer. Besides, how can She sleep here when the English archaeologists came and dug Her up and took Her away a hundred years ago. She may have slept here once, but now She is in a museum in Paris, in France. Your great-grandfather worked on the crew that found Her. What did they teach you in that year at the gymnasium, anyway?"

"They told us about that," Spyro nodded. "But the herders say She was not in the earth at all, but in the sea."

"You say one thing. I say another. Come." Panos rubbed the back of Spyro's neck. "You must give something too. But it must be of yourself, and quietly."

Afterward they walked home by moonlight. Though the November days were warm enough, the nights were cold. When they followed the road into the shadow of the lime bluffs, Spyro could hardly see, and had to blink after his brother, a shadow before him on the night road.

And blinking brought back Katina's face, still before him on the dock, wide-eyed, but steadily watching. "It was my brother," he repeated.

She whispered something he hardly heard, and seemed near running away.

"What?"

"I said," she repeated, " 'It was my dog.' "

"Yours—?" The mucilage that held sound to meaning had come unstuck. Spyro struggled to fix it.

"He came to the café once, when the boys had thrown cans at him and cut his side, here." She touched her ribs. "I put iodine on the cut so it wouldn't run. Then I fed him and let him sleep in my room. Now they have killed my dog—" she dropped her eyes— "and your brother." The last was softer; he watched the small jumping muscle in her cheek.

"But he was in the nets," Spyro said, for the first time trying to explain to himself what had been done. "He was tearing them, and there was no time to untangle him slowly. Each time he turned, he wreaked a day's damage. They had to kill him because he would have ruined the strings beyond retying if they tried to take him out slowly. The sound of tearing nets is like the Lady's laughter. It was an accident he was caught, and there was no—"

Horror had built in her face. "You mean the dog," she said suddenly, comprehending.

"The dog, yes. Of course I mean the dog!"

"But Paniyotis—"

At the name, rhythmic explosions began in his chest. The greatest part of grief is fear. "My brother—"

"It *was* an accident," repeated Katina, her voice hoarse. "Oh, yes. They saw the nets going, and they ran to help, to save those terrible nets!"

He could understand her sorrow over the pet, but the hard, flat anger that struggled under the words was disproportionate.

"What sort of men are they that they could not even see the trapped man for the dog. Oh, yes, it was an accident they killed him—"

"You mean my brother!" Now surprise was his.

"Your brother, yes. Of *course* I mean your brother!" Her voice, emptied of outrage, became subtle and forlorn. "I do not like this island. Here they do not know which is more important, a fisherman or his nets. Someday—" her eyes moved from thing to thing across the dock—"I am going to leave Milos. I will go to Syros, where they have many boats every day, to Piraeus, to Mykonos, and Rhodos. I can go to 'Idra, or St. Orini, or visit my aunt in Athens anytime I want, instead of waiting for the one boat here from Piraeus every Sunday. I do not like it here."

Spyro smiled, having heard her say this before, usually in exasperation at some man in the café. Her eyes returned to him, but Spyro walked back to his stack of fish boxes. A dozen women had been picking among the fish from the other boats. The smaller fish were piled on newspapers or verdigrised brass trays, the medium ones were in wide enameled baskets, and the larger were laid across iced boxes in alternate directions.

Spyro started to take the top box down, then paused to look at four girls, near Katina's age, but of good family, strolling with joined arms toward the dock.

Two old men with string shopping bags nodded and smiled to them, inquired after their fathers, turning to watch them go on. Austinos, the older man, had let it be known that as soon as his six months of mourning were over and the black armband came off, he would take a third wife. Panos had once proposed, against all advice and reason, to Ana, the prettiest and strongest of the four. The existence of unmarried Piope, whose house and dowry had not been settled, aside from his fluctuating income, made it a ludicrous proposition. Her father had instructed Ana to refuse him. Six months would probably see Austinos with her or her sister.

Spyro slid the box across the deck, and pulled back the lid. Beside the mackerel, there were several eels, four black ones and three gold-flecked marinas with long mouths. When all the boxes were open, he planted his feet wide apart and called out, "I have fish here, and today free! Here is a gift to anyone who wants it! Here is fish that the sea gave me for nothing but the sweat on my arms. The price to you is the work it takes to carry it home! Fish! Fish! Free fish here!"

One girl with Ana laughed and began to pull the others toward Spyro's boxes. They were beaten by a little girl who pointed to the largest mackerel and demanded, "That one!" She grabbed it by the tail with her left hand, thought again, and grabbed a second fish with her right, and ran. Austinos, exhorting people to respect his sixty-seven years (they ignored him), pushed a marida in his string bag. A woman jostled him, and the gold and black length slithered from an opening and was crushed by bare feet and booted. Spyro himself pushed away. Women were running toward the crowd. Children streaked off with fish over their shoulders. And one woman waddled away with six in her apron.

Something more powerful than sorrow, but propelled by it,

erupted from him. The full sound clanged in his throat for seconds before he recognized his own laughter.

Katina watched wonderingly from the other side of the dock. Slapping his thighs, Spyro turned from the jetty.

A circle of stone about him. Grass, mud, gravel, and cactus with rotten fronds shriveled among the spears. Still, a circle of stone. This must be something of yourself, and quietly.

But all he had were memories of Panos. They clawed, would not loosen, even though he was exhausted with them: Panos yawning at dawn, cursing at noon, laughing in the evening at the café. The laughter, still on Spyro's face, only netted the beasts. But oh, they turned and tore and twisted.

Below lay the harbor of the Old City, abandoned now for less accessible Adamás from which the brothers had fished. Spyro climbed from the foundation and crossed the terrace. Above were the catacombs from the time the island had been under Rome. She had wanted the mines, of course. At the gymnasium he'd learned that Rome was the capital of Italy. Italian sailors worked on the freighters that carried the obsidian and the clay. The mates and captains let their little fingernails grow long, the same as the bank clerks and the waiter at *Alexi*'s in Adamás, or the Greek sailors from the National Navy who sometimes took their leaves on the island. Spyro knew a war had ended about the time of his birth, in which Greeks fought Italians. His uncle had gone all the way to Albania to fight, and still told stories to anyone who would listen. In class, Spyro had asked if that were the war which had ended the Roman control of the mines and the Old City. Some people laughed. That laughter, which was frequent, was one reason Spyro had left the gymnasium. "Twenty years, two thousand years!" His teacher had exploded. "Does it take such great intellect to distinguish between the two?" With many of the students, both herders and fishermen, this was his most frequent chastisement. When Spyro announced at home he was not going back, Paniyotis had been quietly angry, and Piope had whispered, "I wish I could go to the gymnasium at Plaka."

"What? Like some herder's girl?" Panos snapped, and Piope, pulling her kerchief up over her strange, lovely hair, moved into the corner. But his brother's and sister's disappointment shadowed the house for days; Spyro spent most of his free time in the café over small cups of coffee, playing at tavli or cards with the older fishermen when no money was involved. After all, he was a boy, and must be allowed to do what he wanted.

Spyro dropped to the last rock by the water. The small Aegean tide rilled his feet, and to the right a stone inlet roared with froth. No matter which branch of the possible future he looked at, the fruit was ripe loneliness, to feed the beasts:

Panos flinging an octopodi again and again on the jetty, to tenderize it, till pink froth covered the stone: Panos after too much ouzo, stealing—well, borrowing, since he returned it the next day—the out-of-tune saturi hanging on the wall at *Alexi*'s, sneaking beneath the window of Ana's father the night his proposal had been refused, to set up a tinny racket on the unharmonized strings till the noise ended with her father's curses, and the curses ended with his own laughter: or later, the same morning, when it turned chilly and Spyro climbed to the roof to take a blanket to his brother who had insisted on sleeping up there the rest of the night, Panos hunched at the roof's corner, crying.

Then, again, there was Panos, his hand hard and sweating on Spyro's shoulder, when they danced together in line with the other men at the St. Barbara day festa. St. Barbara was patron of the miners. The weather had threatened since morning. Below the mine shacks the sea ground the rocks. Piope, even with the house rebuilt, was still unhappy, so they had taken her to the party and, when the dancing began, left her with widow Mardoupas and the other women, and joined the line of men who stamped and ducked with arms around each other's shoulders. Costa pounded his drum with his black fist and those that could stuffed hundred-drachma notes in the little hole at the top. Someone from the Plaka had tuned the saturi and hammered out the insistent melodies, while a concertina player, who had come from Sifnos for the day on a fishing boat, razored the winds with his yowling box. There were miners, herders, and fishermen, as well as soldiers from the National Army Airport at the far side of the island, who were only allowed in town five at a time and whose presence most people ignored.

The herders were welcomed this time because they brought three roasted goats. The trouble started when one of the soldiers, who was from Macedonia, took a herder aside and tried to tease him into teaching him one of the goat dances. They danced together, the soldier clumsily, the herder nimbly, miming obscenities at one another. Spyro and Panos watched with the other men, and Spyro laughed till his throat was sore. Then Austinos came over and objected, and some other people who had laughed at first now grew offended and called for an end. The musicians stopped, the soldier apologized and sat down, but the herder kept on. Then his friends came and danced too. The herder women began to sing for the men and stamp their sandals. When anyone tried to stop a man, he would make dirty signs and pull away laughing. Then one old woman, at least thirty, in a skirt made from a silk housecoat thrown out by some woman in town, with necklaces of shells, teeth, and polished wood, started to do the forbidden dance that the women do alone in the mountains. Some of the fishermen cried out. Someone called the herders Gypsies and said they should go away and leave decent people alone. Three boys were suddenly beside her, their light eyes frightened, but their hands knotted. Two older men stepped beside her as well, one with arms like rocks in a sausage skin. The other could have been the goatherd they'd met before on the road. "How come you have men about you, Lady?" It was Costa who called. Though his tone was contemptuous, he still called her *Lady* rather than *woman*. "Who are these standing by you now?"

"These are my sons," she gestured to the boys. "And these are their fathers." People gasped, but she creased her lips back from yellow teeth. "Though I need not one of them to protect me from any man here."

Just then the Orthodox Father, who had been taking a glass of sweet Samos in another shack, came up to see what the confusion was, still holding a half-eaten, winy apple. "Come now, come now," he said, striding through the crowd by the door where the dancing had been going since noon. The sun was down and there was only gray light left in the west. "This is a holiday," the Father said. "A saint's day. There is no time to quarrel." The Father wore his long hair in a little bun at the back, as the herder men did, and most of them respected him. But the women—

The old woman in the bright dress gave a growl of disgust.

Panos, who was holding Spyro's arm, suddenly squeezed. They had laughed at the dance before, but it was suddenly as if the lewdness had been ripped away revealing—evil or good, Spyro did not know, but it was vast as the secrets behind his sister's unsettling stare.

"Be friends," continued the Father. "This is Saint Barbara's day—"

"You dirty Her with a name that can be said by men," the woman answered with drawling contempt that turned to rasping laughter. "You try to make Her a saint, a chattel to your weak little god who can die and be reborn only once. It is Her day, the day of the Earth, that potters and farmers and miners have held holy since before your weakling came to die in his turn as gods before him have died, as gods will die after him, while She rules always."

"My daughter—"

The woman stamped her foot, spat, and everyone, including the Father, jumped. Just then the whole sky split, and trundled into the . sea. The priest went down on his knees with his hands over his face. Some people screamed, and Spyro's heart pounded so slowly and hard his chest ached, and he felt weak. Rain flushed from the clouds as the last light disappeared. When Spyro wiped water from his face, he saw all the herder women were dancing. Fear and fascination ranged through the miners and fishermen who had run from the other shacks to see. Men hustled their wives, sisters, or daughters away so they would not see or perhaps learn from the forbidden steps and rhythms, then rushed back across the mud to watch for themselves. People jostled, pushed, and somewhere a fight began. Panos had to shake Spyro's arm three times before he gained his brother's open-mouthed attention. "Piope! Where's Piope!"

Spyro closed his mouth and shook his head. "I don't—"

"For the sake of Kyrios Jesus, find Piope, before—" Thunder deadened his last words, and Panos lurched away.

Spyro started in the other direction. In a lightning blaze, he recognized his sister. Her scarf had blown off and her hair streamed. He grabbed her hand . . . but the gray eyes that turned to him were a stranger's:

The shell of her ear, the high-boned cheek, the corner of her wet mouth gleamed in yellow light from the shack window. As the rain roared between them, he tried to pull away, but the herder woman grabbed his other hand and leaned close, hissing, or was it singing, in that odd accent between music and laughter, "Come with me, Greek. Lie down on your back in the wet earth, and I will ride you where rider never rode horse—"

Spyro ran. Water struck his face, got in his throat, and he began to cough. He tried to get inside a shack, but it was too crowded, and people were yelling about something. For a long time he crouched under the dripping eaves in the back; then sounds coming through the rain frightened him, and finally he reached the head of the path back to Adamás.

Lightning bleached the rock behind a familiar figure twenty feet ahead, bulling through the rain. "Panos!" Spyro began to run. When he grabbed his brother's shoulders, Panos turned and caught him. Spyro pushed his face against the wet sweater. Then he pulled away.

His brother's back was caked with dirt, too thick for even the torrent to wash away. Spyro ran his hand up through his brother's hair. The front was slick and clean, but the back was filled with mud. Panos started forward angrily. Spyro followed, wiping water from his eyes with his dirtied hand. "Panos, what—"

Piope reached home the next morning while rain still fell. She was dirty, exhausted, and immediately caught a fever that lasted nearly a week. Three months later, Paniyotis had to pay Marias, the carpenter who had lost his arm in a freighter winch last year, and so could never be more than an assistant, five thousand drachmas to take Piope for his wife, and Spyro had to work a month on his sister's new house under Marias' crabby and impatient instructions.

The time just before the wedding was strained, and Piope cried most of it. Once she broke all her shells and ran into the mountains where something unpleasant must have occurred; when she came back three days later, she had strange scratches on her face that couldn't have been from brambles, for they were in ordered, parallel strokes. She refused to tell what had happened. But during the whole time, where many a father or brother would have turned her out, Panos never said a word.

Water lapped from the old bay of Milos, pulling a single file of sand across the rock by Spyro's foot and into the sea. Spyro looked out where She slept. Fear and sorrow tightened his throat. And the fear had to loosen if the sorrow were to leave him.

Suddenly he pulled his sweater over his head and jerked his wrists from the sleeves. He flung his pants back on top of it. Then he crouched, drew in his breath, and leapt.

Water struck cold into the crevices of his body. The winter Aegean warmed to him quickly though. Summer lingered under the sea well into December. Pressure built on his eyes and ears, and he refused to come up, even when over a minute had passed and his chest hurt. He twisted before blurred and blued rock. Then something above dove into the water, plummeting in silver toward him.

At the same moment, directly before him, he saw the stone thing. Twice broken, it jutted from the rock slope, arms twined with carved snakes and shingled weed. Weeds bearded Her gaping face, clotted Her eyes. Spots on Her chipped shoulders glittered gray-black. He was very near, perhaps ten feet. As he turned, She waved a long net toward him. As it settled about him, he thought, She isn't asleep! She isn't asleep at all! He clawed still deeper in the cool tow.

The form above him—a live woman, he realized suddenly—reached him at last, seized his hand through the strings. And string tore.

As they rolled upward, Spyro looked back to see other webs sailing gently from the stone arms. All the lost nets, snagged yearly from fishing boats that dared Her waters, swirled around the huge, pointed, black breasts.

The woman beside him tugged his arm, and air began to seep from Spyro's nose, the bubbles tickling his eyelids. He kicked hard, overtook her, and dragged her halfway up before he lost her. When he broke surface, he was blind with pulsing blood, and he thought for a moment he was going to vomit.

He heard her splash beside him, and took long strokes forward till his hands scraped painfully on rock. Water streamed his face and it was hard to hold his head up. She—probably one of the strong herder women—had been under perhaps half as long as he had. He heard her wet hands slap the rock, a splash, then a slap again as she pushed herself up on the stone lip. He shook hair and water from his eyes, and looked up.

Katina, naked and wide-eyed, sat on the rock, her black braid trailing between her breasts, the ends making little circles against her skin. Her breasts were goose-fleshed around the brown, shriveled nipples. As she gulped her breaths, her stomach, behind the wet braid, took a single crease, smoothed, creased.

"Why—?" Below the water he felt warmth coiling through the place where fear had been. Katina, as though she were reaching for something she did not know was hot or cold, took his wrist. "You better come out."

He nodded, his mouth open—and swallowed brine as a wave washed him. Coughing again, he pushed up on sore hands, then rolled against her. His wet shoulder struck cool against her thigh, then warmth broke through. "Why—" he asked again, "why are you here?"

He thought she was going to brush his cheek. But she said, "I come here too, sometimes—when I'm sad. I swim here, because it's alone, and nobody else does, and . . . and I followed you."

"Why did you follow me—I mean, down there?"

"When you jumped, I thought you didn't want to come up."

"I didn't want . . . ?" Though sorrow was still real, when he had faced Her beneath the water, the fear had gone. And without it, the laughter came up, this time free and freeing. He lay on his back, rocking his head and laughing, his thick hair sloshing against her calf. Then he took her shoulder and pushed himself to his elbow. Water coursed the runnel of his spine. "Not me! No! When I go down, I come up!"

She looked at his horny yellow hand on her shoulder. "Men have felt that way before about brothers. Why else should you come here to where She . . ." She inclined her head toward the water.

Spyro dropped his hand to her knee; it fell palm up, the fingers defining a cup. "Tell me, Katina," he whispered, "if She sleeps here, what was it the archaeologists carried away from the slopes that is now in the Paris museum?"

Katina shrugged. "Just another statue, the same sort as the Turks carried away from here by the dozen. It must have been one the Turks simply overlooked."

"The herders tell the story, *ne?*"

She shrugged. "But the archaeologists should have listened to the herders' tale more closely. The herders say She stood on the top of the tower guarding the Old City that was sacred to Her, until the tower fell in an earthquake. We exported obsidian to Egypt even before Minos flung his net over the seas. But that statue they found was of white marble, from Paros, while we have only poor red marble here; and the herders say She was chipped from black glass." Katina twisted her head to look out again.

"You come to swim here?" Spyro rose to his knees as she turned back. "And you are not afraid of Her?" He stood up.

Katina looked up at him, then suddenly pushed herself back against the rock, pulling in her shoulders. Her lips, gemmed with seawater, parted.

"But you are afraid of me."

Katina shook her head quickly, but her eyes began to dart around and about his body. What light came past his left hip banded the right side of her face and body with gold. Nakedness, a corollary of circumstance a moment past, was suddenly something powerful about himself, glorious about her. Spyro stooped, bending above her till one knee rubbed against her wet arm, and her staring face darkened with the shadow of his. He took her neck in both hands, as she bent back her head, the muscles stretching under his palms, and touched her ear with lips and teeth at once.

A goat's bleating above became laughter. Twigs and gravel burned his back, and Spyro leaped away, nearly slipping.

The goatherds, two girls and a boy, were scrambling up the foundation, looking back, poking each other, and giggling. Glory and power became tingling heat.

Katina was nervously slipping up her skirt when he looked back. Spyro stood a moment, then, confused, reached for his sweater and butted through the wool for the neck. The knit scratched the skin under his arms.

At the foundations, Katina hesitated before accepting his hand. He had hesitated before extending it. When she took it, he saw indecision in her face. He pulled her up over the rock, and she looked at him very straight all the time. "I don't like this place, this little island," she began again. "It is somehow as if we are all caught in . . . like Paniyotis. Then one dives below and discovers even She is bound in the nets of men." Katina shook her head. "I do not like this island."

"I am going to leave Milos," Spyro said.

They were both surprised. Spyro spoke the thought as he'd formed it, and its articulation was strange and amazing.

"You are?"

"*Ne.* I have nothing here. My sister is married. My brother . . . is dead."

"Where are you going?"

"Piraeus, I think. Yes, to the mainland at Piraeus. I will work on the freighters there."

"You . . . really will go?"

He nodded. "*Ne.*"

"And it will not be hard for you, just to leave?"

"Old, waterlogged nets tear easily."

"I am afraid to go," Katina said.

"I am, too," Spyro admitted. "But I'm going." They reached the donkey trail.

The evening star led the crescent moon from the sea. The sky was purple behind the lime bluffs. They had only been walking a minute when Katina said, "I'm going too."

Spyro smiled at her, then looked at his feet.

"I am going to Syros," she went on. "Though I may come to see you in Piraeus. Boats leave from Syros every day, not just once a week. From Syros I can go anywhere. Anywhere!" Suddenly she ran a few steps forward and laughed.

From the high bluff laughter returned, as though another woman laughed above them.

Spyro took her arm and they walked together.

"I am going," she repeated.

"I think you are," Spyro said. Then, a few minutes later, when they reached the asphalt road, Spyro said, "I am more important than the nets I cast."

"Yes." She frowned toward the shadows in the bluff, "I think you are."

—Mykonos
January 1966

night and the loves of joe dicostanzo

She was weeping—banally—in the moonlight.

He was annoyed, but contented himself with taking her luxuriant red hair (really rather mousy before the huge ivory disk balancing on the carbon-paper forest) and changing it to black. Then he coughed.

She turned from the balustrade. Tears rolled under her jaw. Two, like inexhaustible pearls, reappeared from the shadow on her neck. She *was* beautiful.

"Joey . . . ?" she whispered so softly he recognized his name only because that was what she *must* say.

He looked at his dirty knuckles against the top of the wall, then stepped forward, letting his fist roll. On his sleeve the open zipper jingled.

The breeze cast her hair forward from her shoulder, and her eyes (he would leave them green; green in the moonlight. Stunning) flicked down to perceive the change. "Oh, Joey . . ."

He wondered if she appreciated it. No matter. He stuck his hands into his back pockets. The left one was torn.

"You're getting . . . tired of me, aren't you?"

"Jesus, Morgantha—" he said.

The breeze, for a moment, became a wind, and his chin and toes got cold. He curled his toes through the dust. He couldn't curl his chin, so he dropped it into the collar of his turtleneck.

She wore only the green gossamer, fastened at her shoulder with a cluster of gold scorpions. Bare, her left breast taunted the moon.

He said, "Morgantha, you know you're a real—" and then just chewed on his back teeth and made fists inside his jeans.

"Joey—" she spoke with sudden eagerness, backing to the edge of the puddle so that her heels touched the heels of her reflection— "you know, I could be an awful lot of help to you. I really could, if you'd let me. I could tell you so much, about things you'd really like to know. Like why the clocks in the East Wing never read later than three. Or what's in the locked chamber that grumbles and thumps so. Joey, there's a little one-eyed boy coming to try and—"

"Oh, cut it out, Morgantha!" and felt his anger surge. He tried to stop it. But it was too late because the emotion was what did it. There was no ritualized gesture, no motion of control.

Morgantha stepped backward. Not a ripple: she fell straight down while her reflection shot straight up. For one moment reality and image were joined at the waist, like a queen on some grotesque playing card. Then, there was only the green gauze settling, darkening here, there.

Regret had grown to pain in his belly and along the back of his neck, even before the anger peeled away. He lunged forward, grabbed up the wet shift, as if he might somehow retract, retrieve, recall. . . .

Gold insects scurried from the dripping folds, splashed through the shallows to trail dark curves over the flags. He danced back from their scrabblings. A baker's dozen of them, at least!

As he pranced from the largest, he saw the smallest stop beside his other foot, curl its tail, and deliver its sting into his naked instep.

Joey howled and hopped.

Satisfied, the vengeful beasts scurried away, disappearing into the crevices of the masonry, climbing over the wall, or merely flickering out in the shadow.

With a bellow he flung the wet cloth. It stuck on the wall, fold on fold opening down the rock. He turned and hobbled across the roof, the dust first softening under his wet feet, then gritty, then just cool and dry. And the throb; throb; throb.

When he got to the doorway, he dug out his crusty handkerchief, pawed through for a clean spot, took off his rimless glasses, and scrubbed at the lenses. (Jingle, jingle, jingle: the zipper fasteners on his leather jacket.) When he slipped the wire hooks back under the hair clutching his ears, he realized he'd only managed to fog part of the glass so that the moon and the few lit windows in farther towers had all grown luminous penumbras. And his foot hurt.

Joey picked up his unicycle and kicked unenthusiastically at the starter. The third time, which hurt the most, the motor coughed its hot breath against his pants. He manhandled it around toward the dark portal, put one leg over the seat, folded his arms, swayed a bit for balance. Then he picked up his other foot, leaned forward, and caromed, barefooted, down the spiral steps. At each turn, as he racketed around the tower, a narrow window flung a handful of moonlight in his eyes.

Between, was all darkness and thunder.

Joey halted halfway along the East Wing's northwest corridor on the seventh floor.

The motor stopped roaring; purred instead. He got off, and frowned at the line of depressed piling that ran back along the maroon carpeting into the lithic dark.

He dragged the unicycle over to lean it on the wall. "Hey!"

"Joey?"

"I'm coming in."

"I'll be there in a minute if you'll just—"

But Joey strode up the three steps in the narrow alcove, punched the wooden door with both fists: it flew in.

The grandfather clock in the niche in the floor-to-ceiling bookshelf said twenty to three.

"You know, you're a real pain," Maximillian said. "If I were only a fraction meaner than I am, I'd toss you back into whatever bad dream you fell out of."

"Try it." Joey dropped into the leather wing chair in front of the desk.

Maximillian pushed aside two mounds of books and regarded

Joey through his black plastic frames. His fingers meshed into a big, veined knot between olive corduroy. "What's the matter now? And get your dirty feet off my desk."

Joey put his feet on the floor again. "I just got rid of Morgantha."

"Why don't you go somewhere else and complain about your love life?" Maximillian leaned back and put his own loafers up. Two volumes dropped. And his heel had tapped the crystal paperweight which rolled forward and nearly—

Joey caught it.

"Thanks," Maximillian said.

Before he put it back, Joey looked into the flashings and crystal glister. Below the reflected points from the candles set about the room, there was a rippling as of water, beyond a darkness that could have been the edge of a bridge; also, something that might have been shrubbery, and in it: a face under lots of hair with a . . . black rag over one eye.

Joey's attention was broken by a rumbling downstairs that ended in a double thump. The flames in their luminous waxen collars shook.

Maximillian put his shoes down. Both he and Joey looked at the floor.

A gold scorpion ran from beneath the desk, dodged about one of the fallen books that stood open on its spine, and disappeared behind a pedestal on which sat the stained bust of a nameless patriarch.

"*Eh* . . . what's this?" Joey asked, hefting the crystal.

"Oh." Maximillian's eyes came up. His brows lowered. "Usually. it shows the view though the front gate over the drawbridge."

"That's what I thought it was." Suddenly Joey turned and hurled the crystal.

It *thwumped* the thick hanging, which expelled a wall of dust that broke apart: great gray dragons fragmented into medium-sized vultures that finally vanished as small bats. The crystal thudded to the two-foot mound of tapestry on the floor and *churrrrred* across the planks to the side of the desk.

Maximillian picked it up and leaned on his elbows to examine it. After a while he said, "You really are upset about this Morgantha business, huh?" He put down the crystal, took out his meerschaum and tamped it in the baboon's-head humidor beside him. The yellow eyes glanced up, blinked twice, then crossed again to contemplate the flat black, perpetually damp-looking nose. Actually, Joey knew, it was shellac. "Well go on, Joey. Talk about it."

"Max," Joey said, "you are a figment of my imagination. Why don't you admit it?"

"Because you are a figment of mine." Maximillian sucked the flaming flower from the match. After several bubbly explosions he caressed the ocher bowl with his thumb. "I'd rather talk about Morgantha. You're not really going to go through this again?"

"Yes, I am."

"Joey, look—"

"Max, I've finally got it figured out. One day, a long time ago, I decided to make something I couldn't unmake. I was very lonely. I wanted someone around as different from me as possible. So I made a Maximillian; and I made one I couldn't get rid of. Then I made myself forget having made it—"

"Oh, really, Joey! *I* made *you*. And I remember perfectly well making you. I remember before you were here; and I remember even before that."

"Because I *willed* you to have those memories, don't you see?"

"Joey, look: everything about you is preposterous. The way you clatter up and down the steps, and that outlandish outfit. How could you possibly be real?"

"Because *you* could never conceive of making anything that preposterous, Max. You've told me so a dozen times. How could you?"

"That is a very good question."

"If you made me like you say, then why can't you unmake me, the way I unmade Morgantha?"

"I have more self-control than you, for one thing."

"Because you can't! You can't! You can't! I get you furious a dozen times a week. Believe me, if you could unmake me, I'd have been gone long ago." He sat forward energetically. "I make and unmake things all the time. But I've never actually seen you make anything at all."

"I've told you before, I don't think it's something to be abused."

"You're just trying to keep me from getting really mad and unmaking you."

"Quote you back at yourself," Maximillian said dryly: "Just try."

"I have. It never works."

The hands on the grandfather clock had swung around with amazing stealth to two minutes of.

"What's more, I've given you the only explanation that accounts for why it doesn't."

Maximillian sighed. "I remember distinctly making you. You have no memory at all of making me. By all the laws of economy and logic—"

Joey flung his hand out. "Do you see anything around here either logical or economical?"

"That's not the same—"

"Could you make a rock so heavy you couldn't lift it?"

"Of course I could. And that's not the same thing at all as making a rock I couldn't unmake if I happened to see it falling toward me from a balcony."

"Max—" Joey clapped his hands in frustration. "Do you realize I've never seen you outside this *room?*"

"All my needs are provided for here or in the chambers adjoining."

"Come out with me now."

"I'm busy."

"You can't come out. I made you so you'd always be in this one room."

"Absurd. Every couple of days I go for a walk in some of the lower corridors."

"And every time I come here, you're always sitting behind that desk, no matter what time of the day or night. I've never caught you out. Not even to take a leak."

"All the more reason to believe I made you. I never summon you—I suppose I do it unconsciously, because I must admit I occasionally develop a certain fondness for you *in absentia*—while I'm taking a walk, a nap, or a . . . leak."

Joey just grunted. "What are you reading anyway?"

"*Puffins.*" Maximillian picked up his current volume. "M. R.

Lockely. Perfectly delightful book. If you promise to take good care of it, I'll lend it to—"

"Max, you've got to come with me! There's something outside. Morgantha told me just before I got rid of her. There's something outside that's trying to get *in*!" He lowered his voice theatrically: "Over the moat!"

Maximillian's laughter burst out with an introductory sound Joey would have sworn was a "pop." "Go fight your own delusions."

"It's not one of mine; it's one of yours!"

"Cut it out," Maximillian said and turned over Lockely. "You really do make me angry sometimes, you know? You've got to learn to take the responsibility for what's yours and stop trying to assume the glory for what's not."

"Such as?"

The book flapped down on the table. "*You*, for one thing. *Me* for another!"

"Damn it, Max—" In frustration Joey stalked across the room. He turned back, but his outrage was trapped by an occasionally recurrent stutter.

Maximillian had folded his arms and was glaring. The hands of the grandfather clock had crept back to quarter of.

Joey slammed the door.

The direct way to the moat took Joey roaring and bouncing down another flight of steps and off through a rocky corridor whose ceiling was so low he had to hold his head down.

Fires flickered behind iron cages set in niches left. As he passed the black, studded door of the locked chamber on his right—a five-by-five square recessed in the rougher stone—he could not be sure (it may have been vibrations from the engine, as his muffler had fallen off two weeks before), but he thought the door rattled as he shot by. He swung his vehicle around into another stairwell.

Fists bagging his jacket pockets even further, and meer-schaum chirping, shortly Maximillian went for a walk in the remoter levels to ponder his origins. His certainty over the matter, alas, could only be assumed in the security of his study. The farther away he wandered (and he did take at least one goodly stroll every other day) the greater grew his doubt. What he talked of to Joey—and he was fairly certain Joey knew it—was a period some years back when, through overwork, fatigue, and the ever-mounting pressure from the discovery in one of the lumber rooms of a slightly damp eleventh edition of the *Encyclopaedia Britannica,* which threatened to decompose before he got all thirty-seven volumes read, he had hallucinated a time in which he had created not only Joey, but all the rooms, books, staircases, and chambers, vacant, furnished, or locked; as well as the briny waters around them and the brackish woods beyond. Before that, his memories were a little hazy. The only thing certain about that time was that Joey had been there, and the castle, and the wood.

He had been walking in darkness for some time when he became aware that the echo of his footsteps was returning over a very long distance.

Far above and fifty feet to the right was a small rectangle of moonlight cut by bars. Equally far below him, and left, a luminous pearl flickered on shifting water. And there was a distant plash, plash, plash. He had wandered onto one of the stone arches that spanned the castle's immense cistern. As he came down the steps (there were no rails on either side) a dim light resolved into one of the iron cages where the oil still flickered, lighting the wet, high wall as though it were made of mica.

He reached the crumbling ledge and entered a very narrow corridor, where more fires were caged near the doorway. After thirty feet the rough walls gave way to dressed stone. And the ceiling was a bit higher. A little farther and the dirt floor went under planking.

A chair had been placed at a bend. The carved black rungs had nearly pulled from their pegs. The leather cushion had cracked away at the corners and seemed to be stuffed with cardboard. But it was a chair.

Somewhat farther, and the corridor heaved itself out to respectable breadth and width. There were, irregularly, doors on the left and, quite regularly, windows on the right.

One reason Maximillian did not venture from his study more

frequently was the feeling of being observed that grew with the distance. Joey must be spying on him—that was his rationalization. Alas, Joey had never given Maximillian the slightest inkling that he had observed any of his wanderings. Both spying and reticence were alien to Joey's character as Maximillian perceived it. But Maximillian still nurtured the possibility—as a hope.

Between dark drapes a wing of moonlight fell over an immense painting. The surface was nearly black with dirt and overvarnishing. The frame was an eight-inch width of gilded leaves, shells, and birds. Maximillian stopped to gaze into the murky umbers stained to teak.

Behind the frame the canvas had come loose from its stretchers at one corner. A texture here from a brushstroke, there something that was either color or glare from the moon; was that a pale highlight, or a scar where the underpainting and layered glazes had cracked from the white-lead sizing?

Maximillian looked left where a crystal candelabra rewired for electricity had about half the bulbs working. He looked to the right where the chair sat in the corridor's elbow.

He faced the canvas again and cleared his throat:

"Agent XMQ7–34, calling Supervisor of the 86th Sector, Precinct B. Please come in. Please come in. This is Agent, eh . . . XMQ7–34 calling Supervisor of the—"

"Supervisor here. What's the report?"

"The experiment is progressing nicely, sir. The subject is responding well to the evocation of paranoid projection."

"Good."

"He's moving through the prescribed stages exactly on schedule."

"Very fine."

"The psychic tensions have practically webbed in the life force; it awaits only your orders before we move on to the final phase."

"Oh, yes. Excellent. Splendid. But tell me, Agent XMQ7–34, how do you find yourself holding up under all this?"

"To tell the truth, it's a little hard on me, Chief. You know, it's funny, but I'm really becoming sort of fond of the subject . . . I mean, in a way."

"I'm afraid, Agent XMQ7–34, it's a process I'm familiar with.

They try so hard, put up such a battle, that you can't help developing a certain respect for the little buggers."

"That's it, Chief." Maximillian began to laugh. "That's it exactly. . . ." Laughter from the canvas joined his, merged with it, was absorbed by it, till Maximillian's rang alone. He was unable to keep up the charade any longer.

He glanced down the hall, hoping to catch sight of Joey's head pulling back around the corner. But the audience for whom he conjured his voices was, as usual, absent.

As Maximillian turned from the painting, for one moment the vast surface cleared of moon glare:

A small window near the top; on a narrow stone bridge two figures struggled in the shadow of the wall, high above black water. One figure was naked.

But Maximillian had already taken another step. Again reflected light blotted the surface. Frowning, he moved to one side, forward, back, but could not find the spot again where the subject cleared.

Finally he turned and walked toward the chandelier.

Through blue hangings that curtained the open door came the sound of gentle converse. Occasionally a man's or woman's laughter segregated itself.

Maximillian frowned again.

It had been almost a year since he had been in this hall. His last visit had been on an evening when he had been particularly depressed. A disastrous idea, he had known it wouldn't work; still, he had made a party.

He had left early, fleeing back to his study and his books. As he stood there now, he realized he could not recall ever consciously unmaking the gathering. The voices chattered on.

He looked at the electrified chandelier. The black extension cord he had run to the other chandelier inside to light the party room still hung down to the rug, curled twice, and snaked off between the hangings.

His apprehension deepened. The party had been formal. He was wearing only his baggy corduroys. Suddenly, perhaps too suddenly, he pushed through the drapery onto the small balcony.

"Maximillian! Oh, there, I told you he'd be back. Steve, Bert,

Ronny? Max is back! Didn't I say he wouldn't run off and just desert us forever?"

"Well, you certainly took your time, boy. It's almost twenty-five to three."

"Come on down from there and have a martini."

"Oh, Karl, it's much too late in the evening for martinis. Max wants something stronger than that. What about *three* martinis, and very fast—"

"Are you feeling any better, honey? You looked a sight when you ran out of here."

"Oh, Max was just having one of his moods, weren't you, Max darling?"

He held the railing and gazed down into the room.

"I think he still looks sort of green around the gills."

"All he needs is a drink. Max, come on down here and have a drink."

He opened his mouth, his tongue stumbling; he tried to think of something witty to toss before his descent.

"Max? Max! I *am* glad you came back, really. It wasn't something *I* said, was it? Tell me it wasn't something I said. I was only kidding, Max. Really I—"

"Come on, Sheila. Let it go—"

"Max, Ronny just told me the funniest story. Come on, Ronny. Tell Max the one you just told me. The one about . . . well, *you* know!"

"Oh, yes, you've got to hear this one. Gracie laughed so much she lost her shoe. Gracie, did you ever get your shoe back? I saw Oliver doing something with it over there behind the piano."

"Max? Oh, come on, Max! You're not going to run out on us again, are you?"

"Of course he's not. He just got here, right, Max? Max . . . !"

"Oh, don't pay him any mind. You know how Max is. He'll be back."

Maximillian stopped in the corridor. His palms were moist. As he opened his fingers, they cooled. For one moment he tried to summon up the will to unmake what was inside.

The hangings swung. The conversation burbled and wound. A woman laughed. More conversation. A man laughed.

He felt terribly drained. The necessary anger that would erase it all was stifled in him. He swallowed, and was surprised by the breaking sound from his throat.

Hands in his jacket pockets, he hurried down the hall.

The gate's beams, vertical and cross, creaked up into the stone. Joey looked out on the bridge. The trees beyond the shrubbery wrinkled and rolled. A moment later the surface of the water reticulated like foil. And terror divided the focus of his senses into some great fly's eye through which the whole vision before him was suddenly fragmented and absurd. Then the ordinary fear with which he could cope returned.

He stepped from the stone floor to the wooden bridge, paused for a moment with his hand on the seven-inch links of the draw chain, till he remembered it was caked in grease. He looked at the black smears on his fingers, wiped them on his jean thigh, and put both hands in his back pockets without checking again: it would take soap. And water . . .

Something moved in the shrubbery at the head of the bridge. Squinting through the fogged lens, Joey stepped forward. The forest roared softly. The wind flattened the leather jacket to his side; zippers tinkled.

A figure darted forward, gained the boards, and came up short as though it had expected no hindrance.

Joey snatched his hands from his pockets so fast his knuckles stung: he heard more threads go in the left one.

The boy was naked.

Crouched.

Balanced on the balls of his feet.

Hands to the side.

His hair, black as rags of the night itself, whipped and snapped over one shoulder.

". . . What do you want?" Joey demanded above the wind.

A black cloth was tied down around the boy's left eye.

The right one, huge and yellow, blinked.

"Come on," Joey said. "What do you want?"

The boy blinked again. Then he laughed, a skinny sound that twisted out like barbed wire through dry pine needles. His arms came back to his sides. He took another step.

Joey said, "You better get away from here."

The boy said, "Hello, Joey."

"You better get away from here now," Joey repeated. "What do you want?"

There were cuts and scratches on the boy's shins and feet. He held his head slightly to the side in order to see. "Can I come inside, Joey?" and the laughter following was all breath. It sounded terribly wet.

"No. You can't. What do you want?"

"Aw, come on." Another step. The boy stuck out his hand. "I'll tell you when we get inside."

Joey took the hand to shake. "You can't come in." Joey's hand was thick, dry, and gritty.

"Yes I can." The boy's was long and moist. And he was still laughing.

"You get on out of here." But physical contact, unpleasant as it was, made the child less threatening. The eye-rag was knotted across his left ear. A spatter of acne wounds made their red galaxy on his jaw. "Get off the bridge." Joey tried to pull his hand away. The fingers stiffened around his own. "Now, come *on*—" He shook his hand. The hand holding his swung with his shaking. "Hey—!" Now Joey pulled back in earnest.

The boy laughed and pulled against him. He was very strong.

Joey leaned back and grabbed his own wrist with his free hand. The boy leaned too. His free hand waved behind him. The boy's foot touched Joey's; the boy's toes were wet and cold with night water.

The boy grinned.

Joey jerked, slipped, yanked.

Then the boy released all pressure.

Joey staggered backward, almost tripped on the sill, went back three more steps, and sat down.

The boy stood over him, his grip still firm.

The gate creaked down. The splintered stumps of the vertical beams thudded into puddles that had collected in the worn depressions, sending dark rills through the checkered moonlight.

"Told you I could get in."

Something ran out into the pale square where the boy stood, paused to raise its glittering barb, thought better, and scurried off. Joey felt a sympathetic throb in his instep.

"You know what I want?"

As Joey pushed to his feet, the boy helped him with a tug. Joey narrowed his eyes. The boy released Joey's hand.

"I'm going to unlock that room upstairs. I'm going to push back the door, and whatever is inside is going to come out."

"*Huh—?*"

"What do you think will happen once it's let out?"

"What out?"

The boy suddenly giggled and rubbed his wrist across his mouth. "Joey, you know . . ." He looked around the dim hall. ". . . maybe the clocks in the East Wing will get on with their business at last. Perhaps you and Maximillian will decide you don't want to live here anymore, and move away into the forest. Interesting to think about, isn't it?"

Joey tried to focus his discomfort.

The boy's vocal expression suddenly changed. "I've *got* to try and unlock it! Take me up there, Joey. All you have to do is show me the door. I'll do the rest. I'll let it out, and then I can go. It'll be simple. Show me where the chamber is. Once I open the door, I'll go away and leave you alone. . . ."

"*No . . . !*" Joey wanted to give his refusal full voice. But it came out in a rasping hiss. He turned in the echoing hall (the discomfort focused was terror) and ran through the nearest doorway.

"Joey . . . !"

Joey scrambled down the ill-lit steps. At the bottom he turned to see the silhouetted figure, a hand on either wall, starting after him.

He missed the next step. His heel struck full on the stone and jarred him to the head. But he was running again.

Joey swung under an archway, knowing steps would take him shortly up, up where the locked chamber waited. Desperately he tried to think of somewhere, place, direction to—

He crossed a grate and felt his feet press momentarily between cold bars. The steps were close.

"Joey . . . ?"

He practically fell up them, trying to recall some turnoff, some cross-passage to take him away. He scrambled over the length of the hallway in his memory. It opened directly into the low stone corridor not three yards away from the recessed square, five by five.

He remembered the conduit the same moment he passed it. And he was on his knees, lugging away the heavy cover. He shoved the circular hatch from him and heard it clanging down the steps, *ka-tang, tang, tang,* for all the world like his unicycle.

"Hey, what the—!" from behind him.

Joey lunged through the opening. His back and shoulders scraped the sides and roof.

"Joey, you shouldn't have done that—"

He had to crawl with his forearms flat. His own breath raged in echo around his ears. There was water on the floor. And much more softly, at a distinctly different rhythm, somebody else was breathing.

Joey's head tapped the plate on the other end in blackness. He shoved with his shoulder. For a moment it stuck—

". . . Joey?"

—and that was terrible.

Then it pushed away. The *thud* of the fall was duller than he expected. He scrambled out over the metal plate, and crouched on all fours on a rug.

As he stood, as he stumbled, he saw a sideways H of light between the double doors just ahead of him. Behind him was the sound of scrabbling. He pushed the doors apart, lurched out, and was practically blind after his crawl through the darkness.

"Oh, I say there—"

"I told Sheila. I told her, I don't think anyone could have blamed *her*. I mean, after all—"

"Oliver! Come out from under there!"

"Leave him alone, Bert. You know how Oliver is—oh, pardon me!"

"Hey, I didn't see you come in! Are you all right? Here, let me get you a martini."

"For God's sake, Steve, it's too late in the evening for—"

"Dreadfully sorry. Did I bump into you—?"

". . . Joey?"

"Say, I bet you haven't heard this one. Ronny, tell this young man that story about—"

As he pushed forward, Joey felt the electrical cord catch around his ankle. The chandelier shook overhead.

"—Hey, watch it there! Better keep your eyes in front of you, young fellow."

The cord pulled free: the room dropped into darkness deep as the conduit's.

"You're sure I can't get you something? If not a martini, perhaps—"

"I think you're being terribly hard on him, Karl."

". . . after all, he *has* been under a great deal of pressure, you know."

"All *I* know is that if anyone had said that to me, I would have scratched his eyes out!"

"Joey?"

"Oliver? Is that you under there? Hey, are you all right? Oliver?"

Joey was clambering up the steps toward the little balcony.

"After I've gone and mixed this, doesn't anybody want it? Would you—"

"Joey . . . ?"

He beat at the hangings. Then, suddenly, he was through and into the hallway.

He stepped over the extension cord and hurried up the corridor. The air was dusty with moonlight.

By a huge gilt frame he turned to look behind him. For a moment the glare cleared from the blackened varnish: two figures struggled through a richly appointed room filled with men and women in evening dress. One figure was naked.

And someone was pushing aside the blue hangings back in the doorway.

Joey turned again and ran down the hall. At the bend, he punched the wall by the chair. Again he looked back.

"Joey, are you taking me in the right direction? You're sure now this is the way? If you take me there, then I can let it out and leave you alone. You know, you can't lose me. You think you'll just take me around in circles, don't you? But that's not going to work. You'll make a mistake, turn down the wrong hall, and there we'll be, won't we?"

Joey felt the arm of the chair move under his hand. He glanced down: the whole frame swayed, about to collapse.

"Lead on! Right this way to the locked chamber. Is it down there, Joey?"

Joey started along the hall again. He was holding his breath, he realized. He let it out with an aching gasp and sucked in another.

"Right behind you, Joey."

The walls were no longer paneled, but merely dressed stone. And there were no more windows. He had barely noted this when the ceiling dropped to within a foot of his head.

"This long-way-around business is a real waste of time, Joey. Why don't you just give up and show me the quick way, nice and simple?"

The walls were closer too. He moved forward in slow-motion hysteria. Pebbles chewed the soles of his feet. The niched flames flickered. For a moment he had a vision of the hall diminishing to the size of the conduit.

He stopped, because suddenly he was standing in an echoing hollow that stretched out and up into dimness that became blackness and still went on.

"Which way do we go now?"

Joey jumped, because the voice was practically at his elbow. He was thinking about running, was running—

A weight landed on his back. Joey staggered forward, zippers going like chimes. There was the sound of breath, roaring loud; then a sharp pain below his ear.

Joey's shriek vaulted about the echoing cistern. The boy had bitten. Joey went forward, clawing up the stairs. The weight released, and Joey ran ten more steps before he realized he was on one of the bridges. He turned to see the naked boy again, in silhouette from the fires on the ledge.

"Go on, Joey." The boy was breathing hard. "That was just to show you I'm losing patience, though."

Joey backed up another step.

The boy came on two. Beside the sloping rag, the single eye was in shadow.

At the next step pale light caught in Joey's eyes. High, very high above him was a window, broken by bars and filled with moonlight. The beam lit three of the chipped steps before falling over the edge to flicker on the misty ripplings far, so terribly far below. Joey backed up another four steps.

"You know I really am losing my taste for all of this crawling around in the dark." The liquescent breathing lisped among the sounds of dripping. "When are you going to cut this out and show me the chamber? I think I'm going to have to teach you another lesson." Then the figure was racing forward.

Joey saw him pass through the light. The face was creased with rage about the yellow eye. Joey whirled, started up, stumbled immediately. He went down on his hands.

At the same time he heard a high shriek. And something struck his back, slipped to the side— It jerked him, *hugely* to the side. Joey went flat, clutching the steps, cheek pressed against the crumblings.

And the shrieking.

Joey bit the corner of the stone and cried and kicked violently. An amazing weight was hanging from below his waist. There was the sound of ripping cloth. Then there wasn't any more weight.

The splash cut out the noise's core. The echo grew quieter, then even quieter. It may have been the reverberation from his own sobs, but the echo didn't quite stop.

After a while Joey pushed himself up and walked down. He halted at the beginning of the moonlight's wash.

There was a dark smear to the step's edge. At one end a golden carapace was crushed flat, along with clotted maroon.

Stung and slipping, the boy must have leaped for Joey only to catch his back pocket. Joey ran his hand over the stubble of threads on his buttock. Then, jingling softly, he stepped around the moonlit stain.

When he reached the ledge, Joey was holding his breath again. When he let it out, the echo still came back like shrieking.

The grandfather clock showed less than five minutes to three.

The baboon's eyes uncrossed from the gleaming nose, rolled to the left, then to the right. The lips lifted from the yellow teeth. The humidor gave up a sound for all the world like someone clearing his throat:

"Agent XMQ7–34, calling Supervisor of the 86th Sector, Precinct B. Please come in. Please come in. This is, eh . . . Agent XMQ7–34 calling Supervisor of the—"

"Supervisor here," the marble patriarch announced from his pedestal. "What's the report?"

"The experiment is progressing nicely, sir. The subject is responding well to the evocation of—"

"Yes, of course," interrupted the bust. "I know, I know: but you just can't help respecting the little buggers. Oh, yes, yes, I know about all that."

Their mounting laughter was cut off by rumblings from the chamber beneath, punctuated by three distinct thumps, the second much louder than either the first or third.

The baboon rolled his eyes around to observe the grandfather clock just as Maximillian opened the door: seventeen minutes past two.

———

Maximillian had been back from his walk almost half an hour and was making fair progress in his comparison of Apollinaire's *Le Poète Assassiné* with the Padgett translation, when the whine of Joey's unicycle came shuddering through the door.

I tell you truly, brethren, Padgett had rendered, *there are few spectacles that do not put the soul in danger. I know of only one place* . . . Maximillian looked up, frowning. The familiar whine became a familiar roar. . . . *one place you can go fearlessly and that is*—Maximillian closed the book as the motor coughed to silence.

"Max!" The door banged back against the bookshelf as Joey bounded forward. "Max, it almost got in! But I led it on a wild-goose chase! Into the cistern. And it tripped and fell into the—oh, Max!"

"What are you talking about?"

Joey was gasping between each clutch of words. "It wanted to open the locked chamber! Let it out! But I wouldn't let it." He grabbed the edge of the desk. "Max, don't make any more of those! Please, Max, please don't *ever* make any more."

Maximillian shook his head. He wished Joey wouldn't barge in on him. He was beginning to wish it more than anything else. "Make what?"

"Ones like *that*!"

"God*damn* it, Joey, *will* you get *out* of here!" and he was standing now, astounded at his own anger, aware that the tics in the muscles of his face were his own winces at the volume of his voice.

Joey backed to the door. He made three forays into some word or other but kept jamming on the letter "b." Then he fled the room.

Maximillian sat down while the unicycle thundered outside, and couldn't find his place in Padgett at all.

Clacketing up the tower steps, he didn't care if Max didn't know what he had just saved them from. And he didn't care if Max never lent him another book forever and ever. And he didn't care if

Max never went out of his old study anyway. And if he got mad enough, Max better watch out, because he *would* unmake him.

He reached the sill and rolled out on the tower roof. He caught himself on the stone wall as the cycle sagged, got off, and positioned his machine against the doorjamb.

A small moon winked overhead between running clouds. The puddle rippled by the balustrade as the wind unrolled across the roof and swayed through his hair so that it tickled his forehead.

He didn't care if he never saw Max again. He would make a beautiful, sweet, interesting girl who would do everything he said, and would never talk back to him, and be very much in love. With him. He'd make this one colored. And maybe she'd be able to play songs on the autoharp. Yes, she'd have a nice voice, and would sing to him after dinner and be as dark and warm as the shadows in the hallways in the remoter levels.

He picked the green shift from the wall. Then he sat down and leaned against the rock. He held the gauze around his fists, bent his face to touch his chin to it. It was practically dry now, and cool.

He tried to think about the interesting colored girl. But it was chilly and his thoughts kept drifting. The flags were cold under his naked feet and through the seat of his pants (he didn't wear underwear anymore), and soon he would zip his jacket closed over his turtleneck sweater. When he squinted, the stuff on his right lens made the reflected moon explode on the waters beside him in a shower of silent, silver needles. And he was tired, almost tired enough to sleep, right there, but first he would think some more about the girl until he would hear her voice behind him, calling him, Joey? Joey . . . ?

In another tower a clock chimed three. He started to his knees, looked out over the wall. But the chimes had sounded from the West Wing where the clocks were all perfectly normal anyway.

". . . Joey?"

—New York
October 1968

afterword: of doubts and dreams

The request to write about your own work—to comment on a collection of your own fictions, say—is, to most writers, an occasion for distractionary tactics. What you do when you "write a story," like what you do when you bleed or heal, is too simple and too complicated for the mid-level exposition most such pieces presuppose. ("We want something informative, of course—but don't get *too* technical. . . .") What makes it simple *and* complicated is not, oddly, what you do when you write. It's what people have said about writing over many years. To be simple is to say, in whatever way you choose, that they are, all of them, right. To be complicated is to explain that they are wrong, and why.

Simply? You sit down to write a story. The excitement, the sweep, the wonder of narrative comes over you, and, writing as fast as you can, you try to keep up with it till the tale is told.

The complicated part?

Just try it. You see, what comes as well, along with the narrative wonder, is a lot of doubts, delays, and hesitations. *Is* it really that wondrous? Is it even a decent *sentence?* Does it have anything to do with the way you *feel* about the world? Does it say anything that would at all interest you were you *reading* it? *Where* will you find the energy to put down another word? What do you put down *now?* Narrative becomes a way of negotiating a path through, over, under, and around the whole bewildering, paralyzing, unstoppable succession of halts. The real wonder of narrative is that it can negotiate this obstacle course at all.

Just over a dozen years ago I first found myself, through a collision of preposterous circumstances, in front of a silent group of strangers, some eager, some distrustful, but all with one thing in common: all had registered for a writing workshop I had been hired to teach. And I became formally, articulately, distressingly aware how little I knew about "how to write a story."

The workshops recurred, however; and finally I found my nose pressed up against the fact that I knew only—perhaps—three things about my craft. Since I filched two from other writers anyway, I pass them on for what they're worth.

The first comes from Theodore Sturgeon. He put it in a letter he wrote in the 'fifties to Judith Merril, who quoted it in an article she wrote about Sturgeon in 1962. To write an immediate and vivid scene, Sturgeon said, visualize everything about it as thoroughly as you can, from the dime-sized price sticker still on the brass switch plate, to the thumbprint on the clear pane in the unpainted wooden frame, to the trowel marks sweeping the ceiling's white, white plaster, and all between. Then, do *not* describe it. Rather, mention only those aspects that impinge on your character's consciousness, as she or he, in whatever emotional state she or he is in (elated buyer seeing it for the first time, bored carpenter anxious for lunch . . .), wanders over the squeaking planks beside the paint-speckled aluminum ladder. The scene the reader envisions, Sturgeon went on to explain, will *not* be the same as yours—but it will be as vivid, detailed, coherent, and important for the reader as yours was for you.

Number two comes from Thomas Disch, who suggested it at a Milford science fiction writers' conference in 1967 during a discussion about what to do when a story or novel runs down in the middle and the writer loses interest. The usual halfhearted, half-serious suggestions had been made, from "take a cold shower," to "kill off a main character." Then Disch commented that the only thing you can do in such a situation is to ask of your story what's really going on in it. What are the characters' real motivations, feelings, fears, or desires? Right at the point you stopped, you must go down to another level in the tale. You must dig into the character's psychology deeply enough (and thus build up your vision of the story's complexity enough) to reinterest yourself. If you can't, then the story must be abandoned.

Number three has to do with the preparatory story stages, though it can also be used with smaller sections of a tale during the actual writing. It's the one writing notion I've put together more or less on my own. At some point, when the story is still only an idea, an image, or a topic, ask yourself, what is the most usual, the most traditional, the most clichéd way to handle that particular material. Ask yourself what are the traps that, time and again, other writers have fallen into, when handling the same matters, which have made their work trite, ugly, or dull. Can you think of any way to avoid precisely those traps? How do you want your work to differ from the usual? How is your work going to deal with this material in a way no one has ever dealt with it before? Locating a precise writerly problem to avoid (or solve) or situating a particular writerly approach that will set your work apart can often provide the excitement to write it.

I've run into other rules of thumb about writing. When stuck for something to say in a writing workshop, I've even passed them on. Occasionally someone else has claimed to find them helpful. But these three are the only ones I have ever personally used. They exhaust my very tentative, firsthand, "how-to" knowledge.

What you learn in a creative writing workshop, of course (especially if you're the teacher), is how *not* to write. And when writing is looked at as a series of don'ts, then even the three suggestions above turn over to reveal a more familiar side:

Sturgeon's point, when all is said and done, really boils down to: Don't overwrite.

Disch's point, by the same reduction, becomes: Don't let your writing become thin or superficial.

And my own is simply: Don't indulge clichés.

Suddenly none sounds very original. Notice also, as soon as the advice is rendered negatively, it begins to suggest the same list of doubts with which we began. Indeed, whenever you find yourself writing a cluttered, thin, or clichéd sentence, you *should* doubt and doubt seriously. And once we are in this negative mode, we can put together a whole list of other things to doubt as well, hopefully to one's profit. Myself, I doubt modifiers, especially in bunches, particularly when they are prepositional phrases ending sentences. I doubt verbs that get too far from their subjects. I doubt story endings so violent no character left is in any state to learn anything from what has occurred. I doubt story endings so poetic you begin to suspect, really, there was nothing to learn in the first place. I doubt descriptions put down "exactly as they happened." And I doubt descriptions so badly put down they couldn't have happened at all.

What does this doubting mean? It means a writer *may* just let any one of them stand. After all, that extra adjective may not be clutter but an interesting catachresis that allows us to see something unusual about the object. That sentence or paragraph may not be thin, but rather a synoptic account that highlights a quality we might otherwise miss. And that cliché may make an ironic comment on a certain kind of banality that is, itself, what you want to write about. But it means you'd better be convinced.

It means you don't give any one of them the *benefit* of the doubt.

I suspect one reason creative writing classes and workshops are not more successful than they usually are has to do with *when* the doubting takes place.

A unique process begins when the writer lowers the pen to put words on paper—or taps out letters onto the page with typewriter keys. Certainly writers think about and plan stories beforehand; and certainly, after writing a few stories, you may plan them or think about them in a more complex way. But even this increasing complexity is likely to grow out of the process of which I'm speaking. And the fact is, almost everyone *thinks* about stories. Many even get to the point of planning them. But the place where the writer's experience differs from everyone else's is during the writing process itself. What makes this process unique has to do directly with the doubting.

You picture the beginning of a story. (Anyone can do that.) You try to describe it. (And anyone can try.) Your mind offers up a word, or three, or a dozen. (It's not much different from what happens when you write a friend in a letter what you did yesterday morning.) You write the words down, the first, the second, the third, fourth, fifth, sixth, seventh—suddenly you doubt.

You sense clutter, or thinness, or cliché.

You are now on the verge of a process that happens only in the actual writing of a text.

If the word you doubted is among those already written down, you can cross it out. If it's among the words you're about to write, you can say to yourself, "No, not that one," and either go on without it, or wait for some alternative to come. The act of refusing to put down words, or crossing out words already down, while you concentrate on the vision you are writing about, *makes* new words come. What's more, when you refuse language your mind offers up, something happens to the next batch offered. The words are not the same ones that would have come if you hadn't doubted.

The differences will probably have little or nothing to do with your plot, or the overall story shape—though they might. There will probably be much to reject among the new batch too. But making these changes the moment they are perceived keeps the tale curving inward toward its own energy. When you make the corrections at the time, the next words that come up will be richer—richer both in things to accept *and* to reject. And the process doesn't end. Frequently something you've arrived at through this process on page six will make you realize that you now doubt something back on page two. Perhaps it's cluttered—maybe a whole sentence can go. Perhaps it's thin—maybe a whole incident must be added.

If there is a privileged moment somewhere in the arc of experience running from the first language an infant hears, through the toddler's learning that language, to the child's learning to read it, learning to write it, to the adolescent's attempts to write journals, tales, dramas, poems—if there is a moment, rightly called creative, when the possibility of the extraordinary is shored up against the inundation of ordinary discourse that forms, shapes, and is the majority of what we call civilized life, it is here. This is the moment covered—in the sense of covered over—by the tautology against which so many thousands of would-be writers have stumbled: "To be a writer, you must write." You must write not only to produce the text which is the historical verification of your having written. You must write to project yourself, again and again, through the annealing moment that provides the negentropic organization which makes a few texts privileged tools of perception. Without this moment, this series of moments, this concatenation of doubts about language shattered by language, the text is only a document of time passed with some paper, of time spent pondering a passage through a dream.

A teacher can take a page from a story written the night or the month before, focus in on a few sentences, and point out three superfluous adjectives, a dangling modifier, and a broken-back sentence (Damon Knight's term for a sentence carrying too much baggage, often lodged between subject and verb). Truly enlightened, the student may cross out the adjectives, reshuffle the clauses—and the sentence or sentences may now evoke their object with a bit more grace and precision. But the student will not get the immediate charge from having made the corrections at the time of writing, an energy that will manifest itself among the three sentences written next.

Narrative sweep, then, is not only being able to make your criticisms on the run, as it were, but being able to work with the resultant energy.

Doubting over a longer period also, however, produces its changes. One story in this collection, for example, is both among the oldest stories here and is also the fantasy short story most recently completed. I first wrote it sometime around 1962—that is, I wrote out a version in longhand in my notebook (doubting and rejecting all the way), then went back, reread it, doubted some more, and made some more changes. I typed up a rough draft, which involved much doubting and rewriting as well. Then I reread it, wrote in *more* changes; then I typed up a final draft, in which I made even more changes.

The story never placed—which is to say, for reasons mainly

involving forgetfulness, it was only submitted once. In 1967 I discovered it in a file cabinet drawer the same week a fanzine editor asked me for a fiction contribution. I reread it, doubted, and wrote in a lot more changes. Then I retyped it, making still more. Another rereading made me write in a few more. And I gave the story to the fanzine.

When I read the fanzine's mimeographed version, I recall making a few more changes on my own copy—but that copy was shortly lost. Still, by now I'd decided I *liked* the story. Last month, after a twelve-year hiatus, I ferreted out a Xerox copy of the fanzine version, reread it, and, to assuage a few more doubts, made still more handwritten corrections. Then I typed up a draft, which included those corrections plus numerous ones in response to a whole new raft of doubts. Then I typed still another "final" draft, incorporating just a *few* more changes. There were a few more rereadings over the next few days, each one of which produced three to five new changes—and that, along with a few doubts about my typing from the copy editor, is the version here. Copy editor excluded, that's at least twelve layers of doubts spread over seventeen years. I know I enjoyed first drafting the story back in '62. And I certainly enjoyed the rewrites. Yet frankly, the story still strikes me as . . . slight— which is to say the doubting process I've been describing is finally interesting not because it *guarantees* accomplishment, but merely because it happens. At this point we may even begin to doubt the doubting process itself, whereupon narrative becomes only the habits of mind, for better or worse, the writer goes through while writing, and reason only the principal among those distraction tactics mentioned at our opening. Slight as the story is, however, my view of the characters, the landscape, the buildings, and the general decor is clearer for me than it was seventeen years ago. And if Sturgeon's point is correct, the reader's may be clearer than it would have been, at least from the first version.

So much for long-term doubting.

The French novelist Flaubert is known for the immense effort he put into his style. The late Roland Barthes once quipped that Flaubert brought the whole notion of labor to fiction, which made the conservative French middle classes begin to trust it more. Once Flaubert worked for several days on a single sentence, at the end of which time he had only removed one comma. Still dissatisfied (still doubting?), he continued to work on the sentence, and at the end of several more days, he had put the comma back. But now, Flaubert concluded in one of his letters, he knew *why* the comma was there.*

I suspect even this belongs among the simple things one can say about writing. The work, not to mention the final knowledge, is not on the rational level that produces the academically acceptable explanation, but rather in that oddly blurred area where linguistic competence (the knowledge of the language everyone who can speak it shares) is flush with the writer's individual suspicions about how words can be made to mean more accurately and intensely. That's hard to talk or write about. That's why it *is* work.

In conversations about writing, I've occasionally said writing strikes me as a many-layered process, only the top three or four of which have anything directly to do with words. This, however, is another easy metaphor. And when you analyze through introspection, it is always hard to know *how* metaphorical you are being. I do know that just under the verbal layers there is a layer that seems to me much more like numbers than like words. It is a layer controlling pure pattern, where, among other things, places are set up for words that are going to be the same (or very much alike) and other places are set up for words that are going to be different (or highly contrasting). Frequently these places are set out well before the actual words that will fill them are chosen. Once, writing a novel, I realized I wanted a description of a highway light moving down the pockmarked face of a truck driver at night, forming shadow after shadow, to mirror a description of the sun moving down the face of a tenement building at evening, windowpane after windowpane flaring gold. I wanted one description to be near the beginning of the novel and the other to come around the midpoint. The midpoint

---

*More recently I have heard this anecdote attributed to Oscar Wilde.

of this particular novel turned out to be about four hundred fifty pages away from the opening. When I decided this, I had no idea what the actual words of either description would be. But once both sentences were written, whenever one description would be revised, four hundred fifty pages away, the other one would have to be revised too—as I recall, both went through over a dozen rewrites. Then a proofreader's error destroyed the symmetry in the published version, which is why it weighs heavily enough on me to mention it here.

Another example of this same mathematical layer at work: Toward the beginning of a previously published story, included in this collection, a character slips on a rock and gets a foot wet in a stream.

"Why," demanded my original editor,* who was plagued with length restrictions and who wanted to see the story cut, "do you need *that*?"

Because later on in the story another character does *not* slip on that rock and does *not* get a foot wet. The two incidents served as a kind of mutual characterization, an *en passant* comment on the two characters' contrasting abilities to maneuver through the landscape. But (as I was too flustered to explain to the editor at the time— which is probably why I mention it now) that is why I couldn't cut the one—at least not without cutting the other. And again, the incidents' positions in the story and their contrasting nature were determined, at this mathematical level, long before I knew what the incidents or the words that would realize them were. I think, then, that a good deal of the "sweep" part of narrative sweep is the creation of some formal pattern—a structure, if you will—and the subsequent urge to fill it with language that will manifest it.

Besides the fact that both of these cases were challenged by the world (one by a printer's slip and one by an editor), which make them, among the thousands and thousands of such cases that

---

*Edward Ferman, then editor and publisher of *The Magazine of Fantasy and Science Fiction*.

underlie any writer's text, remain in mind, another aspect of their exemplary quality is that the patterns stayed fairly clear from conception to execution. Yet even on this mathematical level, the writing down—and the rejecting—of language produces revelations and revisions in the most formal organization of the story. At any time, on any level, at any moment where you can doubt, at any place where you can say, "No, I want something better, other, different . . ." this sharpening and reenergizing process can take place.

Freud, in his *Interpretation of Dreams* (1900), describes a phenomenon you can check for yourself if you have a cooperative friend, patience, and a cassette tape recorder. Catch your friend within minutes after she or he wakes and ask the person to describe a dream into the recorder. Now immediately have the person describe the dream again. Then have the person describe the dream a third time. It is important that this be done within five or ten minutes of waking—after twenty minutes, or an hour, the phenomenon is far less noticeable. The number of changes in the three descriptions, however, will often be astonishingly high. Sometimes the sexes of minor dream characters will alter. Or the number of characters will vary. Often what people were wearing or what they looked like will shift markedly between retellings. Often the settings will become more specific, while character motivations will become more complicated. Most people, if asked to spot changes in their own accounts, will accurately notice two or three. But the number actual transcription reveals is frequently unsettling. What Freud saw was that, as the descriptions changed, the memory of the dream in the dreamer's mind seemed to change as well.

Dreams, as Freud knew, are closely allied to language. They frequently turn on puns, alternate meanings, rhymes, or other plays on words having to do with something said or read, to or by the speaker, during the previous day. A young woman who has planned to go camping tomorrow dreams she is walking by a post office where she sees an American flag wrapped around the flagpole, which, as she passes, suddenly unrolls to drop a slumbering woman to the street. In this dream a sleeping bag—which our prospective camper, the day before, was wondering how she was going to obtain for the trip—has become a sleeping flag.* As the French psychiatrist Jacques Lacan has pointed out, the analyst does not analyze the dream itself so much as the language with which the dream is recounted. Freud proposed that, on waking, often the dream is not really complete in the dreamer's unconscious—especially a dream that is remembered. The dreamer's own language, then, reenters the unconscious mind and, through more wordplays, puns, and alternate meanings, joins with the still malleable dream material, and the content of the dream is actually emended, even while we are awake. This explains the great changes between these various early accounts and why the changes are so hard to catch except in transcription—since the actual memory of the dream is changed along with them.

Imagining a scene in a story and then writing it is certainly not identical to dreaming a dream and then telling it. But they share enough characteristics that it seems feasible they might be subject to the same mental process. In both cases one imagines. In both cases one responds to that imagining with language. In both cases the language one accepts (or, indeed, rejects) may go back to affect the imagination directly, which in turn affects the subsequent language by which we continue our narration. With writing, however, because of the whole doubting process (even when it doubts itself),

---

*Some years after I had written the above, I was on a bus, one afternoon, from Amherst, Massachusetts, to New York City. I was very tired, and, to pass the time, I was reading a magazine article about rock-and-roll, when the phrase "weeping and wailing" passed under my eye—moments before I dozed off . . . and I began to dream I was standing on the deck of a rocking ship in full sail. I was sweeping the deck with a broad push-broom. I swept my pile of refuse to the deck's edge, where I saw an immense whale had been roped up against the boat. As the boat rolled deeply, I stepped from the deck onto the whale's gray back and continued sweeping—whereupon I woke in the trundling bus. The words "weeping and wailing" had generated a dream about sweeping and whaling, rocking, sailing, rolling. . . . Dreams, Freud tells us, are often put together like a rebus puzzle. From this arose Freud's famous advice as to the best practice for anyone who would work to analyze them: "Do word puzzles."

we have a way to discipline our imaginings through disciplining our language—an endless process of doubts, of rejections, of things avoided, things not done.

These stories, then, include a number of fantasies and a number of science-fiction tales in which I have, well . . . tried to avoid an amount of clutter, thinness, and cliché. The places I've failed, despite my aim, some may find instructive—a modestly direct statement.

The simple ability to write, active talent, and writerly genius lie on a line—and genius is far off and hard to see. In his wonderfully readable *Laokoön,* in which he alerts poets and sculptors to the greater strength of esthetic effects posed through suggestion over those embodied in statement, G. E. Lessing made an aspect of it vivid and visible when he characterized genius as "the ability to put talent wholly into the service of an idea." (In 1766, twenty-two-year-old Johann Von Herder read Lessing's book—famously—cover to cover, in the afternoon and again in the evening of the same autumn day it arrived at his Königsberg bookshop.) Today, wherever we or others—they never coincide—see ourselves on that knotty line, a statement such as the previous paragraph's is as direct as a writer can risk if the distractions are not to become more than the fictions can bear.

—*New York City*
September 1980